D0856512

THIS OLD
HEART
~ OF MINE ~

This Old Heart of Mine

The Best of
Merrill Joan Gerber's
Redbook Stories

MERRILL JOAN GERBER

LONGSTREET PRESS
Atlanta, Georgia

Published by Longstreet Press, Inc.,
a subsidiary of Cox Newspapers,
a division of Cox Enterprises, Inc.
2140 Newmarket Parkway, Suite 118
Marietta, Georgia 30067

Printed in the United States of America

1st printing, 1993

Library of Congress Catalog Number 93-79663

ISBN: 1-56352-091-5

This book was printed by R. R. Donnelley & Sons, Harrisonburg, Virginia.
Jacket design by Laura McDonald
Book design and typesetting by Graham & Co. Graphics

All of the stories in this volume were originally published in *Redbook*.

For Sandra Earl Mintz,
who started this ball rolling

AUTHOR'S NOTE

All of the stories in *This Old Heart of Mine* were published in *Redbook* between 1964 and 1991. My editors and friends there over the years include Sandra Earl Mintz, who bought the first story (and set me on my way to publishing forty-two stories in *Redbook* during those years), Sey Chassler, Neal Gilkyson Stuart, Barbara Blakemore, Margarita Smith, Anne Mollegen Smith, Eileen Schnurr, Deborah Purcell, and Dawn Raffel.

Special thanks go to Jane Hill, who saw the stories in the shape of a book, and to John Yow, who got them between covers.

— M.J.G.

CONTENTS

A Night Out

~

THE STREET LAMP THAT has been flickering for about half an hour in front of the green house opposite ours finally goes out with a purple flash of light, and then the whole street is dark. I know it is probably ridiculous for me to worry, but it is after one and Danny should have been home by ten-thirty. For three hours now I've been sitting at the window in my nightgown. Every time headlights shine down the street I begin to get happy, or at least relieved, and then the car drives past and I pluck another tissue out of the box. I have been pulling up bouquets of colored tissues all evening, and they are crumpled everywhere on the floor like old confetti.

All morning at work I sat at my desk breathing through my mouth and sucking rock candy, and finally I decided to come home early so Danny could make me hot tea and bring aspirins to me every two hours and treat me kindly. Danny wasn't home when I got here, and coming up the stairs to our attic apartment I bumped into a new couple who were moving in on the second floor. It was very awkward; it seemed as if the boy had just moved in their last piece of luggage, and the two of them were standing in the hall smiling at each other just as I came up the stairs. I couldn't pass them unless they both stepped into their apartment—the hallway is so narrow—and they didn't seem to be willing to. Finally, with a shrug and an odd laugh in my direction, the boy leaned forward and swung the girl up in his arms, carried her through the doorway and closed the door. Then I went along up to our attic, realizing on the top step that what I had just seen was a groom carrying his bride across the threshold of their new home. It made me laugh when I understood it, and then when I found Danny wasn't home, it made me cry.

He was at school, of course, but I had hoped he'd be home. It is Tuesday, and on Tuesdays he has a night class at his professor's house, so that meant he wouldn't be home for dinner either. I might as well have stayed in the office with my little plastic bottle of mentholated air to keep me company.

I don't know exactly what made me cry when I found the apartment empty. No doubt it was partly my cold and partly Danny's absence, but mainly it had something to do with those newlyweds, because just like everyone else around here, he was going to go to Harvard and she was going to work, and it wasn't going to be all peaches and cream. And the girl seemed so sweet. She was wearing orange canvas shoes and orange slacks. And here it is the dead of winter, and she was so trusting and happy.

But she'll never be my friend, of course, because it's not as if you can talk to people around here. No one wants to be friendly; everyone is too busy guarding their privacy and mentally comparing marriages and wondering about the stipend of the other couple's fellowship.

And babies—that's another thing people around here don't have. And then sometimes they do anyway, and in a few weeks the wife trots back to work and the husband has to write his dissertation with one hand and rock the cradle with the other.

I saw a baby today, though. While I was watching out the window for Danny, the girl who lives in the attic of the green house came to the window in her robe and held aside the curtains so her baby could look out at the snow. It had just started sprinkling, very lightly, and she held the baby's tiny head against the glass and whispered something to it, and then let the curtains drop again. Now all their lights are off and it's getting to be two a.m., and soon I will probably have to call the police.

We don't have a phone and we don't have a friend whose phone we can use, so that's why I haven't thought of calling the police yet.

Danny's class started at seven and ended at ten, and he should have been home by ten-thirty—he always is. Even if the class ended late, he should have been home by eleven or, at the very latest, twelve.

Maybe he had an accident. But the odds are against it; Danny is a careful driver and it's not too icy tonight. Well, what if someone held him up, hit him over the head with a blackjack? What if he picked up a hitchhiker who robbed and killed him? What if right now, this very instant, I am a widow?

I pull a yellow tissue from the box on the window sill and think about that for a minute. We own hardly anything—all I'd have to do is buy a ticket and fly home to my mother in Florida. Or I could stay at my job and marry Barton Wilky, who probably will soon own half the stock in the publishing house I work in. Then I could live with him on Beacon Hill and have all the babies I want, and never go to work again.

But I have been over this before. Barton Wilky isn't for me. Danny is. But is he, is he, *is* he!

My head throbs and I am shivering, so I go over to the heating grate to see if by chance any stray steam is coming up.

Earlier this evening, every time I opened the grate the strains of sweet violins were wafted up at me, and it was too much—I'd rather be cold. The newlyweds were probably waltzing around down there, beaming at each other.

So I stayed cold and pulled out my wedding album from the closet and climbed under the electric blanket with it, to get altogether sentimental. The thing that shocked me, though, is that when I looked at those pictures I stayed as politely unmoved as a stranger. There was me, in my white dress in this fancy hotel, in a line, shaking hands with everyone right after the ceremony. Big smiles were coming at the camera from all directions, but I don't remember that at all.

What I remember are four or five strangers who were clustered behind the glass door of the wedding hall, just hotel guests who noticed a wedding going on, and all of them were beaming in at me with radiant smiles. And I remember the lady in the elevator who tapped me on the shoulder as I was going up to change out of my wedding dress. She smiled at me and said, "I was married a week ago and I'm on my honeymoon now, and I'll tell you, dear, it's very wonderful." She was about thirty-five and homely, but she looked beautiful to me.

That's the kind of thing I remember, and now I wonder where that lady is today and if she would still tell me it's wonderful. Rather, I wonder what I would tell *her*.

Well, I *was* very happy for a while, but then Danny didn't seem to be turning out right—he wasn't working as hard as I thought he should be. I had this idea that when I came puffing up the stairs after work he ought to be wildly typing his dissertation or flipping through his books at the rate of a thousand pages a second—just to prove to me that he was really going to get his degree as soon as possible, so I could stop working and be a wife-type wife in our little house somewhere, with tricycles on the lawn.

The truth is that when I come home Danny is often asleep or listening to records—or not home at all but at the library, where he spends the day reading current magazines, as it turns out when he finally does come home. At first I waited patiently for him to get to work, and then I began to yell at him, and it seems I've been doing that now much too long for it to be fun, or even useful.

Another picture in the wedding album was taken of me by Danny in Georgia, on our honeymoon trip to Florida. We stopped there one afternoon to visit the Etowah Burial Mounds. When you get there you walk up the mounds on steps carved into the earth, and then you are standing over the bones of hundreds of Indians. It was very sunny out and everyone there had a camera swinging from his neck, and it didn't seem that anyone dead even existed, much less right under our feet. Then we went down and there was this little depressed cage in the earth, and in it, bare to the air, were the skeletons of two Indians, a husband and wife, close enough for us to kneel down and touch. The smaller skeleton—the wife's—was on her side, her back curved toward her husband as if they were sleeping on their own pallet in their own tepee. Their bones seemed to be naturally cemented onto the little platform they lay on, and it was not scary at all, just very sweet and peaceful. I remember turning to Danny and kissing him, and thinking that I would love him when we were alive and then when we were dead.

The picture he took of me there shows me holding onto my sailor hat in the wind. No one looking at it would ever know that the bones of an Indian husband and wife were two feet away from me in an open grave, or know what I had been thinking about then . . .

I decided now that the true nature of anything that happens is always and only in your head, and nothing is as it seems. The strain of that reflection is too much for me—it doesn't explain anything and it doesn't help my cold—and I suddenly feel very sorry for myself.

I don't want to do anything drastic; I just want Danny and me to be all right. But *can* we be unless I stop yelling at him? And how can I stop yelling at him, unless I decide that I don't care about his dissertation or his mental blocks or gardens full of tricycles, but that I only care about *him*? Did that Indian squaw keep nagging at her husband to catch better buffalo hides? Or did she just curve next to him at night and assure him that she would stay with him forever because he was her man and because she loved him?

I just don't know. The world is so lonely, and if I married Barton or flew home to my mother, I would be so lonely I would die. I can't think of *not* being with Danny; he is my only friend and we have no other friends in the world.

But am I *Danny's* friend? How do I know, if he makes my life so hard and makes me sit at the window like this, praying every car will be his? How do I know anything?

Well, I know it's ten minutes until three a.m. and my husband is nowhere in sight, and I just cannot sit here any longer.

I go to the closet and pull out my snow boots and gloves and my winter coat and put everything on over my nightgown. Two blocks down Massachusetts Avenue there is an outside phone booth; that's where I'll go. But whom will I call? Danny's professor, who'll probably be fast asleep in bed? And if that's true, the class was over hours ago, and how can I explain my husband's absence to *him*? And you don't go calling the police when a full-grown man is a few hours late. Well, then, I'll call someone in Danny's class. Who? John Longenecker—that's a name I can't forget. He's in that class. Danny has mentioned him.

It's not snowing now but it's very cold, and dark because the street lamp is out. Under the sink I find Danny's army-surplus flashlight with the red glass on the end.

I stick that in one pocket and a clump of tissues and some dimes in my other and start down the winding steps. On the second landing I stop, wondering if I am insane to go out like this and if I shouldn't just go back up and get into bed and try to go to sleep. It occurs to me crazily that I would be doing the new bride in the second-floor apartment a good turn if I knocked at her door and told her to take a good look at me now. I'd warn her about night classes. There are lots of beautiful girls in night classes, because I've seen them, I'd say. And if they've got to graduate school, they're likely to be brilliant as well. And probably one of them in your husband's class won't have a car, and your husband, being gallant—besides being reluctant and guilty to go home to a wife who has worked all day to support him—will offer to drive her home. She is single, of course, and carries on scintillating conversations. She never complains, and she knows about all the things your husband knows about and you don't.

Then I'd tell her about "having coffee," which is what graduate students do all the time in student unions and such places. Your husband sits around all day with people you never meet, and when you ask him to tell you what they talked about, he'll tell you you never heard of those things and wouldn't really be interested. You might think if the girls he has coffee with are interested, why wouldn't you be, but you never say anything. He doesn't ask you where *you* had lunch or coffee because he already knows; you've already told him—about a hundred times.

You eat lunch at Woolworth's with no one, and you have coffee in the employees lounge with a girl from the art department. He doesn't ask what you talk about because you've also complained about that; the girls talk about clothes and sales in the department stores, and it couldn't be more boring.

Oh, I'd tell her, all right: Sweetie, you don't know what you're getting into. But then again, she may be more tolerant than I am. She may be willing to have a few days of dancing around the heating grate with her husband and then plunge right in like a steady old scout. She may be a better woman than I am.

But—and now I am angry—she may have a better man!

I run down the rest of the stairs and then I am out in the night, with not a soul awake in the world that I can see.

There is a wet fog hanging over the street that will probably be snow by morning. On Massachusetts Avenue there are a few street lights, making the sky appear a chalky charcoal color. I take as deep a breath as I can and begin to march along, noticing it is not much colder out than it was in the attic.

All the stores are dark except the supermarket across the street, which has a pyramid of yellow grapefruit in the window—much too expensive for us to buy at this time of year. Right there in front of the store is where I wait every day for the trolley that takes me underground to the subway at Harvard Square. Maybe I will stop off on the way back and tell that new bride about the subway. But she won't believe me, because at first the subway is very pleasant. You leave your gloves in your pocket and cross your hands delicately on your lap, and then everyone can see your beautiful new wedding ring, the way it glints in the light and the way it tells everyone—all those painted-up old ladies and those young girls losing hope—how you have just made breakfast in a special warm home for a man who loves you and to whom you will go home tonight when the work of the day is over, and that none of this sooty world is real to you. The only real thing is the light in your eyes, which they can see after they notice your wedding ring.

I feel so bitter thinking this that I am almost happy when I am distracted by an attack of sneezing that lasts a full two minutes. So shaken am I by this attack that I hardly see my tissues go flying about as I walk along. Later, when I look back, I see a trail that could be the salvation of a hundred lost Hansels and Gretels.

I still can't see the phone booth and I hope I am not mistaken about its being there. Usually in emergencies we use the phone in the drugstore, but it is closed now. I remember, thinking about phones, how on our honeymoon we called my mother collect from a phone booth in Blowing Rock, North Carolina, and my mother kept saying, "From *where*?" and the operator, exasperated, kept saying, "Blowing Rock, Madam, *Blowing Rock!* Will you accept the charges?"

The thought of that makes me smile, and in quick succession I remember some other funny things about that trip. One night we got lost in the Great Smoky Mountains National Park. Our gas was nearly gone and we were exhausted and tired and the road wound endlessly onward. Finally our headlights grazed the square of a white sign coming up. Terribly excited and anxious, we pulled up; the sign said "Do Not Feed the Bears." We laughed and laughed, rolling around on the front seat, slapping each other on the back. That is one funny thing I remember.

"Ha," I say out loud into the cold air, and I feel very lonely. It seems to me that if I could just see Danny's car coming now, I would be happy for the rest of my life and never complain again.

The other funny thing I remember isn't really funny, but it was wonderful. On one of the nights of that trip Danny and I had to stay in an old hotel in Knoxville that had available only a room with a single bed. It was right next to a bus station, and all night the loudspeaker woke us with announcements of departures for all points north and south; and each time we woke up, one of us started rolling off the bed and the steady one had to catch the other.

It's amazing to me, but it seems I have known only Danny all my life and no one else, not even my parents. The morning after our wedding in Miami, right before we left on our trip, I left our motel room where Danny was packing and went down to the water so I could see the sun come up over the ocean. Danny came after me, thinking I was sad because I had to leave my parents. But when he turned me around I was smiling and I said to him, "Danny, I just can't stop smiling." And then he couldn't stop either. So it keeps seeming truer and truer that Danny is my only happiness, and if that is so, why am I so unhappy? Danny is the only friend I have; what I have to find out is, am I *his* friend?

Finally up ahead is the phone booth. I am very glad because the dark street has really been scaring me, and at this hour of the morning in a big city it is not unrealistic to be scared—especially if you are wearing only a flowered nightgown under your coat. I step into the booth and pull the door shut. Somewhere in my coat pocket I find a dime and get it into the slot while I lift the receiver. As I bring it to my ear the mouthpiece shoots off the bottom and flies past my eyes, hitting the glass door with a clunk. Instantly yards of wire spring out at me from the hole, uncoiling blackly all about my face and making me scream in fright.

Then I am laughing because it is really funny to think a broken telephone is a cobra, and I push my way out of the phone booth, glad to be alive.

A block down I see a dim light in a sandwich shop. It's doubtful that I will find it open at this hour, but I will try anyway. Since I left the house I have been on the street down which Danny must drive to get home, and no car at all has passed. Wouldn't it be funny, I think, if Danny came home and found all the lights on and tissues everywhere and me gone? I am glad to notice I still have a sense of humor, odd though it might seem to someone else. I cannot tell for sure if anyone is in the sandwich shop, but there is definitely a light on, and as I come up I think I see a movement in the back of the store. Quite innocently I pull out my red flashlight and shine it into the dim store to see if anyone is there.

There is a great uproar all at once. Four or five chairs are flung back, and the men who were in them are staring, frozen with fright, at the door, at my red light. I think I hear one of them say, "It's a raid!"

I turn off my flashlight and after a minute the door is opened by a huge man in a T-shirt, who is completely astonished to see me.

"Do you have a phone?" I ask. "I'm sorry if I frightened you, but my husband should have been home four hours ago and I can't find him anywhere, and I have a terrible cold, and I have to call up someone to see if I can find him."

The man looks behind him at his friends, and then he stands back and lets me in, motioning to the back of the store, past the table where the men are. He looks as if he is a sympathizer with my husband—he too is the kind of man who goes home at four a.m. after a night on the town. I march past the men and see cards and beer on the table. They are gamblers, I think to myself. Who knows *what* they are? But they thought I was the police, imagine that.

On the wall there is a phone that, I trust, works. I hear the big man turn the lock in the door and then go back to the table. Then the men are all sitting down again; they are watching me. With my gloves on I can't seem to find another dime, and I am sweating under my coat. I can't, of course, unbutton it, considering what I am wearing underneath.

"You need a dime, sweetheart?" one of them asks. I can't tell if he is sincere or if he is making fun of me. They are all a little drunk, no doubt, and no telling what is in their minds. Well, it will serve Danny right to have to come here in the morning and identify my dismembered body.

"I—I have one here," I say. After an interminably long search I am able to find, in the phone book hanging on the wall, John Longenecker's number, and I dial it.

One of the men says, "Don't worry honey. He'll come home. All husbands do this sometimes."

Now I decide all these men are sweet and wonderful, and I love them all, and wish I were married to one of them. Then I feel unbearably lonely; the world is indifferent when you are alone in it.

John Longenecker's wife answers the phone. I tell her I am Danny's wife and that Danny has this night class with John and that Danny isn't home yet and is John?

Yes, she says, John just came in a minute ago. In fact, Danny dropped him off.

"Well, what *happened?*" I cry.

"What do you mean?" she says.

"Why were they so *late?*"

"Oh, you know how it is—they just got to talking," she says. Then I hear her whisper, "Now, stop tickling, John."

"Anyway," she says, giving me her attention again, "your husband is on the way home right this minute."

I thank her and hang up. Whoever she is, she certainly isn't like me, because she isn't the slightest bit mad or upset. She may "know how it is," but I certainly don't. If Danny tickled me at four in the morning—I mean a morning like *this*—I would knock his block right off. No wonder Danny and I don't have friends; it was all we could do to find each other.

The men are still watching me, and I say, "Thank you very much. I've found him and he's coming home."

"Don't you worry your pretty head," the big one says. "You gotta be philosophical in this world. Don't be too hard on him."

He unlocks the door and lets me out and I wave to them tearfully, feeling I am parting with people very dear to me.

On the street I head for home, seeing my trail of tissues emerge before me. At the sight of them I start sneezing, and then two headlights come beaming along the road. My search is ended—it is my Danny come home. At first I decide I will let him pass me and arrive home to find me gone. But then, like a madman, I am jumping up and down, waving my red flashlight at him and laughing.

He slows, then stops, then throws open the door for me by leaning across the front seat. His face is worried and surprised.

"What's the matter?" he asks. "What are you doing out here?"

"I hate you," I cry, flinging my flashlight wildly at his feet. "Where *were* you? I nearly went out of my mind. I nearly called the police. I could have been attacked by ten men in the back of a beer parlor. I watched out the window for five hours. My cold is so bad I need an oxygen tent and I came home from work so you could make me better and you weren't there, and you weren't anywhere! And we don't even have a phone, and how could you just stay at the professor's house and *talk so much?*"

"Oh, baby," Danny says. "I thought you'd be fast asleep."

"Ho, ho, very funny. Well, I wasn't. I sat up in that freezing attic and thought someone had robbed and killed you, or that your car went into the Charles River and they'd have to chop you out of the ice in the morning. I thought . . . I don't know *what* I thought!"

I begin to sneeze, and when the sneezing stops I begin to cry, and then I begin to beat on Danny's chest, crying, "I hate you, I hate you." And then he is hugging me, laughing and stroking the hair away from my face with his warm hands.

"If you couldn't call, you should have done *something*," I say. "You should have at least . . . you could have sent me a telegram!"

Then Danny is kissing me right on the mouth and I push him away, crying, "My germs!"

And Danny says to me seriously, "I love your germs."

And then it is clear to me at once: Who in the world but someone whose best friend you are could love your germs?

(1964)

Many are Cold

~

ANY IGLOO MUST BE warmer than our attic apartment on a winter morning. Hot, oily air does not start coming up the register in our living room until eight-thirty, and by then I am in my coat, ready to leave for work. Last year I called the landlady to tell her I got up at seven and could she please start the heat earlier, and she said in her cold, lovely, rich Boston accent, "Why, my dear, you have no idea how *costly* oil is."

Which was true, I suppose, but our rent was costly too, because two whole weeks of my salary went to pay it every month. When I told Danny how unfair she was, and how the furniture couldn't even be given to Goodwill as a gift, and how I did the dishes in cold water every night, he said in his calm voice, "Well, please don't yell at me, Janet. It isn't *my* fault."

He was right, of course; but something terrible has to be someone's fault, doesn't it?

I go through this whole thing every morning, when I get dressed and am shivering so badly it is all I can do to keep from crawling back in beside Danny and waking him and telling him it is all over—I'm never going to work another day. All I want is what those other dumb girls want—a nice, warm, modern house with central heating and a turquoise refrigerator and lots of chubby, rosy babies.

Well, I never do it. I get dressed and go out into the snow.

And I always kiss Danny good-bye, uncovering his head from under the sky-blue electric blanket—our only decent wedding present—and reminding him to try to start the potatoes early so that I won't have to do them when I get home at six.

This morning while I am eating my English muffin, the urgent voice of the radio announcer says it is another record day for cold—six degrees at Logan Airport this morning. I listen to this man as though he were my oracle. My heart beats in tempo with the tone of his voice. Twice last year he brought me beautiful news—once that the snow was so deep the trains weren't running; and once that the MTA was on strike—no trains that day either.

Today it is just cold; he goes on to other news and I dump my coffee in the sink and put on my boots.

A rush of air from the register reminds me that I will be late if I don't hurry, so I clump into the bedroom and kiss Danny good-bye. He must have stayed up studying very late last night, because he is really unconscious. He doesn't budge, or even mumble good-bye. The register, as I go out the door, finally sends up its mocking blast of hot air, and I slam the door in its face.

The trolley stop is jammed. All the people who usually drive into the city are taking the subway because the snowplows have to be working all day clearing the streets. There is a parking ban in effect and it is terribly unfair. All the people who usually drive in their heated cars now come crowding in on us, and squash us to death or keep us out altogether. I dread these days more than anything. I can't bear to be so close to a million strangers who avert their faces and poke their briefcases into my bones. Well, it is only an eight minute ride from Harvard Square to Park Street.

I don't know what's making me so cranky today. The sight of Danny under that blue blanket keeps coming into my head, but it's a foolish vision. By now he must be up and dressed—he always gets up when the heat comes on—and sitting at the cracked wooden table with his cup of instant coffee and one of his gigantic books open in front of him. There's no doubt in my mind that he works hard, but sometimes it's difficult to remember what he's doing, when he mainly seems to be sitting around at home all the time with one book or another open on his knee.

Whenever I get a look into one of those books and see what Danny spends all his time doing, I'm more confused than ever about what his books have to do with what *we* are doing. Danny is getting his Ph.D. at Harvard, and I am helping us out till he does. And then I read something in his book like: "We may say, speaking in the abstract, that imperfection is as inimical to the nature of God as complete nonexistence. One way of illustrating the detestable nature of idolatry would be to collect all the solemn denunciations which the church herself has uttered against it."

With a little effort I can usually understand what I am reading, but I don't see much sense in it—all that talk about the existence of God, and good and evil, and neat little phrases like "I think, therefore I am." I know only too well that I am, otherwise I wouldn't be jammed into this subway with a thousand other human beings who know they are. You just can't forget it when someone's umbrella is boring a hole through your spine.

But I suppose Danny is making something of all that stuff in his head, and someday, as he says, he will write it down and then we can start living "normally." I simply have to trust him.

The icy air is a relief after the subway, and I only have to be in it a minute. The elevator man says the same thing he says every morning. In the winter he says, "A real stinger today—six degrees," and in the summer he says, "A real scorcher today— ninety-six degrees." It depresses me to think he lives his whole life talking such surfaces. It depresses me even more to think that I live my life pretty much the same way. I'd rather say nothing than that sort of drivel, but when you work at a job where you can hardly imagine what anyone is really *doing* there, you can't do much but talk about the weather and the news and everything that doesn't concern anybody's *insides*.

When I take off my coat it crackles like frying bacon, and I know I'm in for a shock again. It is always a matter of some entertainment to guess where I'll get it this time—at the drinking fountain or at my desk or, if I postpone it that long, perhaps at the phone. These shocks are another one of the terrible things in my life—I get them everywhere, and am always leaping in pain and being laughed at. No one feels them the way I do. It's criminal to have to be at the mercy of landladies and static electricity and forces like that.

Barton Wilky is already in his office complaining. I can hear him through the thin walls between our offices. He is telling his secretary that he is having another attack of claustrophobia; that they should have left him behind in the old building where the ceiling was cracking but where, by God, a man could lean back in his chair and not hit his head on the file cabinet.

Barton is the science textbook editor. He is the youngest man to be head of a whole department; he is a Harvard man; he is very smart. Most of the time he is damning everyone and everything in the publishing house, but they keep him because he's very promising. He is always stamping down the hall to Harlan Winter's office to tell him that as head of the company he ought to move them all back to the old building, where the heating worked and where you had room to breathe.

I get my shock on the coat hanger, so the suspense doesn't last terribly long. With the worst part of the day over—I am out of that freezing attic and through with the trolley till five and through with my shock till the next one at lunchtime—I settle down at my desk and get to work on the current problem. There are three lady schoolteachers in Kentucky who have collaborated on a grammar textbook. Their names are Beadle, Kent and Simon. Miss Simon claims that since the idea for the book was hers, her name should appear as first of the authors. Miss Beadle insists that the idea was hers too, and that she did most of the work anyway, and *her* name should be first, as is alphabetical and proper. Miss Kent is content to stay in the middle, since all she did was type the manuscript and give suggestions.

It is my job to settle their differences and see that these Kentucky ladies are made happy. Mr. Cowper, my senior editor, says any way I settle it, as long as I settle it, is fine with him. The book has given him a good deal more trouble than it's worth.

In my life, this is all pertinent to nothing except getting the money to pay for my landlady's costly oil. So I immerse myself in the dilemma of the Misses Beadle, Kent and Simon's prestige, and try to figure out what on earth I can do to settle this business.

It is tedious and boring. I know, a lot of the work in this world is tedious and boring. I should consider myself fortunate—it won't be forever. (But hasn't it already been—three years of my very finite life?) This is a nice place where pleasant people work; I have my own office, two coffee breaks a day, lots of complimentary paper clips. And think of what I have at home! A wonderful, handsome husband with an IQ three times my salary, waiting for me in our little love nest. Think of all these pathetic secretaries who spend their earnings on clothes that they wear to impress one another at the office and in the hope Barton Wilky will notice them someday. Think of the good health I have, and the promising future.

Well, maybe Barton Wilky has a promising future, but all I see for me for a long time to come are those demoralizing subway rides every day.

I shove the pawky little letter I have been composing to Miss Beadle into the wastepaper basket and go for my coffee break. In the lounge everyone is holding insulated paper cups full of coffee and talking about how cold it is. The new building seems to have a defect—the architect apparently made no provision in the design for an air-and-heat vent to the lounge. This is what everyone talks about at every coffee break. It is not very interesting, but it is all one can think about because it is so cold.

I stand alone, sipping the bitter coffee, and notice a stirring among the people, who have till now been standing stiff as penguins. They are making way for Barton, who is coming in carrying a large, hand-lettered sign. On second glance it is clear that it was previously his desk blotter. He places it over the counter with Scotch tape. It reads: MANY ARE COLD, BUT FEW ARE FROZEN.

Everyone laughs, including Mr. Winter, who must realize, like the rest of us, that it has taken Barton all morning to make that sign. Promising people, it seems, have certain privileges.

When I return to my work, the mail girl has been by with her cart, and on my desk are two letters. One is from Miss Simon, with new proof that the idea for the book was hers alone. She has enclosed with her letter a sealed envelope, addressed and sent to herself five years ago. In it, she states, is the idea and outline of the grammar book, proof that she had this idea five years ago, before Miss Beadle was even on the faculty.

Busily, I address an interoffice envelope to the legal department, enclose all the papers and pop the whole thing into my out box. Much of the business in this publishing house goes under the category of Pass the Buck.

Lunchtime is approaching. I wish again we had a phone at home so I could call Danny. I just want to say hello to him. But a phone is an extra expense. An education at Harvard, even with a fellowship, is expensive.

I notice the second letter and realize that it is actually for me, with the notation "Personal Please" on it. It is from Roy Bentley, postmarked Mexico. Roy and his wife Sally have been a great inspiration to Danny and me for years. I wonder why they are in Mexico, unless it is for a second honeymoon. They spent a week there when they were first married, and Danny and I agonized together in envy. Our own wedding was at least two years away at the time—till I finished college and could get a job to support us. We sat together on a park bench on Roy and Sally's wedding night and counted dollars and years and hugged each other.

Sally is one girl who has never complained about her lot, and she has a much worse job than this one. She works in some company that manufactures paper cups. She has something to do with turning down the rims. Roy is getting his medical degree, and that is an even harder haul than Danny's Ph.D.

Well, maybe this letter will be good for me today—a pepper-upper.

Dear Janet and Danny,

I'm sending this to the office because I'm in Mexico and don't have your home address with me. I have bad news about Sally and me. We have just, about three hours ago, got a divorce. It all happened very fast, in the last month, and if you had no warning about it, neither did I. Neither did Sally, I guess, until some papercup tycoon convinced her there were better things to do than turn down rims, and now she is having his child. She didn't mean to make a mess, she says, but it got to be too much for her— working for so many years while I read up on gynecology and obstetrics, letting her have none of it. She was twenty-seven in May, and she says that's old enough for any girl to quit thinking she's just a girl and get busy and start living. She said if I didn't know so much about contraception she'd probably still be married to me, and we'd have a darling baby instead of a darling divorce.

Well, I feel all numb and crazy right now, but wanted to write you about this. Stick together, you two, and, Danny, buddy, take my advice and go out and get a job quick, or let Janet quit and the two of you live on relief. There's something lethal in these eternal-student marriages, believe me. I have a deadly document to prove it. Much love to you both.

Roy

I put the letter in my purse, take my lunch hour twenty minutes early and leave the office to wander around the Boston stores. I go to Jordan Marsh's maternity department, sit down on a red plastic chair and watch the pregnant women looking at maternity clothes. I am twenty-five years old, and twenty-five isn't peanuts. There is an especially beautiful black turtleneck maternity dress that I keep looking at, and finally I get up and look at the tag, and it is in my size. I have always been curious about how maternity clothes are made, but I never looked at them because I was reserving that information for when I needed to know it, just the same way I never read books about raising babies, because I was waiting until it would be my time for having one, and then I could do such wonderful things properly.

I buy the black turtleneck maternity dress with the fifteen dollars that is delegated to the grocery envelope in my purse and take it back to the office with me.

When I touch my doorknob I get my shock, and when I yell

Barton comes out of his office and hangs up my coat for me so I don't have to chance another high-voltage encounter on the metal hanger.

He comes into my office and closes the door behind him. I set my package on the floor next to my desk and get out the Beadle file. Barton comes over and sits on the edge of my desk.

"I saw your sign in the lounge," I say.

"Oh? Did you like it?"

"I don't think it's altogether true, Barton," I say. My voice comes out more somber than I intend. "It ought to have read another way."

"May I ask what your improvement might be?"

"Well," I say, "the truth is, Barton, that many are cold and many are frozen."

"Aha," Barton says. "I detect philosophic overtones in that remark."

Barton and I have always shared a certain cynical mode of communication, and he has always let it be known to me that he admires my general attitude toward the world. We never talk about Danny. A few times when Barton wanted to have lunch with me and I was supposed to meet Danny at the Boston Public Library, I said, "I have to meet my husband," and felt very odd about using that word to him.

"Just being silly," I say. "At least, half-and-half silly."

"Where are you coming from with all that built-up electrici- ty?"

"Oh, shopping."

"Wasting your hard-earned money on what frilly stuff?" he says, and reaches down for the paper bag from Jordan Marsh.

Before I can stop him, before I even remember what I bought, Barton has taken out the dress and understood what it is. He reddens and puts it back in the bag.

"Well," he says. "Congratulations. Janet."

"It isn't—I didn't—" I begin, and then I stop and look out the window, where a pigeon is sitting on the sill. I am on the verge of showing him Roy's letter, of telling him how tired I am of working, of talking about how Danny sleeps late, of how slowly his work is going, of how I long for babies and baking apple pies in a bright kitchen and wearing that lovely black, tenty dress.

Barton is sitting there, all sympathy, all tender and single, all willing to listen to me. He's very intelligent and promising, and he already owns stock in the company, and he has a big apartment on Beacon Hill—much too big for only him, he often says. It would be very easy. It is barely a step from him to the paper-cup tycoon, from Boston to Mexico, from my attic to Beacon Hill. It's all possible—I'm bright enough to know that; you can't mistake a moment of possibility like this one.

The pigeon sails away and I remind myself that a moment like this is no accident. I am looking for whatever I get. A girl doesn't buy a maternity dress unless she's going to do something with it—in one fashion or another. Well, I hope Danny will call me right this instant from the library and say something sweet to me over the phone. Either that or Barton will lean across the desk and kiss me. I don't know exactly what I will do with this dress otherwise. It needs to be explained to someone; I can't just take it back. Something too important made me buy it.

"Barton," I say finally, "that dress is a present for my sister. It isn't for me."

"I'll mind my business in the future, Janet," he says. He stands up and adds: "So I guess you'll be here a while longer."

"I guess so," I say ruefully, and we both smile.

When he is gone I realize I have not eaten any lunch. I just cannot bear the thought of going out and eating and coming back and getting another shock and going through all the business of getting involved with Miss Beadle and Miss Simon again. A woman is entitled to some indulgence at a moment of great crisis in her life, and I decide I am going to tell Mr. Cowper I have a toothache and have to go home.

Sometime before tonight when Danny comes home from the library, I will have to decide what to do with this black dress that I have bought, and what to say to Danny about Roy's letter, and about my job, and about our life. I have a lot of thinking to do, and I certainly can't do it here.

Before I think a single thought, though, there are three

things I have to do, and I have to do them right now. First of all I have to eat. Then I have to go home to our attic and put this bag from Jordan Marsh in the corner behind the ironing board. And then I have to spend the rest of the snowy afternoon under our sky-blue electric blanket, getting a better perspective on things.

(1964)

A Daughter of My Own

EVERY GIRL I KNOW who has ever had a baby has had her mother come and stay with her for two weeks—or her mother and a nurse—and each one tells me how wonderful it was and how she never could have survived without her mother's advice and help and soothing presence.

I just don't know. I think I love my mother as much as any girl loves hers, and I think I have always got along better with my mother, on the average, than most girls do with theirs. But if I never have another baby, it won't be because I didn't like being pregnant or being in labor or losing six months' worth of sleep; it will be because I won't know what to do about my mother.

When I found out in September that I was pregnant, and told my mother I was due to have the baby in April, she immediately began making plans to fly up "in February or March, whenever you want me." It had never occurred to me that I would want her at all. I mean, it was my baby, and we were very far away from my parents and they didn't have the money to toss away on airplane trips, and my husband was a student at the time and at home nearly all day to give me any help I might need, and there just wasn't room for anyone. There was hardly room for the baby. Danny and I lived in a three-room apartment near the university, and had figured that by gouging out the shelves from a built-in-the-wall living-room bookcase we could just manage to squeeze in a tiny crib for the baby. We hadn't exactly planned on enlarging our family just yet, and there was quite a bit of arranging to do in those early months. Not that we were unhappy about it—far from it; it just took some adjusting.

My husband was happy to adjust to a baby, but not to a mother-in-law. What bothered him most, to begin with, was that if she came before I had the baby, he would be left alone in the house with her for five days while I was in the hospital. I could see what he meant; my mother wasn't one to discuss Aristotle and Danny wasn't one to discuss the upbringing of children—at least, not with my mother and not the upbringing of *his* child.

It was hard to tell her not to come before the event, because I know what was on her mind. To put it rather simply, she wanted to hold my hand. My mother had always held my hand through crises—I had been a very sickly child, and I think that in those frightening years when doctors loomed everywhere, the grip of my mother's fingers was all that sustained me.

Now I was having a baby. People sometimes died in childbirth, I knew, and even when you made it through, it could be pretty rough. My mother had nearly died having me, and I knew how worried she was and why she wanted to be around to whisper encouragement at the hardest moments. The only difference, I felt, was that this was not a crisis. I was not sick; I was not frightened; I was not even worried. I was in perfect health, I liked and trusted my doctor and I loved the little thumps I was beginning to feel down where my appendix had once been. Most important of all, though, was that I *had* someone to hold my hand if necessary—my husband.

I don't suppose Mother gave Danny much credit for being useful in any situation. After all, we had been married for three years and I had been supporting him—while all he did, as far as my mother could tell, was lounge around in unpressed pants all day reading books.

I tried to show my mother how calm and unworried I was. I sent her diagrams of the fetus in different stages of development with long, technical explanations about its growth. I recommended books on childbirth for her to read that told how simple and safe the procedure was these days. I wrote her with the gain of every new ounce, knowing she believed that gaining weight meant being healthy. I had Danny take pictures of me in different smiling poses, my jolly wave saying, "See? Nothing is wrong with *me*."

Finally I was able to persuade my mother to come right *after* the baby was born. When she agreed, though reluctant and somewhat hurt, I was able to relax and enjoy the remainder of my pregnancy. I saw every old Tarzan movie on television that had ever been made. I sat at the window on gray afternoons with all the lights off and watched the snow come down. I spent long hours staring up at the ceiling from my bed, imaging my baby and imagining me with my baby.

Danny was home nearly all that winter, studying for his comprehensives, and we talked to each other mostly at dinnertime, usually about what names we would like the baby to have and how we wouldn't do to him the bad things we thought had been done to us. It was a fine, snowy, happy winter—wet and icy outside, warm and steamy inside. I bought eight dozen diapers in my ninth month and washed them all three times by hand so they would be soft for the baby. Danny bought a used crib and we painted it and got a new mattress. We read Dr. Spock, *Childbirth Without Fear*, Gesell. We were ready.

The baby started to come on the very day he was scheduled to, which made us think that he had a most reliable character. We saw the doctor in the afternoon and he told us to go home and call him when there was "some real action." So we went home and we timed all the warming-up pains, and soon it was dark out and I was warming up a little faster. We played all six Brandenburg Concertos, while I lay on the living-room couch and Danny sat on the floor next to me with his wrist watch in his lap. At eleven we called the doctor, who said, "This sounds like it. Come on down."

The snow had changed to rain, and it was a very appropriate, dramatic night for racing to the hospital. I knew, though, from the hospital brochure I had, that if we arrived before midnight we would be charged for the entire day, so I cautioned Danny to drive as slowly as he could. We meandered to the hospital—even circling a few extra blocks to kill time—until the baby made it known we had better meander no more.

We parked in the hospital lot at four minutes to midnight. I was game to sit it out till twelve, but Danny was beginning to get glassy-eyed and I was not as confident as I sounded, so we went in and signed the admittance form.

Danny was permitted to stay with me as long as I wanted to be awake, and we stayed together until nearly dawn, having a very sweet, dreamy time, holding hands, and making faces at each other every time a nurse came in to listen to the baby's heartbeat or time a contraction.

When he went away I was floated into an elevator on a very soft, high bed, and in the morning I had a little girl, six pounds, two ounces.

I truly had never felt better. It was a bright, sunny morning, and I was cranked up on my neat white bed and the light was coming in right on my knees, making them warm and comfortable. I had just seen my baby, pink and perfect, asleep, and more beautiful than any beautiful thing I had ever seen in the world.

I drifted about in the bright sunlight for a while and then Danny peeked into the room, grinning like mad, and we had a big kiss and a tremendous long smile together and then I sent him off to see his daughter.

He was with me all afternoon, but occasionally went out into the hall when a nurse came in to poke my stomach and take my pulse and temperature.

He came back one time with roses for me, and I felt like a queen there in the sunshine, all loved and loving, and I thought we had just begun to get happier than we had ever been.

When they came in with my dinner Danny got up to leave, and I remembered that he hadn't called my mother. I told him to do that right away, and he said he would, but it seems he drove home first and had dinner and fell asleep, and it wasn't till about ten at night that he remembered to call, and the baby had been alive nearly twelve hours by then.

Everything started falling apart. My mother called me the next day at the hospital, when I could walk to the phone, and the first thing she said was, "Why didn't Danny call me right away?" So I made up something about his wanting to make sure I was all right before he called, but it wasn't very pleasant to argue and to come out of that gentle haze I'd been in, and I resisted it. I said I had to hang up and go back to bed because I was getting dizzy, but my mother managed to mention that she was coming in two days, when I would be ready to go home.

I spent the rest of the afternoon worrying about her coming and feeling very helpless and unhappy. They brought the baby to me only twice for the first two days, to get her used to me and me to her. There was no sense in her coming oftener, since she wanted mostly to sleep and my milk hadn't come in yet. It was very fine to hold her, and each time the nurse left I would undo her little kimono and examine her tiny body and count all her toes and fingers.

After they took her back to the nursery I would get worried again about my mother, and I'd feel bad till the next time they brought the baby to me. When I told Danny my mother was really coming, tears came to my eyes, and he tried to cheer me up by saying that as long as she *had* to come she would be a great help, but he didn't sound very convinced himself.

My mother arrived the evening of my fourth day in the hospital. I was to leave the next morning. Danny had a night class, so no one met her at the airport, and she took a taxi to the hospital and dragged her suitcase by herself, and when she came up to the desk they told her it was final feeding time and no more visitors were allowed until morning. She told them she hadn't seen me for a year and some kind lady let her up, and she came into my room just as the baby finished nursing. Without a word I held out the baby to her and she took her, and we both were crying, because it had been so long and we loved each other so much and now I had a daughter of my own.

But even though I was so happy to see her, that perfect moment couldn't last very long, and it didn't. Immediately she was asking me if we could pay the hospital bill, since Danny was obviously not earning any money, and then asking again why Danny had waited so long to call her, and asking if I had had "too terrible a time." Nothing had seemed wrong till then, and suddenly I was worrying about the hospital bill and feeling very sorry for myself because it was hard to sit down and my breasts ached while they were getting used to the baby's nursing schedule. I didn't want to feel bad—I wanted to stay feeling like that queen in the sunshine for a while—but it was too complicated; we were talking about practical things and old rifts were coming up.

As my mother left to meet Danny downstairs and go home with him, she said, "Do you want me to come with Danny in the morning when he picks up you and the baby?" and I said, "Whatever you like," hoping she would understand that I really meant, "This is a private time and it would be nicer for the three of us to be alone."

But the next morning she was there, very proud and pleased, giving directions to everyone. "Danny, you go down to the cashier, and I'll stay here and help Janet pack her things and then we'll have the nurse dress the baby." Then she asked me if I had a nursing brassiere and I said no, so she went down to the gift shop and bought me two for five dollars each, and I knew she couldn't afford it and neither could we. Everyone was bustling around so, I could hardly think of what time in my life it was— the time that I was taking my little baby home, where I would be her mother for the rest of my life.

We drove home, my mother sitting in the back seat, leaning over my shoulder all the way and looking at the sleeping baby in my lap and touching her little curled fingers and saying how beautiful she was—which was true, but somehow seemed false with my mother saying it aloud like that. Danny didn't speak all the way home, and when we got to the house he took my suitcase and went inside, and my mother and I sat in the car waiting for him to come out and open the door for me, which he didn't do. After five foolish minutes I had to open the car door myself, nearly dropping the baby and nearly crying, and my mother gave me a look that said all she had always thought of Danny. It nearly broke my heart to have everything ruined when it could have been so fine.

I went inside and put the baby in her crib, but didn't know what to do then. Danny had gone into the kitchen with a book, and was sitting at the table reading. I wanted him to admire the baby and tell me what a fine child I had produced and what a brave girl I was, but he never raised his eyes. It seemed as though I had not seen him in years, and I was missing him because I had been away from him for five days in the hospital and, in a way, all the months before that when, if he so much as gave me a kiss, my already overburdened heart would begin to shudder to remind me that warm kisses would have to wait until the baby did not demand so much blood and energy of it.

And now we were further apart than ever.

My mother took over. "You get into bed," she said. "I'll take care of the baby. You need to rest."

"But I want to look at her," I protested.

"You'll look later—you just got out of the hospital." She took off my coat and led me into the bedroom and tucked me into bed and closed the door, to leave me aching and open-eyed and missing my baby and my husband.

The baby, because she was small, had to nurse every two and a half hours and each feeding lasted nearly an hour, so I was never able to sleep for much more than an hour at a time. The nursing I had loved so much in the hospital became a terrible ordeal at home because neither Danny nor my mother could be in the room together with me and the baby at that time without becoming very embarrassed. If one was in the room and the other inadvertently came in, they both would avert their eyes, as though neither would acknowledge to the other his intimate relationship with me.

The baby and I had done beautifully in the hospital, but now, with everyone avoiding everyone in our three rooms, and doors being closed as they went in or out and me being so exhausted and tense, the baby sucked less and cried more, and made me desperate for relief of some kind—sleep, at least, or a little privacy and quiet. Privacy was what we lacked most—I wanted to be alone with my baby, I wanted to be alone with Danny and I wanted the three of us, so newly a family, to have some time alone. My mother, though, was everywhere. If Danny went over to the crib to look at the infant, my mother would appear and look too—and look at Danny to see his reaction. He would mumble and walk away.

On the third day my mother said, "I've never seen Danny kiss the baby. Doesn't he like her?"

What could I answer—"You haven't seen him kiss me either"? or: "He'd kiss her if you weren't watching all the time"? So I just sighed and asked her to bring me a drink of water. "Nursing makes me very thirsty," I told her.

That week my mother prepared all the meals and called us when they were ready. She washed the baby's diapers every day and hung them up outside. She rocked the baby so I could sleep, she cleaned the apartment from ceiling to floor, she baked my favorite chocolate cake, she fixed the hems of my skirts, she ironed, she labored like ten mules.

And it was horrible. One night in bed—my mother was sleeping on the couch in the living room—Danny whispered to me, "I'm sorry, Janet, if I seem awful to her and to you, but I can't stand this. I don't feel as though this is my home any more. I feel as though I were courting you again and calling for you at your mother's house—the way she calls us to meals and is so polite, and the way she just goes into our closets and drawers as if it were her own house. I feel as if I don't belong here."

I took his head in my arms and held him, but he said, "I really can't stand it, Janet," and then he asked me to please do some of the cooking and dishwashing so my mother would remember it was she who was visiting us and not us visiting her. "I know you're tired and still a little sick, but you have to show her what she's doing to us."

So the next day I started to wash the dishes after breakfast, though I hadn't slept three hours in twenty-four, and my mother asked me if I was crazy and told me to get back into bed that minute. I said no, I felt fine, I was getting stronger every day, and then I fainted.

Which made Danny even sadder than he had been, and soon he just left the house in the morning and went to the library and didn't come back till supper time. He had yet to hold the baby.

So I stayed in bed, and my mother brought my meals to me and brought the baby in for me to nurse and did the changing and dressing. Soon she would not even wake me if it was feeding time, but would make up a formula bottle and give it to the baby so as not to disturb me. And soon I wasn't having enough milk because the pattern was destroyed.

One night when the baby started crying, I leaped out of bed and lifted her from her crib and carried her back to my bed with me, where I was going to wake Danny and tell him to look at his daughter. But suddenly my mother was right in our bedroom, white and disheveled in her nightgown, her gray hair disordered from sleep, her arms out for the baby. "Give her to me, Janet— I'll get her quiet. You go back to sleep."

I couldn't help what I said and it was wrong of me, but I said, "Why on earth do you have to come poking around every minute? Why can't you leave us alone?"

And my mother, horrified, went right out of our bedroom. I heard her walking around in the living room all the rest of the night, while I sat in the bedroom with the baby in my lap till the sun rose.

In the morning my mother's eyes were red; she said it was because she had a cold and she was going to fly home because she didn't want the baby to catch anything from her. It was only the end of the first week, and she had planned to stay two. I knew all I had to do was ask her to please stay, and she needed me to—her eyes on my face were so pitiful—but all I did was say that I was surely much stronger now and could manage alone. Danny spoke for the first time in days, to volunteer to take her to the airport.

My mother and I couldn't look at each other—both of us had tears on our cheeks all morning—and she packed and I pretended to be busy in the bedroom.

On the way to the airport she said from the back seat, "I had to borrow on Daddy's life-insurance policy to get enough money for plane fare. I suppose I should have stayed home. You didn't need me."

"I did, oh, I *did*, Mother," I cried. And then, recognizing the lie exposed by this solemn trip, I fell silent, while my mother fumbled for a handkerchief.

"I thought you would need me," she said. The grief in her voice was so deep that I reached back for her hand, to hold it, but she pulled it away and looked out the window. "A good day for a flight," she said, making her voice steady.

My hand dropped to my lap, where my daughter lay asleep, wrapped in a blanket, and I touched her cheek, thinking: Will you and I ever come to this?

At the airport Danny wanted to go up on the observation deck because we were early, and he paid three dimes to get us through the turnstile. As soon as we got there my mother said, "It's too windy here for the baby. Let's go down." Danny said, "A little wind can't hurt her," and my mother said, "Wind is the worst thing for an infant not even two weeks old yet," and I said, "Oh, please, let's not fight—it is a warm wind, Mother," and she said, "Have it your way. I have to get on that plane."

She went down, and in about two minutes we went down too, and she had checked her luggage and was ready to leave.

"Good-bye, Mother," I said. "Thank you for coming."

She stood stiffly, looking at my face as though she didn't know me, and then she began to walk toward the gate. I ran after her and threw my arms around her and hugged her, crying, "I love you, Mother, I love you." We embraced desperately, as though this were the last time we could ever express our love, and then she went through the gate, her head down, her hand to her eyes.

I went back to Danny, who stood to one side with the baby, and shouted at him, "Why couldn't you have let her kiss the baby good-bye? Why couldn't you? Why did you have to carry her away like that?" He didn't answer me, just put the baby in my arms and then put his arm around my shoulder and began to lead me to the car. When we got outside I did not even look at the plane my mother was flying away in. We walked to the car and the wind blew the baby's cap off, and I yelled at Danny, "It *is* too windy for the baby. My mother was right! Don't you see? She was *right!*"

The cap, filling with wind, flew and bumped across the parking lot, and Danny and I watched it until it got tangled under the wheel of a car, and then we just left it there and drove home.

(1964)

Baby Blues

~

ALTHOUGH JANET SEEMED TO be floating even when the bed was still, she could enjoy a heightened effect by pushing the buttons on the gray, cross-shaped machine attached to the hospital bed. There were six buttons: Head up, Head down, Bed up, Bed down, Feet up, Feet down. Each operation was accompanied by a dull, whirring sound, as the mysterious hydraulic system levitated and lowered her. The whirring could be heard all night, up and down the hall, as other patients felt the need for height or depth. At each extreme a crushing, grinding sound suggested the machines were, ultimately, only of human design, and that the ceilings could not be transcended or the heavens reached so simply after all.

They would not let her sleep. From the moment they had rolled her into this bed at eleven p.m. four nights ago, they had interrupted her reveries and her sleep with constant mechanical ministrations. A hundred different faces had flashed in front of her the first night; all of them looked grimly into space as hands kneaded her uterus with indifferent response to her protests. Now the faces appeared less often and she had more time to think.

A deliberate-sounding cough in the hall caused Janet to start, and then she saw the woman in the blue robe pacing in the dim corridor again. She wore the zombie-like expression of a sleepwalker, but a shrewd intelligence showed in her eyes.

On her third trip past Janet's door she slowed her steps, and before Janet could turn her head away, the woman saw that she was awake and came into the semidark room.

"Why aren't you asleep?" the woman asked. "Have you got something to worry about?"

"Oh, no," Janet said. "It's just hard to know night from day here. I sleep on and off."

"I saw your daughter," the woman said.

"How did you know which one was mine?"

"I know them all on this floor." The woman came up close to the bed.

"What did *you* have?" Janet asked.

"A boy."

"Oh, I wanted a boy so badly," Janet said. "My first was a girl, and another girl seems so much of a repetition—I can't imagine how she can be anyone but the same exact child as my first girl. Besides, girls have a hard time of it in this world. I was hoping so hard for a son." She laughed a little breathlessly. "I don't know why I told you that. I was determined never to mention it. It doesn't matter now. But it *is* nice you have a boy."

"Don't let it bother you," the woman said, "but he was born dead." The woman held out her arm, and Janet saw that she wore a plastic admittance bracelet, not the engraved silver coin on a nylon cord that matched the coin fastened to each baby after birth.

"I'm so sorry," Janet said. She felt frightened, and she had an impulse to ring for the nurse and ask that the woman be taken away.

"I've had six stillborns," the woman said, watching Janet closely. "They all, when they got to a certain weight, fooled the cervix into opening. It was too soon for any of them. This time the doctor promised it would be all right; he stitched me up inside so I could go full term. I felt the baby move when I was in labor—I was so sure I could keep this baby. But it didn't like being sewed up. It had its way."

Janet thought the woman was insane, speaking of her cervix as an intelligent force she had tried to deceive and that had had its revenge.

"I don't know why they don't let me go home," the woman said, suddenly pitiful. "They make me stay here, and I hear the babies crying and see the flowers delivered up and down the hall and watch the carts come out from the nursery at feeding time."

The muscles of Janet's face were frozen in a kind of shock; she tried to think of something to say. Then the woman touched Janet's arm meanly. "Don't worry about me," she said. "Life is awful, but at least my baby doesn't have to have it. Yours does."

Janet lay trembling after the woman walked away. A curse had been uttered, and she did not want to think about what it meant. After the first day or two here she had tried hard *not* to think, only to drift about in a sort of hazy peacefulness, absorbing whatever happened to her passively, willingly, without analysis. But her mind continued to focus on the reconstruction of her labor and delivery. She kept finding new things scattered about her mind that should have been tucked neatly into place.

She had to preserve her experiences because nothing quite so interesting had ever happened to her before—she had been unconscious during the birth of her first child—and she felt she would never be in danger of complete boredom again, having this birth in her memory. Already, though, it was sifting away; and feeling it become less immediate, she longed again for the complete experience. She was feeling empty and increasingly vulnerable. In pregnancy she had believed herself to be protected against sickness and deterioration—her baby was in there, keeping an eye on things, watching out for her. Now she was on her own again. She could hardly recall her nausea, her great weight, the pounding of her overworked heart, the excitement and live promise of the baby's movements, though she had thought of nothing else for months. And now, if she was not careful, she would not be able to remember this birth either.

No matter how often in her life she had actively tried to keep a picture in her mind, saying to herself, "You will remember this moment; it is significant," she had not remembered it. The first sight of her daughter Bonnie, of her husband's face as he turned to her after he had placed her wedding ring on her finger, these and others all had left her, though she had been determined they never would.

During her labor she had commanded herself, "Keep this!" But now only vaguely—and because the knitting pains in her pelvis were not entirely gone—could she recall the grandness of her contractions and the hardness and coldness of the bedrails she had held onto while she counted the breaths it took for a pain to rise and pass. Her husband, who had stood by anxiously while Janet slid her fingers over the rails and gave tremendous concentration to the contractions, clearly did not believe her when she told him in her quiet moments that really, she liked the pains, they were fine and efficient, they did not hurt in a way that frightened because she had no fear.

In fact, the most unpleasant moment of her labor had come when the nurse in attendance had said, "So you're Dr. John's patient too—that poor man has had three deliveries tonight"; and Janet had answered, "Oh, but he loves children so, I can't imagine him minding. He has four of his own, you know, and probably plans four more."

"He doesn't plan any more," the nurse said coldly. "His wife has been dead a year. She died in surgery here."

Janet had been incredulous. All during her visits to him, he had spoken constantly of his wife and how he had seen the knees and elbows of his unborn babies poking through her stomach. This talk had made Janet comfortable—this warm approval of his wife, and of childbirth in general. It was unfair, somehow, to be told this about him now, and Janet resented the nurse's badly timed confidence.

Later in the delivery room, she had suffered an immense wave of compassion for him. Watching him deliver her child, she had felt so grateful for his earnestness and for his care for her life and her infant's that she wanted to repair his deprivation somehow. She would marry him and give him this baby; she would become all his patients, and all their babies would be his . . . and hers.

She knew the experts had written of women falling in love with their obstetricians because of the intimate nature of their relationship. Simply because something was explained didn't make it less true; understanding was not the same thing as undoing—she was in love with Dr. John, and she had been in love with the doctor who had delivered her daughter Bonnie. . . .

Her feelings of sympathy had disappeared immediately when her baby's ear, then face, appeared in the delivery-room mirror, and the doctor put a finger in its mouth, the best grasping place, and said to her, "Don't turn away. Watch." She'd been insulted that he thought she would turn her head away, and then felt he was stupid when he said, "This is your last chance—a boy or a girl?" He had forced her to say what she had told no one—"Oh, please let it be a boy"—and then an instant later he said, "A sister for your big girl," and she had felt humiliated.

Suddenly, though, he was no longer speaking to her, but was tensely doing something to the baby. She saw her infant's completely perfect, human face in his lap—purple, immobile, lifeless, and she thought that after all this her baby was not going to breathe.

She did not breathe herself, only listened to the squish of the syringe as the doctor manipulated it in the baby's mouth and nose. A nurse was running toward him, pushing a metal table with a machine on it, and suddenly Janet heard a whimper. The nurse laughed, and Janet at the same moment heard the whimper renewed, loudly and magnificently; the cries filled her ears and choked her throat till she began to cry. She had cried the same way when the baby first moved inside her.

After that she no longer loved the doctor; she wanted only to see her husband. When she was wheeled into the hall, her husband placed his hand on the pillow next to her, and she rolled her head and pressed her face against his hand fiercely to express, hopelessly, some of what she had felt in the last moments.

The next morning when they'd got her out of bed and shakily onto her feet, she'd walked alone to the nursery to see her baby. As she looked through the window, her eye was carried to the light coming from a window on the other side of the nursery that opened to an outside patio, and there she saw the face of

Bonnie, her big girl, looking in. She thought it was a trick of light or of her own sight—to look into the nursery and see not her new baby but her old. When she saw her husband in the background, she realized that he had brought Bonnie to see the baby through what the hospital called the "Heir Port" window. And then she saw the glass cart under the far window, with her new baby in it, too new even to be thought of by the name they had chosen for her—Jill.

She waved, trying to catch Bonnie's attention, but the little girl was staring stonily at the glass crib.

Feeling suddenly frantic and cut off from the people she loved most by all these walls and windows, she hurried up and down the hall until she found a storage room with a small window overlooking the patio at the end of it.

Pulling it open, she cried, "Danny! Danny, I'm here!" and then she had to lean dizzily on a pile of white hospital gowns.

Danny's face appeared at the window and Janet laughed, and then he disappeared, to return carrying Bonnie.

"It's Mommy, sweetheart," she said. "Mommy had the new baby. Now you have a little sister."

"I don't want it. I want a brother," Bonnie said.

"But we didn't *have* one," Janet said angrily. Her teeth began to chatter and her knees to shake. No one had shown her any gratefulness for this child. It was not fair.

Her daughter, not yet three, looked huge and alien through the window. The blonde, uncombed curls, usually in a neat ponytail, made her nearly unrecognizable, as did the hard expression about her mouth.

Trying to become sensible again, Janet said, "Now throw Mommy a kiss—she has to go back to bed. Soon she'll come home and take care of you again, and we'll all have our new baby to play with. Will you like that?"

"I want to get down," Bonnie said to Danny, twisting in his arms, and when he set her down she ran away, a splash of red dress against the lawn, looking to her mother like any unfamiliar child at a playground.

"There've been so many changes—it's just hard for her,"

Danny said to soothe Janet, but the tears that had started were not because her child did not seem to care about her; they came because she did not care about her child. She could hardly remember that she had loved her, and she did not know how the betrayal had come about. Just the day before, driving to the hospital, she had been terrified that neither of them could survive this first separation. Apparently they had not. Now she felt tender only toward the new baby, and hostile and resentful toward Bonnie—resentful even of her existence, because it meant a reduction in discovery and delight with her second baby, who could, by definition, of course not be her first.

She had passed through so many firsts now—the first kiss, the first night, the first child—how much more was left for her to be moved by?

"You'd better get back into bed," Danny said, and she assented, moving out of view of the window and sinking down against a stack of towels. "I'll see you at visiting hours," he called. She did not answer him, but just sat there looking at the stacks of sheets, towels, pillowcases, packages of sanitary belts, pads and tissues.

A nurse found her that way, half asleep, and led her toward her room. As they passed the nursery, Janet peered in the window and pulled away from the nurse's arm.

"That's my baby vomiting!" she cried. "Look—she's choking, she can't breathe, milk is coming out of her nose!"

Hysterically she pushed open the nursery door and found a nurse sitting at a desk. "My baby's choking! Why aren't you watching her?" Janet cried.

"What's your name?" she asked, studying the card clipped to the crib.

Janet told her.

"Well, this isn't your baby," the nurse said, beginning to wipe the child's mouth with a diaper.

Outraged, Janet said, "Yes, it is! I ought to know—I *had* her."

She brushed past the nurse and lifted the silver coin around the baby's arm. "There," she said. "Read the name. She's mine. You have her in the wrong crib."

"Well, well," the nurse said, amused. "We have a new student nurse. She's a little confused by all these screaming creatures."

Janet was not amused. The other nurse, waiting in the hall, came forward and took her arm again and put her to bed.

When the baby was brought to her later that afternoon, the nurse who wheeled her in smiled and announced that they had put a tube down the baby's throat and pumped her stomach of mucus. "That ought to take care of the vomiting. She'll be fine now," the girl said. "She seems to have a little infection in her mouth, but it's not serious."

When the girl had left, Janet set down the bottle of formula she'd been handed and put the baby to her breast. But it was too soon for both of them—the baby wanted only to sleep. Janet opened the baby's mouth gently and counted nine white blisters on the lining of her tiny cheeks.

She leaned back and held the baby close against her. The word "cradle" came into her mind, and she remembered a part of a ballad:

> Oh, little did my mother think
> When first she cradled me
> The lands I was to travel in
> And the death I was to dee.

It was a fine, sentimental song but it was true; little did she know how this baby would live and less did she know how it would die. And she had placed it on earth, without extreme consideration, to do both.

A flicker crossing her baby's face caught her eye: the baby —Jill—was smiling.

It was an act of faith—it could be nothing else. The child had had nothing but tortures acted upon her during her brief existence. Already she had been smacked, stuck with needles, stung with eyedrops; already she had lain in her vomit, had a tube put down her throat to pump her stomach, been tested for proper blood, been poked for hernias, hammered for reflexes. Germs had attacked the lining of her mouth; ammonia had seared her tender skin. And yet she could lie against Janet asleep, with the corners of her small mouth pulling themselves into the most delicate, beatific smile Janet had ever seen. It seemed to Janet that behind those eyelids a vision of glory was coming to her baby, a picture of supreme happiness, a dream of life that could tempt the first dimple into her cheek, promising—to Janet at least—that she would be a beautiful child, if one deluded by a specious dream.

Guilt again, for this mindless act of creation made Janet lift the child and kiss her tiny lips. She had neither wanted children nor not wanted them. She had simply followed the lines of human life, desiring what were promised as fulfillments and experiences, unable to know what else she could expect from her existence. For the second time now, she and Danny had made a life, without knowing really what a life was, without the power to explain its origin, its purpose, its meaning, its end.

And there was where the knife turned—its end. By now, Janet believed and expected she would die, and not profit by doing so. Worse, she believed that everyone she loved would die, probably before her own death. It was a fact she hated, feared, and accepted.

But to make a new person who, when grown, would have to come to this same conclusion, would feel the same helplessness and rage—possibly that was the prime sin. Was it fair? The old questions arose—was it better to have a life—to have a look at the sunshine—than to have nothing? Probably yes. But if the price of life was death?

She had not got far enough to know.

Again the ghostly smile illuminated her infant's pale face, and Janet gave it up—this useless thinking. Where could it lead anyway? She was cursed with dying her own death a thousand times before it came. Perhaps her children would be smart enough to die only once, at the end of their lives.

She reached for a magazine. She had been told that thinking happy thoughts was good for making lots of milk; at this rate, she would starve her baby to death before it had any fun at all.

She smiled to herself and then she felt better. She was having a happy time—really she was. She had loved this birth and she loved this baby. Why couldn't she enjoy her *happy* times, at least?

And she had tried. On the second day she had addressed birth announcements. Placing the envelopes one by one in the mail slot gave her an immense satisfaction. Then she decided it was time to reward Dr. John with payment for his services, so she took her checkbook from her purse and wrote out a check for his fee. She hesitated, wondering if the bank would cash it if she signed it "Love, Janet."

At visiting hours Danny came, with books and chocolate bars, which she read and ate in the hours she was left alone. Danny did not bring Bonnie again, and Janet found it an effort even to ask after the child. She knew she should: Is she eating; is she taking her vitamins; does she mind having the sitter look after her?

But she did not have the energy to care, and the presents she had taken to the hospital, wrapped in pink tissue, to send home to Bonnie day by day, stayed untouched in her suitcase. She did not ask herself if it was a "normal" reaction. Whatever it was called, it was horrible. Before Jill was born, she had loved Bonnie more than her own life.

When the announcements had been mailed, she found it best just to float, to float and sleep and put off thinking.

She had often noticed the woman in the blue robe, but never until this fourth day had she spoken to her. Everyone's sadnesses . . . they were not her fault. From down the hall she heard the cries of a woman in labor and felt no sympathy. The squalls of the babies did not move her; pain, separations, birth, deaths—why should she have to worry all the time?

She lowered her bed, climbed out gingerly and packed her suitcase. The doctor said it was her choice when to leave—well, she was ready.

In the morning she called Danny and told him to be at the hospital before eleven. "Should I bring anything?" he asked, and she said, "Not Bonnie."

The dress she'd packed did not fit her at all, and she had to wear only her coat over her slip. The nurse brought in the baby for her to dress and left a parting gift—a blue, plastic shoe with a slot in it for coins, compliments of a local bank. Another nurse, coming to sign her out, saw the blue bank and her pink baby and said, "Who has the funny sense of humor?"

Well, so she would never have a son. She had made enough babies already.

In the car she held out her arms for the baby, but the nurse could not relinquish her until the silver coins were removed from both mother and child. They made a little ceremony out of it, with Danny cutting the cords with nail scissors. She put the two coins in her purse and they drove away.

When they pulled into their driveway, the mailman was coming up the walk, holding a sheaf of letters. Ah, Janet thought, already the announcements were bringing back congratulations, checks, cards—celebrations of the new life.

He came up to the car and handed her one brown envelope through the window. He didn't notice the baby in her lap, and she could not bring herself to announce that this was a great day, a moment of great importance in their lives that he was missing. When he had walked to the next house, Danny helped her out of the car and she looked around, hoping some neighbor would be at a window, some witness somewhere to this moment.

When they got into the house, the teenaged girl who was staying with Bonnie said the baby was cute, and Bonnie came over with a crayon in her hand and tried to write on the baby's head.

Janet thought she would ask Danny to turn on the tape recorder so that they could have a record forever of this event— the baby's first cries, her first minutes in her home. But it was too complicated to explain; she did not really want to bother to open her mouth.

She put the baby in her crib, blanket and all, and, still wearing her coat, sat down at the table to open the letter she was holding. It was a letter from their bank, returning the check she had written to Dr. John and stating that it had not been paid because of insufficient funds. She looked in her checkbook and found that because of a mistake in her arithmetic, Dr. John, whose wife was dead and who was both father and mother to his four poor children, had not been paid his due. It was the first time in her life that a check of hers had bounced, and she put her head down on the plastic tablecloth and began to cry.

The teenaged girl who had been staying with Bonnie came running over to her, saying, "Please don't cry. Let me read you something."

Janet raised her head and saw that the girl was holding a book taken from the bedroom bookcase, called *A Happy Pregnancy*. Breathlessly the girl began to read:

> Every new mother, after her baby is born and everything is going along beautifully, suddenly bursts into tears one day during her recovery and has a good, long cry. There is never any reason she can find for it but nothing can stop her—she simply cries and wails for a good half-hour, and when she is through she says, "I don't know what came over me." If this happens to you, don't worry. It is called "Baby Blues" and once it's over, it will never happen again.

"So please don't worry," the girl said. "It won't ever happen again." And Janet dried her tears and said, "I don't know what came over me."

(1965)

Explain That to a Baby-Sitter

~

I REALLY DON'T LIKE to go away from home at all, though I'm always saying to Danny, "Why don't you take me some place? I'm so bored sitting home all day, with only the children to talk to." I usually go on, in hardly a kind voice: "You go away every day, you see people, you talk to *adults*, you drive around, you eat lunch out. You have an *interesting* time."

It's not quite true, I know. Danny gets up very early and he works very hard, and the people he talks to are mostly his students, who say he didn't give them a fair grade, or the men in his office, who are always trying to get him to join one teachers' union or another—and he doesn't like to be political—so it isn't really true that he has such a wonderful day while I stay home and eat cereal with the children for lunch.

But when I get that cranky, miserable feeling in me, the tone in my voice is just aching to be aimed at someone or I will never get relief from it. The thing is, Danny agrees with me. "I'd be glad to take you somewhere, Janet—in fact, I've been wanting to for years. Don't I always tell you that? Just find some kind of baby-sitter and we'll go out. Tonight, if you want to."

And that's where the trouble comes in—I don't like to go away from home and leave the children. It's so disturbing when I think about it that I always decide I'd rather stay home and be bored.

But unless I am some kind of idiot, I just can't go on complaining that I never go out and then refuse to go when Danny wants to take me.

So I decided I will really make an attempt. Till now I have been using our big girl as an excuse. When she was three years old she had a terrible croup attack, and after that no one could expect me to leave; because if it happened again, no baby-sitter could be expected to know what to do—which is first to run the hot water in the shower full blast with the bathroom door closed and to make her breathe the steam, then to cover her crib with a heavy blanket and take out the vaporizer and point its nozzle under the blanket, to make a steam-filled tent to put her back into. That is, if she has caught her breath and is breathing more easily. The important thing is not to get her too excited or to show her you are alarmed. I remember—too often—how the night it happened I read her a book about a circus train, I sitting on the tiles of the bathroom floor and she on my lap, wheezing as if the air would never get into her lungs. My nightgown got soaked from the moisture filling the room like a smoke screen, but I just kept reading blindly, feeling her little back heave against my chest, every gasp keeping the life in her.

There are other procedures to take if things don't improve. I have a bottle of syrup of ipecac in the medicine chest, which would make her vomit (I still don't know how that would help), and as a very last resort there is one more thing to do. I got a book called *Emergency Procedures* from a medical publisher (I wrote for it, implying that I was a doctor), which describes how to do an emergency tracheotomy—that is, how to cut a hole in her throat between the ridges of cartilage in her neck so that air can get into her lungs.

Now, would you want to have to explain all *that* to a baby-sitter?

The truth is, it's been over two years since she had the attack and she hasn't had another, so the likelihood is very small that she ever will. Of course, the little one is just at that age now, and she or the baby just might have an attack, but to worry about that is decidedly neurotic, since they are different people and both in very good health.

"All right," I tell Danny, almost defiantly, on Friday morning. "I am going to get a baby-sitter for the children so you can take me out tonight."

"Good! Wonderful!" he says, and kisses me good-bye. For him, it's as simple as that. And off he goes.

I think suddenly that I have nothing to wear. When you don't ever go out, you don't waste money buying pretty clothes or having your hair attended to. Around the house I wear any old things. Neat, of course, but old. But in a dark movie who will know or care what I wear?

I start out; I am not completely without resources. I put the baby in the carriage, and the little one holds on to the left side and the big one to the right side, and I lock the front door and we go down the block to the undertaker's house. I have never met him, but I have heard that his old mother does baby-sitting. The carriage goes fast because the street tilts downhill. They live about five houses away. I have seen the undertaker's children playing in the street. They look very serious—I can imagine what the talk at their dinner table is like.

The undertaker's wife opens the door and is very surprised. In all the years she and I have lived on this block, the only time we say hello is when the bread man comes by and toots his horn and we both go out to get bread. She takes her whole wheat loaf and nods to me and I take my dozen powdered doughnuts and I smile at her, and that is that.

"Hello," I say. "I understand that your mother-in-law likes to baby-sit sometimes. Do you think she might want to take care of my children for an evening?"

"Come in," she says, and I take the baby out of the carriage and wrap her up and knee the two bigger ones into the house. (Even preparing for *this* trip away from home was a lot of trouble. I had to take a bottle and pacifier and diapers in case the baby needed them and I had to make ponytails for the two big girls and change my own clothes.) Inside the house, the undertaker's wife yells, "Ma!" and an old lady comes out of a bedroom, her gray hair all blued and curled and red polish on her fingernails.

On the dining-room table there is a mountain of unfolded laundry, which the undertaker's wife begins automatically to fold. "This lady"—she smiles at me apologetically ("I never really learned your name," she says, but she doesn't stop to ask it then, either) "—this lady wonders if you'd like to baby-sit for her."

"I'd like to," the old woman says. She doesn't glance at my children. I can see that the undertaker's wife would be glad to have her out of the house for an evening. It's clear that the old woman wouldn't consider lifting a finger to help with the laundry.

The transaction is so simple that I have all kinds of doubts again.

The old woman says, "Everyone calls me Mom Williams."

"Could you come tonight?"

"Yes," she says. And it seems to be settled. We don't discuss price because that is not the issue in my mind. I have five years of staying home that I am supposed to make up for tonight. It doesn't matter what it costs.

"We live in the yellow house on the corner," I say. "Do you think you could walk over this afternoon for a minute so I could show you where things are and so the children could get used to you? There may not be time to do that later."

"Oh," says the old woman. "I can't walk up that hill. I have a bad heart. Your husband would have to come and get me in his car tonight."

My own heart lurches. How is this woman going to take care of three children—undress them, lift them, carry them—if she is on the verge of heart failure? I am having heart failure myself, thinking how close to catastrophe I have come. I would come home and find her dead on my kitchen floor with all the children screaming in terror.

"Well, Mrs. Williams . . ." I say, and she says, "Just call me Mom Williams," and I try not to run out the door. I say, "Let me find out what our plans are, and I will call you later."

I stand there in the face of my lie while she writes down our phone number. I shudder, walking home, pushing the carriage up the small hill to the house.

Still, there are other possibilities. There is the Cuban lady Juanita, across the street, who brings me roses from her rose-bushes. She is very sweet, she loves children and she has none of her own. Whenever she sees mine, she swoops down on them to hug and kiss them. My big girl just stands rather stiffly, enduring it, but my little one always runs to me in tears because she thinks Juanita is going to carry her away from me. The baby at the moment isn't choosy.

So I steer the carriage across the street. Juanita always lectures me that I should go out more, that I owe it to my husband, that my children will grow up and never thank me. I know all that. What she doesn't understand is that I don't want thanks from my children in twenty years; I just want to be calm *now*.

She is in her garden and she sees us. "Aah, my darling angels!" She rushes at the little one, who turns in panic and grabs my leg. "Aah, why you no like to kiss Juanita?" Juanita says. Her smile is clear and lovely, and simple as the sky. She just doesn't understand. "And you, my precious darling? You no like Juanita?" My big girl smiles stiffly, like a grownup. Children learn to dissemble so quickly. Juanita bends over the carriage. The baby, only two months old, yawns, showing us her little tongue. There is a white coating of milk on it; she was fed just before we left the house.

"Ooh," says Juanita. "You don't give her water to wash out her mouth?"

"She doesn't need water," I say. "She just had five ounces of milk."

"No, no, no," Juanita says. "You listen to me—I know. They need water. To clean the tongue. You don't want her to have a sour tongue."

"Maybe," I say noncommittally.

"And you, you darling," she says to the little one. "Your mama gives you tonic? You're so pale."

"What kind of tonic?" I ask.

"For the blood," Juanita says. "I have a big bottle. You come in, I give her some. Then her blood will be red, her face will be bright."

My children have red blood. I know from their scraped knees. But I am discouraged again. I can see it all: Juanita comes to baby-sit: She scrubs the baby's tongue with scouring powder; she gives the little one a quart of blood-reddening tonic to drink; she gives my big one—what? An enema, a mustard plaster? There is no end to it.

"And you," she says to me. "Why you not let me come to your house and you go out with your Danny? For so many months you have that big belly, you can't move, he cannot get near to you. Now you have to go out, be with him again, have a good time. Your Danny needs you. You think too much of the babies—not enough of you goes to your man."

"Soon," I say, refusing to consider the truth in her words. "Soon." And before we leave, Juanita gives us roses.

In the house I unload the baby, change her diaper, send the children outside to play. There is one more possibility: my in-laws, who now live nearby.

I don't consider too carefully; I just dial my mother-in-law's number. Otherwise I will just give up.

"It's Janet," I say. "Do you think you could watch the children tonight for a while? Danny wants to go out." I put the blame on her son.

"All of a sudden?" my mother-in-law asks. "For five years you've never gone out."

"So isn't it time already?" I say—a kind of joke.

"I'll be glad to," she says. "Only today I have a bad headache."

"Oh." I am so relieved. "Well, some other time, then."

"No, no. Dad and I would be delighted. We were going to go over our checkbook tonight, but there's no rush."

"But that's more important," I say.

"No, not at all," my mother-in-law says. "What time do you want us there?"

"Around seven," I say, wishing she had said she would be glad to come and mean *be glad*. You don't pay off that kind of debt at seventy-five cents an hour.

We make arrangements. I hang up. Living is so complicated.

Now—I first have to get to work. The house has to be cleaned. When you go out and your mother-in-law is going to be loose in your house, it has to be clean. Not only that—I have to start hiding things. Letters on my desk, bills, my checkbook, our bankbook. My mother-in-law is very curious. I can see her poking around like a policeman, trying to discover all the things we have never told her, like how much rent we really pay, how much money we have saved.

I wash the kitchen floor; I move out the couch to vacuum under it, the first time in years. I find huge networks of cobwebs on the walls I have never even noticed before. The day is rushing by. When Danny finally comes home, I am stricken with panic. The evening is really upon us. We have to go out! But why? I'm not bored any more. I've spent the whole day busier than I have ever spent a day—knocking on doors, talking to people, cleaning my house. Now I need to rest, to stay home quietly. I have no *strength* left!

We eat dinner. I tell Danny his mother is coming so we can go out.

"Fine," Danny says. "That's wonderful. Where do you want to go?"

I haven't even considered it. Out. *Out!*

"You decide," I say. "Pretend you are taking me on a date, like long ago."

"But it's up to you," Danny says.

I almost feel like crying. "I don't *want* it to be up to me! Everything is always up to me! Why can't you make a simple decision? Why can't you be a man?"

But why can't I be nice? Why am I being nasty? It's so long since Danny took me out. So long since those starry walks along the beach, when we sat in empty lifeguard towers and watched the water. It was so nice then—even to see a rat run across the sand was a pleasure. The forces of life were all around us—wind, water, love, rats. The pull of the tides was in us then. What is in us now? Work, worry, hurry.

"Do you want to go to a movie?" Danny asks.

I shrug. "I don't care," I say. I am sure nothing can be worth all this bother.

Danny finds the Sunday paper, looks at the movie ads for the week. He shrugs too. "Nothing any good," he says. He looks up at me, waiting. He wants us to have a nice evening. He wants me to change channels, to get on a happy track, to put the whine away. He smiles. "We don't have to go to a movie. There are lots of things. Plays, concerts."

"No," I say. "I have no patience for those."

"Then what?"

"I don't know," I say. And I add, "Your parents will be here soon."

I do the dishes quickly; I put the cooled formula in the refrigerator. I still doubt that we will really go. I am waiting for something: a war, a hurricane, an earthquake. We are not destined to have an evening out.

And suddenly I hear a crash from the children's bedroom. I *knew* something would happen! I am in the room before I remember moving. The little one has toppled the dresser over on top of her.

"She was using the drawers for stairs," the big one cries, to clear herself.

The little one is flat on her face; any instant she will start to cry. I pull her out. The dresser drawer is on her foot, but I am sure she is not really hurt. She is only scared. I turn her over, waiting for the flood of tears, but she cannot get them out. She has drawn breath to cry, but the breath goes neither in nor out. Her lips have lost their color. As I watch, her face turns dark red, then blue. She is turning black: she is not breathing.

"Danny!" I scream.

He runs in.

I am shaking the little one, screaming, "She isn't breathing!"

"Give her to me," he says.

But I rush away with her, shaking her, crying, "Breathe!" Her face is black; her eyes are closed. Her head lolls loosely; there is no tension in her body. She is unconscious.

"Why is there so much excitement?" I hear the big one say in a shaky voice, as if from a distance. I am faint with terror.

Danny says, "Stop shaking her. Give her to me."

"But she isn't breathing," I beg him. "She'll die." I am sobbing, pressing the little one against me.

The she gasps. Her face gets less black.

"I think she's going to breathe," I say. The words feel like a prayer.

She gasps again. Her lids flutter.

"She's going to be all right," I say. I sit down, trembling, with the little one in my lap. She takes a deep breath and her face lightens. She opens her eyes and looks around, dazed.

The big girl laughs in relief. Then the little one starts to cry, a single sob, and then she stops. She seems very tired. She doesn't seem to know what has happened.

In a minute she slides off my lap and walks to her crib to get her blanket. She rubs her thumb over the silky binding.

The doorbell rings. Danny's parents.

I am about to say, "How can we go? How can I leave now?" but I know that is what Danny expects me to say. It is what I expect of myself.

But there the little one is; she is smiling, perfectly well. Nothing else can happen today.

While Danny answers the door I pull out my Doctor Spock book. I read that children sometimes hold their breath till they turn blue, that it is nothing serious but that parents are often scared out of their wits. I love that wise old doctor; he has saved my life before, many times.

Danny and his mother and father come into the bedroom.

"It's late," his mother says. "You're not even dressed yet."

"I'll get dressed right now," I say.

"Where are you going?" Danny's father asks.

"We're not sure," I tell him.

Danny says to me, "Do you want to go to the Folk Palace? They have the Nitty Gritty Dirt Band there."

"The Nitty Gritty Dirt Band! Are you serious?" I gasp. Those seem to be the funniest words I have ever heard. I begin to laugh, and Danny, sharing my hysterical relief, begins to laugh with me. His parents think we are crazy. We laugh till tears run from our eyes. We cannot control ourselves; we are heaving to and fro with laughter. Danny staggers across the room to me and puts his arms around me and we weave back and forth, laughing, choking "Nitty Gritty" till our heads knock together.

"I'll get dressed," I manage to say, and I stumble out, giggling madly.

"Must be funny," my father-in-law says behind me.

We really do go to the Folk Palace. It is filled with smoke, which obscures even the fake Tiffany shades hanging from the ceiling. In the lobby they sell *The Free Press, The Oracle, News From Underground*, psychedelic coloring books, posters recommending Mellow Yellow. I have colored lights in my head already without outside help, and I am still weak from laughing. I hardly remember leaving the house. I kissed the children; I left no instructions, no doctor's number, nothing. We have to take chances in this life.

Danny and I sit at a little round table as big as a poker chip, and the waitress brings him a menu. "How about Cleveland Sparkling Grape Juice?" Danny says, and shows it to me on the menu. It costs a dollar fifty a glass. It is the second funniest thing I have heard this evening. I nod, unable to speak, and Danny starts to laugh too. We laugh until the waitress returns, and Danny orders two glasses of Cleveland Sparkling Grape Juice.

The Nitty Gritty Dirt Band is the most awful thing, but Danny and I have never seen anything funnier. They jiggle around on the stage with their washboards and long hair and coonskin hats and they dodge in and out of the stroboscopic lights, yowling their music, and Danny and I laugh and drink our grape juice. Danny takes my hand. I have never had so much fun.

They are singing some awful song, "Been gone so-o-o lo-ong baby . . ." and they rock and jiggle under their guitars and disappear in the smoke. I have been gone from Danny so long; for years I have done nothing but worry about the children.

When we get outside the air is like a jewel. We are under

some kind of spell. We hold hands till we get to the car and we drive even farther from home, toward the beach. It will be 3:00 a.m. before we get home. I don't care if we stay away a year. For the first time in years, I feel separate from my children. I feel like myself.

We walk on the pier, breathing the air. I don't say, "It is so late—I am tired. How will I ever get up tomorrow?" We stand against the cold rails, watching the lights of a ship, and then Danny kisses me. It is like a kiss after a long separation.

The evening no longer seems funny; it is even better than that.

Danny says, with an almost shy smile, "Should we call home and tell then the car broke down?"

I almost ask, "Why?"—but I know.

"Then we can stay at a motel on the beach," he says. "Would you like that?"

I feel shy too. It is like a proposal of marriage, but nicer because we are already married.

The words are as good as the deed, perhaps better. We have our own home. We hurry to the car to get to it.

As we park in our driveway I see, across the street, Juanita's rosebushes. She is a dear person; she is very wise about some things; she loves my children. It would do them no harm if she gave the baby water, gave the little one some of her miracle tonic. Children survive many things, a baby-sitter the least of them. I will just warn her—not too much tonic. And I will leave sterilized water for the baby so she can have a sweet tongue. What difference can it make?

In the house I don't see Danny's parents too clearly. The smoke from the Folk Palace is still in my eyes. I don't even rush in to look at the children. Danny asks, "How were they?" and his father says, "The baby screamed for two hours," and Danny says to his mother, "Why? Didn't you let her have the pacifier?" We know his parents disapprove of pacifiers. "It will be better for her if she learns to do without that piece of rubber," his mother says, admitting it. At any other time I would have been furious. Now I float past them. I want them to go home, to leave.

"It's late," Danny says to them. "You'll be exhausted tomorrow." He gets his mother's jacket out of the closet and holds it for her. I could kiss him.

I understand that is what this whole day has been moving toward. In fact, as soon as they leave, I plan to.

(1968)

What Do I Want to Do Today?

~

ALREADY THEY HAVE HAD a good laugh, and her children and husband are generous enough not to remind her of the tears they witnessed that morning. The goat is chewing; he has come over to them in the little enclosure where the children are permitted to play with tame animals and sidled up to the baby, almost as if to pose for a picture. Then, quick as lightning, his head has darted toward her purse, in an outer pocket of which she has tucked the yellow zoo map, and in an instant he is rapidly crunching yellow paper between his teeth as the children yell with excitement.

The crackly paper has almost disappeared between his loose lips, and he is chewing fast so as not to lose his advantage. He no longer looks adorable, but crafty and sly, and his guarded eyes are already calculating the new family that has just come in the swinging wooden gate.

Well, sooner or later she is going to have to take back the unfair words with which she slandered these animals this morning and admit to her husband the real reason for her coming along. But for a little longer let her pride be intact; let them think she is here to take care of the baby properly; let them understand her conviction that only she is equipped to be absolutely sure the little ones will not wander off.

This day began for her at the hour all her days started since she became a mother—sometime in the nether regions of the night when the cry of the newest baby shattered her dream, left her with her heart pumping fast and her sleep in pieces. This morning she found herself in the kitchen, heating a bottle, before she was entirely awake. It was freezing cold in the dark house, and the dream—whatever it had been—still lingered like a piece of secret excitement in her mind. Something had been happening—real, vital, relevant to her inner self. Something highly dramatic, like a lovers' quarrel or a separation. The reality around her, by contrast, seemed so dull—her husband heavily asleep (he never, *ever* heard the children's night cries); the cranky baby, who might or might not go back to sleep after her bottle; the toys all over the house that she would have to pick up sooner or later.

She went back to bed and was wakened next by her middle daughter, to whom, too, dreams were more real than actual life. And then—somehow—the true light of day arrived and she had to get up again, entirely weary, as she always was these days, to prepare breakfast.

It was then, as she stumbled around in her robe, making separate dishes for all of them, that Danny said, "Well, where shall we go on our ride today?"

"The beach!" Bonnie shouted.

"Yay! The zoo!" said Jill.

"Da doo," said the baby.

"What about Mother?" Danny said.

"Yes," said Janet. "What about *me*? Where do you suppose *Mother* would like to go?"

"Where?" said Danny, and although Janet knew it was not the beach or the mountains or the zoo she wanted to go to, she could not think of where in the world she did want to go—that is, with her husband and three children.

But because it was Saturday, and because the choice was either going out for a ride or staying at home to hear the children complain that they had nothing to do, she began the long process of getting ready that a ride required. She cleared the breakfast dishes and dressed the girls. She made braids for the two older ones and changed the baby's diapers. She dressed herself, packed the suitcase that any trip with a baby demands, made up bottles and piled on the couch the sweaters and jackets they would have to take along in the car.

She even—knowing that Danny would probably not think of it and regret it later—found the camera and loaded it.

And all the while her mind was lingering on her dream. If only she could remember it, find out the source of that delicate sorrow, that delightful sadness, that had come from whatever went on in the dream! She knew there had been a lover in the dream; she thought it was Danny. But Danny in a different dimension. Not Danny the Father. Not Danny the Taker-for-a-Ride.

Finally she was ready. She sent the older children for a last trip to the bathroom and called out, "Danny, we're ready!"

But Danny was not in the house to hear her. Danny had disappeared, and when Janet located him, he was in the garage, taking apart the motor of the lawn mower, which had not worked in some months.

"Danny!" she cried. "We're all ready for a ride! What do you think I've been doing all this time? I was getting the children ready for the ride you said you wanted to take! We have our sweaters on. We're at the *door*, ready to *leave*!"

"Oh," he said, not raising his head from the greasy pieces he was studying. "I didn't know you were really getting ready."

"Well, I was, and now *you* get ready," she said, "because pretty soon it will be lunchtime and then the baby will need her nap, and that will be the end of any outing today."

"Do you really want to go?" Danny asked, "I thought you didn't really want to go to the zoo."

"Of course I don't *really* want to go to the zoo," she said between clenched teeth, "But that is where we are getting ready to go and that is what I suppose I will do to get through this particular day."

"Well, then," Danny said cheerfully, "I'll just go wash my hands and get ready to leave."

But first he had to collect all the pieces of the broken motor, and then he had to change his clothes and scrub his hands, and by the time *he* was ready the older children were engrossed in playing a game they called "Mickey and Minnie Mouse" (which involved, as far as Janet could see, their running back and forth across the living room, one calling, "Did you find it, Minnie?" and the other answering, "No, Mickey, not yet") and they did not want to go anywhere, because leaving to go on a ride would interrupt their game.

Janet, standing again, with her purse and the jackets over her arm, said, "Let us *go*, for heaven's sake. We have been getting ready for this great trip for two hours. Let's *leave!*"

And her oldest daughter began to yell, with tears in her voice, "We always do what you want to do! We never do what we want to do! We want to stay home and play our game but we always have to do what you want to do!"

"Well!" Janet shouted, dropping the jackets in a heap at her feet. "Do you think that's what *I* want to do—go to the zoo to watch a bunch of stupid animals all day? I have enough stupid animals to contend with at home! Oh, no, that is not what I want to do at all!"

The fervor in her voice attracted the attention of all of them. Even Danny, who was busy adjusting the camera around his neck, stopped still to listen to her. She thought she might as well go on—she was shaking slightly; she thought she must say what she felt. At that moment they all disgusted her; her life seemed extraneous and foolish, and the busy, intense energy she had expended this morning utterly wasted and extremely useless. She had to protest.

"I'll tell you what I'd like to be doing right now," she said to her husband and her children. "Since you seem to want to know, I'll tell you. I wish I were somewhere by *myself*, in my own house, and I were just getting out of the shower to get dressed. Now, this would have been a most unusual shower—in it I spent a full fifteen minutes without someone once kicking at the door and running in to cry about this fight or that injustice. I would be getting ready to meet a friend somewhere—at a restaurant, for instance; and at this restaurant this friend and I would have a quiet, interesting talk over dinner; and I would not once have to mop up spilled milk or cut up meat on three plates other than my own and no one would beg me for dessert when all the vegetables were still on the plate. This friend and I might then take a pleasant walk or go to a movie, and then I would go home, by myself, and walk quietly into my own house, where there would be no toys waiting to be picked up by me, and no dinner waiting to be prepared, and no diapers waiting to be washed, and particularly no children waiting who had to be told a minimum of ten times to brush their teeth and get ready for bed."

Her audience was rapt. She felt as if she were a breathtaking stage presence. Every eye was upon her.

"And," she continued, "then I would actually get into bed and read for a full half hour without being bothered, and then—wonder of wonders—I would turn out the light and sleep till morning. I would sleep for an entire night without a single scream for attention from anyone. Without someone crying because of a dream monster or kicked-off covers or needing a drink. In other words, I would spend a day without infinite interruptions in *my* life. You get angry if your game is interrupted, but what if your entire *life* were? I would spend a day without interruptions, without being frustrated like a mouse in an experiment who is blocked at every turn, who can never complete a single thought or action. I would be able to sleep and eat in peace. I could think about myself, about what *I* wanted to do, for once in my life. You see? That's what I would do this afternoon if I could do what I wanted to do. Oh, no," she said passionately, tearfully, "oh, *no*, I do not want to go to the zoo to see a bunch of stupid animals."

She stepped over the pile of jackets at her feet and went blindly into her bedroom, closed the door and lay down. She heard Danny talking in a low voice to the children and then she heard sounds of movement—children being sent again to the bathroom, and doors opening and closing.

Finally the bedroom door opened slowly and Danny said in a gentle voice, "I'm going to take the children to the zoo myself. You need some time by yourself. You'll have a little quiet if I take them. I'll put the stroller in the car and then we'll go."

He backed out and closed the door again, and before she

could appreciate his offer she felt panic. They would drive away and the house would be utterly quiet. She had a vision of the endless afternoon—the shadows in the living room getting longer and the light running deep gold as the sun set. She saw herself sitting in a chair, staring at the wall.

Then another, more realistic vision followed the first. She saw herself picking up toys, doing the laundry, washing the kitchen floor, since no one would be at home to track it up for a few hours, preparing some complicated dish for dinner, now that she had a little time to follow a recipe that was not entirely simple-minded. And then, herself bored, falling asleep, till finally her people came home, tracking in dirt, full of news of their outing, with the older children outshouting each other till again there were pokes and hair-pullings and all the jolly rest of it.

She was like a person with a desperate choice to make within ten seconds; all the possibilities of this day reeled before her; and her choice—inevitable, she decided—was the one she had refused and denied moments before. It was this third alternative she now pictured in her mind: herself wheeling the baby in her stroller up the steep hills and turns of the spacious zoo, stopping to point out the amazing skyscraper-high nose of the giraffe and the weird horn of the white rhinoceros. In front of her were the two older girls, running, their braids bouncing, and Danny trailing behind all of them—Danny the Photographer, stopping here and there to snap a funny monkey or, more likely, over and over, herself and the girls—now all of them standing at a fence, with only the tail of the lion visible, now the girls dripping frozen custard on their dresses.

With a profound, physical embarrassment, Janet knew she must admit that she did not wish to be "by herself," to sit quietly inside her own mental blankness. Her dream last night had been a specious temptation; she was no longer fitted to daydream, to moon about a sad and fictional parting from a faceless lover. She was *not* parted from her lover, and if her lover had a camera around his neck and wanted to trek all over a zoo (not holding hands with her, but photographing *her* holding hands with their children), then that was her dream, and a living dream it was, as well. She did not want to sit with a friend (what friend?) and talk about interesting things (what things were interesting now?), nor did she want to read for a long, quiet evening (what book? what long, quiet evening?). She wanted to go to the zoo with her family. She wanted to run out the door and catch Danny before he drove away and say, "Take me with you. *I* need a ride too." But she could not admit these things.

Instead, to save face, she went outside a little belligerently and found Danny just closing the back of the station wagon.

"You won't be able to handle the baby by yourself," she said, not quite looking him in the eye. "You don't know her schedule for her bottles and you won't be able to change her diaper"—it was true; he had never learned to put the pins in properly—"and if you have to push the stroller, no one will be able to hold the girls' hands in the crowded places and they might get lost. So I'd better come along."

"Are you sure you wouldn't rather have some quiet time to yourself, alone?"

But for an answer she was already bending into the car to strap the baby into the car seat, which of course Danny had not remembered to do.

He accepted her decision to accompany them without question. He believed in letting people alone, was never at them to explain their reasons for this or that. She wished, in a way, that he would question her more closely so that she could explain all her ambivalent feelings to him. He was going to make it hard for her—hard to confess that her projected afternoon of delight had been a false and fabricated vision. In fact, she wondered if he had paid any attention to her eloquent speech at all. Maybe it was the children to whom she needed to confess. Danny, perhaps, understood her all too thoroughly. Well, she would do what was required as the day progressed . . .

The goat, having digested his snack of yellow paper, takes off for the peanut-vending machine in the enclosure, and pathetically tips his nose up toward the vending spout.

Danny bangs Janet energetically on her back and laughs. "Let's get going before he starts eating our clothes," he says, and they all laugh.

They proceed to the monkey colony, where a gorilla pounds himself on the chest and waits for applause and in another corner two monkeys battle for a raw potato, then turn to the audience to bow before they resume their act.

An infant elephant, across the road in a small enclosure, is being fed milk from a gallon container with a nipple as long as a pencil on its end. The pretty young girl who is attending him strokes him affectionately and removes the bottle from his mouth: he immediately tickles her back with his trunk to beg for more.

"They aren't stupid animals at all," Janet says offhandedly to her daughters, but they are swinging on the pipe fences just like little monkeys, and like all young animals they are conscious only of the moment. The past has no meaning for them. They are content just now.

In every section of the zoo Janet sees parent animals with their young. The mother monkey embraces her baby and fondles it while the male does hand-springs around the cage. The baby elephant stands with his head underneath the mother elephant while the father hulks around them, flicking his ears and appraising them with his intelligent eyes.

The kangaroos hop together, the old and the young, from one end of their run to the other; and the giraffes, parents and offspring, parade regally back and forth, their heads passing through the treetops.

None of them seem to have anything very important to do, but all of them are busy, living and watching the young grow.

Janet begins to sing, as if it is an old song she has always known:

"The animals in the zoo
They don't have nothing to do!"

And when Danny says her grammar isn't the best, she says she doesn't care, because it is pleasant here at the zoo and she feels like singing.

(1969)

The Ultimate Friend

~

"YOU ARE IN A VERY dangerous position," says my sister-in-law, who has lately been considering divorce. We are sitting in the kitchen over cups of instant coffee; my sister-in-law has given up smoking cigarettes, and the fumes of her miniature cigar are permeating everything in the room so that tomorrow, I am sure, my violets will smell like the smoking car in a train. My four-year-old daughter, in a pink, one-piece bathing suit, is perched on a breakfast stool, waiting for me to take her to her swimming lesson. My two other children, who already know how to swim, have been taken away by their daddy for a ride to places unknown.

"Take my word for it," says my sister-in-law. "You don't have a single friend—you said so yourself. If anything happened to Danny, or *between* you and Danny, that would be it. Nowhere to turn. No one to talk to. No hope!"

"I suppose you have friends?" I say. It is only partly a question.

"Yes," she says. "Of course! Or where would I be now?"

Maybe still happily married, considering your friends, I think to myself; but it would not be suitable to get into that so I do not say anything.

"Yes," I say, "you are probably right. I really do need some friends."

"When you *really* need them, it's too late to start thinking about it. *So think now!*" She rises, and with a flourish and a click of her heels salutes me farewell. I admire her style.

When she has driven away, I consider the truth of her advice rather than the outcome of her own personal acts. I have no friends at all. I have only Danny and my children. It seems to be enough, this houseful of my people. But I did not receive a guarantee with any of them—who knows what lies ahead?

But what is a friend, when you have been married for ten years and already your seven-year-old daughter is waiting for the day when curves will appear under her Charlie Brown sweatshirt?

The word "friend" seems to be in a category with movie-star scrapbooks and cherished ticket stubs from football games. The friends I can recall with any emotion are the girls I spent all those pajama-party nights with and with whom I exchanged the greatest confidences. Will I be flat-chested forever? Will I be an old maid? If I am, at what age should I decide it isn't worth it, being a virgin any more? When a man . . . makes a baby with a woman, do you think it takes a minute or a half hour?

Oh, yes, in those days I certainly had real and dear friends.

But what makes a friend now? I ask myself. According to the adults I know, a friend is one of the most commonplace conveniences in the world. People everywhere, all the time, say things like: We had dinner with some friends; or: A friend just called and invited us to sail on his boat this weekend; or: Last night some friends of ours dropped in.

Well, the only genuine article that drops in on *us* is rain, right through the hole we have in our kitchen roof, and the very last real and dear and true friend I made in the world was my husband Danny.

When I was a girl and the phone in our house rang and it was for me, I could see my father thinking: Oh, I'm glad it's a call for Janet. I'm glad she's getting popular. I can just see Danny thinking to himself when the Salvation Army calls, asking me to leave old clothes outside for their truck: Oh, I'm glad my Janet is popular these days!

The difference, of course, is that my father was waiting (just as I was) for that one boy, the *ultimate friend*, to call me. My husband, it so happens, *is* that boy, my ultimate friend, so in what light may I consider this advice I have just been given by my sister-in-law? Who shall I pray will call me now? How dangerous, exactly, *is* my plight?

My daughter Jill is making lovely, graceful pirouettes in her bathing suit, and I think I would be doing her a service to forget the swimming lessons, which she is so afraid of, and take her instead to Ramon's Ballet Studio. On the other hand, she could never *plié* her way out of a swamped rowboat, and I owe it to her to see that she learns to swim.

"Come on little fish," I say. "Get your bathing cap and we'll proceed."

"I won't have to go under, will I?"

"Whatever Jim says. You have to listen to your teacher," I say, and we set out on the three-block walk to the public pool. I decide on the way that it is only sensible for me to try to make friends—and to start today. If not friends, then *a* friend. There are hundreds of people at the municipal pool; surely some of them are nice. Surely with a little effort I can find a friend and reduce the danger of my treacherous, friendless footing. What if Danny and my other children find a carnival somewhere, shoddily set up in a parking lot, and go on a rickety Ferris wheel? What if a bolt slips and they all plummet to earth? What if, while this very swimming lesson is going on, my phone is ringing with the black news? Whom would I turn to? What would I do? My heart is pounding with the terror of the thought. Yes, I am going to stop this complacent, contented life I have sunk into. I must worry a little. I must put out some effort. I must make a friend.

The children's pool is glimmering in the sunshine. Floating dolls bob in the current of the hot water coming in from the hoses; little red plastic doughnuts ride on the tiny waves.

Jim is already in the water; at the deepest part it is barely to his waist. We are the first ones there. He says to Jill secretly, like a conspirator, holding out his arm, "Come in with me. We'll have a head start on all the others."

My daughter casts an uncertain look at me, but already she is extending her little arm and going forward down the steps of the aqua pool.

"A—ah," he says, "that's a good girl"; and he swirls her by the hand till her shoulders are wet. "The water feels smooth and warm, doesn't it?"

His voice is very calm, very reassuring. He is about nineteen. His shoulders are dark brown—he has been teaching swimming all summer. He is wearing red nylon bathing trunks—all the instructors wear the same style of suit—and he has curly brown hair, which grows in wavy sideburns down his cheeks.

More people are coming—mothers, children. The other Tiny Tot instructor, a girl named Betsy, steps into the pool at the other end, where five little children are waiting on the steps for her. She wears a red, one-piece, nylon bathing suit. It clings in a breathtaking, straightforward way to her perfect, swimmer's body. She takes a blue plastic pail, fills it with water and dumps the contents over a little boy's head. He looks as if he will cry, but he manages to laugh instead. She tosses back her three feet of blond hair, fills the pail and does it again to each of her little students. She is far less gentle than Jim.

He is still with my daughter. He holds her delicately under the arms, as if holding a flower that he is about to place in a vase of water. He bobs about with her in the turquoise water with his chin pressed against her forehead. He is whispering steadily to her.

He is so sweet, so gentle. I think I will make *him* my friend. Why not? He would be dependable in a crisis. He loves small children. Look how he has enchanted my child. Even as I think this he lowers her head absolutely under the water till she is gone, and then, just as surely, he raises her up. When the water clears from her stuck-together lashes she finds him smiling great approval at her.

"*You did it!*" he says jubilantly, and my child sees me on the bench and cries, "Mommy, I did it!"

"She did it!" Jim says to me, seeing me, I am sure, for the first time in the weeks I have been coming here. Then he gives Jill a little, happy push and places her on the steps in order to take another child out.

I decide I am going to talk to him after the lesson. I am going to tell him what a wonderful, gifted teacher he is; what trust he inspires; how he, alone among teachers, has actually got Jill to do the hardest thing—go under the water, away from the life-giving air. My goodness, I am going to make him *happy* (has any other mother taken the time this summer to tell him just how good he is?) and—I am going to make him my friend.

But now the other instructor, Betsy, is wading quietly from her end of the pool toward him; his back is toward her; she is holding high her plastic bucket of water. She sneaks up behind Jim, who is helping a little boy to float, and hardly able to contain her joy, dumps the bucket of water over Jim's head. He snorts in surprise. His hair nearly covers his eyes; water streams down his face and he gulps for air. Then he sets the little boy back on the step, takes two giant steps toward the girl in the red suit, dives for her knees and upsets her into the water. She falls with a huge splash, laughing, and grabs for his suit, nearly pulling it off his hips. He says something in a low, intense voice to her and her laugh stops. She pushes her weight of hair away from her face and smiles at him. I feel myself blush. I turn hot all over and I swallow for shame. In my very wallet is a picture of Danny at seventeen, in swim trunks, with his muscled arms at his sides and his chest covered with black hair. He is the only boy in swim trunks that I am going to be a friend of if I am in my right mind.

On the walk home with Jill I thank myself for my good judgment. I have saved myself from making an idiotic spectacle of this young woman that I am. Young—but not eighteen.

But . . . is my phone ringing? As I get in the front door of my house I think I hear it give one last jangle and stop. Where is Danny? Why isn't he home by now? What if . . . But let me not get into that again.

However, there, mowing her lawn, right next door, is my neighbor Linda, who has borrowed no fewer than three dozen eggs from me in the year we have lived here. And why, I ask myself suddenly, isn't *she* my friend? She's always been very *friendly*. But that isn't the same, I acknowledge now. More than eggs have to be involved. We must give more of ourselves.

"Morning," I say loudly, coming to watch her push the lawn mower. "Where is that man of yours? Don't you think you ought to let him do that kind of hard work?"

"May he walk under a falling brick!" she says sweetly, making a U-turn and puffing away over the grass.

"Oh, my. Is something wrong?"

"*Is it ever!*" she says. "Why don't you come in for a cup of coffee?"

And here it is—pure opportunity. Here is my chance; I am finally going to make a friend.

"Jill is in a wet suit," I say. "Maybe I ought to change her first."

"No, no," says Linda, killing the motor. "It's hot. Please, come in."

Her sons do not seem to be home—they are older than my children—but she finds a puzzle for Jill to put together in the playroom. In her kitchen, on the table, are a pile of bills. The top one is from Happy's Liquor Store.

"Isn't Howard home?" I say. "It *is* Saturday, isn't it?"

"Howard hasn't been home for about five weekends. He's out, bringing home the bacon. He's been working days and nights now, weekends and holidays."

"You sound so annoyed," I say. "Don't you feel he's doing it for you and the children? Don't you *need* the bacon?"

"My God," says Linda, "I don't need a whole *pig!*"

She sets coffee down for us and says, "Janet, how many cars do we need? How many cabins at Lake Arrowhead do we need not to be able to make it to every weekend? How many king-size beds can we fit into the bedroom, for heaven's sake? What on earth does he think we are going to do with all this money he's so desperately collecting for us?" Linda moans, "I don't need *any more money*. All I want is to see Howard sometimes. Before he kills himself, before his ulcer works its way up to his head and down to his toes. I want to have him *go* with us to the cabin on the lake. But all he does is take this client and then that client to dinner at some fancy hotel while the kids and I have macaroni. And then he flies to the home office in Washington, and then he flies to the branch office in Morris, Minnesota, and then he flies home for two days and then he's off again. You're lucky. Your Danny is a teacher. You don't have those problems."

I nod. Neither do we have a cabin at the lake, but it's true—I don't have those problems.

"No, you really don't," she says belligerently. She stirs her coffee and looks up at me. "What kind of problems *do* you have with Danny?" she says, and I sense that this is the moment of truth. Friendship is born either now . . . or never.

I think. And I think. "Danny is . . . very nice," I say lamely.

"Well, he can't be perfect."

"Oh, no, he's not. No one is."

"Well?" Linda says.

I finally think of something. "He's not very polite to my mother," I say, blushing even to betray him this much. "Sometimes when she comes to dinner, he just reads a book through the whole meal."

"Oh, my God. *That's* your problem?"

"I didn't pretend I had a very serious one," I say, trying to defend myself.

"Honey," Linda says, "you don't know what serious is."

"No," I say. "I suppose not."

"Howard drinks," Linda says.

"Oh." I just cannot match any of these confessions. I think of one more thing to offer. "Danny listens to records a lot. Sometimes a whole Sunday will go by and he won't have said a word to me."

"You're not even warm," Linda says, touching my arm.

"Well maybe I better stop trying, then," I say. "I just can't do any better than that."

"Sweetie, I hope you never can."

Linda stands up. The interview is over and I haven't qualified.

"Well," I say, "if Howard is really making that much money,

why don't you hire someone to mow your lawn?"

"Because I hope I have sunstroke and he comes back to find me passed out in the grass, being eaten by ants."

"Oh, Linda," I say. "I wish I could do something for you."

"You can. Lend me a couple of eggs. Would you have a few to spare?"

I call Jill, and the three of us cross over the boundary between our homes. I go inside and bring out not two eggs but six. It is really all I can do.

"Thanks, love," my neighbor says. "You're a doll."

Linda goes home and I am alone with Jill. Alone and friendless.

The phone rings. This could be it. My sister-in-law was right. Anything could happen at any time. I am not protected. I am in a totally vulnerable situation. I have, as it were (minus a few more now than this morning), all my eggs in one basket.

I steady myself and answer the phone.

"Hi," says Danny. "We're down at the playground. I thought you might want me to pick up something for lunch and bring it home."

"Oh, yes!" I cry. "That would be a wonderful idea. We have hardly any eggs."

"Were you planning on eggs for lunch?" says Danny.

"Of course not," I say. "Why should I be? We just had eggs for breakfast."

"Oh," says Danny. He is silent for a minute. Then he tries again. "I thought you might like me to bring home a pizza."

"Oh, yes," I say. "That's a marvelous idea. Pizza will be wonderful. But please . . . come home soon."

"I'm coming, but first I have to get the pizza. Nothing is wrong, is it?"

"Jill went underwater," I say.

"Did she drown?" Danny says.

"Of course not," I say. "She can almost swim."

"Well, that's fine," says Danny. He will never know what this day in my life has been like. "I'll see you in a few minutes."

"Hurry," I say.

I hang up with the full knowledge that anything could happen in the pizza parlor. The ovens could explode. The Louisiana Shrimp could bring on toxic poisoning. But Danny *is* my one and only friend, and like having only one heart and taking the risks of *that*, I am going to keep my one friend, and worry when the time comes.

(1970)

Poor Katie

~

THE MOUNTAINS ARE AFLAME. The whole crest is burning and a few moments ago with the binoculars we were able to see the darting flames jumping hundreds of feet into the air. Danny has just left with the children, who are in their bathrobes and slippers, to walk down to the main street, where there is a clear view of the holocaust. All the girls were asleep when the fire trucks started shrieking by, and although sirens are a common sound in our city, the endless succession of screaming engines woke them in fear, and then Danny and I looked out the front window to see the sky all orange, the glow lighting up the entire northern horizon.

"Don't cry. It can't get to us," Danny promised the girls. "No one's life is in danger. It's just the dry brush up on the mountain; it's going to burn itself out when it gets to the firebreak."

Bonnie's teeth were chattering, Jill was sobbing as if doom were imminent and Myra—just three—was screaming wildly, so Danny said, "Come with me. We'll go out and watch it for a while. The firemen are going to be able to handle it without any trouble."

He looked at me with his eyebrows raised in question, and I nodded. They weren't going to get back to sleep in their beds anyway—not with the added sounds of helicopters and planes coming in with fire-fighting chemicals, and more emergency trucks roaring down the street a block away.

The night was hot. The Santa Ana winds had come in from the desert that afternoon, as they do suddenly every fall, bringing with them skies so clear that we had had to readjust our eyes which had been adjusted all summer long to the dull outlines of shapes in the smog. And with the winds came a treacherous heat and dryness that were, directly or indirectly, the cause of forest fires all over the Southern California mountain ranges.

The spectacle out the window now is tremendous; I have a feeling of exhilaration and excitement—a spark could drift onto anyone's roof; the distant glory could become our own. And beyond those thoughts is another one—can such a fire really start by itself?

Neighbors all up and down the block have come outside. Most of them are walking to the street where Danny has gone—there are no trees there to block their view.

I lie down on the bed and close my eyes. The fire engines have stopped coming, and now there is only the occasional sound of the helicopter's rotors reverberating loudly and then fading away. The street outside our open window seems silent and deserted.

Suddenly I hear a man's voice, loud and urgent, call, "Katie! Katie!"

So—she is missing again. For at least the hundredth time this year. Usually it is not so late, though—usually she delays coming home for dinner just long enough so that everyone eats without her. Well, with a family like hers, I would prefer to eat alone too. Her father's voice is fierce now as he shouts, "Katie! Katie!" He sounds as if he is angry in advance—angry that he will find her, for his little girl always shows up. I have seen her often enough coming carelessly up the street, her head tilted back as she drops candy corn into her open mouth, her feet bare, her hair unkempt and stringy—her fat legs strolling along as if there were no such thing as being home on time and no such thing as furious parents.

I expect that in a moment her father will go into the house and slam the screen door; he never keeps it up very long, his yelling, his search. It is just some kind of token attempt, a way to prove to the neighbors that he and his wife are decent parents, that they want their kids safely home just like everyone else.

But I am surprised, for a new voice joins the first. A woman's voice is now calling, "Katie! Katie!" Could it be her mother? I get up and go to the window. Across the street Katie's mother stands on her front steps, her hands cupped to her mouth, shouting. Drifting like a halo in the sky is the red glow of the fire. It is eerie to see. The father, farther along the street, looking one way and another, calls the girl's name, and the mother, on the steps, echoes it with a trace of hysteria. Perhaps they are afraid Katie has gone up the mountain to look at the fire, and that she will get too close. Perhaps they are afraid (and I see it now in a triumphant deduction) they are afraid she *started* it! They think her capable of anything. They are not fearful for her safety, but for their own should she be caught. I am excited by my conclusion; I wish Danny were at home so I could tell him my idea. We have always known she would get into bigger trouble. Where else could she be headed—a nine-year-old girl who had total charge of her own life, who was unsupervised from morning till night, who had only the example of her wretched older brother and her disgruntled teenaged sister to follow?

The shouting goes on. "Katie!"

"Katie!"

A high note and then a low note.

I go back to rest on my bed and think of Katie. A fat little girl with pretty features lost in the flesh of her face. She is never without food. In the beginning, when she used to call for Bonnie, she always had in one fist a sack of potato chips or a can of soda pop or a dripping ice-cream stick. Whatever she ate had to be fattening and messy. And it had to be something she could drop on the lawn when she was done with it. I say "the lawn" because after the soup incident I did not allow her in the house. On that day she had rung the bell to ask if Bonnie could play.

"Come in," I told her, and I noticed with half my attention that she seemed to be holding something behind her back. She came in after me and I went to the kitchen and she went to the living room, where my girls had set up their dollhouse. Later, when I walked through the living room, I found a great, messy red stain on the cream-colored rug.

"What's this?" I said, and as I said it I saw in Katie's hand the can of tomato soup from which she was eating with a plastic spoon.

"My God, Katie! Did you bring that in my house?"

"Uh-huh," said Katie.

"Well, get it out and never, *ever* bring something like that into my house to eat! Do your eating at home before you come here. My children are only allowed to eat in the kitchen. No one ever brings food into the living room."

Katie, expressionless, got up slowly with her can of cold soup and went out the front door without a word. I turned on my children and shouted, "She is not to play in the house ever again—do you hear? I don't want her dirty bare feet all over my furniture!"

"Sometimes I wish I could go out in my bare feet," Bonnie said.

"Well, you can't," I said. "We've been through that. It's ridiculous and dangerous."

"And we do sometimes eat in the living room," Bonnie persisted. "When we have company, or if you offer Daddy and the rest of us peanut brittle."

"That has nothing to do with this! And if Katie didn't eat all that *junk*, if she didn't eat so much candy, she wouldn't be so fat."

Then, my heart pumping, I sat down and tried to clear the rage out of my head. How could her mother allow her to grow up like this? How could she expect Katie to be welcome in the houses of people on the block if this was the way she treated other people's things? And why should I have Katie in my house day after day—why should I be, in fact, baby-sitting her—when my children had never set foot inside Katie's house or played with her toys or gone to her birthday parties? Not that I would ever let them go, with no adults at home and that queer brother of hers playing his rock records or his electric guitar and her sullen-faced sister painting her fingernails and toenails—one day purple, the next day green. The only time I ever set eyes on Katie's mother is when I see her get in and out of her car.

But we all know why Katie's mother works; Katie has told us often enough. They are going to get a swimming pool just as soon as Katie's mother has worked long enough to get the money for one.

Which, as I lie here thinking now, brings me to the incident of the swimming pool—our pool. It's a small one, as pools go, and it's right beside our house, not more than three feet from the sliding glass door in the family room. It has a high brick wall around it protecting it from the street, and a little wooden gate leading from the pool area into the driveway. When I think of the pool Katie's mother is going to build I think of flowered lounge chairs and floating beach chairs with a place in the arm for a cocktail to float along with you. I think of perfumed suntan oil and sexy music from a transistor radio and that woman's back getting darker and darker from the sun.

My pool is different. It's a place where I work. It's a place where I never relax long enough to take a deep breath. Before we even get *out* to it, my children's shoes, socks, panties and dresses have to be picked up from wherever the girls threw them in their haste to get into their bathing suits. Then I come out in my faded shorts with an armful of clean beach towels and I sit down—and the work begins.

"Don't jump in so close to the side, Jill. You'll hit your head on the concrete. No—not that way! Jump toward the center!

"No, Bonnie, you *can't* wear three tubes at once, one around your neck and one around each ankle. You might get tangled in them.

"No, Myra! You absolutely may not jump in at the deep end. You can't swim yet. You have to stay on the step. If you want to go where it's over your head, you must wear the life jacket. No! You can't. And if you do that one more time, you will come right out and I won't let you go in again!"

I am sure that however unluxurious my pool seems to me, the splashes and gurgles sound delicious on a hot day to whoever is on the other side of the wall. It is no wonder that Katie appeared that day at the gate, opened it without invitation and came in and sat down on one of the webbed aluminum chairs. This was not her first visit to our pool. Early in our first summer at the house we had been so unsuspecting as to invite her to swim with us. She accepted gleefully. At eight the next morning (as soon as her mother had left for work) she appeared with her bathing suit on, ready to go in again. We let her swim that second day too; but on the third day, when she arrived before we had even had breakfast and we found her already in the pool (she looked exactly like a pig, coming up snout first and snorting for air), I told her that we were not using the pool that day because the chlorine level was too low, and that in the future she could come only when she was invited. Which of course was never again.

But last month, when she quietly opened the gate and came in, I thought, Well, what harm can it do? That child is desperate for something to do and someone to be with. And to her credit, she sat fast on that beach chair all afternoon in the heat, watching my children swim and jump and dive. They even appreciated her company, and kept calling to her, "Watch me do this, Katie. See how I can find my barrette on the bottom? See how I do a somersault?"

The next day I had just taken out a clean pile of towels when Katie once again unlatched the gate. This time she came in and sat down on the edge of the pool with her bare feet on the top step, just in the water. She was in a bikini, from which her fat stomach stuck out horribly, and I wanted to say to her, "Katie, you'd look so much better in a one-piece suit—the kind Bonnie has." But Katie didn't seem to know how she looked. She only moved her feet carefully down from the first step to the second and—pretending to reach forward to push away an inflated octopus—moved her bottom onto the first step. Within ten minutes, because I had not said anything (how could I?), she was standing up to her waist in the shallow end of the pool, and within twenty minutes she was crashing in off the diving board, sending huge overflows of water out of the pool, covering the lenses of my sunglasses with cascades of water and drenching every towel around.

My children did not seem to object. They were fascinated at the display of so much flesh and noise. Why should I feel so much anger? When Danny jumped in, all one hundred and seventy pounds of him, and drenched the towels, I only laughed and went inside to get some dry ones. Why did I find everything Katie did so calculated, so scheming? Why couldn't I simply view her as a child who just wanted to go swimming? It was not so evil a desire.

But the next day when she arrived at the pool gate, I said to her, not looking at her eyes, "Katie, my children have to swim without company today. I am not able to be a lifeguard for so many people at the same time—it is not safe. Any children who come to swim here from now on have to have their mothers come along to watch them."

Without a word, without even a blink, her head simply disappeared from the top of the gate. But the next evening Danny had to fish a strange brassiere up from the bottom of the pool, and I realized that she had made her reply.

It's strange, but as I rest here in the dark and listen to her parents calling her name in this fiery night, I can't seem to work up my old anger at some of her deeds. I can't keep my mind on the image of her letting our bunny out of his cage, after which he was lost for three days. I see her instead calling to the ice-cream man and offering any child within reach of her voice an ice-cream bar. She has always had money to spare, and up and down the street she tries to buy friends, just as her parents try to buy her favor. A couple of boys take her up on it—they are no fools—but the girls on the block always say, "No, thank you, we can't eat ice cream so near to dinner," or, "Thanks, but my mother keeps ice cream in the freezer for us."

Katie shrugs. She eats her ice cream alone, sitting on the curb, her fat knees wide apart, her hair in her face.

Sometimes we hear Katie's sister calling to her from the house: "Do you have homework? Come on in and do it, you little pig." Her sister is about sixteen; it must have been her brassiere that we were the recipients of. She always has a bitter look on her face; at sixteen it already looks pretty bad up ahead to her. The brother speaks to Katie only when he finds something wrong: "Did you fool with the mirror on my motorcycle? Did you leave my tape recorder on? If I catch you the hell near my stuff again, I'll break your head."

Katie always says, "No." No, she has no homework. No, she didn't touch his motorcycle. She sits on the curb, eating her peanuts or her chocolate bar or her cold hot dog, and she looks up and down the street. If she sees one of the neighboring mothers, she says very politely, "Hello, Mrs. Stone," or "How are you, Mrs. Wilson?" She sounds so polite, you almost want to trust her. But of course Mrs. Stone and Mrs. Wilson are not idiots; at one time or another, they have had Katie in to play with their children and also have been the victim of Katie's upbringing—just as Katie is—but they don't have to stand for it. Their children eat at mealtimes and wear shoes and know where they are welcome. No one is required to tolerate Katie, and no one does for long.

Sometimes when I am sending my big girls off to school in the morning Katie passes our house, wearing a miniskirt and her black leather boots, and looks at the scene on our doorstep.

"Do you have your lunchpail? Do you have your Brownie dues? Don't forget to give that permission note to your teacher so you can go to the dairy farm with your class. Here, Jill—let me put your barrette in better. Cross at the crosswalk, where the crossing guard is. Yes, I love you too. I love you both. Yes, I'll kiss you again. Good-bye. Have a nice day. I'll see you this afternoon."

Katie makes her own lunch. Bonnie says she eats funny things, like cans of bean soup or just bread with ketchup on it. Bonnie and Jill neither walk with Katie to school nor eat with her there. Once when Bonnie did eat with Katie, the lunchroom teacher walked by and discovered half a dozen chocolate cupcakes in Katie's lunchpail, and Katie had been sent to speak to the principal. I told Bonnie then that it was best for her not to be associated with Katie; if their teachers considered them friends, she might suffer for it. I explained my feelings carefully to the children: that it was not *exactly* Katie's fault the way she was; it was just that she was not properly cared for; and she was just not a very nice person as a result of being so neglected.

And yet last week, when Bonnie lost her Brownie pin in the grass, Katie saw my girls hunting on the lawn and joined them in the hunt. On her hands and knees, her stomach nearly brushing the ground, Katie crawled inch by inch over the grass. When my children got tired and complained of bugs, Katie kept right on, crawling without worry through the shin-deep ivy, raking her fingers through places that my children were forbidden to explore for fear of spiders and snakes. When I called my children in for dinner, Katie said, "I'll just keep looking. Sometimes I'm good at finding things." Finally, when it was getting dark, I had to tell Katie to go home. The sight of her out there on all fours was disquieting, and after all, a new Brownie pin cost only a quarter.

But at nine that night, when my children were already in bed, there was a quiet knock at the front door.

"Yes?" I said.

"It's Katie."

"What do you want?" I said, opening the door a crack.

"Could I speak to Bonnie?"

"She's in bed. Why? Can you tell me what it's about?"

"Well . . ." And Katie smiled in a shy, crooked way and extended her hand through the crack in the door. "I thought I could give Bonnie this—my Brownie pin." The pin shone gold in her chubby palm. The nails on her curled-up fingers were bitten to the quick. "I'm not a Brownie any more—my mother can never bring refreshments or anything to meetings, so she doesn't want me to be one—but Bonnie can have my pin."

"Oh," I say. I almost add, "That's very nice of you, Katie," but I say only, "Oh, just a minute; I'll call Bonnie to the door." I don't even ask her in, but let her wait on the step in the dark. I can't keep from smiling as I tell Bonnie that Katie wants to see her, and I feel very happy suddenly. Bonnie goes to the door and is back in her room much faster than I expected her to be.

"Well?" I ask her. I am still smiling.

"Oh. Well, Katie wanted to give me her Brownie pin. But I told her, 'No, thank you.'"

"Why?" I cry. "Why did you say that? You *need* one. She *has* one. Why didn't you let her give it to you?"

"I thought you wouldn't want me to take it," Bonnie says.

Jill says, "She probably stole it somewhere," and I want to slap her; I want to slap both of them.

"She's trying to be nice!" I say. "Can't you see that? Maybe people have to let her be nice to them once in a while! How would you feel if no one would let you be nice to them?"

"Oh," says Bonnie, her face tight and reserved, "I thought you thought she wasn't a nice person."

I remember how this summer Katie announced that she was growing Super Seeds in her back yard. She told Bonnie she was growing giant watermelons and four-pound tomatoes. Bonnie told her we were growing pumpkins. She took Katie under our bedroom window, where our pumpkin plant had exploded in three weeks from a little shoot to a five-foot vine with all kinds of buds and yellow blossoms and curling green tendrils that crept around leaves and rocks and even tufts of grass. Every day when Katie went by she would call to the girls, playing outside, "How is your vine doing? Mine has ten watermelons on it!" and one day Bonnie cried, "Oh, come see! We have a pumpkin starting." The pumpkin was about three inches long, dark green, and very heavy for its small size. Within a week it had quadrupled in size, and the children talked about having it ready for Halloween. Katie listened.

Jill said, "Our daddy is going to carve it with a big smile and then put a candle in it. Then he'll take us trick-or-treating."

Bonnie said, "My mother always makes popcorn for all the kids who come on Halloween. She lets us help her."

"My father," Katie said, "won't answer the door. He turns off all the lights and makes my mother sit in the dark. But I always go out myself and get a whole pillowcase full of stuff."

"And you eat all of it the day after Halloween," Bonnie said. "You know you wouldn't be so fat if you didn't eat all that candy."

"I don't care," Katie said.

Every day my girls and I watched the pumpkin grow. Soon it was big as a cantaloupe. It was marvelous—so heavy and green that it almost seemed alive. Bonnie watered it every day.

The morning after the Brownie pin had been lost, when I went out with the children to wave them off to school we saw that the pumpkin was not there. Rather, it was there—smashed to pieces. The pale-yellow seeds were everywhere on the grass.

Bonnie began to sob. "What could have happened? Who could have done it?" she cried furiously.

"Only one person could have done it," I said between my teeth. "No one knew it was there but Katie."

"I hate Katie," Bonnie cried. "I'd like to smash *her* in."

There is the sound of an argument outside my window now. I get up from my bed and look out again. The glow in the sky is dimmer, and perhaps the fire is not going to spread very far after all. The children and Danny should be home soon; it must be after ten already. The screen door at Katie's house slams, and I see that her father has just gone in and that her mother is running down the street. I wonder if they prosecute little girls for setting mountains on fire. I feel nearly hysterical myself as Katie's mother screams Katie's name over and over as she runs down the street, smoke from the burning ridge hanging in the air above her head.

I even think I will go out into the street and call Katie once or twice myself. I think of the times she offered to buy my girls ice cream. I think of the Brownie pin. I think of how young she is, of her fat little face that hardly ever smiles, and of the terrible clothes she is given to wear. Not cheap or shabby clothes—just all wrong for a little girl, all wrong for a child's world.

I stare out, and in the faint glow from the fire I see under my window the stripped pumpkin vine. Another fruit never grew there. And now I have to admit it to myself—in the last week I have seen two boys walking across our lawn; twice I caught them picking oranges from our orange trees. How can I be so sure it was Katie who smashed the pumpkin? Why do I insist upon it? In fact, if pressed to describe what those boys were doing under my bedroom window the other day, I would have to say that they appeared to be checking the pumpkin vine for new additions. How is anyone to know anything in this world?

Now I hear the whine of a fire truck again, but it is less urgent.

It is coming back; the emergency must be over. People are returning up the street, although flames are still creeping along the crest of the mountain. They will probably be there all night.

Then I hear very fast, loud footsteps, and a yell: "If you ever go there again, I'll kill you. I'll just kill you. Do you hear me?"

Katie would not be the only one to hear her mother; everyone else on the block must hear. The mother keeps saying that she will kill Katie, but what I hear is not the voice of a woman who is going to commit murder but that of a woman who is hysterical because she so long ago lost control.

The screen door across the street is flung open and the father comes out.

His wife shouts out meanly, "I've got her!" and the father runs onto the sidewalk, calling, "Where was she?"

"In the pool hall! Can you imagine! The little bitch was in the pool hall."

I can no longer see anyone clearly because the father has moved to meet them in the darkness away from their door.

"Katie," the father says, "is *that* where you were?"

There is no pool hall in this town. What the mother must mean is that Katie was at the recreation center—the new community building two blocks away, which has thick blue carpets and a ping-pong table and a beautiful pool table in front of a fireplace, and a chess-and-checkers rooms and a dance floor for teenagers. For a dollar a year a whole family can use the facilities every evening from seven to ten-thirty.

But "pool hall" was how they thought of it—how they needed to think of it. Just as they needed to call her a bitch, just as her sister needed to call her a pig. For if she were at the pool hall and not the community center, if she were a bitch and not just a brat, if she were a pig and not just a child who liked sweets—well, then, if she were all these things, she deserved the treatment she got from them, and any fate she found would be too good for her.

It seemed we all needed to blame Katie for our own sad reasons; it was so easy for neighbors and me to pin every assorted neighborhood evil on her. Tonight even a forest fire had not seemed too large an act for her hand.

Now I hear Danny coming quietly in the front door and I go to meet him. Myra is asleep on his shoulder, and the two older girls have a blank look in their eyes, as if they are sleepwalking.

Danny carries Myra to her crib and I guide the girls to their bedroom. Jill gets in the lower bunk and is asleep before I can unbutton her robe. Bonnie climbs limply up her ladder and says, "The fire really is too far away. I'm not so scared now."

"Good," I say, and kiss her. "Go to sleep now. All good children should be asleep at this hour."

"Katie is awake," Bonnie says. "She's outside. They're yelling at her."

"She should be asleep too," I say. "Listen—do you remember that Brownie pin she wanted to give you, Bonnie?"

"Umm," Bonnie says. She cannot seem to keep her eyes from closing. "You know, Mommy," she says, blinking, "I really wanted to let her give it to me that night."

"Why didn't you then?"

"I thought you would be angry. But sometimes I want to be friends with her. I think she's nice sometimes."

"Sometimes I think so too, Bonnie. And maybe you should do what your feelings tell you to do and not only what you think I will approve of."

"Well, then—I want to tell her I'd like to have her Brownie pin. Do you think I could?"

"I don't see why not."

"You know what?" Bonnie says, leaning over her guard rail and touching my shoulder. "I don't think she's going to have a very happy life."

"If there are enough people like you in the world, Bonnie, she has more than a fair chance." I want to bless her for her generous heart in spite of me.

"Then can I play with Katie tomorrow?"

"It's up to you," I say, and I kiss Bonnie good night. "A lot of decisions from now on are going to be up to you."

(1972)

Sadzia, the Sultan's Sweetmeat

~

GREAT THINGS OFTEN BEGIN inauspiciously, don't they? That's why I believe the best cure for depression is just living a little longer. All the philosophers say so. You've probably heard it a hundred times: *It's always darkest before the dawn;* and: *Just put one foot in front of the other;* and: *The air smells less smoggy on a new day.* I admit I made up that last proverb—but what is meant, I suppose, by all this advice is that time passes. And things change. And if they change, they get different. And if they get different, and if you've been depressed, you get undepressed.

It's so simple, any fool should be able to figure it out. But, my Lord, I was so depressed when this summer started, I couldn't even figure the way to get out of bed!

Why should I go into it too heavily? You probably know most of the details already: three kids under nine (all home for the summer) and a house with a white kitchen floor. Add to that a husband away on an extended tour of six European countries and you have the proverbial last straw. Danny—even-tempered, hard-working, earnest husband, voted as having the "most interesting class" of all the history teachers—was off for the summer as the chaperon of thirty of his students, half of them peach-skinned, gorgeous and bra-less.

Never mind. I didn't discourage him. I'm a modern wife. He's a modern husband. He felt we needed the extra money. (Who doesn't?) I felt he would benefit from eight weeks in Europe. (Who wouldn't?)

There was no question about my tagging along with three young daughters who still had trouble eating anything as exotic as mushrooms on their pizza.

"Don't worry about us," I assured him. "You go and enjoy yourself—broaden your horizons." (I should have bitten my tongue. What I really was thinking was that he would come back broadened and find me so narrow that I had almost disappeared, and we thus would be rendered incompatible.) "We'll find lots to do," I said. "We'll be just fine."

Well, in a limited sort of way we found lots to do, all right. I signed the girls up for every other course that was offered at the local recreation center. On Mondays, for example, they took a cooking course. (Let them spill honey all over the rec center's floor; I was more than glad to pay for the privilege.)

On Tuesdays the girls were enrolled in Karate, or "Self-Defense and the Study of the Martial Arts." I often went along to pass the time, of which I had much to pass. Imagine watching your seven-year-old (and rather delicate) daughter screeching "Ki-aaay!" and digging two fingers into the neck of your nine-year-old, who then lunges for your five-year-old, who proceeds to throw the oldest one over her knee and onto the mat with a resounding thud. There is no question but that roles have changed in American life. At least I am glad my girls will have the training to defend themselves.

Then on Wednesdays there was a course in Horse Care. (You have to provide your children with all kinds of knowledge, don't you?) And on Thursdays was Cardio-Pulmonary Resuscitation for Children.

I was beginning to feel I might need some resuscitation myself, one of these endless days (not to mention the silent, solitary evenings). My two good friends were unavailable all summer, since they both were back in college, working on master's degrees in education. They, like half the women in the world, were tired of cleaning kitchen floors and wanted to fulfill themselves. In my case, the trouble was that I already *had* a master's degree in education because I had had great foresight in my youth. My miscalculation was this: It would never occur to me for a minute now that I could fulfill myself by spending my days in rooms full of other people's children, when it was all I could do to stay in rooms with the very flesh-of-my-flesh that I myself had borne.

It did not make matters better to get my first call from Danny one night from the Cafe Europa in Frankfurt. It was early afternoon on my kitchen clock when the phone rang, but it was hot time in the old town tonight wherever he was. The music was so loud, I could hardly hear him.

"Hi, Janet. How's everything, honey?"

"We're . . . managing, I guess. Where are you calling from?"

"Oh, we're all at this little nightclub. I'm a bit surprised they put this place on the tour, if you understand me."

"No, I don't understand you, actually."

"The first act was an Egyptian belly dancer. I rather expected folk singing or poetry reading—something like that."

"Did you like her?"

"Ah, well—yes. I would say belly dancing is of great historic interest, you know. It's as old as life itself. This dance has mesmerized kings."

"I *thought* you sounded a little breathless."

"We've been having apple wine and pretzels."

"Go easy on the wine, Danny. You know how too much makes you weak in the knees."

"The pretzels here are really tremendous. I can't get over them."

"I'm so happy for you. Why don't you write us some long letters?"

"I will. Did I tell you one of the girls broke her toe in the Vatican? She had to fly home."

"Do they let your female students into churches in those . . . T-shirts they wear?"

"Listen, Janet, the intermission is over. I have to get back now for the next act. I wish you could taste the pretzels here—they're about three inches thick."

"Bring me home a couple."

"I will. Kiss the children for me."

"What about me?"

"Kiss yourself too."

"Thanks."

"Auf Wiedersehen, Janet."

Nuts.

That night—Friday—the children had to attend their Origami class. It was too complex for me in my deteriorated state of mind. I left my children busy with their squares of colored paper and wandered down the hall. In the next room was a course in the Care of Ten-Speed Bicycles. I passed that one by. Beyond that was a room in which a rubber lady lay on the floor. The instructor blew into her lips and her overly ample bosom rose and fell like the balloon built into her. It looked as if a fatal accident had just occurred, with all those people crowding around. This was the adult version of Cardio-Pulmonary Resuscitation. Since I was already feeling morbid enough, I wandered on . . . past the Senior Citizen Square Dance Circle, past Billiards for Leisure Enjoyment, past . . .

But what could be going on behind *that* door? Was this the Cafe Europa or was this the rec center? A low, thrumming drumbeat came from behind the closed door of the room, with a rhythmic accompaniment of metallic clicks. The high wail of some exotic instrument filled the hallway. I leaned my head against the wall. I felt my blood moving. Something was engaging inside my head. My cloud of crankiness seemed to be lightening all around me. I opened the door and went in.

A circle of women, clothed in swaths of chiffon, turned and swirled on the carpeted floor of the big room. Gold coins clicked and danced on their bellies, on their breasts, even on their foreheads. Gold circles on their fingers flew like lightening to convey an insistent signal to their arching bare feet and moving toes.

I could not tear my eyes away from those exposed bellies (for indeed, all that chiffon flowed from well under the hipline). When the music slowed, the bellies quivered and breathed like living souls. They swayed, they undulated, they twisted and shuddered.

Did I have this marvelous equipment under my shapeless summer shift? Should I unzip right now and check? What beauty! What glorious womanhood!

"Will you join us?" the gorgeous young woman leading the class suddenly said to me. She wore a jewel in her navel.

"Well . . . yes, I will," I said. I couldn't believe my own ears. Was this *me*? I slipped off my sandals and kicked them out of the way, and would you believe I was an absolute whiz at it? I joined right in and started rotating the bones of my pelvis and found them to be marvelously lubricated with the oils of Araby. My powers of imitation, which I didn't know I possessed, were miraculous. The teacher, named Nefertiti (no less), would do a hip-lift ("Down-*up*, down-*up*, remember to keep your arm curved low to accent the moving hip, the other arm held high,") and my hip would do what it was told, immediately, while I watched it over my shoulder in amazement. When the command came for the double hip-lift ("Down-*up-up*, down-*up-up*"), the flesh I had always deemed too ample shuddered and bounded with absolute grace. My long-denounced cellulite had finally come into its own. Truly the skinny girls just did not convey the essence of the dance as well as those of us who had something to call a belly.

Before the evening was out I had learned to steer my heretofore ordinary abdominal region (useful in the past only for growing babies and digesting milk shakes) through a formidable course of flutters, undulations and back bends, while my hips traveled through long, slow circles, figure eights, and loops within circles. All around me, in deepest concentration, were ordinary mothers, wives, daughters—even, it seemed, a grandmother.

When it was time to try the shimmy I pretended I contained a built-in electric vibrator, and I could hear myself rattle like *dembones*. What a sense of exhilaration! For the first time in ages I was feeling fantastic.

And I was being watched.

My three little girls, holding Origami storks in their hands, had appeared in the open doorway and were staring at me. The little one's mouth hung open. The three of them looked like variations on the village idiot. I ignored them.

Nefertiti did one last, spectacular back bend, brushing her black hair along the rug, and when she rose up under a shoulder shimmy she said, "The effects are all in your heads, girls. Remember to *think* the way you want to look—get your mind where it's at. That's half the battle. Okay? That's all for tonight. See you next week."

I rushed up to her.

"Do you think I can join the class? Am I too late?"

"How many years have you studied and who was your teacher?" she asked me. She had a tiny rhinestone glued to the side of her nose. She had silver-snake circlets on her upper arms.

"Are you kidding?" I said, "I never danced at all . . . anywhere."

"Once in a while a natural comes along," Nefertiti said. "Sometimes it happens that way. You're lucky. Get together some kind of costume and some zills and come next time. You're really very good, but you'll need a lot of practice."

"I will, I will!" I promised. I would have sworn on her golden coins, on Allah himself, but she had walked off to gather up her records, doing a little shimmy shake as she traveled.

The only time I had ever danced and laughed with joy was when my father whirled me around the floor at my wedding. As hard as he had tried, Danny never learned to dance. In my secret heart I had always wanted to dance—at least once—until dawn. Now, a late starter, I danced home from the rec center with my children.

"Don't shake like that in the street, Mommy. You look funny."

"Funny? She'll probably get arrested."

"Why were all those ladies wiggling like that? Just to show off?"

"The belly dance, children," I said, "is as old as life itself. Kings have been mesmerized by it since the beginning of time."

"Can we go to the zoo next week? You said one day while Daddy was away we could go to the zoo."

"No. Next week we can't do anything. I'm busy. It's absolutely imperative that I get some zills!"

... Whatever they were.

~

On Monday, while the girls were making Cinnamon Toast de Luxe at their class, I was disassembling the yellow chiffon dress my sister had worn at my wedding. (It was so out of style, she had given it to my girls for dressing up.) By adding two of my best sheer nightgowns as underskirts and by stitching on some two-inch gold fringe around the hip band, I made a graceful, long skirt.

I found a bikini bathing-suit top and transformed it by attaching two hours' worth of sequins, fringe and coins from an old belt. I sat in my rocking chair, smiling to myself and sewing.

My temper mellowed remarkably. When the children spilled a pitcher of orange-slushy on the white kitchen floor, I said quite airily, "It's merely a spill, girls. Get the sponge."

They looked at one another and made circles in the air around their ears.

On Tuesday, when they went off to Karate, I drove downtown to Ali Baba's Cave and bought zills. When I asked for them ("Some zills, please") I was prepared for anything. Was it going to be Arabian underwear? Jewels for my belly button? If the man had returned with a dozen Arabs, each of them playing a Middle Eastern musical instrument, I wouldn't have batted an eyelash.

He put on the counter a set of four brass finger cymbals. I immediately slipped them on by their elastic bands and clicked out "Left-right-left. Right-left-right." The man stared at me.

"I'm a natural," I explained to him.

My next secret foray occurred on Wednesday when the children were studying Horse Care. In the record shop I found an album called "Let's All Belly-Dance." On the cover was a picture of a magnificent, flawless belly decorated with at least ten thousand little coins and bells. Could any human belly be that perfect?

When I got home I checked my stretch marks. They were inevitable, I consoled myself—the scars of living. You don't have babies and come away unscathed. But having babies is an experience and all experience is broadening (some, I admitted, literally and some figuratively), and even if Danny was in Europe getting experience, he would never have babies. Or stretch marks.

This line of reasoning was getting me nowhere. Also it was threatening to bring me back to that low state I had been gloriously free from for several days.

Thursday, during Cardio-Pulmonary Resuscitation for Children, I made my private debut. I moved the full-length mirror into the living room, donned my costume, my zills, some silver bracelets and earrings and turned on the record player.

I thought of Nefertiti and tried to put my mind where it was at. I swirled, I curled like a snake, I shifted my rib cage (which I had never known before could shift), I engineered my hips through startling maneuvers and I double-hip-lifted to the shouts of the Turkish singers until I was sweating and laughing with joy.

When the record had played on both sides I had blisters on my toes, and when the girls came in from their class I was collapsed, panting, on the couch.

"Let's resuscitate Mom," my oldest said.

"We have to wipe her lips with alcohol first," my youngest said.

"Never mind," I said.

"Here's the mail," said my middle child. "It's an air-mail package from Daddy."

I ripped it open. There in white tissue paper lay four German pretzels. How can you complain about a man like that?

Thereafter the summer ceased to be a torture. Every day while the girls were out, I belly-danced. Every Friday night I was instructed by Nefertiti. Several times she brought to class the man she called "my drummer." He nodded somberly at the introduction. He carried a drum made of fish skin stretched taut across a large pottery jug. He was very tall and thin, with long, wavy brown hair, and he always wore a tan silk shirt, brown suede pants and high leather boots. His features were like a marble sculpture and as inscrutable. He'd sit at the front of the room on a low table and Nefertiti would instruct us: "Basic step forward, then add the crossover, hip-lift and maybe go into a shimmy. When the beat slows, go into the slow circle, and then the camel walk. Keep those arms up and rounded, but limp at the wrists so the zills hang downward. Bend your knees as much as possible. Now go."

The drummer would begin and we all would advance, following Nefertiti, swaying and leaning our way forward till she had moved herself directly in front of the drummer and was dancing in place, her coins swinging and brushing his leather-clad knees. He never smiled and she never smiled. Their eyes held, not six inches apart, and she worked her amazing muscles into a wild and desperate shimmy. He wasn't only her drummer. And wasn't *that* interesting?

Everything was suddenly interesting to me. Life was. Danny could tramp through old museums all summer, and all winter too, if he wanted to. *I* had an interest in life. I—could it be?—had found my calling. I was fulfilling myself.

Let's not be ridiculous. Can you fulfill yourself if you dance only in absolute secrecy when your children are away? Can you fulfill yourself if you don't get paid (even a little?) doing it?

Then at the end of summer Nefertiti called me.

"Look, Janet, I was supposed to dance at a party Saturday night, but the girl who dances at the Aladdin's Lamp Restaurant fell off a ladder and broke her ankle. They need me to stand in for her, so I told the party people I thought I had a replacement. I told them your name was Sadzia and that you were very good. They pay thirty dollars, and you only have to dance for a half hour or so. Sometimes a guy will tuck a dollar bill into your waistband, sometimes five. That's okay if it happens. So will you do it?"

"You told them my name was . . . *Sadzia?*"

"Well, you know—Janet, Sadzia—it sounds better. Will you help me out?"

"How about 'Sadzia, the Sultan's Sweetmeat—formerly Janet,

Mother of Three'? That sounds even better."

"So you'll do it. That's terrific. I'll do the same for you some-day. Be sure to be there by eight-thirty."

"Oh, my God."

"What is it?"

"Saturday night is the night my husband is finally coming home from Europe."

"Well, leave him a note, or something. You wouldn't let me down, would you?"

"I would never let you down, Nefertiti. Never."

For the rest of that week I practiced dancing ten hours a day. The children, whose classes at the rec center were over, for lack of anything else to do began to dance with me. At first they gig-gled and made faces and moved as awkwardly as possible, but then something got through to them and they each began to take it quite seriously. I found the youngest one standing naked in her bedroom, practicing figure eights before her mirror. Her face was full of concentration—she waved me away. I taught them how to do hip-lifts and loops within circles. Soon they could shimmy better than I could. One afternoon I made each of them a danc-ing skirt strung with loops of tiny beads and bangles.

On the night of the party my sixteen-year-old baby-sitter arrived at eight o'clock. She stared at my costume. "Wow!" she breathed. "I don't believe it's you."

"That's the whole idea," I said. "Live and learn, grow and change. Now, listen. My husband's plane is due in tonight. I think he'll call home as soon as he gets to the airport. Maybe in the next half hour. Tell him an emergency came up and that I will be at this address . . ." I wrote it down for her. "Give him my love and tell him I'll see him as soon as I can."

Just then my girls came shimmying into the room in their new skirts.

"This is too much!" the astounded girl said. "What are you guys into?"

"Freedom of the spirit," I said. "We are broadening our hori-zons."

"Even my mother's going back to college," she mumbled.

"It's a whole new world. See you later, kids."

I didn't mingle with the party guests because it would have spoiled the effect of my entrance. I was rushed into a small bedroom by the hostess, who was about fifty years old and was dressed in a navy suit with a gold pin at the collar.

"What kind of party is this?" I whispered politely. (I had imagined anything but this—a stag dinner, a pot party, a salesman's convention . . .)

"This is the Temple Sisterhood's annual dinner," my hostess explained. "We're so delighted you could come."

"Me too," I said.

She left. I sat there for at least a half hour, memorizing the wallpaper. I was sweating so hard, I checked my zills for rust spots. Finally the bedroom door opened again. Nefertiti's drummer stood in the doorway.

"*Shalom*," he said. No one had warned me about this! Was it really he? The tan silk shirt was there, the suede pants. But where had that long, drooping mustache come from? A week ago it hadn't been there. He had his drum with him. The door opened again and another man came in, this one with a beard. "My *oud* player" the drummer announced in his low, poetic voice. The bearded man saluted me with his instrument, which resembled a guitar with a round belly.

"Shall we?" the drummer asked, taking my arm.

My entire life flashed before me.

The hostess stopped us in the hall. "I forgot to tell you—there's going to be a sultan. The men are drawing for it now. It's our door prize. The winner gets to sit on the floor while you dance around him."

"I can't," I said. "That is, I'm not really trained in that aspect of the dance."

The drummer leaned his stony face toward mine . . . and winked. Then he grinned at me. I laughed, he began the Balady rhythm on the drum, his friend began to play the *oud*, and suddenly I was dancing out into the living room of the Temple Sisterhood's annual dinner party.

Can you imagine belly-dancing to *Havah Negilah*? It's absolutely perfect. I had never danced so fast, so recklessly, before. The drummer was extremely skillful; I knew exactly what to do by what he did with his fingers on the fish skin. Coins began to fall all around us. I laughed and spun and hip-lifted in a frenzy. When the music slowed I moved hardly at all; my belly swung around the world; it was the center, holding everything together.

A short, roundheaded, bald man came into the center with me, grinning. He folded his legs under him. My hostess appeared with a turban for his head. She fixed his hands in a position of prayer. I must have lost my rhythm for a moment, because he looked up at me and said: "Don't worry, sweetheart. I'm a grandfather, myself."

My drummer played faster; I shimmied and shook until cries of encouragement nearly brought the roof down. At the end of my final twirl, with the drum and my zills and the applause ringing in my ears, I swept out of the room and down the hall.

But not before I saw my husband standing back against the wall, near the front door, watching me. The hostess rushed to me, where I stood panting and soaking wet.

"Sadzia, your husband is here—he says he just came from the airport."

"I know," I said.

The applause was still ringing. There were shouts of "Encore, Sadzia! Encore!"

Danny came down the hall toward me. He was grinning madly as he held out his arms to me. "Sadzia!" he said.

"Janet to you," I said.

It was a little blurry, seeing my way back into the living room for my encore.

What else do I remember about that party? The drummer gave me all the coins he gathered from the floor. Men stuck dollar bills all over my costume. Women took my phone number for parties they wanted me to dance at. Danny stood back and watched me, a smile of wonder and approval on his face.

At home we paid the baby-sitter and watched her cross the street to her house. We looked in on the sleeping children.

"They dance too," I whispered. "You have a harem now."

"Will you dance for me alone?" he asked. "May I be your sultan?"

I wrapped myself in my veils and turned on the music softly. I unveiled very slowly. There was no other sound but the gentle shimmer of my coins.

Afterward Danny said, "You're marvelous. I didn't know you had that in you, Janet . . . I love it."

That pleased me immensely. But the truth was that I hadn't done all this for him. I had done if for me. And that made the difference.

(1975)

I Am . . . the Queen . . . of England

"I AM REALLY SICK."

She said it aloud for the novelty of speaking with no voice.

"I am . . . the Queen . . . of England."

Nothing at all. Not even a squeak. Last night there had been at least a hoarse croak.

"I definitely think I'm dying," she said clearly, and no message entered the atmosphere. Then she filled her lungs with air, and cupping her hands to her mouth, she screamed with all her might.

"*Fire!*"

In the kitchen, Danny kept on whistling.

Janet began to cry. She knew him—he would whistle happily unto eternity there in the kitchen while she expired here in the bedroom. He had not looked in on her for two hours, simply because she had told him to stay out so that he wouldn't catch anything.

"You're right," he had said. "Someone has to stay well."

Well, did it have to be *him*? She probably didn't mean that. But two hours! If there *were* a fire, she could be devoured by flames. Imagine it—a fire could easily start because the gears on her alarm clock were rubbing together too fast, and she had no voice to call for help and no strength in her legs even to stand up by herself.

She leaned toward her nightstand and took a pad of paper out of the drawer. She would write him a final message:

"You are heartless. I have no voice; my teeth are chattering all over the place; I have a cough, a headache, a sore throat; I am a captive in a firetrap and *you* are whistling. I'll never forgive you. You're the only one I know who can eat with a good appetite while your wife is dying."

She put the pad back in her drawer. If her mother were here, she would be sponging her brow, spooning soup into her mouth. Earlier Danny had called down the hall: "Janet—do you want anything to eat?" and she just had not answered him. She hadn't known then that she couldn't have answered if she'd tried.

But did her silence bring him dashing down the hall? Not at all. She heard him say to one of the girls, "Mommy must be sleeping. Don't go down there and don't make any noise."

This was the first time she had ever got sick before the children did. Usually the girls brought a cold or a flu bug home from school, and it went the rounds of the three of them and *then* she got it. Danny never caught anything.

Not that she actually resented it—but wasn't it just amazing that she lay down with every cold and flu in the district and Danny never did? It wasn't that she wished illness upon him (she couldn't be that immature)—it was just that he didn't understand what it was like to be sick. He refused to worry when the children were down with a high fever and strep throats, and he thought that her restless, worried nights when they were sick were "overreactions" to perfectly normal conditions. "All children get sick and then get well. Children are tough."

But did they all get well automatically while their mother slept like a dead one through the night? No, they got well because they were tended to lovingly—fed and sponged and medicated and watched over and loved. Sleeping snugly didn't kill germs. Mothering killed them. No doctor had ever written a treatise on that, as far as she knew.

Janet moved her legs very slowly, lifting them with her hands one at a time over the side of the bed. Reaching forward for the wall, she leaned her way out of bed and crept dizzily toward the hall. If she didn't get herself some tea or soup, she was going to die for sure. And no one was bringing any in to her—there was no doubt about that.

She shuffled her way, step by step, into the kitchen. There was a mirror in the hall that she tried not to look into. Who was the wild woman with the sunken eyes and the witch's hair?

"Well, look! There's Mommy," Danny cried to the girls. "Are you feeling better? Do you want to eat dinner with us?"

Janet glanced at the table. They were eating yogurt and salted peanuts.

She ignored him. She lifted the kettle and tried to fill it with water, but as soon as the water started to go in she dropped the kettle. It was too heavy. She leaned over the sink and tried to stop the spinning in her head.

"Why don't you take an aspirin?" Danny asked, standing up.

She wondered if that was a sign of his wild concern, his standing up.

"I can't stand up long enough to find the aspirin bottle," she said, forgetting that she could not talk. "I can't talk," she explained, but of course he didn't hear that either.

Crying again, she shuffled back to her bed and collapsed into it. Nothing was more annoying than not being able to sob *loudly* when you needed to.

In the morning Danny, fully dressed, tapped her on the shoulder.

"How do you feel today?"

She stared up at him. How did she know yet? There were all kinds of tests to take before she could answer that. She would have to see if she could breathe through her nose, if she could swallow, if she could lift her aching head off the pillow, if she could talk. She would have to see if her fever had gone down, if she could get her legs out of bed on their own power, if she could stand up. She would have to see if the will to comb her hair had returned. How did he expect her to have an answer right away?

"I'm taking the kids over to the drive-in for an egg sandwich. Want us to bring you one home?"

She stared at him with what she hoped were hollow, sunken eyes. Did she look like a person in the mood for an egg sandwich?

"What day is it?" she said. The only word that made the transition into sound waves was "is."

She was going to say that if it was Monday, which it well could be, then he ought to get the girls ready for school. But if it *was* Monday, then *he* would be getting ready to go to work, and she would be alone all day. She decided to let it go. Better someone whistling in the kitchen when the alarm clock caught on fire than no one home at all. If it was Monday and no one knew it, it was just as well.

"You rest," Danny said, patting her cheerfully. "You'll be just fine soon."

She was sleeping again when they got home, all of them singing a song about a loony rabbit with goony ears.

Bonnie came down the hall and stopped in the doorway, waving an ice-cream cone. "This is the first time," she said, "that we've ever had ice cream for breakfast dessert."

Jill appeared in the hall behind her. "This is the first time, actually," she said, "that we've ever *had* dessert after breakfast."

Janet smiled wanly at them. Who were they, exactly? They looked so big and tough and they seemed so loud! And unkempt. They weren't well-cared-for children at all.

"Why don't you comb your hair?" she said. A sound like a door creaking came out of her throat, but at least it was a sound.

The children threw her kisses and seemed to disappear. Janet put her head down on the pillow.

Again Danny was poking her shoulder. Why didn't he leave her alone?

"How are you now?" he said. "I think you should eat. Do you want some dinner?"

"What?" she said. The word actually came out.

"Chili and peanuts," he said.

"Bring me ant poison," she said. "I'm of no use to anyone . . ."

And then she closed her eyes again.

"It's only the flu," Danny said. "Don't be so dramatic."

"Shut up," she said. "You were not born to suffer like the rest of us."

Sometime in the middle of the night, she felt much better. Danny was sleeping beside her. The house was quiet. She got up and walked slowly into the kitchen She filled the kettle easily. She leaned against the stove till the water began to boil, and she made a cup of tea. She put six teaspoons of sugar in it. It was delicious.

A child cried out from the bedroom: *"Mommy!"*

She carried her cup of tea down the hall.

"I'm sorry, but I have to throw up," Bonnie said sadly from the top bunk of the bunk beds.

"Me too," Jill said from just below.

"That's impossible. You can't," Janet said. "You only do that with stomach flu. The kind I have is the other kind."

"Don't argue," Bonnie said, but by then it was too late.

In the bedroom, Danny slept peacefully.

The monster.

For a few days they had two flus. Janet caught the stomach flu from the girls and they caught the upper-respiratory flu from her. There was so much activity, Janet couldn't believe it. People were sneezing and coughing, people were vomiting, people were running to the bathroom. People were crying. The washing machine ran constantly. Aspirins were consumed by the ton. Three thermometers broke. Janet drank a cup of tea every hour, with ten teaspoons of sugar. She could navigate the house very well now. She could talk. She talked several times on the phone to the doctor, who said, "Hang in there. Just try to stick it out. It has to end soon."

"Is it catching?" she asked.

"Are you kidding?" he said. "With four of you sick, you ask me that?"

"There are five of us," Janet said.

"Tell him to pray," the doctor said.

Janet omitted to relay the doctor's advice to Danny. Neither did she pray for him. Her anger at him was intense. She could hardly stand to look at him. They were no longer on speaking terms. She assumed the excuse he was using to stay home from work was to "look after them." That is, he sat in the living room, reading old magazines and eating peanuts. Where did he find so many cans of peanuts? Had she been planning a party she'd forgotten about?

She was so tired, she was falling over her feet. She still hadn't combed her hair. Each time she lay down on her bed, a child cried out, "Mommy!"

"Call Daddy," she said. "Can't you call Daddy for once?"

"He's no good," Jill said.

"I wish he'd heard you say that," Janet said.

"Should I get out of bed and tell him?"

"Never mind," Janet said.

In the night Myra, her youngest, had a croup attack. Janet was asleep when she heard the barking cough that only a few years ago had sent her into paroxysms of fear. Now Myra was old enough so that the danger of her suffocating was slight.

Janet poked Danny in the back. "Get up," she said with clenched teeth. "You have to get the vaporizer plugged in."

"Huh?" he said, half sitting up.

"Myra. Croup. A little variety, so things don't get too monotonous."

"Go back to sleep," he said, lying down.

"She's coughing. Can't you hear her?"

"It's just a little cough," he said. "She's had a cold. Leave her alone."

Janet kicked him. "Do you want your child to die?" she shrieked. "Get the vaporizer!"

She ran to start the hot water in the shower. Then she carried Myra to the bathroom and held her face near the steam rising from the tub. The barking cough subsided immediately.

"I'm sleepy," Myra said. "Where's my bed?"

"You must stay here a little longer," Janet insisted.

Danny was standing, dazed, in the bathroom in his nightshirt, filling the vaporizer under the tap. "Why don't you just let her sleep?" he pleaded. He looked hairy, wild, like a gorilla.

"You mean," Janet said, with exquisite venom in her voice, "why don't I let *you* sleep?"

"Well, yes, damn it, if you must put it that way. Why don't you let us all sleep, instead of running around, ringing alarms, feeling heads and taking temperatures like a madwoman? It's only the flu. It isn't the plague!"

"What do you know?" Janet cried out. "You don't know how dangerous the flu can be, how rotten it can feel. You're exempt from human ills. You're Mr. Superhuman."

Myra slipped out of Janet's arms and padded back toward her bedroom. "I'm going to sleep," she said.

"See?" Danny said. "All we all need, including you, is a little rest around here."

"What do *you* have to rest about? You haven't been off the couch in a week!"

"I'm staying home in case you need me," Danny said reasonably. "I'm trying to take care of you. And it's no picnic, let me tell you. I keep asking you if you want anything or need anything and you refuse to answer me."

"Well, you shouldn't have to ask! You should *know* what I need! I need tea and soup, not chili and peanuts. You don't know how to take care of sick people. What do you know about being sick? About worrying about children? All those years when the children had croup, when they couldn't breathe, when they turned blue, what were you doing? Sleeping!"

"Well, what were you doing?" he said. "Racing through the house, spreading fear and panic, terrifying the children, sticking your finger down their throats."

"They would have died if I hadn't!" she cried. "You never believed then and you *still* don't believe there was any danger. You just don't know!" She could hardly see him in the steam-bath atmosphere of the bathroom.

"I really hate you," she said, sinking down suddenly on the bath mat. "If I live through this nightmare, I'm going to leave you."

"Shh," he said to her lifting her up and leading her down the hall. "Come with me. All you need is a little sleep."

"First I have to check Bonnie," she said.

"Bonnie's sleeping. Leave her alone."

"She had a fever of a hundred and four degrees this afternoon. I have to feel her head."

In the dark bedroom she reached up to the top bunk. Bonnie was all the way over, against the wall. Janet climbed up on the wooden ladder to reach her. The ladder slipped sideways and Janet screamed. She landed on her back on the floor.

"Are you okay?" Bonnie cried, scared, peering over the edge of the top bunk.

"How could I hit so hard?" Janet said. "I'm not that heavy."

"Why don't you get up?"

"I can't."

"Should I call Daddy?"

But Daddy was already lifting her up and was carrying her into bed.

"Leave me alone!" she commanded.

"Quiet!" he said fiercely. "This is an order. There will be no more taking care of sick people in this house till everyone gets well."

In the days following, everyone seemed to be getting well, though Janet's tailbone was very sore. Danny no longer asked her what she wanted. He brought her the heating pad and lifted her up with one arm while he slid it under her with the other. He brought her meals to her. He usually served yogurt and peanuts. Sometimes it was strawberry yogurt, sometimes blueberry. She drank lots of tea. She didn't ask about the girls. She was too tired to care. She didn't talk to Danny. She took his service as if it were her due and she ignored him. He didn't talk to her either. When the mail came, he dropped it on the foot of the bed and went out. He took empty plates with him, glasses, medicine bottles.

The girls no longer sang about the loony rabbit with the

goony ears. They left her alone and they left Danny alone. From her bed, Janet heard her children coughing and sneezing now and then. She wasn't concerned. It was natural for children to get sick. They got well. She was not going to worry again. Keeping life going in herself and in her children was out of her hands. It had never been in them. Understanding that made her indifferent. She could relax because the work of staying alive was really none of her business. For a long time, since her first child was born, she had been mistaken in believing that it was her concern, and hers alone.

On a sunny afternoon (was it a week—two weeks—since she'd got sick?) she walked to the bathroom and took a shower. She washed her hair. The water was hot and marvelous. She knew that if she wanted to sing, she would be able to. She had her voice back. She had her health back. Why did she feel so sad?

She wanted her family back. She'd scared the girls and Danny away, somehow. She wanted to be able to make contact with them, but she didn't know where to start. *They* didn't know where to start. She knew this illness hadn't started out as solemnly as it had ended.

Janet combed her hair and powdered her body. She was really well. She wanted a reason to be glad to be alive. The sun was gilding the ceiling, the hallway, the buttons on her robe. And yet a coldness was everywhere. Now she was in isolation when she no longer needed to be. She needed contact and warmth. She wanted so badly to touch someone. The fear of spreading germs had kept them apart at first, and later something else.

She walked slowly back to the bedroom and saw at once that there were clean sheets pulled tight on the bed. She could see Danny in the living room, sitting on the couch, reading a magazine. How had he managed that so fast? And so neatly? But then she saw the children, peeking with serious faces at her from the doorway of their bedroom, waiting for a sign from her.

She made her way to her bed and crept between the smooth, clean sheets. She looked at her alarm clock. The minute hand raced along, sweeping great circles of time away. The gears of the clock were turning, rubbing together. She could not allow any more of this sour time to exist; she had to do something to try to make things right.

Then she did it. She filled her lungs with air, and cupping her hands to her mouth, she screamed with all her might: "FIRE!"

(1975)

How We Spent Our Summer Vacation

~

WILL SOMEONE TELL ME where vacations got such a good reputation? As I look up and down this block I can't believe the enthusiasm I see all around me. My neighbor to the left is at this very moment loading the family camper with enough groceries to support a fortress of pioneers against a three-month siege by Indians.

My neighbor to the right is also getting ready to leave—school has been out a full two weeks; perhaps that is the legal limit set by the Board of Mental Health for staying at home with the children, and *her* family is really going to rough it. No camper there—just a couple of tube tents and a prayer. Everything goes in the back of the station wagon: sleeping bags, fishing poles, hibachi, sun umbrella, folding table, fly swatters—the works.

Right at this moment I see her loading her survival gear—the tarpaulin and the bucket and the three-foot rubber straw for extracting water out of the desert sand, the snake-bite kit, the bee-bite kit, the hammock to double as a litter, the hatchet, the flashlights, the packets of dried beef and deconstituted apple-sauce. Her husband comes out with the fire extinguisher, the first-aid kit with a big red cross on it, and a large green metal oxygen container with a dial mounted on it.

I turn away from the window and consider my own "Vacation List." I have been adding to this list for ten days now (our vacation is only going to be three days, starting tomorrow) and I have managed to check off only the first item: "Think positive."

Following that are these various other instructions that I have found in articles that are published in the newspapers at the start of every summer.

"Cancel newspaper, mail and milk deliveries and inform police of absence." The articles say it is very important not to have old newspapers accumulating on the lawn, letters in the mailbox or milk cartons on the front step. This precaution is to foil burglars, who might otherwise think that we are away and that the house is an easy target. The fact is that even when we *are* home there are often yellowing newspapers sticking out of the ivy (these are generously thrown away on my lawn twice a week); and as for the milk cartons, when they aren't on the front step filled with milk, they're on the front step filled with aphid eggs or butterfly cocoons.

The next item is "Make reservation." Of course, the question is *where*. By the time we all agree on our destination, there won't be a room left in America. The children want to go to Disneyland to see the parrots in the Tiki Room, Danny wants to go to San Diego to see a production of *Othello* at the Globe Theater and I . . .

Well, two weeks in Italy and two in France wouldn't be a bad idea at all. Better still, I'd vote for a trip in a riverboat down the Nile, complete with Humphrey Bogart at the helm and Masai warriors hiding in the tall grasses. I've never told Danny this because he might laugh, but even though I'm not much on camping, I think I'd do splendidly on a safari, wearing khakis and hiking boots and carrying my full load just like any man. I could even get used to the sight of crocodiles yawning at my toes. (No doubt, after some experience I would not even scream.)

But the Nile is not a possibility, and a vacation within a hundred miles drive is. I consult my list again.

"Return library books, get money from bank, take the rats

and goldfish to Linda's, take the anthuriums to Mrs. Johnson's, cancel music lesson for Jill, do last minute laundry, *find top to bathing suit*, get heels on white shoes, have zipper on suitcase fixed, buy upset-stomach medicine, buy film.

That, of course, is only *my* list. Danny has a list (getting the car in order, cutting the grass), the children have lists, and the ones I am referring to are only the lists of things to do at *home*. Then there are the other lists of what to take along with us.

At the bottom of my list, in red marker, is the P.S.: *"Leave house clean!"*

I contemplate scratching that. However, I have always had a strong feeling that I must leave things in order. If all of us are caught in a tornado (should we go to Kansas), I want to be sure the relatives find the kitchen neat when they and the police make legal entry into the house.

I wonder, *Are* we going to Kansas?

Myra is wondering too. "Have we decided on a place yet?" she asks, running into the kitchen.

"We're deciding right now," I announce. "In fact, you and I are going to decide this minute." I go to the cabinet and pull out a pile of brochures I've been collecting over the winter at various restaurants and places of entertainment.

I sit down at the table and Myra deposits herself on my lap. We examine the brochures one by one.

"Wax Museum?"

"Too creepy," Myra says.

"Hearst Castle?"

"Again?" she moans.

"Sea World?"

"Goody!" Myra says. "I love to see the dolphins hula."

"Well, I don't," I say. We pass quickly down the list: Fisherman's Wharf, Fun World, Hawaii (Oops! Wrong pile!) . . .

"Why don't you ask Daddy?"

"He says it's up to us. He's agreeable to anything." Just as I am about to give up in despair, my eye falls upon the last brochure. It says: "Visit the Black Heart of Africa Park and Animal Reservation. Let our seasoned guides show you the secrets of the

Dark Continent, see the eyes of lions peering out at you from the brush!"

"This is it!" I cry, standing up and nearly dumping Myra to the floor. *"This* is where we're going!"

The timer on the stove dings to tell me the bank will close in fifteen minutes. I take the bell as an omen. I have picked the perfect place.

"Announce it to everyone." I tell Myra. "Get your gear together. We're going on a safari."

∽

In the motel we finally pull up to, well after dark, there is a cheery fire burning in the lobby fireplace.

"I don't like the looks of it," I whisper to Danny as we walk in the door. "It was a hundred and one degrees this afternoon."

"This is the first motel in sixty miles that has had a vacancy sign," he whispers back. "Let's not blow it by having hunches."

"A room for yourselves and the three kiddies?" asks the clerk at the desk.

"Yes. If possible, we'd like separate beds for the girls; they aren't used to sleeping together. So if you have some cots . . . "

"All we have is one room left, and what's in it are two double beds," he says. His head is bald, like a buzzard's.

"Well, I guess we can manage with that," Danny says, looking at me for confirmation. "Us in one bed. Bonnie and Jill in the other, and Myra can bring in the slumber bag we have in the car. She doesn't mind sleeping on the floor anyway."

"We don't allow sleeping bags in the rooms," the clerk says, the smile gone from his face. "You never know who's *been* in them or what's *creeping* in them."

"Only *I've* been in it and nothing's *creeping* in it!" Myra says angrily, astonished.

"That's all right dear," I say. "We'll manage without it."

"The three children can easily fit into a double bed," Danny says. He turns his back on the man and winks clearly at the children, who close their mouths suddenly at the first lie they have actually witnessed their father engage in.

We follow the man to a room with a pink door, and he lets us in with a master key.

"I smell gas," I say. I look at the clerk. "Don't you smell gas?" I ask him.

"I most certainly do not," he says, standing stiffly at the door. "Now, will this do?"

"The air conditioner is about two inches from the head of that bed," I point out. "Whoever sleeps there will get pneumonia."

The clerk's face is turning darker and darker red.

"No problem, no problem," Danny says, waving his arms grandly. "We'll leave the air conditioner off, sweetheart," he says to me.

Since he never calls me sweetheart, I shut my mouth.

"This is fine," Danny says. "May we have a key? We'll be going out for dinner in a little while."

"There is no key," the clerk says. "The last people in here— they didn't turn it in, and we can't have another made till after the weekend."

"Well," I say, "how can we expect to go out and have dinner if we can't lock our things in here after we unload?"

"Don't *worry*," Danny says. "Nothing of value to worry about."

I am thinking: camera, binoculars, my precious odd-sized bikini with a size A top, size Z bottom, which took me months to find in the stores.

"It's all right, *sweetheart*," Danny says, as he follows the clerk back to the office to sign the register while I try to open the stuck windows to air out the gas leaking from the heater.

At the coffee shop I once again have to confront the reality of having to pay a small fortune for a hamburger meal for the five of us. I have never forgiven nature for deceiving us into thinking, when the children were babies, that the five of us could easily eat well on a two-hamburger dinner, plus an extra order of French fries and three glasses of milk. Nature, having enlarged the children in the normal course of events, has tripled our restaurant costs.

Since it is our holiday, the girls all order cups of hot chocolate topped with whipped cream. The waitress brings these confections a full fifteen minutes before the hamburgers arrive. By
that time the children are no longer hungry, and furthermore,
they claim they are thirsty and have nothing to drink with their
hamburgers.

I point out the water.

The water tastes like laundry bleach, they say.

In the meantime I am trying to eat my hamburger, discreetly
depositing strange bits and pieces from my mouth onto the side
of my plate.

"God!" Bonnie says. "There's glass in my hamburger."

"There's rocks in mine," Myra says.

"I have seashells in mine."

"Just a little bone and gristle, girls," Danny says, valiantly
chewing his hamburger. "They don't always buy the best grade
of meat in these places."

"Don't eat it," I tell my girls. "Just eat your parsley and put
lots of ketchup on your potatoes . . . I don't want that stuff in my
children," I explain to Danny. The implication is that he is an
adult, and if he chooses to nourish himself on refuse, that is his
business.

The waitress sails over. "Is everything fine and dandy?" she
sings, smiling perkily.

"Just fine, just fine," Danny says.

I kick him under the table. He shakes his head at me. This is
our vacation. He doesn't want any fusses. His look says that he
hopes we'll eat better tomorrow.

The waitress places on the table—as I guessed she would—a
bill for as much as the motel room.

"Thank you, sir," she says.

Danny takes out several dollar bills and places them on the
table. Waitresses, he feels, have a hard lot in life, on their feet all
day, taking orders, carrying dishes, wiping tables, picking up
soggy crackers from the floor. (He has never noticed, I am sure,
that as an American housewife I not only take orders and carry
dishes to and fro; I also shop, cook, and wash all the pots!)

The manager, a man with a mustache, takes our money graciously at the cash register and says, "I hope you enjoyed your dinner and will come back again soon."

"We'll never come back," Myra says suddenly. "There were rocks in my hamburger."

The man smiles at my little girl, but his lip curls slightly. He looks at us questioningly.

"Look," I say, "the truth is, we all left our hamburgers, even my husband, who usually can eat anything. The meat was entirely inedible."

The waitress is called. The evidence is still on the stainless-steel clearing wagon—all hamburgers present, one bite out of each. (Two out of Danny's.) Apologies ensue. The manager, of course, has nothing to do with the ordering of the meat. The head office takes care of that. He's so sorry. He charges us only for French fries and drinks. There is a generous refund. He still hopes we will come back again soon. We drive back to the Open Door Motel. It is hard to believe that our vacation has only just started.

Never mind that at two o'clock in the morning someone starts to sandpaper a chest of drawers in the alley outside our window. Never mind that Myra, sleeping in the surreptitiously hustled-in sleeping bag (full of whatever creeping things) is snoring ten inches from my ear. Never mind that the double bed sags brutally and that Danny, as much as I love him, is too close for comfort or the possibility of sleep. At three o'clock a party moves into the next room and sends out for pizza. By four o'clock they are dancing in there. At dawn the gas heater goes on automatically, creaking and clanking. There is nowhere to flee to. How long will this go on? Well, at least there is The Black Heart of Africa Park and Animal Reservation to look forward to.

～

The children and I drink from a water fountain while Danny buys the tickets. It is so hot this weekend that steam rises from the piles of coins catching the sun behind the cashier's window.

"This is just like Africa," Danny says bravely. "This is what the ivory hunters experienced when they tramped through the veld."

"Could we buy a souvenir stuffed animal?" Jill asks.

"Did the ivory hunters buy souvenir animals?" Danny asks.

"They got tusks for souvenirs," Bonnie says smartly. "What do we get?"

You get a slap on the behind, I think meanly, but silently. The heart of darkness is getting to me.

We are lined up to board the tram. The trams are loaded by men wearing khaki shorts and hunter's helmets. There are rifles hanging from their belts. One young hunter has a small transistor radio in his shirt pocket and is listening to rock music. The long lines move up. The third tram loads and it's going to be close. Will we manage to squeeze on or not?

We'll manage. There is one wide seat left at the back of the tram. With relief, Danny steps in to reserve it, and the three girls climb in after him. As I step up the hunter blocks my way.

"Sorry, full," he says. "You'll have to take the next tram."

"This is my *family*," I say.

"We have strict rules, ma'am," he says. "You wouldn't want to fall over the side and into the waiting jaws of the lions. Only four allowed to each seat."

"But I want to be with my children!" I cry.

"If you like, your family can unload and wait for the next tram. Then I can seat all of you in the same vehicle, but still only four to a seat. One of you will have to sit alone."

I notice Myra, our youngest, is leaning her head against the silver railing of the tram in exhaustion, sweat on her forehead. I am not going to ask her to climb out of her little patch of shade for me. I'll be brave. I'll take the next tram alone. I'll see the Black Heart of Africa on my own, like a big girl.

"Give me the binoculars," I say to Danny.

"You can stay with the girls and I'll take the next tram," he offers.

"No, no," I say. "Let me have this great adventure alone."

There is a toot and my family pulls off. Soon they are lost to sight in the jungle.

When the next tram arrives, I am seated first. Here I am, having longed to feel adventurous in an army jeep, and instead I am riding in a surrey with a fringe on top.

A teenaged couple, both with long hair and dressed alike in blue jeans, are loaded on next to us. A Japanese businessman with three cameras around his neck is added to complete our arrangement.

The sun is getting hotter. The loudspeaker suddenly shrieks in my ear: "Welcome to the Black Heart of Africa. Keep your hands inside the tram at all times and do not lean over the edge of the car. We keep our animals fed, but not that well fed. That's a joke. Ha-ha."

The couple beside me aren't worrying about privacy. They're hugging and kissing as if the world will end when the ride is over. The Japanese man is twirling the dials on all his cameras and is half standing, aiming this way and that at the invisible ostrich. He sighs and sits down. We are thumping out into the open plains, which look like nothing so much as a bunch of dirt hills and piles of rock. Not a blade of grass, just a few trees. A lot of gray trucks here and there.

"Out to your right," the guide says, "you will see a mother rhino with her brand-new baby rhino. Actually, probably not all of you can see the rhino because she's behind that tree, and you can't see the baby because she's behind the mother. Maybe we'll get a glimpse of them when we come back the other way."

We rumble on. "The lions, which, as you know, are the fiercest creatures in the jungle, probably could be seen if it weren't such a hot day. It happens that the coolest place around is under the tracks on which this tram travels. So if you had x-ray vision, you could see through the floor of the tram and all the lions would be down there, resting in the shade. However, we caution you not to lean over to try to see. They're not that well fed, as I said before."

I listen for the ha-ha, which this time does not come.

"To your left you'll see a gray maintenance truck. The animals are great friends with the maintenance men. Behind the truck is the hippo. If we're lucky, we might get a glimpse of him on our way back around the other side."

The Japanese man is still setting dials and aiming his cameras—first one and then another. Finally he leans way back and takes a picture of the couple kissing.

He smiles at me and I smile at him. Then he takes a picture of me.

"Look!" someone cries from the back of the tram. "Look at the gazelle!"

I twirl around and I catch a shimmer of movement out on the plains.

"Luckily, many animals are blessed with nature's camouflage," the guide says. "Now you see it, now you don't."

"I don't," I mumble to myself.

The Japanese man is chuckling out loud.

"What? *What?*" I cry.

"Got picture of giraffe," he says. "Just head sticking out of tree. Hardly see it now, but nice when I blow up."

"Next time you see one, will you let me know?" I ask.

I begin to take the binoculars out of their case.

"See one," my friend says.

"Where?" I look for giraffe heads in every tree.

"Not up. Down. Lion," he says.

A lion! Will I finally see his yellow eyes peering out at me from the brush?

"Too late," my friend says. "Licking lollipop on ground, come out of shade a minute."

I haven't seen an animal yet. I do see, in the great circle of dirt that comprises the African countryside, several other trams with red-striped awnings. I raise the binoculars, and to my delight, as I focus I see through my glasses my husband and my children seated in the rear of the tram that has just turned around for the final half of the ride.

I am so excited, it's as if I have just sighted a rare goola bird. There they are, *my* people, my favorite species, my lover Danny and my darling children.

Of course they don't know I am watching them. Danny has

his arm protectively around the back of the seat, and with his free hand he is pointing out things (maintenance men? trucks?) to the girls. I can see their faces as if they are a foot away. Bonnie's face is getting long and thin; her nose is clearly growing up before the rest of her face. Jill is grinning at something. All the gaps from her missing teeth are evident. She says something, a joke—she laughs. Danny brings his arm down and hugs her. The youngest, Myra, seems to have fallen asleep. Her head is on the railing of the tram, her blond hair blowing slightly in the breeze of the moving car.

Danny is wearing his jaunty sailor hat and his "Freakie" T-shirt, bought for him by the children as a surprise birthday present. He has his camera around his neck, and his pocket full of money he is planning to spend on his family, on their vacation.

They are beautiful, they are mine, and this moment is my vacation.

The Japanese man reaches over the kissing couple and taps my arm. His eyes are asking me what I am looking at so long that is causing me to smile so happily.

"Oh, it's just my family I see," I tell him. "My husband and my children in that car—see? Right there."

"Permission please to take picture of them for you, zoom lens?" he asks me. "Promise I send to you."

"Delighted!" I say. He takes the picture; I give him our address. In a few moments the tram slows; the safari is coming to an end.

"Enjoy vacation, surely," my new friend says in farewell.

"Surely," I say. Vacations are just a matter of new perspectives.

(1976)

The Three Princesses

~

THERE IN THE NUMBER-ONE ring is Anna, the maternal grandmother, playing a Beethoven sonata. Note the cultured expression on her face. Note the practiced way her shapely legs control the piano pedals. See the crowd gathering around her—already she has charmed the majority, two out of her three granddaughters staring with wonder at her flying fingers.

And there in the number-three ring on the couch is Aunt Gert, the maternal great-aunt, embroidering a luscious red rose on a piece of white linen. Her silver needle flashes under and over the hoop; her range of elaborate stitches is astonishing. Note the rapt attention of the single, yet perhaps the most impressionable, observer, her youngest grandniece.

And here in the center ring, half dead after serving Thanksgiving dinner to everyone, is myself—Janet, the maternal mother—slumped unnoticed in a rocking chair, wishing I could figure out a way to effect a reconciliation of opposing camps.

The truth is, I am not really a dispassionate observer. By virtue of my birth and perhaps because of an innate loyalty to my mother, I am definitely an advocate of the art displayed in the number-one ring, where my mother's inspired *Appassionata Sonata* is shaking the dusty chandelier. After all, I was raised on the airwaves of those chords, even though I spent at least half my childhood in Aunt Gert's apartment learning the romance of the rose, crocheting pot holders, sewing aprons, drying dishes and struggling to master what was to me the pointless art of ironing.

It has always seemed to me a stroke of amazing fortune that my mother preferred to allow the air to dry her dishes rather than to insist on her daughter and some linty dishcloth. And even in those days before "permanent press," she had the good sense to buy us clothes of flannel and wool and corduroy, avoiding as much as possible those rigid, starched cotton dresses that needed constant pressing. Compared to Aunt Gert's manner of living, our household was terribly straightforward and unsentimental.

Aunt Gert's closets are full of scrapbooks, photograph albums, diaries, boxes of old letters and a precious collection of valentines. On every doilied surface of her living room she always had a display of greeting cards to commemorate whatever recent event had taken place in her life—a birthday, an anniversary, the New Year, the flu.

My mother scorned greeting cards. "If I want to say something to someone, I write a letter," she said. "I don't need to pay good money to have someone else write some nonsense for me."

When she occasionally received a greeting card from someone who didn't know her preferences, she'd glance at it and toss it into the wastebasket. "I'm not going to put them up on the walls like your aunt does," she would say to me.

The question (always in my mind when I was young) was, did my mother *like* my Aunt Gert or not? After all, they were sisters, just as my sister and I were sisters, and we were supposed to like and respect each other even if we didn't feel like it. In fact, my mother required it of us. "Sisters share the same mother and father. There will never be anyone again in your life who has so much in common with you. You are in a unique relationship to each other, and it is very important that you always be close, because when you're grown up no one else will understand quite what your childhood was like but your sister."

I wish suddenly that my own sister were here tonight so that we could exchange knowing, amused glances, and burst into private giggles over matters that are funny to no one but the two of us. It is definitely true that I love her in a way that I love no one else on earth—and I love her more as we grow older.

I wonder if my children think of themselves as loving one another at all. At the moment, the two older girls are beginning to step on each other's toes as they shift restlessly from one leg to the other. Beethoven does go on and on.

Finally Aunt Gert calls out: "Enough culture already, Anna! Give the children a little fun now. I could use some myself. Why don't you play the routine you used to do when we were girls—the Three Princesses Story?"

"Yes, do it!" Jill cries out. She is eight; perhaps it is asking too much of her to be a serious listener this long.

Bonnie, older and eager to appear as mature as possible, says in an adult voice, "No, do go on and finish the piece, Mom-Mom."

My mother lifts her hands from the keys and spins gracefully on the piano stool to face us, her hands poised on her knees.

"Your aunt," she says to us pointedly, "can't take too much culture at one time."

"Oh, feh," Aunt Gert says, never breaking the even in-and-out motion of her needle. "You fill the children full of fancy airs; you try to make them think there are no other important things in life but the things you like."

"Such as?" my mother asks. "Cooking? Sewing?"

"Yes, cooking, sewing!" Aunt Gert says firmly. "Don't be so fast to put them down. Didn't Janet make a beautiful dinner tonight? Didn't we all enjoy it? Isn't such joy important?"

My mother's eyes flash and the children see we are in for a real conversation, the kind they are not usually present to hear. The two older ones fold their knees and settle down on the carpet. Myra moves closer to Aunt Gert and touches her arm.

"Give me a kiss," Aunt Gert says to her. "Give me a vitamin, darling," She points at me. "Your mother," she explains to Myra, "when she was little, used to call it giving me a 'raisin.'"

My mother sneers. This is just the kind of precious talk she can't stand.

"I suppose," she says, "that Janet should be preparing her girls to start sewing their trousseaus."

"That would be wonderful," Aunt Gert says. "If it weren't for me, you never would have had a trousseau."

"So?" my mother says.

Aunt Gert stops the movement of her needle. My mother has gone too far and realizes it.

"I don't mean that," she says. "You made me some beautiful nightgowns. Really beautiful. Even Abram thought they were amazing."

"He should rest in peace," Aunt Gert says.

At the sound of the words my mother folds her arms over her breast, as if a cold wind is coming across the room toward her. Despite all the Thanksgiving nights that have passed since my father's death, his absence from the table does not get less shocking with the years.

"You want my sweater?" Aunt Gert says.

My mother shakes her head.

"Still," Aunt Gert continues, "even though he's gone, you should be willing to cook for yourself now and then. There's no need to eat out so often. If it weren't for me, you'd never get a decent meal."

My mother turns to the keys and plays a nervous C scale. It is clear that she wants to change the subject.

But Aunt Gert goes on: "And for you I leave out the garlic because you can't stand it, even though Harry loves it."

I hold my breath, knowing what my mother might well say. She has told me often enough: So don't do me any favors, Gert. Don't leave out the garlic and don't invite me to dinner. Make your pot roast the way Harry likes it and leave me in peace with my frozen chicken pie.

My mother catches my eye and I shake my head. I hope that I am a comfort to her. She has one satisfaction, at least—Aunt Gert has no children.

Finally my mother says, "I don't think trousseau sewing is what Janet has in mind for her girls."

I try to laugh. "You know what Danny says? That when it's

time for their weddings, we're going to hold the receptions at McDonald's."

"Not funny," Aunt Gert says. "Not funny, Janet. A wedding is too important in a girl's life. I should know. I had two—late in life, but still two. The first when I was thirty-nine, the second after I was widow for two years, when I was fifty-four. Such emotion I had on those days!"

"I'm sure Janet thinks a wedding day is fine, but not a reason for her beautiful, brilliant little girls to waste their lives cooking and sewing."

"Playing scales on a piano isn't wasting? Is that how you want them to spend their lives?"

I can't believe these women, these sisters, are at it again. Hadn't I seen them helping each other up the steep driveway— holding hands—just a few hours ago? How can they be from the same family, from the same mother and father?

We hear Danny and my uncle Harry in the family room, fooling around with a tape recorder that hasn't been working properly. Into the silence I say, "Who wants to play Scrabble?"

But they are too far into it.

Aunt Gert is stitching furiously, speaking into her lap. "Your mother has these airs now because she was a career woman. She's so self-important because when she was twenty she put on her fancy tailored suits and her leather shoes and went out into the world to be a high-class secretary to good-looking lawyers and rich judges. If my father hadn't died so young, maybe my life would have been different. But I was the younger. I had to stay home with my sick mother and keep house while Anna went gallivanting all over New York City."

"Gallivanting? I was putting bread on the table, Gert. I was paying the mortgage so you would have a roof over your head. And I was only eighteen years old, not twenty! I was just a child, and I had to take the subway every day, and what did you do? You stayed home and cut out valentines and baked cookies."

"But I also cleaned chickens and I dragged out the garbage. And when Mama needed me I was there to take care of her. Don't you know I would have given my arm to be doing what you were doing? All I did was go to school and take care of a sick mother."

"And don't you think," my mother says suddenly, "that I would have liked to do what you were doing? To stay home and finish high school, and not have to rush out into the business world and lie and pretend I had experience and knew everything when I knew nothing?"

I know what's coming. But my girls don't. She looks at them and says, "My first job was with a lawyer. What did I know about law? I lied and told him I'd had all kinds of experience. He liked me—he hired me. That afternoon a man came into the office and said to me, 'Where's the process server?'

"I began opening and closing drawers in my desk.

"'What are you doing?' he said.

"'I'm looking for the process server,' I told him! I thought it was like a cake server. How was I to know it was a man? That's how smart I was."

"But you had a career!" Gert almost moans.

"No, I didn't. I never did!" my mother says. "I was a secretary—but to me it was only a job, and I wanted more, I *wanted* a career, I wanted to learn about music, to study it and play it and become someone. But there was too much responsibility on my shoulders. I had to support a whole household."

"Nevertheless," Aunt Gert says.

"But what is the point of all this? There are three lovely, intelligent young girls growing up here, and the question is, what do we want for them? To be cooks?"

"To be players of scales?"

"To be married at the Beverly Hills Hotel and then nothing?"

"Who says nothing?"

"I say."

The sisters stare daggers at each other. My eye lands on the coffee table, where I see the little gifts they have brought for the children. My mother bought them each a set of crossword-puzzle books and my aunt bought them each a Modern Miss Manicure Kit.

My aunt and my mother are looking at me, waiting for something, and I realize it is not really my girls they are talking about.

It's me. They are still battling for control of my soul. My mother thinks I have defected because I cooked a good turkey dinner and because I sewed the kitchen curtains. Aunt Gert thinks all the years she spent with me have been wasted because I don't iron my sheets or set my hair.

My mother wanted great things for me and instead she got from me three grandchildren and merely nice things. Aunt Gert dreamed of looking in my drawers and seeing my husband's handkerchiefs in beautiful, neat piles and smelling the odor of sachet among my lace slips. Instead what she sees are crumbs all over the floors, a great disarray of books and papers on all surfaces and a niece who hasn't worn a dress in six months.

"I was thinking I might be an anthropologist," Bonnie says suddenly, as if it is relevant. "But I could keep taking my violin lessons to see if I get better, too."

"I haven't made any plans yet," Jill says. "I have to find out more about what there is."

"I'm going to be a famous singer, more famous than Cher," Myra says, and begins to sing "Oh! Susanna." My mother swings around to face the piano keys and accompanies Myra to the end of the song.

Aunt Gert resumes sewing calmly.

"Anna," she says gently into the silence after the song, "play for the children the song about the three princesses. You make magic when you do that."

My mother smiles and all the wrinkles seem to leave her face. "Shall I?" she says cheerfully.

The children don't know what to make of it. They have not yet learned that it's hard to keep up a thirty-year-old argument, which is also boring and tiring. They are eager, though, for a change.

"Play it! Play it!"

My mother begins in a hushed voiced, her fingers poised above the keys.

"Once upon a time there was a king . . . [some royal music].

"He had three daughters. One was tall . . . and . . . skinny . . . [high, squeaky music].

"And one was short . . . and . . . fat . . . [low, loud, music].

"And one was young and beautiful. [A springtime waltz.]

"In the village lived a young and handsome prince. [Stirring chords. Vibrations shake the room.]

"He loved one of the princesses.

"Not the tall and skinny one . . . [high, squeaky music].

"Not the short and fat one . . . [low, loud music].

"But . . . the young and beautiful one. [Flowers and butterflies.]

"One day a villain came to the village. [Heavy, threatening thunder.]

"He was also a prince, and he wanted the young and beautiful princess. He took her by the arm and said: 'Gimme a little kiss, will ya, huh?'

"She cried, 'No, no, never!' Along came the handsome prince, confronted the villain and challenged him to a duel. [Fierce battle music.]

"Alas, it was very sad for the villain, because . . . [somber tones of a funeral march] . . . the strong prince killed him. [*Clunk.*]

"Then he married the young and beautiful princess and all about the land were heard wedding bells. [Tinkling, chiming wedding bells.]

"'Here Comes the Bride' was played from the mountains to the valleys." [Dum-dum-da-dum.]

"A year later they had a baby, and this is what they sang: 'Yes sir, that's my baby . . .'"

My mother sings the chorus and finishes with a flourish (de dum, de dum!): "The Happy End."

Everyone is grinning. Aunt Gert is wiping her eyes with the edge of her embroidery cloth. My mother is flushed and animated with pleasure. The children are enthralled.

"Well, enough of that," my mother says, standing up. "Now let's see what needs doing in the kitchen." As she leaves, Aunt Gert says to me, nodding her head, "Your mother has more romance in her heart than she even knows herself."

She puts down her sewing and follows my mother into the

kitchen. I know without looking that my mother is washing the dishes, and my aunt, trying to ignore the condition of the dish towel, is drying.

The children stretch out on the rug and begin to do their crossword puzzles. I'm thinking: Wedding bells. I'm thinking: Handsome princes. What has all this to do with the children? They'll figure it out themselves. In the meanwhile I really ought to point out to them that they are sisters and exist in a unique relationship to one another. Not only do they share a mother and a father, but they share this evening, this great-aunt, this grandmother. No one but the three of them (and me) will ever understand exactly what it was like.

They're too busy to be interrupted now. But when the appropriate moment arrives, I'll tell them.

(1976)

A Gambling Woman

~

AS WE ALL KNOW, certain things are good. Beauty is good. Wealth is good. Health is good.

Gambling is bad. This I learned from my grandmother when as a child I would sit on the edge of the bathtub as she bathed and scrub her back for her.

"He was a gambling man," she said of my grandfather, shaking her white head ruefully. "He nearly ruined us all."

Just as my grandmother did not bathe in a red-tiled, heart-shaped, four-foot-deep bathtub (such as the one featured in the brochure of the Las Vegas hotel we are presently headed toward), neither, I am sure, did my grandfather do his gambling in a casino studded with crystal chandeliers and carpeted in lush, blood-red wool that appears from the brochure to be two feet deep.

My heart pounds in anticipation of the bad, bad vacation Danny and I are on our way to enjoy.

How two-faced I am! There I was, just a few hours ago, in the parking lot of our local sports arena—a concerned mother seeing her three girls off to a wholesome, character-building, Girl Scout camp for a week, at the same time harboring in her heart visions of what might be considered the world's least wholesome, least character-building entertainment.

"Do you have your insect repellent? Remember to rub it on

every night. Only use your flashlight when you need it or the batteries will wear out. I know the biffies smell bad, but be sure to go to the bathroom often anyway. Every Girl Scout needs to experience the primitive joys of an outhouse. Be good—be careful—yes, don't worry, the cat will be just fine at Mom-Mom's—have *fun.*"

Two hundred girls in sun hats and with canteens over their shoulders being waved off by at least three hundred mothers and fathers, four huge buses loaded with sleeping bags and duffels (at least one of them, I knew, containing a teddy bear), and all those shining faces at the windows. "Good-bye, Mommy!" . . . "Good-bye, darling. Have a good time!"

If there was a tear shining on the face of my youngest, never before separated from me for this long a time, I refused to see it. For once in my life I was not just *seeing off* and going home to wait. This time I was off to adventure myself.

Danny was astounded at my toughness. I turned my back to the bus before it had driven ten feet down the road and I hurried to the car, my shoulder bag heavy with my jewels (my rock tumbler beads, paper-clip bracelet, and varnished seed-pod earrings—surprise gifts from my children). Indeed, I was not thinking about Girl Scout precepts like thriftiness—I could hardly wait to get busy gambling, to carry on the family weakness and to see what real sin was like.

Danny squeezes my leg pleasantly now that we are truly on our way, heading east across California. For the first time in years and years we are free to be alone together for a few days. I laugh out loud at the thought.

Even the blank Mojave Desert, which I have never crossed, seems exciting. It is one hundred and five degrees, which the radio says is moderately warm for July. The principal scenery consists of strange, bristly little Joshua trees and distant outcroppings of rocky mountains. I drape Danny's head with a dripping washcloth and I drop an ice cube down my dress.

"In the old days," Danny says, "it would have taken travelers weeks to reach a landmark like that dry lake bed in the distance. But watch—we'll be there in ten minutes."

The car seems to be flying along the perfectly flat, straight road. I have the sensation that the wheels have already left the ground and we are ascending.

"Danny, the speed limit is fifty-five."

"But this road was built for safe speeds of seventy or more," Danny explains to me. "The police know people have to get across this desert fast or they'll cook. I don't think we'll be stopped. I'm willing to take a chance."

A gambling man, I think. Oh, Grandma, I've got one too . . . And we haven't even arrived in Las Vegas.

In Baker we stop for a soft, swirly ice-cream cone, and it melts and runs down our fingers instantly. A powerful wind knocks us about and pelts us with sand. We return to the oven of our car. A sign pointing the way to Death Valley seems almost morbid, under the circumstances. We drive on, faster than before, and eventually pass an exit to Zzyzx Road. Can any of this be real?

I am already feeling not myself. Is it true that I am the mother of three children? Did I really spend the past week shopping for mess kits and new bathing caps and little travel tubes of toothpaste? Was that *me* last night on my hands and knees in the living room, panting, trying to roll up three sleeping bags tightly enough to tie them with strings that were too short?

And if that was real, then who is this woman on her way with her lover to a heart-shaped bathtub, to sumptuous meals and elegant nightclubs? Is it the same woman who generally spends her vacations going to zoos, beaches and Disneyland?

I open my purse and count my special money. There it is, twenty ten-dollar bills, which I absolutely do not need. I know this because I have decided it; it is no more to me than Monopoly money. (It already seems foreign, almost the wrong color green.) I know I do not need it because if I am going to gamble it, I can't possibly need it. Besides which, I may very well get rich on it in the next day or so. After all, what is two hundred dollars? A few trips to the doctor would take care of it. Or new tires and brakes for the car. Or the washing machine going kaput. Or one mortgage payment. I spend two hundred dollars all the time on boring things like that. And I don't worry about it; I just consider it necessary. So why should I worry about this money? I don't. That's all there is to it. In fact, I could hold it out the window this minute and watch it blow away in the desert wind.

Danny says, motioning to the bills in my hand, "Do you think maybe we should only use half that much?"

"Don't back down now, mister," I say. "We're in this all the way!"

The bellboy cheerfully takes our one small suitcase (which either of us could manage easily), and as we go up in the elevator he asks, "Do you folks sleep by day or night?"

Who sleeps "by day" unless he has a job as a night watchman? Danny informs him of our regular hours. Once in the room, the bellboy deposits our suitcase and pulls from his pocket a newspaper. He trades it with Danny for a bill and says, "Shall I remove the adult entertainment pull-out section, sir?"

"That's all right," Danny says.

By the time the door is closed I have zapped the newspaper from Danny and have spread the adult entertainment pull-out section on the bed. I read aloud:

"'Twenty-four hour massage boutique—every selection a beauty!'

"'Don't come to us, we'll come to you. Just state your preferences.'

"'Our escorts do more than escort. For a full range of services . . . call.'

"'Do you favor some unique posture?'"

I giggle and roll on the bed, throwing the newspaper into the air.

Danny says, "Hey, you haven't even looked at the bathtub yet."

"I'll get to it," I promise. "Give me time."

As soon as we come down in the elevator to the casino, I hand Danny fifty dollars and wish him luck. He is going to play blackjack, which he has been reading up on at home, and I am going to play the slot machines. Since I sometimes am reduced to counting on my fingers when balancing the checkbook, I don't intend to make a fool of myself at the blackjack tables.

I see a Change Girl and I ask for ten dollars worth of nickels. She's got wild red hair, and her face looks pained from the constant noise of jackpot bells ringing and coins clinking and the raucous shouts of men around the crap tables.

"Good luck," she mumbles.

Five rolls of nickels weigh more than I would have imagined. I choose a slot machine and set my purse down on the floor. An elderly lady taps my shoulder. She is playing a slot machine across the aisle. "Honey, don't you ever let your purse out of your hands! There's people waiting around every corner to snatch it away."

I look around—and don't even see any corners. Just long rows of flashing machines and pleasant-looking ladies playing them, but I thank her and hitch the purse straps over my arm.

When I try to peel open my first roll of nickels, she comes over to me again. "Look, sweetheart, do it this way." She hits the paper roll expertly on the sharp lip of the change bowl, and it splits open. Then, pushing with her index fingers on both ends, she spills the nickels out into the bowl.

"And don't forget your free drink," she adds. "When the girl comes around you just tell her what you want." Her eyes shine. "I adore Las Vegas," she says. "I just adore it."

I study the infamous contraption before me, the "one-armed bandit." There are three vertical reels of symbols in the little window on the front of the machine and three horizontal lines the symbols can land on. Actually there are five lines, if you count the diagonals.

The first nickel I put in the slot lights up the center line. I pull the black ball of the handle and immediately a bell rings and two nickels come back. Not so bad for a beginner! I see, after the fact, what did it. But what's this? There on the bottom row are three yellow bells. The legend on the side of the machine says that three bells in a row return eighteen coins. Now I see the fallacy of the nickel play—I haven't paid for the option of the bottom line. One nickel gives me the odds only on the center line. For two I get the top line as well; three nickels adds the bottom; four and five nickels buy me the diagonals.

Well, okay. I put in five nickels and all the lines light up. I pull, and to my delight, three oranges line up on the top line. Ten nickels pour out, with bells clanging. This is more like it! I put in another five nickels and pull—and nothing lines up. Well, it's all probability, and I've got lots more money and I feel lucky, and probably, as I see it, this is going to be fantastic fun!

There's no clock in the casino and I must have left my watch up in the room. Since I have no appointments, it probably does not matter what the time is anyway. I use up another three rolls of nickels. Now and then I get three plums (fourteen nickels) or three oranges (ten) or two bells and a bar (eighteen), but most of the time the winning combinations just slip by—by one symbol! Oh, if only the reel had stopped just a fraction of a second sooner. Or later. Well, there's a good chance it will next time.

On and on I pull, putting in five nickels at once now. I just love this. The old lady has gone away, so I put my purse on the floor again. The cherries come up with great frequency, and there's always a clang or two as two nickels come back with one cherry, five with two cherries.

Once I drop a coin on the floor, but I wait till I have the reels spinning again before I stoop to retrieve it. When I do kneel down to find it, I'm at eye level with the hole the money comes out of. Something hits, the bells ring and I watch from an inch away while the machine spits nickels into my bowl. But they don't stop after two, or five, or ten, or eighteen. They just keep coming and the bells keep ringing. I watch in fascination as they pour out. I don't even want to get up to see how many I'm going to get. I just watch, entranced, as the endless stream of money comes dropping out. My God, it isn't stopping even after the bottom of the bowl fills up! I can't stand it. I want to scream for Danny.

Someone hurries over to look at what kind of gold I've struck—a middle-aged man, smoking a cigar. "Three sevens on the fifth line!" he shouts as I stand up. "You got yourself a hundred and fifty bucks, lady!"

I simply cannot believe it! Luck is real, luck is mine. I wonder how I could have waited so long in life to discover the joys of gambling!

The machine is now screaming like a siren, along with the bells, although finally the coins have stopped falling. All kinds of onlookers have gathered, as if at an accident. A young man touches my arm. "Hope you don't mind," he says. "Maybe some of it'll rub off on me." I am as hysterical with joy as if I had just inherited a kingdom. I simply cannot think straight.

Finally an attendant arrives to stop the siren and bells. She check to see what I have won, and says, "Ten dollars is there in coins. I'll give you the rest in bills."

She counts one hundred and forty dollars into my trembling hands. Have I won a minor sum of money or have I won eternal joy? There seems to be no difference. This is probably the highest point of my entire life.

"Would you like a drink?" A shapely casino girl wearing a skirt two inches shorter than the top of her legs comes by with a tray.

"Not just now, thank you," I tell her. I think I am beyond human appetites, like thirst. I must find Danny! I begin scooping up the coins by fistfuls. They fill two paper cups, which are conveniently available on the tops of the machines.

I go to search for Danny amid the smoke and crowds of the casino. I pass through what looks like a little theater; people are sitting in seats, looking at what appears to be lots of little white ping-pong balls whirling about in a revolving gold cage. As the balls pour out of the hole one by one, a screen lights up certain numbers. The game is called keno. I'll get to it later. I pass the roulette wheel, the baccarat tables, poker tables, the bingo room and a giant silver-dollar slot machine with seven reels (the prize for which is a sports car, parked just next to the machine).

I can see the endless variety of chance available to me here. I feel as if I've hardly begun and I am filled with greed and excitement. I think I understand what must have been in my grandfather's heart.

Danny is sitting at a blackjack table with a five-inch pile of silver dollars in front of him, plus another pile of five-dollar red chips. He raises an eyebrow at me and looks back at his cards. He is concentrating and I can't disturb him with my news. He has a ten and a queen. One the betting circle before him are three silver dollars. The dealer, an immaculately groomed young woman with an impassive face, goes the rounds of the table. Two men scrape their cards on the table, signifying they wish to be "hit," and the dealer gives them each another card. A woman and Danny place their cards under their betting coins, which means they "stand" on the cards they have. The dealer turns her cards face up, adds another and another and another—and goes over twenty-one. (I am counting on my fingers.) So all four players win the round and Danny gets another three silver dollars to add to his pile.

"What did you start with?" I ask softly.

"Just ten." He must have forty-five dollars or more now.

"Well, don't faint, but I just won a hundred-and-fifty-dollar jackpot on the slot machine."

Danny looks totally shocked, and then relieved. "Let's stop while we're ahead."

"No! Let's not!" I cry. "Play more! We're lucky tonight."

I stand and watch him for another twenty hands or more. Three times he loses, but mostly—it's incredible—he wins.

As he is placing a five-dollar bet I notice that he must not have wound his watch today. It reads noon. I look around for the right time somewhere and see that the watch of the man on my right also reads noon.

"Danny," I say. "The time!"

He is as confused as I am. Midnight! But we haven't had dinner! The last thing we ate were containers of yogurt I had brought with us on our trip across the desert. Is it possible we aren't hungry? Aren't tired? When at home we eat at six and go to bed by ten-thirty?

My hands are as black as a miner's. The lady playing blackjack notices me examining them. "Go over to the change window, dear," she says. "They give away those damp tissue things there."

"We better stop," Danny says. "We better eat."

Before we finish our hamburgers in the coffee shop it is one a.m. We both are too tired to use the heart-shaped tub. And now I know what the bellboy meant by his remark: "Do you sleep by day or by night?"

Only we don't seem to sleep by day either. At six a.m. the desert sun pierces the drapes and comes blazing across the room; we are up, our pulses racing, our pockets still heavy with coins and chips. Why waste a minute? Even Danny, the schoolteacher, has caught the spirit. I'm proud of him.

We brave the heat of the morning sun and drive down the Strip to another gigantic hotel, which is shaped like a showboat. The chill of the air-conditioned casino is a delight. Danny thinks we should have breakfast, but I want to play and I accompany him to a blackjack table that already has two players at it. One of them hands the dealer a five-hundred-dollar bill. She taps the table and calls out to the pit boss, "Change for five hundred." She gives the man his chips, places the bill across a slot in the table and presses it down out of sight with a clear-plastic wand.

The man bets a hundred on the first hand.

I catch my breath and walk away. I don't want to see him lose it. Or maybe I don't want to see him double it. I'm full of mixed emotions. I had thought I made a big killing with my jackpot, and now I see how insignificant it is in the serious world of real gambling.

I find a slot machine I like, but for some reason today things go badly. I use up both cups of nickels and cash another twenty-dollar bill, but I get no return other than the clink produced by an occasional cherry. I change machines and try for watermelons and bars. Soon I am walking up and down the row, trying one machine, then the next and then the next. I change more bills into coins. I lose count of how many. I never put in just one nickel—then I would lose the chance for the big jackpot. I always put in five. In the progressive machines the jackpot goes up one cent for each nickel put in, which must mean that for a jackpot of four hundred and sixty-seven dollars an awful lot of nickels must have gone in and not come out.

But nothing happens. I get impatient and act dangerously. I get twenty dollars' worth of quarters and find a twenty-five-cent machine. In a few minutes they're gone, especially at five quarters a pull. Now I'm getting scared. Shall I go back to nickels? Why did I do so well yesterday and so poorly today? I probably should be trying bigger and better things. After all, I have one hundred and fifty dollars of house money to play with as well as what's left of my two hundred. Why not? Surely if people here bet a hundred dollars at a time, I can bet five or ten.

So I do, I switch to roulette and place ten dollars on red. The wheel spins, stops on black. I put ten more on black; the ball comes in red. Then I place ten on each of four numbers, both red and black; the ball comes in on double zero and the board is wiped clean.

No one else who loses makes a sound, but I feel as if I am gasping for breath. I rush over to the keno game and black out fourteen numbers on an eighty-number game sheet. They're all lucky numbers, the ages of everyone in my family that I can think of. If they all come in, I can win (it says) up to twenty-five thousand, depending on the size of my bet. Well, why not? The money is free money; I'll bet (I swallow in terror) fifty dollars. I am truly in a panic. It's now or never.

The balls spill out of the golden cage like little monsters, and not one of them is a number I've chosen.

I won't tell Danny what I've done. It was a terribly rash decision. But maybe this is just the wrong casino. It's unlucky, definitely unlucky. I rush back to the blackjack table to tell Danny I want to go somewhere else. He does too. His pile of red chips is gone and he has three silver dollars left.

Our step is less light as we walk to the car to drive to another hotel. Danny says we have to eat; it's lunchtime and we still haven't had breakfast. I hardly care, but I agree. In the next hotel's coffee shop we count our money. There are only a few small bills left, so I have to tell him about my keno bet. But did I really buy that many nickels? Did Danny really lose *that* many silver dollars?

Well, it's only money that we don't need, and I really don't care. Danny looks weary and pale. He doesn't look as if he's having very much fun. I eat fast, and so does he, so we can get back to business.

By dinnertime, I've broken open at least ten more rolls of nickels. I've never worked so hard in my life. The tendons in my arms ache and there are blisters on the palm of my right hand. This time Danny comes to find me. "All gone," he says, holding up his palms. "It just all . . . went."

"My God!" I say. "We'll have to go home. We were going to stay at least another day, but now we can't. We're all out of money, unless we cash a check."

I look at him hopefully. In a way, I do desperately want to; maybe we can get another hundred dollars and try to win back what we have lost.

I see the same feeling in his eyes. But he doesn't have my genes, and he says, "No." I think we both feel ill.

My heart has been racing since the moment we arrived. It *wasn't* money we didn't need. There *is* no money that no one needs. It could have paid the doctor's bill or bought new tires and brakes for the car or paid for a new washing machine. Was what we did any different from tossing it into the desert wind? I must have the wrong attitude. How can it be that I am so close to tears? A sore loser. A crybaby. Not my grandfather's true grandchild. A gambling woman doesn't carry on this way.

"Look," Danny says, "we haven't had one minute with each other and this is the first vacation we've had alone together in years. We haven't gone swimming in the pool. We haven't gone to a show. We haven't enjoyed one meal."

"We haven't used our heart-shaped tub," I say, my voice shaking.

"We won't leave early. We'll stay, but we'll do the rest of it differently—okay?"

He guides me firmly out of the casino and we stop at the gift shop to buy the children souvenirs, little slot-machine necklaces. It's so odd—I hesitate to spend two dollars apiece for some novelty jewelry that will delight my children, when moments before I was tossing bills away like confetti. I feel as though I'm recovering from an illness. My perspective is returning and money is regaining its normal green color.

Choosing something for the children makes me remember them and who I am and where my life is. I give a deep sigh.

"You know," I tell Danny, "if only we had the girls here with us, we could take them to see Hoover Dam."

"It's a hundred and twenty-two degrees today at Hoover Dam," Danny says. "I heard the bellboy say so. They're much better off at camp."

"Well, then, lets buy some picture post cards to send them right now so I can tell them how much we miss them."

(1977)

I'm Fine, Where Are You?

~

WHEN, LATE IN JULY, Danny read her the brochure about a three-week Bach festival and lute-building workshop to be held during mid-August in a picturesque beach city up the California coast, Janet said cheerfully, "Why don't you go?" She said it reasonably, deliberately, generously and maturely.

She had been dusting in the living room, and she noticed with detachment that as she spoke she had come into the kitchen—where Danny was eating a late lunch—picked up the catsup bottle and dusted it. Her offer was sincere, though her heart pounded as she made it. The summer was getting very stale; they all were home all the time—she and he and the three girls—and she was oppressed.

None of the girls had wanted to go to camp this year. A vision of all the flies, the sticky spaghetti and the pain of homesickness had come upon the three of them on the day their Brownie and Girl Scout leaders had passed out brochures and application blanks, and in complete agreement they had promised they could enjoy nothing more than a summer at home, full of useful projects. Since all of their friends had gone to camp or were away on vacation, they had no playmates, however. So all they seemed to do was smother the cat with kisses (often pulling him out of one another's laps to do so) and listen to an idiot disc jockey named Dr. Wacko.

Danny too was without direction. For the past five summers he had taught summer school at the university, but since there was a shortage of assignments now, he had been tactfully asked to sit this one out. He claimed to be enjoying these three months off, but Janet knew he was restless. He'd get up at seven (in contrast to the girls, who peeped out at the world no earlier than ten) and the two of them would have breakfast together. Then he'd shower, shave, wander around in the back yard for a little while and end up back in bed with a magazine. He was bored. Boredom was not a new house guest for Janet. She knew it well, especially during those long, gray winter days when everyone was in school—but alone, at least she was able to cope with it. Somehow now the weight of the boredom of four other people was making her own boredom intolerable.

"Why *don't* you go?" Janet said that day to her husband. "Seriously, we would be just fine here, and you would get a rest from us and be doing something you'd enjoy. You've often talked of going to something like this and you've always wanted to build a lute."

He looked at her nervously, as if she might have an ulterior motive. "I didn't know you believed in separate vacations," he said.

Right at that moment she felt as if she could bear a little separation. If only he could take the children with him too—give her a little peace, a little relief from the constant filling of the sink with glasses, from the constant awareness that everyone was marching in place, herself included, yet without purpose, disorganized and unproductive.

Jill wandered through the kitchen with the cat draped around her neck, his golden fur clinging to her dark-blue T-shirt.

"What happened to all the projects you were going to start this summer?" Janet asked her.

"I need some frozen yogurt," Jill said. "For energy to think."

Danny was studying the brochure carefully. Janet turned her back on him. She knew he was going to do it. He had taken the dare and she felt both exhilarated and scared. Would she be able to handle it?

~

On the morning Danny left, he wore a jaunty straw hat and a two weeks' growth of beard. He was already changing his image—no longer a father and husband, but a traveler, an adventurer, a student thirsting for knowledge and experience. She had counted out ten T-shirts and eight pairs of undershorts for him; she had seen that all the necessary odds and ends were in his suitcase. She felt supremely generous, giving him this chance, this freedom, this gift. As they packed, Myra asked him, "Doesn't going away make you feel a little scary, like not knowing where the light switch will be in your new room?"

"It *is* scary," Danny admitted. "But exciting."

Janet said to her, "When someone goes away from home he has new thoughts and ideas and feelings, and he comes back with memories. If a person always stays home, what will he make of the time or remember of it? It's so much the same at home, it's almost like not living."

She wondered if what she had just said could be true; after all—she was home herself all the time.

Danny kissed them all good-bye in the driveway. Too late, she felt cheated of a longer, more loving kiss for herself, but it did not at the moment seem appropriate, nor did she feel particularly loving just now. She blamed him for not having thought of it the night before. She'd been busy looking for his eyeglasses case until well after midnight, and he'd been charging the battery of his car until nearly 2:00 a.m. Just now her bare feet were burning on the hot pavement and she wished he'd get on with it.

Finally he backed out of the driveway. They waved until his car was out of sight, and then Myra said, "I've decided to go to camp, Mommy. Do you think there's still an opening in the Brownie Pines Unit? Do you think I can be ready to leave in two days?"

Then there were only three of them. The house became vast.

It stayed neat. The older girls conspired to start a secret project that Janet had absolutely no interest in asking about. It was enough to know that they were out of her way, behind the closed door of Bonnie's room. She closed the door to her own bedroom. The blanket on her big bed was taut and smooth. She tried resting on the very edge of it—*her* side—and the bed looked as endless as a meadow. She stretched out, smiling. Then she got up and looked through a stack of old magazines piled on a shelf under the window and chose a Playboy to leaf through. Looking at the centerfold, she felt gorgeous and sexy. She thought with abandon that she could, if she wanted to, give a party. Then she realized she didn't know a single male person who might be considered her friend. What was she going to do with all this freedom, anyway? She wanted to turn a cartwheel. Instead, she went into the kitchen and opened a can of little round beets, a vegetable Danny hated, and she ate all of them cold. They were absolutely delicious.

One night she took her two daughters to dinner—not to a hamburger place but to a fancy Mexican restaurant called The Zesty Onion. The waitresses swished their flounced skirts and bent countless times over the tables, displaying their bountiful breasts, which spilled out from their peasant blouses. It was a party—not like the one she might give but the only kind possible for her at the moment. Janet, who never drank anything but an occasional glass of wine, ordered a Margarita. She saw the drinks being carried about in tall-stemmed glasses, foamy confections. She was a woman alone (the children notwithstanding) and she was grown up.

She began to speak to her children of independence, of competence, of the liberation of women, of never trying to own or control another person. Husbands and wives must do their own things, just as Daddy was doing. You had to follow your own star, married or not. That was why it was important, she said, for them not to feel bad or left out or left behind, but to enjoy the new sensation of the altered family shape and style for the short time Daddy would be away.

Bonnie said she didn't feel the slightest bit left out, and Jill said that when Daddy was home they never went to fancy restaurants like this one. She scooped up a mouthful of beans covered with delicious, stringy melted cheese and smiled through it at her mother.

Janet noticed a man eating alone at the opposite table. He was perhaps thirty-five; he ate his *enchilada* quickly, with head bent. Once he glanced up and saw her staring and immediately picked up the wine list. Why was it, she wondered, that when she ate with Danny in a restaurant she never noticed the people around her? Her senses were heightened because he was gone. It was an amazing, refreshing change.

After dinner, in a continued mood of festivity, she took the girls to see *Rocky* at the local theater. It seemed to her that when Danny was home, she had a license to ignore the children far more than she was doing now. The new circumstances put upon her the pressure to communicate with them, to help fill the emptiness they might feel—though not admit to it—because he was gone.

When Rocky, in his undershirt, swung by his muscled arms from an overhead pipe and towered over the shy girl from the pet store, Janet's heart leaped. When he kissed the girl in the corner of the room, when they both fell to the floor, their legs folding in the weakness of passion, she dreamed of herself as the girl in his arms—the kind of dream she had not entertained since high-school days. It was not only Danny who was having new thoughts and feelings on his trip. She was having her own trip as well.

In bed that night she longed for her husband sweetly, with the kind of longing born of deprivation. She savored it. She wished they might not see each other for a year, so that they would have time to write love letters, have erotic dreams of each other. She thought, What is he doing now? Is he asleep? What is he wearing? Is he thinking of me? Is he thinking of me in *these* ways?

At home he was always there, always available, in view, dependable, predictable. She never wondered where he was going when he was *not* in view—she was relieved to have the time to get her work done, her thoughts thought (though they were never such sweet, delectable thoughts as she was having now). She was excited and filled with joy by his absence. Her heart was growing fonder. The mock pain was exquisite.

In the morning she checked the mail, knowing he would not write. He had said he would call only if something important came up. No mail, no calls and a week had passed. She suffered but felt no fear. It was a charade. She was carrying on handsomely.

Somehow, though, she did not sleep well. If she fell asleep at eleven, she woke at one, certain it was time for the day to start. She watched TV horror movies that played until dawn. There were moments when she heard strange noises in the house, and they alarmed her. One morning she and the girls were in her bedroom, going through old photograph albums and telling wonderful anecdotes—"wasn't that the picnic where Jill swallowed the ice cube whole?"—when the front door clicked open. They reached for one another in terror.

"We're all in here," Jill whispered. "There's no one else it could be."

Janet shook the girls loose, her heart palpitating. "I'm coming," she shouted crazily down the hall.

"The wind, the wind," she explained coming back. But her knees trembled and she had to lie down on the bed.

On the news that night she heard that a Girl Scout had been raped and murdered in a camp in Oklahoma. She thought of Myra, asleep in some tent in the mountains—no locks, no fences. "What kind of security is there?" she said aloud. "I was crazy to let her go."

In the morning she listened to the radio and heard that a hurricane was moving in from the Pacific and coming straight into the same mountains where Myra was. By nightfall, the report was that six inches of rain had fallen in the mountains, the roads were closed and flash floods were driving people out of their homes.

She lay on her bed, which was flat as a desert, and watched the rain all day. It was one hundred degrees outside but it looked like the dead of winter. Her daughters argued about the project they had started; it seemed they were trying to train the cat to jump through a hoop. He had bitten one of them and clawed the other. They blamed each other. She screamed at them to stay apart if they could not get along. They each took umbrellas and went out for a walk, slamming the door behind them. She went back into her room and cried. Danny had been gone almost two weeks now, and no letter, no phone call. She knew where to reach him in case of an emergency, but what was the emergency? Her disappointment? Her wanting him to lean over her the way Rocky leaned over that shy, neglected girl? In all these days and nights no one had touched her gently, no one had given her a single stroke.

Not only was her baby daughter being washed down a mountain in a flood, but also her refrigerator stopped keeping things cold. She called a repairman and as she watched him fiddle with wires and dials she knew he knew her ignorance. He spoke of humidity, compressors, condensers. The refrigerator was hopeless, he said, but he could have a new one there that afternoon. If Danny were home, he would have gone to the library, read Consumer Reports, shopped, calculated and compared before he bought anything so expensive. But it was pouring rain, the milk was warm, the ice cream was like cream of wheat. "Bring the new one," she said. She waved her checkbook like a drunk. "How much? How much?" she asked. What did it matter anyway? Her husband was out on the town, eating at good restaurants, meeting new people, probably female people. Who knew what he was doing behind that beard?

She looked at the repairman, considered flirting but changed her mind. He looked no more than twenty-three; he had a drooping mustache; he carried a radio on his belt so that he wouldn't miss a single dumb song played on the Dr. Wacko program.

"You'd better cook the fish right away, ma'am," he said. "It's all defrosted."

"Would you like to stay for dinner?" she almost said.

~

The camp officer said that no news was good news. If her daughter had drowned, she would have heard. "Why not think of the storm as a grand adventure your daughter is having?" the lady at the Scout House said. "Besides, the rain is stopping." It was. And as soon as it stopped, the grass grew four feet tall on the front lawn. Janet wheeled the new lawn mower out of the shed and nearly dislocated her shoulder trying in vain to start it. The next day the grass seemed to be six feet tall. She found a device in the garage called a Weed Whacker. She cut the grass with it, five strands at a time. It took her all day, but her yard looked like the grounds of a castle in England when she was done with it and she was proud of herself.

However, after her shower she was too depressed even to take the children to McDonald's.

"Find yourself something to eat in the new refrigerator," she said.

"There's nothing in it but rotten fish," Bonnie said.

"C'est la vie," Janet said.

Jill began to eat a prune. "God, I'm bored," she said.

"Don't complain. You're young. Your boredom's more promising than mine. Something's *bound* to happen in your life. I think mine is over. Why don't you just go to bed?"

Janet spent the evening in the kitchen, staring at the phone. At eleven o'clock it rang, and she felt she had willed it.

"ESP," she said cheerfully into the receiver. "I was just thinking of you. Three weeks are up."

"Guess where I am?"

"Tahiti?"

"I'm at my mother's."

"Oh."

"I'm going to stay here a couple of days. It was so close by, I had to stop in and see them. And now they want me here for the weekend."

"Oh. Well."

"How's everything? How're the kids?"

"Just fine. The refrigerator broke down and I bought a new one."

"A new one? Are you sure the old one couldn't have been fixed?"

"As sure as a woman with a degree in English can be," she said shortly. "Also the lawn mower didn't start," she added. "So I cut the grass with the Weed Whacker."

"That's not what it's for!" Danny said. "You could have broken it. And how come the lawn mower didn't start? It's only two months old."

"Oh, was it supposed to work for *longer* than two months?" Janet said.

"You know the Whacker is only for weeds," Danny insisted, ignoring her sarcasm.

"It's done," Janet said coldly. "When you are here you may make a decision of that sort." Was she actually yelling at him? The hollow place in her heart was aching madly. She was going to die right here of loneliness and she was yelling at him.

"How was the Bach festival?" she asked.

"It was fine."

"How did your lute turn out?"

"Very well, I would say."

"How was your hotel room?"

"It was nice."

"Did you meet any people?"

"Oh, yes, quite a few nice people."

She almost, but not quite, said, "Male or female?" But she was not going to stoop to that, or play this game of Twenty Questions. If he called, she had to assume he called to tell her something.

"Did you want to tell me anything special?"

"No, no, nothing special," he said.

"Well, we're doing just fine," she said, "and we're looking forward to seeing you in a few days." (Is that how a woman talked to her lover—*I'm looking forward to seeing you?*) "Myra will be home from camp tomorrow." He had not even asked about the poor child, didn't know about the rapist, the murderer, the floods she had escaped. In fact, he had not even known she was at camp. Janet had borne this tremendous weight all by herself.

"Well, bye-bye," he said, and in the background she heard his mother call out, "Bye from us too."

She hung up and staggered to her bed, the only refuge. When they were in college and he had felt constrained talking to her from his parents' home, he would go out for a walk on some pretense and call her from a phone booth. He never said much from there either, but tender silences were possible—even, at rare moments, the sound of a kiss over miles of lines.

Now it would be ridiculous to imagine he might do that. Right now, no doubt, his mother was plying him with his beloved marble cake and his father was offering shirts and jackets of his own that he wanted Danny to take home because he felt *his* taste in clothes was much better than Danny's. But maybe Danny was a snazzy dresser now. Maybe he had bought a whole new wardrobe. Who knew what changes might have taken place in the last three weeks? She'd probably not even recognize him with his five-week beard. He would be a stranger. He would have a new taste for adventure and go off again and again—perhaps permanently. Her curse would be to eat forever alone, reading the wine list in The Zesty Onion.

What *right* did he have to question her purchase of the refrigerator? Or her failure to start the lawn mower? She would use the Weed Whacker for whatever damn purpose she wanted to. She would whack off his beard when he came home.

She marched back to the phone, preparing the torrent in her brain. She would call him back, rail at him, accuse him, threaten him, make him suffer as she had suffered, cruelly abandoned as she had been all these weeks with nothing to do, no fun to have. She dialed the first three numbers of his parents' phone number and then remembered the day he'd read her the brochures, how she had said to him, "Why don't you go?" That mature, sensible, sensitive wife. That wife so secure in love that she could free him from her voice, her arms, her influence, for all that. Go to bed, she instructed herself. Cool down—it's only marble cake you're jealous of.

She had bunched the pillow against her chest for protection when the phone range, muffled, down the hall. She leaped for it.

"Hi. It's me. I went out to get a newspaper. Or so I said."

"Oh, Danny. This is killing me."

"I know. Me too."

There was a long silence.

"Did you want to tell me anything special?" she whispered.

"No, no," he said. "Nothing special." He sighed. "I had to stick it out, you know."

"Of course you had to," she said. "We both did."

"I'm going to leave for home tonight."

"No, don't. It's too late. You might as well sleep there."

"I can't sleep well without you," he said. "I might as well be driving."

"You might as well be eating marble cake and do this right. I think we both can stick this out until tomorrow."

"Okay, then. But no more separate vacations."

"Agreed," she said.

(1978)

A Peaceable Kingdom

~

ON THE SAME MORNING that the frog, Flippy, stretched out and died with his eyes open, the gentle quail, Sherman, keeled over, skidded on some seed and passed on. All the children were at school. Janet, knowing this was going to be some day, went to check the situation in Myra's room, and sure enough, the last three of the fourteen baby guppies were washing, belly up, in the tide. On the windowsill behind the fishbowl were jars full of moth and butterfly cocoons. On Myra's dresser, below a print of "The Peaceable Kingdom," five Coturnix quail eggs were glowing in a yellow plastic incubator. Their hatching date had passed by a week, but desperate for a miracle, Myra kept the bulb burning, the humidifier filled with water.

It was really getting to be too much. It wasn't that Janet was fastidious about bird droppings and too-seldom-changed fish water, but where was it written that in addition to nurturing, loving and cleaning up after three children she also was indentured to all manner of flying, swimming and crawling creatures both alive and dead?

With her sterling silver soup ladle—a wedding present, which Myra had convinced her, in a weak moment, would get far more use as a guppy scooper—Janet skimmed the dead fish out of the bowl and disposed of them in the usual place without so much as a prayer to guide their souls. The frog, which she had not liked much at all—with his guttural complaints, his squeaky-wet, slimy skin and his convulsive, powerful leg muscles—she carried in his tank of cloudy water and dumped unceremoniously into the deep ivy at the edge of the garden.

She could no longer bring herself to dispose of animals in the garbage as if they were so much trash. Once, because the garbagemen were coming down the street and the ground was frozen solid with cold, Danny had put their dead pet rabbit in a plastic bag and included him with the empty milk cartons and soup cans. But the image had haunted her for weeks. She had watched from behind a curtain while the trash collector, in his ignorance, dumped the contents of the garbage can into the grinder, and then leaped up into the debris in the truck to tromp down some stubborn areas that had not flowed smoothly into the crusher's teeth. Death without dignity, she had thought. The poor bunny, with his twitching pink nose and his delicate ears. Should he really be viewed more sentimentally than the chicken carcass in the same load of garbage?

Janet wondered suddenly why there was such a history of dead pets in her mind. Was her family harder on pets than other people? Did every family with children experience such a wide range of grief, almost *constantly*? There had been a succession of small tragedies for years—rats, hamsters, turtles, toads, lizards and fish.

Their cat, Starshine, had simply wandered away last New Year's Eve and never returned. Their most recent (and last) dog, Peanut Butter, a beautiful but extremely stupid basset hound who had howled constantly while in the yard and barked and whined constantly while in the house, they had finally (in desperation, after complaints from neighbors and visits from the police) given to a farmer, who could, she assured her daughters, give him a much better home.

But the grief after each loss! The hysterics! The taking to bed and pulling of quilts over heads!

"Pets are good for children," Myra's second-grade teacher had told Janet after the horrible accident with Tippytoes, the little white mouse. "Pets teach them about life."

"I don't know of any adult to whom so many gruesome experiences happen as often as they do to my children," Janet had said. Myra was seven then. The mouse was a tiny, delicate thing whose spine was like a quivering feather. Janet (who never refused to appreciate how soft, how cuddly, how scaly, how slimy, a pet was) had herself been touched by the tiny, curious, energetic creature. Myra decided to train it. She closed herself in the bathroom with the mouse and taught it to leap over her foot. The mechanics were tricky. She let it scurry across the floor, and as it came close to her, she put her foot right in its path. When the timing was right, the mouse leaped over her foot in a long, graceful arc. When it wasn't, it stopped short and scurried in another direction. She practiced with the mouse for hours.

One evening when Janet was setting the table for dinner, she heard a hideous shriek from the bathroom. Running toward the sound, her heart pounding, Janet took in the scene at once: Myra completely hysterical, the mouse crushed flat on the floor. The child was hopping on one foot, her murderous sole in the air, and she began clawing at her mother, almost unable to draw breath in her guilt and pain.

What could a mother say?—"It's all right," or, "You should have been more careful," or, "We'll get you another mouse"? There was nothing to do but hold her daughter close, hug her until her breath came back and try not to add her own tears to the flood. She had wanted to cry then—not so much for the little dead mouse as for death itself, that it existed, that her child had to witness it, that her child had to see the permanent end of life for a creature she had loved.

It had taken many days before Myra returned to a state of normal cheerfulness. They had had endless discussions about the nature of grief. "I'll never feel happy again—I know it," she had told her mother as she lay curled on her bed, gripping the silky crib blanket that she still treasured from her baby days.

"It may not feel as if you will," Janet had said, "but the fact is, the image will fade; the scene in the bathroom that you keep thinking about won't always be so sharp. Soon other things will come in and fill your mind."

"I know I'll never be completely happy. When you lose something you love, you can never be happy again."

"I'll tell you something," Janet had said. "You know my father died the year before you were born. I loved him as much as I love you, as much as you love your daddy. But look at me. I don't cry all day, do I? You see me laugh. I have fun—right? Sometimes I even make up sillier riddles than you do. The grief will get less. Believe me."

But though the memory of the mouse's death did recede, new griefs had a way of filling the spaces immediately—a newborn baby rat, blind, pink and hairless, eaten by its mother, or fifteen guppies born with tails and one born without, and Myra wanting to rush the latter to the vet for surgery!

Just thinking about the vet made Janet's blood pressure rise. She felt it was finally time to call a halt to servicing animals and supporting animal doctors. The *money* she'd paid the man! For altering the cat, for the dog's rabies shots, the wormings, the ear mites, the flea baths, the setting of the quail's leg! For indeed, just over a month ago Sherman the quail had taken one too many awkward flights across the room from Myra's hands and landed square against the brick wall of the fireplace, chipping a beak and breaking a leg at the same time. Never mind the cost of medical care for the children—the family had some insurance for that. It was the animals that were bankrupting them!

If Myra were home this morning, she'd want the frog and the quail autopsied so that she'd know for sure why they died. Maybe the quail's meal worms were too big. Or maybe the flies they had to catch by hand for the frog weren't the right variety. Janet stood before the quail's cage in the TV room and studied the dead bird. His leg had healed. And now his heart had stopped.

He lay on his side, his breast white against his brown and black feathers. While in life he had always been twittering and tapping across the swinging cage, always nervously twitching his beak, flashing his black eyes in agitation, now he seemed entirely remote. She had never seen such stillness. It was indeed a peace that passed understanding. She understood one thing, though. This was the last death for a long time. She was through. She would bury this bird, but it was the last funeral she was going to attend for a hundred years.

No more animals. No more having to ask neighbors to come in to feed the fish or bird or cat when they wanted to go to the mountains for the weekend. No more boarding dogs or paying vets. No more reminding children to change the fishbowl water, empty the litter box, clean up the dog's mess in the yard, change the paper in the bird cage. It was as simple as that. She'd put in her time. She'd done her good deed and let her children have the experiences of feeding and loving and sometimes hurting their pets. But this was it—*finis!*

She got her gardening gloves and a big shovel, and in the far corner of the back yard she furiously dug a foot-deep hole. "I mean it, kids!" she shouted to no one in particular as she jumped on the shovel, trying to dig into the hard earth.

Back in the house, she lifted the quail from the cage, wincing as his stiffened legs caught at the edge of the cage door. He was still soft, very heavy, but rigid.

She finally worked him through the wire, and gasped involuntarily as a claw caught on her sweater. "Oh, Lord," she said, realizing she was sweating and shivering at the same time.

She carried the quail down the length of the back yard and placed him gently at the bottom of the square hole. "You were a nice pet," she said. "You really were." She shoveled dirt over him, glad that, unlike the frog, his eyes were closed. She put a rock as a marker on the grave and went to sit on the redwood picnic table to get her breath. The fact was, she had been attached to the quail. For Myra's last birthday she had ordered the yellow "chick hatcher"—a plastic incubator with a seven-watt night-light bulb in it and a dime-store thermometer. It had cost ten dollars for the outfit, which came from a Georgia quail farm and included five quail eggs and a promise that offered the "miracle of birth." For years Myra had wanted a bird. Janet recalled how, as a child of three or four, Myra used to stalk sparrows and jays on the front lawn by hunching forward, creeping along with infinite patience like a hunting cat, her arm cautiously outstretched as if in a moment she could snatch up a bird and bring it joyously into the house to be a beloved pet. But the birds always flew away. Then later, when Starshine the cat lived with them, it seemed too dangerous to have a bird.

But in the spring, just in time for Myra's birthday, the mailman delivered the five miniature eggs and the clear-domed incubator. Together the family had watched, for eighteen days, while Myra turned the tiny gray-and-black-speckled eggs end over end twice a day and saw to it that the temperature was always one hundred degrees.

Then, on exactly the specified day, almost to the hour, a tiny tapping and peeping was heard from one of the eggs. After a time a small, triangular hole appeared and a crack was tapped out. The whole family crowded around Myra's dresser. Bonnie and Jill, the older girls, were just as excited as Myra. "Look—another crack! He's using his egg tooth! Oh, that was a big tap." "Look—look—I can see his beak! His feathers are black! Oh, I wish I could help him get out of there, he's working so hard." They vowed to stay up all night if necessary.

Finally the circle was complete. The tiny chick heaved and heaved, pushing the two sections of the egg apart. Once he seemed to be almost able to push out, but he fell back exhausted and did not move at all. Myra had gasped, "Oh! He can't die from all this work, can he, Mommy?" At midnight he burst out into the sunny yellow warmth of the incubator, all beak and claws, wet and black and gasping from exertion.

Even Danny, who had come to watch the final moments, seemed excited. Janet hugged them all, laughing in spite of herself, and invited them into the kitchen for cups of hot chocolate before bed.

After the baby bird had slept the night, he was transformed into a fluffy chick who slipped and clambered about the tiny incubator. Myra transferred him to a box lined with layers of tissue and warmed by a gooseneck lamp. She offered him chick mash and he pecked and ate immediately. He drank. He ran about with little nervous steps, exploring. He fell asleep in Myra's patient palm held under the light bulb.

As he grew and the fluff turned to feathers he took his first, tentative flight from her hands to the couch. She fed him meal worms from her fingers, took him out in the yard to peck for pill bugs and ants, hovered protectively above him so that he would not fly away, so that no cat could spring upon him. When he was two months old he began to crow, a three-note cock-a-doodle-doo ending with a trill, which was harsh and piercing yet very beautiful. He—now known to be male—trusted Myra so much that he would fall asleep in her hand, his small feet hanging straight down into thin air.

"I'm his mother," Myra said proudly. "I'm imprinted on him, you know. He loves me best of all."

Janet slid off the redwood table and glanced down the garden toward the new grave. She had known something was wrong even last night, when the bird seemed too heavy for his legs, when she offered him a scrap of lettuce and he stared at it but didn't leap for it, didn't dart for it with pleasure.

"Nuts," she said. She dropped the gardening gloves on the patio steps and went into the house. "Nuts," she said, picking up the phone book and turning to the Yellow Pages. The other four eggs that had come in Sherman's clutch had been unlucky. Myra, a serious surgeon, eventually had opened each egg with a toothpick, pecking in, tap by tap, as she had wanted the chicks to peck out, and found half-formed chicks packed in black, lifeless circles inside. So eager was she to repeat the cycle, to feel once again that jubilation of seeing a chick emerge into the world, that Janet had agreed to order another clutch of eggs in the hope of obtaining a mate for Sherman. Those eggs, way overdue in the incubator now, probably were merely getting hard-boiled by this time.

"I must be crazy," Janet said to herself as she dialed a number. "Hello? Would you be able to tell me where I might get some quails or quail eggs locally?" She called eight pet stores before she was referred at last to a man who raised game birds.

Once she had his number, she went back to look at Sherman's empty cage. She could clean the cage, empty the water and seed from the dishes and store the whole thing in the garage. Or she could clean the cage, line it with new paper and freshen the water and seed bowls. She could also have herself committed to a mental institution.

She felt almost lightheaded driving to the address the man had given her over the phone. He was waiting on the front porch of a small frame house, a man of about sixty-five, stubble-cheeked and genial-looking. He waved to her as she pulled up at the curb. He looked a little like her father in the curve of his cheek, the slant of his forehead, his smile. Her father would be about this age now—but she had not seen him grow old.

"I'm the lady who called . . ."

"Yes, yes," he said, taking the empty cage from her hand. "About the quail. Just come this way—they're all out back."

He even walked a little like her father, a little round-shoul-dered, a little humbly. Her father had bought her a dog when she was eleven. It had been the most passionate love of her life.

"Watch out for the clothesline," he said. "And keep your eyes on those tree branches." They stepped through a line of wet work pants, back toward an area of chicken coops, tarpapered and closed in with chicken wire. There was a strong odor of bird feed and bird droppings all about.

"Now, there's the button quail," he said, setting her cage down, pointing at some tiny little birds scurrying about in a large coop. "And there's the blue-scale quail—and there's the golden pheasants."

"They're so beautiful," Janet said. "I've never seen such plumage. Do you display them at shows? Or do you just raise them to breed and sell them?"

"Oh," the old man said, "none of those, really. It's funny, but my daughter, when she was a little girl, she got into all this, and I built her all these coops and cages—and now she's married and gone and here I am, living alone, keeping company with the birds. Now and then I sell a pair or two." He took a cupful of seed out of a giant sack that leaned against the fence and distrib-uted it among several cages. "Yes, yes," he said, stroking the gleaming feathers of a pheasant, "that's my beauty, that's my girl." He stepped along the narrow pathway. "Over here—here's the kind of quail you asked about. The Coturnix."

A beady-eyed pair sat staring at Janet from the back of a dark cage. They looked nothing like Sherman. Their beaks were hooked and pointier, for one thing. They both were larger, and seemed puffed up with hostility.

She took a step back. "Oh, I don't know," she said. "I'm just not sure."

"Oh, they're nice fellas . . . even the girls," the old man said, laughing, opening the cage and scooping up a bird in his hand. "Here you go," he said to Janet, depositing the bird in her palm. It began to coo like a pigeon. It was soft and heavy and very pliant. Its neck feathers flowed like a river of light as they moved in the sunshine. Gingerly she patted its head. It seemed to settle down lower, relaxed, assured.

"I'll tell you," she said suddenly to the man. "My little girl's bird died today—a quail like this one. I don't know now if I'm doing the right thing—getting a substitute bird, making a quick switch, as if she wouldn't know the difference. I mean, dead is dead, you know. I keep letting her get new animals and then they die, and half our lives are spent discussing how sad we are. I'm so tired of feeding animals and burying them."

The quail was warm in her hand. She felt a slight shift of its weight every time it breathed.

"It *is* a pain," the old man said, "taking care of creatures—I know. I bury quite a few myself. But that's the way things are. It's just better to have moving things around. You know—livelier." He took the second quail from the cage.

"This is her mate. You'll want the both of them to stay together. The big one here, she lays an egg a day. When she's laid six or seven, you can set them in an incubator. Don't wait more than ten days to set them, though. Here's this week's batch right now." He reached up to a wooden shelf and took down a little plastic cup lined with leaves. Inside rested six gray-and-black-speckled quail eggs. "It's not substitution you're talking about," he said. "It's just going on."

He placed the quails, one at a time, in Sherman's cage. They looked foreign there, shockingly out of place. But they looked handsomer now. And they were lively. She would get used to them. She paid the man the few dollars he asked, and he offered her a tin of mash and scratch for the first few days' feed.

"You're all set now," he said. "Birds to make eggs and eggs to make birds."

He walked her to her car and helped her place the cup of eggs and the cage securely on the back seat. "You might bring your little girl over to see the other birds someday," he said as Janet got into the car. "Could be she might want a couple of button quail too."

"Oh, I don't think so!" Janet said, but the way the old man leaned hopefully against the car caused her to reconsider.

"Well, why not?" she said, turning the key in the ignition.

He stepped back and smiled.

"Why not?" she said to herself as she drove away.

(1979)

Touching Is Good for Living Creatures

~

"CAN'T YOU PUT IN mayonnaise?" Myra asked. "The baby birds won't like it that dry."

"Do you think birds eat mayonnaise in the wild?" Janet asked, mashing away. Bits of egg were flying out of the bowl and landing in the clean glasses in the cabinet.

"Well, they don't eat hard-boiled egg in the wild either."

"All right," Janet said. "Put in mayonnaise. Put in ketchup. Put in sauteed mushrooms, for all I care. Here—you mash."

"I don't have time. I have to catch the school bus."

"But I have time?"

"You're home all day, Mom," Myra said. "It stands to reason." She wiped her hands on a dish towel and hurried down the hall to the bathroom. Janet heard her turn the barrette box upside down on the counter. Of course she would leave the box open. She would leave it there with ribbons and rubber bands and colored combs strewn about and Janet would have to put it away.

The baby birds must have heard her unscrew the top of the mayonnaise jar. *"Beep-beep! Beep-beep!"* They were craning their skinny little necks over the top of the shoe box, crowding together under the bulb of the gooseneck lamp for warmth and pleading to be fed.

"They're hungry again, Mom," Myra called down the hall. She appeared with her book bag over her shoulder, her hair held back with a red, white and blue ribbon. "Be sure to feed them every hour. Don't give them bread—it expands in their stomachs. And stroke them so they can move their bowels."

"Anything else?" Janet asked. "Anything else you want me to do for you while I'm just home all day?"

"Would you feed the bunny?" Myra said. "And Creamy? I forgot to feed him. And the kitty too."

"The *kitty*? Is he still around? Didn't Daddy say not to encourage him? You *know* how Daddy feels about two cats. One is too many, as far as he's concerned."

"*You* gave the kitty milk last night, Mom. I *saw* you."

"Only because I don't want him dying on my doorstep. But Daddy doesn't want anyone feeding him. He'll be ours forever then."

"Yeah," Myra said. "Wouldn't that be super?"

"We *can't*, Myra. We're overextended. The vet bills, the cat food, the carrots, the eggs!" For emphasis, Janet tossed a spoonful of mashed egg in the air, and it landed in a clump on the floor. "*Me!*"

"You don't cost anything," Myra said. "*Luckily.*"

They heard the brakes of the school bus squeaking down the hill.

"I've got to go. Would you open the door for me? I have to carry this poster to school."

Janet opened the front door for Myra and leaned over to kiss her good-bye. Myra turned her head away.

"Hey," Janet said, "I just want a good-bye kiss. Touching is good for living creatures. You always tell me that when you spend hours petting Creamy."

"That's okay," Myra said. "You kissed me yesterday. And you touched me enough when I was a baby . . ." She dashed out the door, running on her skinny long legs toward the bus stop.

As soon as the bus was out of sight, Janet pulled up a stool to the kitchen counter and began to croon to the baby birds. "Yes, little ones, food is coming. Be patient." She dipped her eyebrow tweezers in the mashed egg, pinching a morsel with the silver tongs. The babies peeped and screamed, reaching their open beaks in desperation toward her hand. Each beak, huge in proportion to the bird's frail body, was outlined in fluorescent yellow. "Bull's eye," Janet whispered, poking food into one eager beak and then the other. "Yes, you love it, don't you?" The birds chirped and gobbled, vibrating the tweezers in her hand with the enthusiasm of their hunger. "One for you. Now one for you. Now your turn, now yours." The birds were like teaspoonfuls of life, all beak and fine new feathers, hollow bones, air. One day, having started life on her egg salad, they would fly over rooftops, soar into the blue sky. Myra had found them beneath the plum tree after a night of high winds; the cat and kitty were homing in on them like pointer dogs.

"Oh, no! Don't get involved in a rescue mission again," Janet had said when Myra carried them into the house. "You know how they always die. Anything can go wrong—it always does. Then you'll be depressed for a week. Let nature work it out."

"Do you want Creamy to bite off their heads?" Myra asked. "At least we can *try* to save them."

"But you mean *I* can try. It's always me that does it. You go away to school and *I* feed them, *I* watch them, *I* pray for them . . . and then *I* bury them."

"What can I do, Mom? I didn't blow them out of the tree."

"No," Janet agreed. "You didn't."

Now that the children were no longer babies, were all in school, Janet had finally begun to relax her vigilance just a little bit. Even Danny had commented on it. One night, coming to bed in a soft new nightgown, she had simply closed and locked the bedroom door behind her.

"Are you leaving the door closed?" he asked quietly, looking up from his magazine.

"Isn't that okay?"

"Well, yes, of course," he said. "But I thought you liked to be able to hear the children."

"They'll be okay," she said. "I'm not worried about them any more. They're healthy. They breathe perfectly well all night.

They've outgrown their croup attacks. If they want me, they can call me."

"Well . . ." Danny said, with a smile, putting aside the magazine and holding out his arms. "That's *certainly* a good idea."

The gray kitty had wandered into the driveway while Danny was washing the car one Sunday afternoon. It had a tiny face, the bluest eyes imaginable and eight toes on each front paw. Janet had two contradictory reactions at once. "We can't keep it," she said, sounding a stern warning to Myra, who was in the driveway shining her bike while Danny washed the car. For Danny's benefit she added, "It's definitely not going to live here." The kitty began pitifully lapping at the bucket of soapsuds. "It would need shots, it would need to be sterilized, it would need worming. It probably has fleas." And even as she said it, as Myra picked up the kitten and began to stroke it, Janet felt a profound softening in her breast, a sweet weakness, an overwhelming tenderness toward the beautiful mewing creature.

In a glance, Myra knew what she could ask for and get. Secretly she met her mother at the side door and together they gave the kitten milk. "But I mean it," Janet whispered to her. "We really can't go on this way. It's adorable, I know. But Daddy doesn't like all these pets taking over the house. He'll accept Creamy because we've had him for so many years, but not *another* cat. Daddy doesn't understand animals. He never had any when he was little—his parents thought they were messy and dirty."

"So are kids," Myra said.

"But Daddy likes kids."

"Who knows?" Myra said. "Maybe not." She walked away and Janet felt something different in her breast, a hollow shock, some kind of fear. Maybe she had given her children the wrong father.

The baby birds went to sleep, one on top of the other, cuddled together under the light bulb. With no one home to pretend for, Janet sat and watched them a long time, remembering the looks on the faces of her sleeping babies, the way their hands had fallen out limply between the crib bars, their delicious soft cheeks, the curve of their eyelashes resting on the rosy skin.

Refusing to care for the pets was a stance Danny had forced her to adopt—he thought she did enough work for the kids as it was, more than she ought to, now that they were growing up and ought to do more for themselves. He wanted to claim her back—she knew that. He was tired of having to share Janet as generously with the children as he had all these years, and now he wanted her to come back to him, to give him at last the lion's share of attention, which he was more than willing to lavish upon her.

She knew she was supposed to show exaggerated relief: Thank God, they're growing up. I have some peace now. She *was* glad to see them grow. Of course she was. But with it came Myra's turning her face away from her kisses.

Janet's anger at the birds, at the kitten, at the mess of bunnies and fish and frogs, had nothing to do with the creatures themselves but with Myra and her sisters, who no longer needed to be fed, teaspoon by loving teaspoon. If pressed, Janet would have had to admit that she really loved the animals, loved their needing her, their unbiased affection, their goodness. When she fed and petted them, she felt a transcendent sense of contentment.

Now she went out into the yard to feed the bunny, and the gray kitty mewed at her from the yew tree. His tiny, triangular face peered out from the thickly twined leaves and branches and he cried pathetically.

"Are you in there *again*, you little mischief head?" Janet said. "Come on, now—reach out to me and I'll put you down."

The kitty offered a paw, but when she moved to grasp it he pulled back, disappearing into the depths of the tree. She heard a scrambling and a rustling, and in a moment he appeared three feet higher, crying more loudly and desperately.

"Well," she said, "shall I wait till you figure it out or shall I get the ladder?"

She went inside and came out carrying the stepladder, and found that now the kitty was at the very top of the tree. She climbed up the ladder and reached perilously to get him; it was risky, she knew. No one was home and she could break her neck doing this. With both arms up in the air for him, she had no way to balance herself or to catch hold of anything. She hoped for the best and then pulled his front legs toward her. Tiny as he was, he resisted leaving his safe perch. They struggled; she caught him but lost her balance. Together they flew through the air, separated, and came down, each of them, on all fours. After a minute she managed to stand up and brush off her hands. A close call. Her heart was pounding. She scooped the kitty up in her arms and carried him into the house, where she sat down on the couch, holding him close against her. She could feel the pulsing of his heart. Soon, though, he began to purr, a rough, sweet rumbling deep under his fur. His coat was smooth, electric, magnificent to stroke. She petted him till they both calmed down and dozed off. Later, when she woke up, she left him on the couch, still sleeping, till just before the children came home from school.

"What's this?" Danny asked, holding something between his thumb and forefinger as they sat having their breakfast at the dining-room table. "And look! There's another one that just landed in my coffee!"

"Fleas!" Myra gasped.

Bonnie and Jill automatically lifted their feet off the floor. "Yuck!"

"Don't blame me, Daddy," Myra said. "I haven't let the kitty in once."

"Then who did?" Danny demanded, looking around the table.

"Not I," said Myra.

"Not I," said Bonnie.

"Not I," said Jill.

"What is this? `The Little Red Hen'?" said Janet.

"Fleas don't have their own key to the house," Danny said, "do they?"

Just then something stung Janet's ankle. She looked down and saw four black dots digging into her tender flesh. When she leaned to grab one of them, they all leaped as if on tiny springs to her other leg.

"My God," Danny said, "they're all over the place!"

"We *can't* have fleas," Jill said. "Creamy has a flea collar."

"The kitty doesn't come in the house!" Myra pleaded.

"Never mind how it happened—that's it!" Danny said. "No more cats in the house from now on. That means Creamy, too."

"You can't do that," Myra said. "He'll be insulted. He *lives* here."

"Well, now he will live in the back yard," Danny said. "In fact, *only* Creamy will live in the back yard. As for that kitten, you will just have to find someone to take it, or give it to the pound. You absolutely cannot keep it."

"You're cruel!" Myra cried. "Anyone who doesn't love animals is sick."

"With bubonic plague, which fleas carry, I'll be even sicker," Danny said, pushing away his contaminated coffee cup.

"Danny," Janet said quietly, "would you like me to pour you another cup of coffee?"

When they all had gone for the day, Janet went through the house and stood in the center of each room. Within seconds, fleas clung to her legs like iron filings to a magnet. It was her fault. She had let the kitty in every day, let it follow her around, let it sleep on the beds. Now she was in bad trouble.

She fed the baby birds their breakfast—mashed egg that was laced with cooked oatmeal—and then drove to the pet store in the mall and had a long talk with the proprietor.

"Aah, fleas," he said. "They're like wild armadillos on pogo sticks. You can't catch 'em, can't find 'em, can't kill 'em. *Unless* you're willing to go to war."

"I'm willing," Janet said. "Under these circumstances I can't conscientiously object."

He outlined a plan for her. She would have to vacuum every inch of the house, strip the beds, wash the blankets and bed-spreads, seal the food boxes in plastic, remove the eating utensils and plants from the house and buy insecticide bombs at the hardware store. The bombs would cover the fleas and everything else in the house with a poisonous mist. Luckily, human beings were bigger than fleas, so the chemicals that would kill the fleas would probably just give human beings cancer in thirty years or so—which was better than being eaten alive now. "Life is a trade-off," the pet-store owner said philosophically. Then he added that the cats would have to have a flea treatment on the same day as the bombing.

"Anything else?" Janet asked.

"Wear a gas mask," the man said.

At the hardware store Janet was told the bombs didn't work too well because they couldn't get the flea eggs. In a week the eggs would hatch and there'd be twice as many fleas in the house as there were to begin with. So instead of bombs, she was persuaded to buy "Murder 'Em Kennel Dust," which, if raked into the rugs, would get the eggs too. Coming home, she hid the lethal materials in the trunk of her car, determined to get rid of the fleas so that she wouldn't have to get rid of the kitten. She wasn't sure just how to work on Danny; he had spoken his final word on the subject. But she certainly couldn't approach him about keeping the kitten while scratching her shins!

The next morning, Janet fed the baby birds and then drove them—with all her house plants and cereal boxes—a block away from the house, where she parked the car. Returning to the house, she put on plastic eye goggles, a surgeon's mask, rubber gloves and an orange poncho (nonporous) and began skulking through the house, bent over, shaking "Murder 'Em Kennel Dust" over her pure-nylon rugs. When every room in the house was covered with a layer of powder, she got the red garden rake and began earnestly raking the stuff deep down into the rugs. She was worried. Ecologists had warned that by wiping out the snail darter, humanity might have changed the whole ecological balance. God only knew what would happen if fleas became extinct. She began to cough, sure that the poison was penetrating her surgeon's mask. She saw clusters of fleas holding on to the laces of her tennis shoes as if to a life raft. She was sweating under the poncho. Once she looked up into the mirror on the living-room wall and screamed in surprise.

"It's all right," she said to herself. "It's only me."

The doorbell rang and she opened the front door.

"Can I help you?" she said to the fleeing backs of two women and a child. They had left religious literature on her doorstep. Maybe they didn't feel that mutants needed to be given a conversion speech.

She walked from room to room through the powdery fog till she was convinced she had raked the seeds of destruction deeply enough. Then, gasping for breath, she ran out into the yard, where Creamy and the gray kitty lay in the sun, playing with each other's tails.

"Come over here, you guys—you're next. I bought you peppermint-scented 'Murder 'Em Pet Spray'—I'm doing this all the way!"

She didn't want Danny to know that the fleas had invaded the entire house, or that she could possibly be the cause of a cancer he might get in thirty years, so she vacuumed the powder sooner than she was supposed to. That night, collapsed, exhausted, in front of the TV, she ordered Myra up off the poisonous floor. "It's drafty," Janet said. "I don't want you to sit down there."

"We always sit on the floor," Myra complained.

"The TV gives off radioactive rays," Janet said. "Sit on a chair."

"Tell her the truth," Danny said. "Just tell her you don't want her to get bitten by fleas."

"I forgot to tell you," Janet said. "The fleas are all gone. Miraculously. There isn't a single one around. Maybe they weren't fleas. Maybe there were just ashes blowing out of the fireplace."

"*Biting* ashes?" Danny said. "By the way, where are the cats now?"

"Outside," Myra said. "Banned from their own home. Creamy is having a mental breakdown."

"Let him call the family-counseling talk show on KABC," Danny said.

"Phooey," Myra said, getting up off the floor and throwing her arms around her father's shoulders. "Who wants to watch TV anyway?"

"Mommy and I do," Danny said. "*Alone,* if you don't mind."

"You don't love me," Myra accused him. "It's obvious."

" 'Torn between two lovers,'" Danny sang, imitating one of Myra's favorite songs. " 'Breaking every rule . . .' We have to try to keep it a secret from Mommy, sweetheart."

"Oh, shut up," Myra said, and stormed off to her room.

Janet was reassured. It was clear that they were friends. She wondered if she ought to tell Danny what a good father she knew he was, after all. But enervated from her day's labors, she lay there like a dead person, too weak to move, to speak, even to return the pressure of her husband's hand. Danny had been right. If the children were no longer exhausting her, now it was the pets who drained all her energy. Like the poisoned fleas in the carpet, her very libido was lying limp and impotent in her hidden crevices. If she weren't preoccupied with the fleas, it would be the birds, and it if weren't the birds, it would be the cats. Poor Danny—there never seemed to be a time and place for him. She would have to give up the kitten. It was her destiny. She lay there, beaten, sorrowful, while Danny switched channels with the remote-control device.

A program zipped by showing a woman giving another woman a sensual massage. Danny clicked back to it.

"This program will explore," the voice-over said, "the hidden meanings and power of human touch and the exquisite responsiveness of the touch-receptive cells in the human skin."

Danny ran his finger across Janet's upper arm. She wondered if he could tell it was made of numb rubber, the arm of a mannequin. A cluster of monkeys came on the screen, hugging and embracing one another. A mother and her baby were shown entwined, and then the little monkey was separated by a glass barrier from its mother and almost at once it displayed symptoms of extreme grief—first a desperate pawing at the glass and then, later, a slumped-over posture, head bowed, little hand to its forehead—classic sorrow. "Monkeys who are deprived of touch," the voice-over said, "eventually display signs of severe disturbance and aggression."

Now there were happier scenes—of an infant at his mother's

breast, of parents cuddling a crying child, of an old woman playing with her cat, of a young man roughhousing with his dog, of a little girl rubbing noses with a kitten. "Pets," the voice-over said, "enhance the lives of those who live with them. The give-and-take of affection, particularly the cuddling, holding and stroking of pets, has been shown to improve the quality of life for their owners. Touch is the matrix of our social and emotional relationships with others. People who own pets are calmer, more secure—and may even live longer."

Danny, still resting his arm on Janet's shoulder, reached up and gently stroked her cheek with his forefinger.

"Ummm," she sighed. Feeling seemed to be returning to her flesh. She shifted on the couch and embraced him, sliding her hand up his sleeve. As the TV screen flashed again to the restful expression on the face of the woman being given a massage, Janet massaged Danny's biceps muscle. As the picture returned to the monkeys, then panned to the old woman playing with her cat, to the young man with his dog and to the child with the kitten, Janet stroked Danny's skin with sweet sensuality. Then very quietly she stood up and excused herself for a second. She opened the patio door and returned with the gray kitten in her arms.

"Look," she whispered to her husband, placing his large hand on the luxurious fur of the kitten's back. "Feel that," she said. "When I stroke him, I feel calm, happy, full of well-being. All my senses come alive."

"They do?" Danny asked.

"Feel," she said softly, drawing his fingers through the fur. "It's almost electric." She placed her own hand over his and together they stroked the kitten, who had begun to purr loudly in contentment.

"He keeps me company when no one is home," Janet said. "He's so sweet, and when I pet him, I can hardly wait for you to come home I can pet you."

"Ummm," Danny murmured. He had put his head back against the edge of the couch and closed his eyes.

"I love his rough little tongue," she said. "It's scratchy, just like your cheek when you kiss me and your whiskers rub my face hard."

"Oh, yes," Danny nodded.

"And people who love pets live longer," Janet whispered. "They're better lovers . . ."

Danny was totally relaxed, given up to the moment. Janet reached over and switched off the TV. In the dark silence she continued to nourish the touch-receptive cells of the three of them, breathing in, as she did so, the sweet, peppermint aroma of the kitten.

(1981)

Good-Bye, Arny Goldstone

~

"YOU REALIZE THIS COULD be the saddest day of your life, don't you?" Donna asked, maneuvering the car along the curves of Prospect Park on their way from Manhattan. "You can't go home again and all that?"

Janet's eyes were fastened on two women in bright red jump suits, standing on a hill.

"Hookers," Donna said. "Did they have them here when you lived in Brooklyn?"

"I don't think so," Janet said. "At least they didn't—well—parade around like that."

"The first of many surprises," Donna said, leaning over and patting her knee. "Just hang on and be prepared."

"Why are you so *negative*?" Janet said. "Why shouldn't this be wonderful? Going back to the house I grew up in, seeing my old neighborhood, my old street . . ."

"Because it isn't going to be your old anything," Donna said. "Because twenty years is a long time. Nothing will be the same. The nice old people you knew when you were a little girl are dead, and the young people have married and gone, and the middle-aged people have moved to Florida or Long Island or—like you—to California."

"But I was so happy there," Janet said. "I spent the first twelve years of my life in that one place. I knew everyone in every house, and I knew their mothers and fathers and sisters and brothers, and their grandmothers and grandfathers, and they knew me and my sister and *my* mother and father. . ."

"All right, all right," Donna said. "I get the gist of it. But I went back to Philadelphia a few years ago to where I knew everybody's grandmother, and instead of my house I found a condominium, and instead of old Mrs. Esposito next door I found a pool hall, and instead of my elementary school I found a factory that makes paper cups."

"Oh, that reminds me," Janet said. "Could we drive by my old elementary school too? P.S. 238? I get a chill just thinking about how I had my first proposal of marriage there, when I was eleven."

"Tell me about it," Donna said.

"Well, it was during a fire drill. We were all standing out on the street by someone's hedge and Arny was stripping leaves off the bush by the handful, and then suddenly he stuck his face next to mine and said, 'Janet, you're not the prettiest girl in seventh grade, but there's something about you that makes me crazy and I hope I can marry you someday.'"

Donna laughed. "Ah," she said. "*Now* I know why you wanted to come back to Brooklyn. You want to look him up!"

"Look up Arnold?" Janet said. "That's ridiculous. He wouldn't be here anyway. You just said all the middle-aged people have moved to Florida or California. He probably lives in L.A., a ten-minute drive from me."

"What's his last name?" Donna asked.

"Goldstone," Janet said. "Arnold Goldstone."

"Perfect!" Donna said. "It's just right. I love it."

They were driving down Ocean Parkway now. Janet's heart leaped at the familiar sight of the benches, the leafy trees, the pipe fence separating the bicycle path from the promenade.

"But where's the bridle path? And I don't see any bicycles either. And the fence—it used to have little pointy knobs on every post. God, I had never even heard of phallic symbols then!

I can almost feel how smooth they used to be. Gold—the knobs were gold."

"You're really thinking about Arnold Goldstone," Donna said. "Confess."

Janet laughed. She was delighted. The trip *was* going to be worth it all—the expense, leaving Danny and the girls for two weeks, coming back here to visit after so long. It was a trip with a practical purpose too; she was going to attend the eighty-fifth birthday celebration of a favorite aunt of hers.

When the invitation came, Danny had urged her to go. "It will be good for you to have a change," he said. "Get away from the children for a while, have a little vacation."

"But I'll *miss* you," she had said. "It's scary to think of going away from you for so long. It seems *risky.*"

"If you don't take a risk now and then," Danny had said, "you won't have any new experiences."

But now she was remembering an old experience; Arnold Goldstone at her twelfth birthday party; how, during a kissing game, he wouldn't let her out of the dark sun porch where they were playing Post Office, how he blocked the door with his long arms and held her there, demanding yet one more kiss, his body heat making her limp, confused.

"One more kiss, Janet—I have to have one more. I dream about you every night, you know."

"I thought you probably dreamed about Wendy," she said, for it was true that Wendy, who let boys do anything to her, had often been seen in the playground, behind the rest rooms, with Arnold.

"What has she got to do with it? You know about *her,*" he said. "She's nobody. The only kisses I want are yours."

But she wasn't sure she could handle another kiss. The first one, given formally—it was, after all, part of the game—had been of a different quality from the wet, awkward, hurried smacks she had experienced at parties. Arnold's kiss was rough and hard; she thought she felt the knuckles of his fist pressing into her back; her knees lost their tension, went watery; and she felt a kind of swooning surrender swirl through her head, something delicious, scary, uncontrolled and possibly very dangerous.

"Tough," she said. "You can't have a second kiss, Arnold." She had pushed past him into the party room, blinking at the bright light, feeling a cold chill now that she had stepped out of the aura of his passion for her, realizing with sorrow that she had made the first of many practical, sensible choices in her life.

In school on Monday he had humiliated her. On the blackboard in his spidery handwriting was the terse message: "Anyone can see inside Janet's dress." She was wearing a loose, sleeveless pinafore on that hot spring day, no bra under it. She had sat all day with her arms pressed against her sides, trying to control her tears and anger.

She had never talked to Arnold after that. And then at some point her parents had moved away from Brooklyn. But every now and then, unexpectedly, as she moved through her happy domestic life, the image of his face would come to her, those wild, sexy eyes, his hoarse, nasal voice, his desire for her, his thrilling demands. The first was always the best. Her husband Danny was handsome, tender, totally suited to her. But no one except Arnold had ever demanded kisses of her like that—"the only kisses I want."

"Avenue O," Donna announced. "It's coming right up."

"Oh, look!" Janet cried. "There's the apartment house where the bad man lurked in the basement. On snowy days I liked to cut through the basement on my way home from school—the hot-water pipes were so nice and warm. But my grandmother warned me about the bad man who would get little girls and do bad things to them."

"So of course you didn't take the short cut," Donna said.

"I didn't—no, of course I didn't. I was a good girl," Janet said. "Always have been—a good girl."

"So you froze your butt off."

"I froze it off," Janet said. "Turn right here. Oh, God, this is *my street!*"

The trees were lacy, beautiful, just as she remembered them. She felt lightheaded, buoyant. When she actually saw her house, dappled sunlight coming down upon it, she began to laugh and cry at the same time. "Look! The stoop where I played stoopball. The sewer where all my balls went—"

"They're probably still there," Donna said.

"The lilac tree! Oh, my God. That bench. It's the same bench my grandmother used to sit on. She would sit there, knitting, and say to me, 'Don't run so much. Rest—you'll live longer.'"

Obediently Donna was looking at the little house, as if she were trying to see the young Janet running, puffing, red in the face, playing stoopball, catching the flies as they came off the points of the brick steps.

"And there's Myron's house next door! Myron—we used to play Monopoly all the time on his back porch. His mother hit him at every meal because he wouldn't eat enough. Once she swung at him and he ducked and she broke her wrist!"

Janet was nearly levitating in her seat as Donna parked the car. "Look. There—across the street. That's where Rachel lived—she was this unbelievably sexy girl. She outgrew her bras every week; her mother kept complaining how she had to buy her so many new ones. And she was a champion jacks player, better even than me. Do you think that was fair, to have a shape like that and to beat me at jacks, too?"

Donna was laughing. "Do you want to walk around a little, or shall I just tie a string to you and you can float?"

"The tree! My wishbone tree!" Janet cried. "When I was four or five I used to sit in the vee of it. And now look how huge it is!"

The front door of the house opened and a little old lady wearing a blue apron looked out. "Hello, girls," she said. "Could I do something for you?"

"Oh . . ." Janet said. "I used to live here when I was a little girl. This used to be my house. Is it all right if we just—well, stand here for a while and look at it?"

"Isn't that wonderful!" the old lady said. With her white hair, she looked the way Janet's grandmother had looked. But her grandmother had been dead fifteen years now. "Maybe you'd like to come in and look around?"

Donna gave Janet a warning glance, meaning, so far so good;

but what if you go inside and it's all different, all wrong?

"I'd love to look inside, if you really wouldn't mind," Janet said. "I have a little camera. Do you think I could take a few pictures?"

"Darling," the old lady said, "do anything you like. Make yourself at home. It's a wonderful house. As soon as we saw it, we bought it right away for the basement. My son liked to build models, so we wanted him to have a basement."

"The basement terrified me," Janet said. "The furnace—the way the pipes clanked every morning when the heat came up. I used to think it would explode. Once I looked inside at the roaring fire . . . my father said I must never open the door of it." Her father been dead ten years.

"So come in, come in already," the old woman said.

Janet walked, knees shaking, up the front steps and Donna followed. Janet had a photograph of herself at the age of two climbing these steps. This was like stepping into another world, another existence. The numbers on the door, her address—405—were the same. The stained-glass porthole in the heavy door—it was all the same; the same sun sending light through the colored glass, making the same colored patterns on the floor of the sun porch where she had slept for twelve years. It was unbelievable that she was here. All those years in between—she had finished college, got married, lost her father, had three children . . .

"Go wherever you like, sweetheart," the old woman said. "I'm Mrs. Berkovsky. Would you like a cup of tea? Some honeycake, maybe?"

"No, no, thank you," Donna said. "But tell me a little about your son. What does he do now?" She nodded at Janet, meaning, Go, do what you have to, we don't have too long.

Janet traversed the three rooms downstairs, the continent of her childhood. Upstairs, tenants had lived. There in that corner had been the old GE radio; there under the window, her dog Spotty. The rooms were their old shape; Mrs. Berkovsky's polished furniture vanished under her hungry eyes and in its place she saw *her* things, her precious memories. Her mother broiling lamb chops between two wire grates on top of the stove, flames leaping upward toward the ceiling; in the back yard; her father pruning the peach tree, shirtless, his bare chest strong and tanned. Herself on the glider on the back porch, reading, writing in her diary, preparing for life, dreaming of the adventures to come.

Going down the cellar steps, her camera ready, she felt the chill of the dark, her fear of the roaring furnace and of the open hole under the house where the bogeyman lived and waited to strike. The green wooden storage benches were still there, exactly as they had been. That was where she'd kept Halloween costumes, games, puzzles.

"I don't believe this," Janet heard herself whisper, clicking her camera at everything, at anything. She was in a time machine; she was eleven years old. It smelled the same. The cracks in the cement in the alley were the same. The tiles in the bathroom were the same; when she had had stomachaches, she had sat in the bathroom, doubled over, counting the tiles.

Finally she emerged from the cellar into the kitchen. Donna, sitting with Mrs. Berkovsky, was leafing through the phone book. "Guess what?" she said, handing the book out to Janet and pointing. "Look at that."

"Arnold Goldstone!"

"None other."

"It can't be the same one," Janet said. "Impossible."

"Call," Donna suggested.

"Call?"

Mrs. Berkovsky said, "Use the phone, if you like, darling. It's in the front room."

Janet followed Mrs. Berkovsky into the front room, her old bedroom, the sun porch where Arnold had come toward her with his long arms, where he had demanded her kisses. On that night the street light had barely filtered through the Venetian blinds into the blackness of the room. The same blinds were open now, letting in the sun.

"So you'll have privacy," Mrs. Berkovsky said, shutting the door behind her.

Sitting on the day bed, she dialed the number. Her throat closed when a man answered the phone.

"Is this Arnold Goldstone?" she said at last, her voice trembling. "My name is Janet. I used to go to school with a boy named Arnold Goldstone. . . ."

"Janet!" the man said. "Oh my God, Janet. I was just thinking about you today. In fact, I think about you all the time. I pass your house and I remember you. I remember your grandmother and her white hair. And your father, and all the junk in the cellar. Your mother used to make us milk shakes after school."

His voice was unmistakably the same, a little whiny, nasal, Brooklynese, marvelous. She felt herself smiling ridiculously, her mouth stretched wide, joy welling up within her.

"You *remember* me?"

"Remember you! Janet, you were my *first love*. You were the only girl I really loved. Oh, yeah, I had other girls for fooling around, but you were really something. You I could just sit and talk to for hours."

"Yes, I remember," Janet said.

"Are you still cute?"

"*Am I still cute?*"

"You know . . . you were the sexiest thing," he said. "I always dreamed about going to bed with you."

"With me? I was such a skinny kid."

"That's the way I liked 'em," he said with a low laugh.

"My God, Arny, if only you'd told me this twenty years ago, my whole self-image, my whole life, might have been different!"

"But I want to apologize for something while I have the chance," he said, his voice going to a whisper. "I've always regretted this one thing."

"*What?*"

"Just a minute—let me close the door here in my office."

"Oh, hurry," she said.

"Okay, I'm back. Do you remember once, it was a summery day, you weren't wearing a bra, maybe some of the girls were by then, and maybe your dress was slightly too big, or something . . ."

Do I remember?

". . . and all the guys were making remarks, you know, and I wanted to stop them, but I didn't have an adult mind then so I just went along with it. . . ."

"Went along! You wrote that awful thing on the blackboard, Arny."

"Not me, Janet. Pinhead wrote it. You remember that moron in our class, Alvin Pinetta, we all called him Pinhead? He wrote it."

"I always thought you wrote it."

"I would never do that to you, Janet. When you love a girl, you don't want everyone looking in her dress, you know. I wish I had punched every one of those guys in the face. It's funny, but I think of that pretty often and I still feel bad about it."

In a mirror on the sun-porch wall, Janet could see from her reflection that she was crying.

"So how long are you in town?"

She took a breath. "Just this afternoon, Arny. A friend from Manhattan drove me in. I live in California now. I have three girls. My husband . . ."

"Yeah, I figured that would happen," he said. "I always wondered, but in my heart I knew. What else could it be? A husband, kids . . ."

"And you?"

"A wife, kids. What could you expect?"

"But is it okay?"

"Yeah, it's okay. And I made a lot of money. What do you think of that, Janet? That dumb kid, he got rich."

"You were never dumb, Arny."

"And I'm still pretty good-looking. My daughter tells me I'm really handsome. I work out every day."

"I can imagine."

"So maybe you could drop by with your friend. I have this restaurant on Avenue P now, Arnold's Salami Palace. That's where I am now, that's the number you called me at. Don't laugh at the name, Janet. It's a real good business. Remember my father—he had Irving's Appetizer Store? It's the same building. Modernized."

"I don't know, Arny. I think my friend has to get back to the city."

"Well, leave it open," he said. "If you come, you come. But, hey, I'm so happy you called. You have no idea how happy I am, I'm smiling all over the place."

"Me too. I'm happy too."

· "So listen, try to drop by. It would really be something to see you."

"I'll try," she said. "Good-bye, Arny Goldstone."

"Hey, kid, I still love you. . . ."

She hung up softly, sobbing with such exquisite pain and joy that the light coming in the stained-glass porthole of the front door swam before her eyes in swirls of fiery, brilliant colors.

She fell back on the day bed and recognized the light fixture on the ceiling of her room. This *was* her room. Of all the rooms in all the places she had lived or would live, this was her room.

It took her ten minutes to compose herself, to set her face straight, to open the door and walk to the kitchen, where Donna, with her sweet patience, was still talking to Mrs. Berkovsky.

"So," Donna said, "was it really your old friend Arnold?"

"Yes, it was," Janet said, smiling. "And would you believe he actually remembered me? In fact, he runs a restaurant right on Avenue P, a block away."

"Do you want me to take you over there?" Donna asked, watching her face carefully.

"Oh . . . I don't know, let me think about it," Janet said.

Donna took Mrs. Berkovsky's hand. "I do think we've taken enough of your time. You've been wonderful. Thank you *so* much."

"You're such sweet girls, come back any time," Mrs. Berkovsky said, hugging them.

As soon as they were in the car, Donna glanced sideways at Janet. "So shall I swing around to Avenue P?"

"Okay—why not?" Janet said, her heart roaring.

"It's a little risky, no?"

"This hasn't been the saddest day of my life so far," Janet said.

"Well, let's keep it that way. But if you want me to, I'll drive down to Avenue P and you think about what you really want to do."

And there, next door to the place where Janet once took ballet lessons, where Irving's Appetizer Store had been, stood Arnold's Salami Palace. Janet could almost smell the mustard out on the street. It was so pungent, beads of perspiration stood on her forehead.

"Stop or go?" Donna asked.

"I didn't say for sure I'd stop by. I told him I'd leave it open."

"And?" She slowed the car.

"No, go on. Just keep going. I think it's better to leave it open."

(1982)

Drastic Reductions

~

"WHAT ABOUT ALL THESE old skeleton keys?" Janet asked her mother. She was down on her knees behind one of the antique store's showcases, pulling out the contents of the storage drawers. On the dusty floor beside her was a pile of odd pieces of costume jewelry, old buttons, broken candles, string, extension cords and light bulbs.

"I don't know. Why not put them . . . No, never mind. Just throw them out."

"Oh . . . let's not throw them out!"

"Why not? Can you use them?"

"It's not a question of 'Can I use them?' How could I use them?" Janet straightened her back and brushed her hands together. The keys were rusted, some ornately curved and filigreed, others heavy and utilitarian. The box of them weighed several pounds.

Her mother, standing in silhouette against the light coming through the iron bars at the store's glass front, began to walk towards her slowly. Her legs were very thin; she walked like a blind person testing the floor to see if it would hold her weight. She had fallen some weeks ago and injured her shoulder and hip. Janet's aunt Gert, who liked to delineate causes, claimed that Anna was careless and never looked where she was going. She had said this to Janet as they waited outside the lab while her mother was being x-rayed for possible broken bones.

"Do you really think it's productive to blame her at this point?" Janet had asked.

"No one is productive in their seventies," her aunt had answered with her special logic.

Now, in the windows at the front of the store, Janet could see the two signs she had made for her mother with her children's red poster paints a month ago. Under the peeling and faded "Goldman's Antiques" sign hung her own hand-lettered messages. One read: "DRASTIC REDUCTIONS"; the other: "LIQUIDATION SALE AFTER 20 YEARS OF BUSINESS." After painting the signs on the picnic table in her back yard, Janet had stood them up too soon and the red paint had run, making the words bleed tear-shaped droplets.

"If only your father were alive," Aunt Gert had said the day of Anna's fall as they waited for her in the medical building. "Then Anna would have someone to cook for." Gert had three or four subjects she liked to talk about. The future of her sister Anna was one. "Now that she's giving up the business, at least your mother will be at home like a normal woman. Maybe she'll start to cook. Even if she didn't break something this time, she will the next time, because she has no meat on her bones."

More than aware of her mother's growing frailty, Janet had driven in to L.A. today with a coolerful of food she hoped would tempt her.

"How about we take a break now and eat lunch?" Janet asked, standing up on creaky knees and putting the box of keys near her purse. She wasn't used to this much physical work. It astonished her that her mother had done this kind of heavy labor for years, each day dragging four or five pieces of furniture out to the sidewalk, where they would attract attention to the store, and then, inside, polishing brass and silver, dusting crystal and china. In the evenings she often went on calls, following up on newspaper ads to find new merchandise.

"I'm not hungry," her mother said. "Here—give me those keys and I'll throw them out. What do you need them for? They're worthless."

"The kids might like to have them."

"What would they do with them?"

"I don't know. They're *mysterious*. They make you think about other lives, of all the people who must have opened doors with them."

"One life is just like another," Anna said. "The good years go fast, and then you get old and everything comes to an end."

"Ma," Janet said, "you're not really so old. Why not consider this a beginning, not an end?"

"What is there to begin on at my age?" she asked. "Next Wednesday is my last day here. Ten years here with Daddy and then ten here alone. I don't know what I'll do the day after I close the door."

"I'm confident you'll think of something," Janet said. Because her mother found reasons to reject the suggestions she made, Janet had stopped making them. To the idea that she might take up something new, like card playing or bird watching, Anna had said, "I'm not a card player and a bird is a bird."

"Well, in any case, I think you'll be relieved to be out of the store," Janet said.

They both knew too well the many reasons Anna was giving up the shop. She had been robbed at gunpoint and was afraid it would happen again; there were holdups on the street several times a week; the rent had been quadrupled. All these things were causing the neighborhood storekeepers to close down one after another. Then there was Anna's health. How much longer could she follow up on ads to buy antiques, to haul furniture, handle the demands of making police reports, keeping records, paying insurance fees and bills?

Sitting on a shaky carved chair with threadbare upholstery, Janet unwrapped the lunch she had packed for them—cold turkey slices with relish and mayonnaise on *challah*, black olives, sour pickles, hot coffee in a thermos, chocolate cupcakes. "Come on, Ma. Sit down and try some of this."

Her mother ate an olive.

"Look, Janet," she said, "I want you to take home whatever you want." She motioned around the shop at all the unsold things: statues, English china, engravings, oil paintings, vases, cups and saucers, platters, candlesticks, clocks. There was also the huge china cabinet.

"What you don't take, I'm sending to auction and it will bring practically nothing, so I mean it—take whatever you want." She paused and looked at her daughter. "So tell me—what do you want?"

Janet suddenly had trouble swallowing.

"Tell me what you like," her mother insisted.

What did she like? All her life she had made it a point not to like anything antique. Her parents had been in a business; antiques were simply stock on the shelves like cans in a super-market. The items were bought and sold, handled like pro-duce—for profit. Never had Janet felt that those goods were works of art, expressions of beauty, culture, history. But there *had* been one thing she'd loved—a small glass figure of two dancing girls caught in a moment of time, their gowns swirling. The glass was opaque, misted, so that the dancing girls seemed shrouded in fog, one reaching out to the other, their delicate fingertips nearly touching, like God's and Adam's in the Sistine Chapel painting. One day many years ago, when her children were still quite small, Janet had come to the shop, opened the door of the immense antique china cabinet where the piece was displayed and picked up the figure.

"Be careful!" her mother had called out. "That's Lalique."

Whatever it was, Janet felt a strong emotion rise within her. The glass felt cool in her hand; the dancing girls were delicate but powerful, yearning in their dance but confident. She wanted it.

"I really love that," she had said to her mother, putting it back in the cabinet beside a silver mesh purse. "It's so beautiful."

She looked at her mother, waiting. She had never, ever, asked for anything from the shop before.

"What would you do with it?" her mother had said, dismiss-ing her. "You have no place to put it."

Janet considered; it was true, she had no high shelves, no curio cabinets, no mantelpiece. Her house was a masterpiece of smooth surfaces; no dust collectors for her, no frills. Just modern utilitarianism.

"The kids would break it or the cat would knock it over," her mother said matter-of-factly. "And what would be the point of storing it away in some closet?"

"I guess you're right," Janet had said.

"And besides," her mother said, "it's very collectible, very expensive."

Later, when her mother was taking care of a customer, Janet had opened the china cabinet one more time and turned the coveted piece over to glance at the price. It was marked six hundred dollars. That settled the matter for her—she was not about to take home a little statue worth that much; if her mother could sell it, it would pay the rent in the store for three months. And that was the end of it. Except that whenever Janet visited the shop afterward, she'd pause by the cabinet, light the light within and renew her longing for the dancing girls. They reminded her of how she felt when she watched ballet dancers. She knew that if only she could free her body, she would fly as they did, defy gravity, express in the poetry of movement all the grace she could find within herself.

But two days ago her mother had sold the dancing girls. She had called Janet and said, "Guess what? I sold that little glass statue you liked."

"Oh . . . you did?" Janet said, keeping her voice cheerful. Somewhere in her chest a heavy feeling collected, a weighted chill, like ice deposited there, melting. "That's good, I guess. I know you can use the money."

"Well, I didn't get very much. But after all, it's my last week, time is running out and I had to take what was possible."

"How much did you get?"

"A hundred dollars."

A *hundred dollars!* Janet had bought each of her three daughters gym shoes last week, and they had cost a total of a hundred dollars. In a few months they would be worn out or outgrown.

"A hundred dollars!" It was a moan—she could not help it.

"Well, you didn't want it," her mother said, "and every penny helps."

Janet was unable to speak

"You didn't really want it, did you?" her mother said, a tinge of uncertainty in her voice. "I remember you said you didn't have any place for it."

"I probably could have found a place," Janet said softly. The place was her heart, now empty.

"You never cared much about antiques," her mother said over the phone. "It's odd, growing up in the midst of it, how you didn't know cut glass from pressed glass, silver plate from silver."

"No one ever taught me much about it," Janet said.

"You weren't all that interested," her mother accused her.

"No," Janet agreed. "I really wasn't."

Now she took her mother's hand and pulled her into a chair. "Eat your sandwich, Ma. You need strength. We both do."

They had a great deal of work waiting for them. The showcases had to be emptied and all the china in them packed in cartons. The mirrors and paintings and jewelry had to be packed for Anna to take home, to be sold as she needed money to live on.

"So what old and beautiful presents would you like?" Anna asked as she ate her sandwich mechanically, without interest. "Anything you like, or want, or can use, or think the children would want, I want you to take home with you today."

Janet looked around. Her eyes landed on a brass opium pipe. "How about that?"

"With children in the house?" Anna asked.

"I'll tell them it's an antique oil can," Janet said, smiling.

"Fine. Take it. It's yours. Anything else? Pick another. Daddy would want you to have everything if he were alive."

The buzzer of the electric eye sounded, and they both glanced up, alert. Her mother had had it installed after a man had held her up, threatened to kill her, a year ago.

"Well, there's your aunt Gert," Anna said to Janet.

"Hello, darling," Gert said to Janet. "I came to help, and I brought your mother a little warm chicken soup." She set down a paper bag on her mother's desk; her hair, like Anna's, was perfectly white.

"Janet already fed me," Anna said. "But I'll take home the soup and have it for dinner."

"Soup is not a whole dinner!" Gert said sharply. "I'm counting on when you're done with this store, that you'll cook real meals for yourself."

"I haven't cooked since Abram died, and I'm not about to start now."

"You'll start, you'll start," Gert said. "When you're a woman of leisure, you can get domestic."

"Never!" Anna snapped. "Not me domestic—oh, no!"

"So what will you do if you don't cook?" Gert asked.

"Who should I cook for? A ghost?" Anna said. "You at least have a husband to feed. Don't worry," she added angrily. "Don't you all worry about me—I'll find something to do." Putting down the half-eaten sandwich, she began to snap up sheets of newspaper from the floor and wrap them around a huge platter. "You'll take this turkey platter," she said to Janet. "It's English, it's very desirable." She put it into a carton and began to pack a cut-glass decanter. "And you'll take this. It's beautiful . . ." She turned it upside down to check its price. "It's marked two hundred dollars."

"But . . ." Janet said.

"Don't give her all the good things," Gert said. "Take them home; then you can have a sale from your apartment."

"I'm giving her anything she wants," Anna said to her sister. "What she doesn't want goes to auction. I don't want to look at these things, once I'm out of here."

"She has no place to keep them," Gert said.

"That's really true, Ma," Janet said. She had a vision of her house filled with dusty horrors, rusty keys, tarnished silver.

"Well, you'll have the china cabinet. I'm giving you the china cabinet."

Astonished, Janet turned to look at the cabinet. It had stood in the store for as long as she could remember, massive, its mirrored back gleaming, its beveled glass door and shelves glistening. A hidden light illuminated the treasures within; a golden key, sitting in the keyhole, would secure them against harm. It was a museum piece, elegant, weighted with consequence. It had been the store's finest piece, its pride, its masterpiece. Her father had bought it a lifetime ago. Her parents had been so proud of owning it that they had put an impossible price on it—three thousand dollars.

Gert gasped. "You can't give it away," she said to Anna. "Think of your future. You've got to sell it—you can live on it for a year."

"I'll get nothing near its value at auction," Anna said, "and I want Janet to have it. I want her to have something she loves from this store before it's gone." She turned to Janet. "Tell Gert how much you've always loved this cabinet," Anna commanded.

Janet took a deep breath. If she loved it, she loved it as one loves a landmark, a bridge, a building, a view—not a love that requires ownership. "Well," she said finally, "it's truly an amazing piece."

"So you'll take it. Now that that's settled, let's get busy and pack some more stuff," Anna said, suddenly energetic, officious. "Would you like this pink lobster dish? And how about this carved wooden fork and spoon from Germany? And the Chinese brass bowls? And the jade tree. I'll wrap the jade tree, and also the soapstone grapes. And the pair of Austrian vases with the hand-painted landscapes. Be careful with these. Don't lift them by the handles—one has a tiny crack in it."

Anna was wrapping, wrapping, her fingers turning black from newspaper ink. She filled a carton, wrote Janet's name on it with red marker pencil. "I think you'll have room for all this in the back of the car," she said.

Aunt Gert had walked to the front of the store and was sitting on a rickety throne chair.

"I only hope you know what you're doing," she said to her sister. "You shouldn't end up in the poorhouse."

"Don't lose sleep over it," Anna said. "After Janet chooses what she wants, then you take home what you want. If I end up destitute, I'm sure the two of you won't leave me out in the street."

She turned to Janet. "Now, let's keep going. How about this

silver candy dish? It will look nice in the cabinet. And this vase from Czechoslovakia. And this sugar and creamer from France, each one made in the shape of a pear."

"Presents! Presents!" Janet said, laughing uncertainly.

"After this week, the age of presents will be over," her mother said sadly. "So don't refuse anything now."

On the appointed day, Janet was moving furniture to make a place for the china cabinet when she thought she felt the house rumble. Earthquake! she thought instinctively. Volcanic eruption—some kind of catastrophe. When she saw the truck parking at the curb, her mother's white head on the passenger side, she knew she was right. Doom was upon her.

Oh, God, I don't want it, she thought in a panic. I don't want heavy things to weigh me down, to hamper my life. I don't want to be caretaker of objects I did not choose, guardian of breakable glass, precious metals, fluted vases and hand-painted shepherdesses.

Even as the thoughts babbled through her head, she dutifully made room for the cabinet, pushed her Danish walnut fold-out dining table to another place, moved Danny's simple leather reclining chair farther toward the corner. I must bear this burden, she thought; and then she laughed at her own melodramatic posturing. She had women friends who would be wild to have this good fortune—the contents of an antiques store at their command, all free!

From the window she could see the two young men her mother had hired as they unbolted the back of the rented truck and began to raise the hydraulic platform to the level of the truck bed.

This was the part she hated, had always hated—the struggle of man against matter, muscle against dead weight. Her father had made his living this way, pushing and straining against furniture that was no longer rooted in some English drawing room or French bedroom or Early American kitchen. When she was a child, Janet had watched him as he dragged and hauled furniture into his antiques store or sweated and gasped as he balanced it on a dolly and inched it into his station wagon for delivery somewhere. She had been nourished all her life by the sweat running down his face, by the veins bulging in his neck. From his efforts her clothes were bought; from them her books, her dolls, her bicycle and skates were given her.

There were times she would have gone without all of it to spare her father that desperate, bursting exertion. Other fathers carried briefcases: her father carried—single-handedly—massive chiffonniers, armoires, library tables, bookcases. Once, hauling a desk for her into the house, a wonderful thing full of pigeon-holes and secret compartments and a locking, fold-down writing surface, he had broken two ribs. He set the desk down and clutched his chest. When Janet and her mother begged to know what was wrong, he laughed, but his eyebrows were tilted as if he were crying and he said, "Oh, it's nothing, I just broke something. I'll be all right."

No—she didn't want to experience that again. She and Danny had bought furniture that between the two of them could easily be moved or pushed around. On the day that her refrigerator was to be delivered, she had managed not to be home.

And now here it was again, coming up her front walk as her mother supervised—a china cabinet made from a grove of mahogany trees, denser than lead, wider than an ocean. *I can't look*, she thought, seeing one of the two young men stumble, regain his balance. *I'll get them something to drink, ice water, tea.* She hated it that she could do only these useless things, jangle her hands in the ice-cube tray, while men, like her father, like these young men, staggered and struggled to make it easy for her, make it pretty and convenient and nice so she could enjoy it . . . whatever it was.

She clutched her throat while the young men came through the entryway and across the rug, grunting like cavemen under the weight.

"Right here," her mother said to them. "No—a little more to the left. Move it back against the wall a little more. Good—that's fine. Thank you very much."

While her mother took out her wallet to pay the movers, Janet offered them the iced drinks, thinking, I ought to give them diamonds, jewels, for doing this for me—a stranger.

"Shall I go back into town with the men?" her mother asked.

"No, no! Please stay for dinner," Janet said. "I want you here. The kids will be home from school soon and they'd be upset if they missed you. We'll drive you home later."

When the rumble of the departing truck had faded down the street, Janet shaded her eyes and looked at the china cabinet as if she were looking into the sun. Her house seemed transformed. Her living room had taken on a new dimension, a serious and majestic splendor, as if a king held court there. The wood of the cabinet was burnished and glowing; she realized her mother had polished it for her, to banish the years of dust it had accumulated in the store.

"Well . . . how do you like it?" her mother asked as she carefully swung back the beveled glass door, pulled out the cord at the back and switched on the hidden inner light. A thousand darts of light, rainbow prisms, shot out from the angled mirrors. Janet felt her mother's eyes upon her, was aware of the plaintive, hopeful tone of her voice. Now that Anna had forced this invasion upon her daughter, she seemed to be worried.

"Do you think it goes with the other furniture in the room?" she asked, as if afraid Janet might change her mind and tell her to take it back. For a moment Janet had a sense of her father's presence in the room, his strong hands on the cabinet as he must have carried it when it was first brought to the store, twenty years ago.

"Yes," Janet said. "I think it goes very well. I think it's really beautiful."

"Would you like to unpack some of the things and put them on the shelves?"

"Yes, let's," Janet agreed. "We can surprise the children when they come home." She hurried out to the garage and began carrying in the cartons that she and her mother had packed the week before. Gently they unrolled the treasures from the newspapers.

"Well, you know the store is completely empty now," her mother said. "Everything that was left after Aunt Gert took a few things was taken away by the auction people yesterday.

Tomorrow I turn in the keys to the landlord and that's it."

"I think you've done a wonderful job, Ma, handling all of this," Janet said. "I'm proud of you."

"But you know? It's harder to end a business than begin it," Anna said. "Endings are always harder than beginnings."

Janet looked up to see if her mother might be crying, but Anna was sternly unwrapping a cut-glass water bottle. "Why don't we put all the glass and crystal on the top shelf?" she suggested matter-of-factly. "The knife holder and the decanter, and this crystal bowl."

"And this little Sandwich glass plate?"

"How do you know it's Sandwich glass?" her mother asked. "Have you been studying the books I sent home with you?"

"No." Janet laughed. "It says so on the price tag!"

"Oh, you must take those off," Anna said.

"At least let me leave them on till I learn the name of each piece."

"You don't have to bother for my sake," Anna said.

"But I want to," Janet said. "Now that these things are mine, I want to know about them. I really do."

Her mother placed a hand-blown bud vase on the top shelf, where it sparkled among the crystal like a diamond. Then Anna came toward her and touched her face. "Janet, I'm sorry I didn't give you the Lalique dancing girls. I regret it ten times a day."

"That's okay, Ma," Janet said, taking her hand and squeezing it. "You didn't know I was going to have a china cabinet to keep it in."

"But it would have looked so lovely with the crystal. There— right in the center."

"But the other things look wonderful. I'm beginning to love how beautiful they are."

"I was afraid you wouldn't want any of it. I thought you'd say, 'Mother, I can't clutter up my house with this stuff—it just isn't *me*.'"

"But it *is* me, Ma, it *is*." And to prove it, Janet leaned forward and smiled into the mirror at the back of the china cabinet so that her face filled the entire second shelf.

(1982)

What to Do About Mother?

~

SMALL THINGS, BUT TELLING. Janet's mother had left the flame on under the teapot till it boiled dry, and when she set it down on the cold tile counter, the teapot exploded into a thousand rainbow-colored splinters of glass. In her fright Anna had jumped and hit her hipbone hard against the side of a table. Her hip, she told Janet, was still black and blue. Then, just the night before, she had accidentally taken the wrong pill as she was watching Jessica Tandy and Hume Cronyn in *The Gin Game* on TV.

"I didn't want to miss a second," Anna told Janet on the phone, "There they were, two interesting, intelligent people in this old-age home, playing gin rummy. I was sure the play couldn't have a happy ending, but I was hoping it would, hoping it *could*. So I didn't notice that I picked up my medicine instead of my vitamins. I never did that before. Then suddenly I realized I'd taken my medicine for the second time that day—the one my doctor told me never, never to take more than once a day. I panicked. I remembered he said that taking too much of the medicine could slow down my heart, possibly even stop it! So you can imagine how I felt, Janet."

"Yes," Janet said. "I can imagine. So what happened?"

"I was awake all night, waiting for my heart to stop. I didn't want to call you in the middle of the night. What could you have done? And I didn't want to call my doctor. What could he have done? So I left a little note on my night table," she said apologetically, "so you and your sister would know what happened, just in case. It said, 'Children, I assure you this wasn't intentional. I accidentally took an overdose of Fenapin.'" Anna laughed.

"Well, a miss is as good as a mile," Janet said, trying to sound cheerful but feeling her heart pounding as she imagined what it would have been like going to her mother's apartment, using her key to get in, finding that note. "We'll talk about it more when you get here. Danny already left for your house, so he should be there in about half an hour. Don't forget to bring your laundry with you, Ma," Janet added. "Danny can just toss it in the car when he picks you up, and then you won't have to deal with it yourself. Why should you have all the hassle of the laundromat when you can bring it here and do it in a leisurely way?"

"Oh, you don't really want me to drag my dirty laundry all the way to your house, do you, dear?"

"Sure, I do," Janet told her. "Whatever will make things easier for you."

But as Janet diced onions for the spaghetti sauce, she asked herself just how far she was willing to go to make things easy for her mother. Yesterday she had been driving on the freeway and had seen a little pink stucco house being transported somewhere on a great wide trailer rig. All it lacked was a foundation. She could even see the doorbell in the front and a little decal of Donald Duck on one of the bedroom windows.

We should buy one of those little houses for my mother, she thought. We could put it in the backyard. Then she wouldn't be alone. She could have dinner with us every night. But then she imagined how isolated her mother would be in her little stucco house in the backyard, and thought once again, No, I'll give her Bonnie's room (empty now that Bonnie was at college). It was right next door to her and Danny's bedroom. I have a right to my privacy, she thought. Her eyes teared as she squeezed two cloves of garlic through the press. This is all academic anyway, she assured herself. *These problems are all still years away. I don't need to deal with them yet.*

Her mother came slowly up the walk, holding her arms out as she walked over the flagstones like a person on a high wire. She wore huge amber sunglasses. On her shoulder she carried her purse, as heavy as a sack of sand. Janet came out to greet her. She kissed her mother's cheek and tried to take the purse from her shoulder, but Anna hung on tightly.

"Here, let me take it, Ma. It's so heavy! What do you have in here? Gold bullion?"

"I only wish," Anna said, tugging it back. "Leave it, Janet," she added with just a shade of irritation. "I like to have my purse with me. I have everything I need in it—my keys and my medicine. I like to know exactly where it is."

Danny closed the trunk of the car and came up the walk behind Anna with two huge laundry bags slung over his back. Janet glanced at him to see how the long ride with her mother had gone. Danny's look was noncommittal. But she knew she didn't really have to worry about Danny; he and Anna got along very well.

"Just put the bags down," Janet instructed him. "I'll start a load in just a minute."

"I think I have at least five loads there," Anna stated. "I brought everything I own: nightgowns, underwear, sheets, towels. As long as we're doing it, I even brought along my shocking-pink bath mats. They're new; they've never been washed yet."

"Well, good," Janet said, casting her practiced eye on the laundry bags. "It won't be any problem. There's at most three loads there."

"I like to give my clothes plenty of space," Anna said. "Plenty of water to slosh around in. Five loads is what *I* think."

"I'll take care of it," Janet said. "Don't worry. I do laundry all the time, and I know just how much my machine holds."

"You never get your towels perfectly clean," Anna accused her. "Forgive me for saying this, Janet, but why you never sort colors from whites is beyond me. That's not what I taught you."

"Oh, things get clean enough for me," Janet said with a laugh. "I don't have time to sit and sort. Come in the living room and relax for a while, Ma. The girls are down at the park playing tennis. They'll be home any minute."

Anna sniffed. "Is that garlic I smell? You're not cooking with garlic tonight, are you, Janet? You know garlic doesn't agree with me."

"You'll hardly taste it in the sauce," Janet said. "I always make my spaghetti this way and you've always liked it."

"Not if you've been putting garlic in it," Anna said decisively. "I can sense it a mile away. I'd know it if you'd been putting garlic in your spaghetti sauce all these years. You never have."

"Well, maybe it wasn't as strong," Janet said weakly. "I'm pretty sure I've always used just a little bit."

"Oh, goody, Mom-Mom is here already!" Myra called out as she came in the front door. "Hooray for Mom-Mom!" She dropped her tennis racket in the hallway and came bounding into the living room, with her sister Jill coming in more sedately behind her. Both girls, long-legged and well on their way to being young women, bent over Anna and kissed and hugged her with as much enthusiasm as they had had when they were small. Anna laughed with delight.

"Oh, my big girls!" she said. "How did you get so tall? Just yesterday you were only up to my knee. Remember when we used to play sheriff and posse?"

"And we used to go on treasure hunts," Myra said, "in the backyard. Remember how you would leave little notes in the playhouse, Mom-Mom, and under the flowerpots? That was *so fun!*"

"I'll play treasure hunt with you tomorrow," Anna said, "if you big girls have time for your old grandmother." When Anna smiled, Janet saw that she had a dimple in her wrinkled cheek in the same spot as Jill had one.

"We have the whole weekend reserved just for you," Jill said, pulling off her sweatshirt. "We wish you came more often, Mom-Mom! How come you don't?"

"I can't put your mother and father to all this trouble every weekend," Anna said. "Pick me up, take me back, carry my laundry, cook me dinner. I have to be careful not to wear out my welcome."

"You never could," Myra said. "Never in a million years."

Janet began to drag the heavy laundry bags toward the kitchen.

"Five loads," Anna reminded her. "The little dish towels go with the colored things because they have red borders."

"Don't worry, Mom," Janet said. "I could do this with my eyes closed."

After dinner, as they listened to the rumble of the clothes dryer, Anna said, "Do you have a mint, Janet? All I taste is garlic. Not that your spaghetti wasn't delicious. It was. I never eat so well at home, but that strong taste . . . I could use a peppermint."

Anna and the girls were playing Scrabble on the kitchen table. Anna's hair shone brilliantly white in the light from the fixture overhead. For once the girls weren't squabbling with each other as they played a game. They gazed admiringly as their grandmother made triple-score words. Janet handed her mother a peppermint cane leftover from Christmas. Anna took it without looking up from the game board.

In the living room Danny was cleaning the heads on his tape deck. Janet stood and watched him for a minute. Then she whispered to him, "You know, I think the girls love to have my mother here. Don't they all seem to be having fun? And she adores being with them. I should insist that she come more often."

"I'd be glad to drive into the city to get her any time," Danny offered. "You know I don't mind."

"You don't think that maybe we should think about having her come here to live with us, do you?" Janet said. "It's really getting too hard for her to shop in those crowded supermarkets in the city. And it's dangerous there. She can never go out at night. And if she should get sick, there's no one to take care of her."

She waited for Danny to counter her arguments, to assure her that her mother was just fine where she was, that she had her life and her activities there, but instead he said, "It would be fine with me. I think it's a good idea." He dipped a Q-tip into a bottle of something that smelled very harsh. "We have plenty of room for her now that Bonnie is away. And I think she'd enjoy all the activity that goes on around here."

"Are you serious?" Janet said.

"Why not?" he said.

"I don't think you've thought this over very carefully," Janet said. She felt anger rise in her and she wondered how Danny would have reacted to the suggestion that *his* mother come to live with them. "Do you realize how close Bonnie's room is to our bedroom?"

"That wouldn't bother me," he said.

"It *wouldn't?*"

"Would it bother you?"

"No, no," Janet said. "Why should it? We're not teenagers."

"Well, good. Then maybe you should bring up the subject with your mother."

"I was planning to," Janet said, feeling extremely confused. "Why do you think I mentioned it in the first place?"

When the Scrabble game was over (with Anna as the uncontested winner) Anna went into the bathroom to take her various pills.

"Be careful you take the right ones," Janet warned her.

"I'm not senile," Anna said impatiently, closing the door firmly behind her. She was in the bathroom a long time. When she finally came out, Janet watched her carefully for signs of heart failure.

Anna said, "I see you keep the bathroom window open. Don't you think that's a little dangerous?"

"I always leave it open a little, Ma," Janet said. "For air."

"Well, you're taking unnecessary chances with your family's safety," Anna said. "I've warned you about that before. And you leave the back door unlocked all the time."

"Only when I'm in the backyard."

"Still, with the crime rate what it is, you shouldn't take a chance. You don't pay attention to what I tell you, Janet."

"Not if it's irrational," Janet mumbled under her breath. She had been noticing during the course of the evening that her mother carried her purse with her from room to room, wherever she went. At one point Janet tried to catch Danny's eye to see if he noticed, too, but he was reading the paper, oblivious to it all.

After a while, Anna said to Janet, "Don't feel that the two of you need to stay up and entertain me. Why don't you just go to bed, and I'll take care of myself?"

"Ma, it's only nine o'clock."

"Well, you work hard. You should get a lot of rest. Don't you agree, Danny?"

During the night Janet dreamed she was in a crowded shopping mall with her mother, who was very old. They moved slowly, their arms linked together. Anna wanted to stop at a K-mart. Janet said, "You shop and I'll just walk around for a few minutes and come right back." But just then a white-winged horse swooped down from the sky and invited Janet to leap upon his back. She knew her mother would worry if she disappeared, but she mounted the beautiful creature anyway and at once they flew away in a great arc above the earth. The wind billowed her hair about her head like a cloud, and stars and comets flashed before her eyes, lighting up the universe.

At breakfast, she felt the invitation she had planned to extend to her mother dying on her lips. While Anna ate the French toast Jill had made, Janet went into Bonnie's room and pressed the mattress on the bed. Too soft. Not good enough for an old person's back. (Janet had been aware all night of mother's presence in the next room.) The closets were still full of Bonnie's clothes. It wouldn't be fair to Bonnie to give away her room when she might be home summers. Of course Bonnie could always take the top bunk in Jill's room; it was perfectly adequate. The girls had shared a room for years before they'd added the extra bedroom onto the house. They often enjoyed sleeping in their bunk beds, for old times' sake.

When Janet returned to the kitchen the girls were discussing old age with their grandmother. "You don't really feel any different," Anna said. "When I wake up, I'm always seventeen."

"I'm always twelve," Myra said, "and I always *want* to be seventeen."

"I change every year," Jill said sensibly. "This year I'm fourteen, next year I'll be fifteen."

"Sometimes I'm twelve, too," Anna said. "Or twenty-five, or forty-five, or sixty. By the time you're as old as me, you can be any age you choose, because you've had them all and you know what they're like."

"I wish you lived here, Mom-Mom," Myra said. "You're so interesting to talk to and it would be fun to have more people here. Just Mom and Dad around all the time gets *boring*."

"It might not be so much fun to have an old person like me around all the time. I'd always be after you about something. You know, wanting you to do it my way. It would be *very* boring after a while. I have my funny ways, you know."

"Everyone has funny ways. Do you know what the Eskimos used to do with old people?" Jill said. "They set them out on an ice floe to die. My teacher told us this story about an Eskimo boy and his father who took the boy's grandfather out to the ice and left him to die. The father said, 'That is what we do with old people, son.' And the son said, 'And that is what I shall do with you, Father, when you are old.' And that frightened the father because he realized that the way he treated his father was how he would be treated by his son."

"Well, luckily," Anna said, "we have no ice floes in California."

The girls went to their rooms to get dressed and Anna called into the laundry room. "What are you doing in there, Janet? I see you folding a sheet. Don't be folding my laundry for me. I need the exercise."

"Just let me do it, Ma. I do it automatically. It's not even work. Don't worry."

"I'm not worrying. Just don't do it."

"Can't you let me do something nice for you?"

"I'd rather do something nice for you. I'm your mother. That's my job. Come sit down here and I'll make you scrambled eggs the way you used to like them when you were little."

"I just had French toast, Ma."

"So you'll eat again. You could use a few pounds."

"You're the one who could use a few pounds. I've been thinking, Ma . . ." The words rushed out of her mouth. "Danny and I were both thinking . . . maybe you'd like to come here and live with us. We have plenty of room and the girls would love to see more of you, and we could feed you and I'd try never to use garlic, I swear."

Anna got up from the table and walked slowly into the laundry room. She picked up a dish towel from the top of the laundry basket. "I thank you from my heart, darling. But you know, I could never live with a housekeeper who throws the colors and the whites together in the same wash. You don't even use bleach. You didn't listen to me, Janet. You didn't do my things in five separate loads, did you?"

"It would have been a waste of water, Ma."

"You're telling *me*, your mother, how to wash clothes?"

"I do things my way, Ma, and they work pretty well."

"And I do things my way, too, Janet. By now you should know that." Anna took the sheet from Janet's hand and dropped it back in the basket. She came forward and put her arms awkwardly around Janet's waist. She hugged her. Janet could feel her mother's delicate bones under the wrinkled skin on her arms. Both of them lost their balance and stumbled, which made them laugh.

"You're the best daughter in the world," Anna said. "The best child a mother could have. But darling, even though I'm grateful for your offer, even though I'm an old woman and I'm not as spry as I used to be, the fact is, I feel I'm still entitled to my privacy. I don't want to move in and take Bonnie's room and feel that if I wanted to listen to the radio at 3:00 a.m. I would be waking you up. And I like my activities in the city. I like my little apartment. You may think it's lonely, but I'm used to it. It's quiet there, and at my age I need quiet. If I want peace, I have peace. If I want to eat, I don't have to tell anyone not to use garlic. I'm not afraid to be alone. I have plenty to think about at my age."

Anna picked up a white towel and began to fold it. It was streaked with shocking-pink dye that had run from the bath mats.

"You should have listened to your mother," Anna said. "Look at these pink stripes where there shouldn't be stripes! Your mother can still teach you a few things. And she can still walk on her own two feet for the time being. Your old mother can't fly, that I'll grant you, but she *can* walk perfectly well."

"I had a dream about flying last night," Janet confessed, feeling close to tears. "I climbed on the back of a beautiful white horse with wings and I flew away with him and I left you behind in a shopping mall. In fact, I abandoned you in front of a K-mart! I feel so guilty, flying away from you like that in my dream."

"I know *exactly* what your dream meant," Anna said, reaching over to hold Janet's hand. "I'll interpret it for you. It's a beautiful dream, a generous dream. It shows your concern for me. You left me standing in front of a K-mart because you knew I had to buy new towels."

"It *wasn't* a generous dream, Ma . . ." Janet said. "Not at all, it was selfish . . ."

"Are you telling me I don't know my own daughter?" Anna insisted. "Look how you take care of me, cook delicious spaghetti for me, give me wonderful granddaughters! Look how you do my laundry for me, fold my sheets and towels. So what if they used to be white?"

Anna bent down to the laundry basket and handed Janet one of the sheets. "Here darling, if you want to take care of your old mother, fold her clothes. Why shouldn't I let you? I did enough for you when you were little, right? So now, if you don't mind, I'll go and enjoy myself with the children. Your girls and I will play Old Maid. We'll play Go Fish. You stay here like Cinderella, and your old mother will go to the ball. Whatever makes you happy."

"It *does* make me happy to do things for you, Ma," Janet called after her as Anna walked slowly away.

"You think I don't know that?" Anna said, pausing to turn and look back at Janet. "You think that at my age there are things about you I don't know? Please, darling, fold my laundry if you like. For now that's all I want you to do for me. In ten years, if necessary, we'll sit down and discuss other matters."

Anna picked up her purse from a kitchen chair, hoisted it over her shoulder and walked carefully down the hall till she was out of sight. In the living room Danny put on a tape of a Beethoven symphony. In the laundry room, Janet snapped her mother's bed sheet to unwrinkle it and felt it billow out as it filled with air. Her hair lifted in the gentle updraft. She had a sense once again of ascending high into the sky on the beautiful white-winged horse of her dream, while down below in the K-mart her mother smiled and waved her on from among the rows of sheets and towels.

(1985)

What's a Family For?

~

MY MOTHER CALLED EARLY on Thanksgiving morning to tell me she didn't want any transients at her funeral. I was surprised to hear her voice, since I expected her here later to have dinner with all the relatives and we usually didn't have our long daily talk by phone when she was coming here. We both understood that we needed to save some news for our face-to-face conversations.

"Your aunt Gert," she said with contempt in her voice. "She's been reading obituaries in the newspaper and she wants all that flowery baloney when she dies—'adored wife, beloved sister, devoted daughter, cherished aunt.' But I want absolutely none of that. Just my name, if anything. With the words 'Private services.' I don't want a bunch of strangers gawking at me, crying crocodile tears. I haven't got a friend in the world! All those people who knew me from the antique store when Daddy was alive—they're all nothing to me. They never call me. They never want to know how I am. So I don't want them at my funeral, coming back to your house for a party in my honor, Janet, stuffing themselves with food that you paid a fortune for and pretending they're heartbroken that I'm dead."

I stopped myself from pointing out to my mother that she didn't even like me to have parties in her honor when she was *alive.* She was always against my making Thanksgiving dinner;

we had the same argument every year. "Why knock yourself out? Your aunt Gert and I could just as happily stay home. She'll cook some garlicky thing for Uncle Harry at their place, and I'll stay here and put a chicken pie in the oven, read the paper and have a nice quiet day to myself."

The vision appalled me: my mother alone in her little apartment on Thanksgiving Day, just like all the other days she was alone there; the world revving up for the holidays—cars filling the freeways, families visiting together, and my mother alone with the *Los Angeles Times* and her pale little chicken pie burning around the edges in her uneven oven.

"I've already bought an eighteen-pound turkey," I told my mother on the phone. "And it was really cheap; there's a price war going on. So don't worry about that."

"Don't you hate to handle a dead turkey?" my mother asked. "They're so cold and slippery." She paused. "Did I ever tell you," she said in a totally different tone of voice, "that the first week Daddy and I were married, I tried to cook a chicken? And I left all the giblets in the brown butcher paper in the neck of the bird? Daddy said to me when I served him, 'What's this? Baked paper? A new kind of stuffing?'" My mother giggled. She sounded more like seventeen than going on seventy-five.

"You have to come," I said. "We have to have your birthday party." My mother's birthday fell just after Thanksgiving. I always baked her a chocolate cake and wrote her age on it in whipped cream.

Her tone of voice changed again. "Why should you go to all that trouble?" she asked almost angrily. "What for? So we can get crumbs all over your rug and give you and Danny a big headache? I don't want you cleaning up after us. You have more important things to do."

"What could be more important than having everyone together? And this year Carol lives right across the street."

There was another pause as my mother struggled with her thoughts. I wondered if she was going to say it. She did.

"At least *he* won't be there with all his craziness."

Taking my silence for criticism, she said defensively, "You

remember how he always walked right in and started looking for wine in the refrigerator? Don't you remember? It always annoyed you. The way he would start eating before we all sat down. The way his eyes darted around."

What I was remembering was something a little different about what had happened last Thanksgiving, when Bard, my sister's husband, was still alive, when my sister's eyes hadn't yet taken on that hollow look, though even at that time she was full of fear. It had started to rain very hard during dinner, and Bard, in his nervous way, had leaped up to check on our new awning. Danny had just installed it the past summer, and in the sudden downpour the rain was puddling the rubbery plastic, weighing it down until it looked like a swollen belly about to burst.

"Get me a broom," Bard had instructed me from where he stood on the darkening cement of the patio. "Get it now." An icy wind blew in from the door. I exchanged a look with Carol. She said quietly, "Get it for him. He needs to be a hero."

Danny said sternly, "Don't worry about it," meaning that this was his house, his awning, his responsibility. But I got Bard the broom anyway because I was afraid of what might happen if we thwarted him.

I could remember him standing out there in the darkness, his body outlined against explosive flashes of lightning, jousting at the heavy water balloon of the awning, poking it fiercely with the broomstick, deaf to the thunder and our calls to come in, until finally, and to no one's surprise, he pierced the awning and was nearly drowned in a cascade of freezing water. His hoarse scream of shock, of disbelief, of failure, still echoed in my mind. I'd given him Danny's bathrobe to wear during dinner; he sat there limply, in my husband's yellow terry robe, his hair and beard wet, staring morosely down the length of the table.

The next day, when the stores opened for Christmas sales, I bought Danny a new bathrobe and threw out the one Bard had borrowed. Bard didn't kill himself till five months after that.

"It was pure luck that Carol found a house right across the street from you," my mother said now on the phone. "Sisters should be near each other if they get along. Thank God you and

Carol are not like Gert and me. Can you *believe* we're sisters? We have less in common than the Arabs and the Israelis. Carol is so thankful to have you near to depend on. Now at least I can die in peace, knowing he's gone and won't be a danger to her. I know you'll take care of her and the boys. I know you'll do your best."

"I'll try," I said, feeling uncomfortable. "So let's all have a nice Thanksgiving dinner, Mom. Just come with Aunt Gert and Uncle Harry and put away your grievances and let's all try to have a happy time."

～

"Oh, God!" Carol giggled as she looked out my kitchen window. "Welcome to the Salvation Army."

I wiped my hands and went to look out the window. Uncle Harry and Aunt Gert were helping my mother out of the car. The three of them began to load up with paper bags and cartons from the trunk.

"Boys," Carol called to her sons, "why don't you go out and help everyone carry in the stuff?" The boys, Abram, eleven (named for my father), and David, nine, were building a fire in the fireplace.

"Go," Carol instructed them. "There might be goodies for you. You never know."

"Yeah," David said, making a face. "Like the last time. They brought *cantaloupes*. They tasted terrible."

"They saw a big sale," Carol explained. "They can't resist bargains."

Aunt Gert was carrying a big silver tray in her arms as she same up the walk. She had insisted on bringing the stuffing. She called three times while she was making it.

"Do I have to use mushrooms?" she had asked on the first call. "Your recipe calls for mushrooms."

"It would be nice," I said.

One the second call she asked, "I only have canned mushrooms; fresh are too expensive. Will that be all right?"

"Fine," I said.

The third call informed me that she had chosen to do without the mushrooms. "The Pilgrims probably didn't use them," she said. "How could they know which ones were poisonous and which ones weren't? So I'm sure they didn't use them at all."

Danny, who loved my Thanksgiving stuffing and looked forward to it all year, wanted me to make my own recipe and pull a quick switch just before dinner, but I told him he would have to bear up and make some sacrifices like the rest of us. "I'll make my own recipe tomorrow. We'll have our own private Thanksgiving with the leftovers," I had promised him.

As my relatives, laden like nomads, squeezed through the front door, I half wondered if I wished this day were over and they had already gone home. I was feeling the strain of having got up at 6:00 a.m. to put the turkey in the oven and cleaning and cooking for hours nonstop since then. I was sorry I had bothered to dust, because now my mother, aunt and uncle were covering every available surface with their bags and boxes and offerings.

"Bear up," Carol whispered to me, squeezing my arm. I looked at Danny, afraid that he might do what he had once threatened—go outside and get a huge trash can and suggest that they all immediately toss everything into it.

"Don't kiss me," my mother said. "I think I may be getting a sore throat." She was wearing big plastic sunglasses that hid half her face. The part of it I could see was small and delicate. Her chin was pointed and her cheeks were sunken. Her short white hair looked pixieish and gleamed like fresh snow.

"Your hair looks nice, Mom," I said.

"Your aunt says I look like a pinhead." She snorted in Gert's direction. "She'd like me to have one of those bouffant beehives she's so fond of."

"No, I wouldn't," Aunt Gert said. "It's just too severe that way. It's not feminine."

"You and your ruffles," my mother said.

Aunt Gert was wearing a black wool cape with white piping that matched her white hair. She was busy unloading things from a paper bag and handing items to Carol's sons. "This I got at a City of Hope luncheon, little table favors. I thought you boys could play with them," she said, handing each of them a little pink plastic cow with a bell around its neck. Carol's sons exchanged glances. "And where is Danny?" Aunt Gert asked, an artificial lilt in her voice. My husband stepped forward. "This is for you." She handed him an article torn from the *Reader's Digest* about saving money on taxes. Danny thanked her.

Now it was my mother's turn. She had the real bargains: twin-packs of discounted paper towels, a gallon of apple juice, some bars of soap, some cans of tuna. She always cleaned out her cupboards for us. With a flourish she held up three boxes of macaroni-and-cheese dinners.

"Who can use these? Carol? Janet?"

Ready for this, we answered together, with enthusiasm: "*I* can use them!"

"Well, you'll just have to share," my mother said. I was feeling giddy. I grabbed the boxes, handed one to Carol and put one down on the rug for myself. The third one I opened, ripping the cardboard top, and told Carol to hold out her hand. Laughing, I poured half the elbow macaronis into her palm. Her sons guffawed as the noodles spilled over onto the rug.

Even my mother was smiling. "That's what I like to see," she said. "Sisters who get along. So when I die there won't be any quarreling over who gets what."

Aunt Gert made an angry noise. "Your mother is so *negative*," she said fiercely. "She likes to spoil everyone's good time." She began to hold up *her* contributions. Coupons, for one thing. She loved to offer us coupons from the newspaper for fifteen cents off on margarine, fifty cents off on detergent. "With double coupons," she instructed us, "you can really save a lot."

Carol groaned. "I have coupons," she said. "I stand there in the market and they go flying all over the floor, and they've always expired, or they're for the super-jumbo size, or the checkout lady tells me I didn't cut the edges straight enough."

"You have no right to be fussy," Aunt Gert said, her voice unforgiving. "You, in your situation, can't turn down the chance to save a few pennies." She looked over at my mother. "You haven't raised your children right," she said. "They're spoiled. They think the world owes them a living."

"I'm sure you could have done better with them," my mother shot back, her eyes flashing. "If you're so smart, you should have had children of your own."

"I wasn't as lucky as you," Gert said. Then she looked at Uncle Harry, who was standing in the living room, slope-shouldered and a little dazed, still wearing his coat. "But God was good to me and I met a good man, even if late in life."

"Hi," Myra said, coming down the hall. Everyone turned to look at her. I knew immediately what my aunt was thinking: that it was a shame all that adolescent beauty was wasted on such a sloppy child. She was examining Myra's shapeless, oversized sweater. (It had belonged to her uncle Bard; she had claimed his sweaters, his black raincoat, his sleeping bag, on the day my sister was throwing everything into cartons for the Salvation Army.) Aunt Gert was frowning at Myra's non-hairdo, at her lank blond hair hanging in her face. She was thinking how much prettier that face would be with a little makeup on it. I prayed she wasn't going to ask Myra again if she was using acne medication; that would be the end of Myra for the day. I would have to take her a turkey leg in her room.

"How about a little vitamin for your old aunt?" she asked.

Myra dipped her head grudgingly and stepped forward to peck Aunt Gert on her cheek.

"Did I ever tell you . . ." Aunt Gert asked Myra for at least the millionth time, "that when your mommy was a little girl she used to come over to me and say, 'Could I give you a vitamin?' and then she'd kiss me on the elbow? She used to call it 'belbow'!"

"I know," Myra said. She looked around at the junk on the coffee table; then she turned around and went down the hall toward her room.

"Remember to turn off lights when you're not in a room!" Aunt Gert called after her. "Later I'm going to spank your little bottom if I find lights on all over the house and no one's in the rooms."

Myra grunted. She held the opinion that Aunt Gert made her light patrol march as an excuse to check the condition of the bedrooms. She was probably right. As a precaution, I always made my bed when Aunt Gert visited. Myra refused to be manipulated. She considered her room her sacred, private space. She was willing for Aunt Gert to think ill of her; she was braver than I.

"A cold soul," Aunt Gert said to me in Yiddish. "Why doesn't she have your affectionate disposition?" She looked at Danny as if the fault were clearly in his half of the genes.

"Fifteen is a hard age, Aunt Gert. I think you remember me as being affectionate when I was very small. I don't think I sat in anyone's lap when I was fifteen."

"At fifteen you had already met Danny. I'll bet you were in his lap plenty."

Danny about-faced and walked down the hall. I heard our bedroom door close quietly. Uncle Harry said wisely, "Myra misses her sisters."

"This has been a hard year for her," I said. I was referring to all her losses: one sister getting married, one sister gone to college, Danny's father dying of cancer, Bard's suicide. And two schoolmates of hers had died in terrible accidents. Suddenly I felt it had been a hard year for me too. I went over to my mother and put my arm around her frail shoulders. She was rummaging around in a plastic bag for newspaper articles she had clipped for me. She lost her balance and fell against me. I led her to the couch and sat her down. I had a memory of walking with my grandmother that way, when she was very old and I was about ten.

Something flashed in Aunt Gert's mind as well, for she said, "You ought to wear flat shoes, Anna; remember how vain Mama was? She didn't like those black old-lady oxfords with laces. She refused to wear them. Remember when she turned her heel and fell and we had to get help to pick her up?"

"I remember," my mother said warily, waiting for what was coming next.

"So you shouldn't wear those shoes."

My mother was wearing high heels because of an arthritic spur on her instep; flat heels caused her pain. She reminded Aunt Gert of this. "I can't even go to the bathroom in the morning without putting on heels."

"But you're looking for trouble in more ways than one," Aunt Gert reminded her. "Remember what that man said?"

"What man?" I asked, and Aunt Gert was satisfied. Now my mother would have to tell the truth about her heels.

My mother smiled in spite of herself. "I was walking in the parking lot of City College, where I take my music class, and a young man came up behind me and said, 'You really shouldn't walk like that around here.'"

"Those high heels make her swing her fanny," Aunt Gert explained. "And in that neighborhood—an eighty-year-old woman was raped in one of the bathrooms last year—your mother shouldn't let her skirt swish around."

"Can I help it if my skirt swishes?" my mother asked, and we all laughed. Carol laughed with us and then continued to laugh hysterically. She couldn't seem to stop. My mother was pleased. Aunt Gert was chastened.

"I'm hungry," Abram said. "When do we eat?" He and his brother David had made a four-foot pile of logs in the fireplace. There wasn't even room to get a match between the layers of wood.

"Oh!" Aunt Gert said. "I'd better get this stuffing into the oven to warm. By the way, Janet, did you tell me to *boil* the onions and celery or brown them first?"

"Brown them."

"Well, I boiled them. But what's the difference?"

The table looked elegant. I had unpacked the crystal water tumblers from the antique store, the Limoges turkey platter my father had given me, the hand-painted celery-and-olive dish, the hand-carved napkin rings of burnished wood with tendrils of lily of the valley curling around them. The brass candlesticks were gleaming; the points of flame on the red candles were shooting out stars of light. I had outdone myself, it was true. I was using all the precious things I had kept hidden for the last few years. I wondered if Carol would notice. When Bard came to our Thanksgiving dinners, he had always broken something, either by accident or by design. He'd test things, challenge their strength, balance delicate dishes one upon another or clink a glass too powerfully in making a toast to a happier, more prosperous year for us.

I counted only Bard missing; my elder daughters would be with us again for future family gatherings, and my father had been dead so long that I no longer saw him looming bigger than life, like a Thanksgiving Day parade balloon, over the table. And yet the thought of him brought back the memory of a dream I had had last night. I closed my eyes to shut out the shimmer of the flickering candles. In the dream my father had told me that he had discovered the cause of his leukemia: little, colorful, plastic elephants and dinosaurs, like the kind found in babies' teething rings, were bobbing along in his bloodstream; his blood was transparent as water. But he was also cured! He had discovered that the cure for cancer was embalming fluid! My father sat up in his coffin to tell me this amazing discovery; his hands held on to the sides of the casket as they might have held on to the edges of a rowboat.

"The trouble," he said in the dream, "is that they cut out my heart during the autopsy. So even though I'm cured now, I can't live. Your mother gave away my heart too easily."

I looked down the length of the table to where my mother was holding her wine glass in her quivering fingers and remembered her fear and guilt on the day she signed the autopsy papers for the entreating physician.

"Let's have a toast," Danny said, raising his wine glass. Myra raised her glass higher than anyone.

"To life," Aunt Gert said.

"To health," my mother said.

"To love," Myra said.

"To less inflation," Uncle Harry said.

"To all of us," Danny said. "To Bonnie and to Jill away at college."

"And let us all be here again next year," my sister said.

"And to those we love who aren't here anymore," I added,

feeling my eyes fill unexpectedly.

"Pass the turkey," David said. He reached across the table and knocked over the gravy bowl. He apologized profusely. Myra, who was sitting next to him, hugged him hard with both arms and kissed the top of his head.

∽

"It's too bad we have no men in our family," Aunt Gert said as we cleared the table. What had brought this on was my warning her not to drop anything down the sink because the disposal had been broken for a month.

Abram, who was carrying in the platter with the remains of the turkey, said, "My dad could have fixed it. He could fix anything."

"Danny plans to fix it," I said. "He just hasn't gotten to it yet."

"We need more men," Aunt Gert continued, scraping turkey bones and yam skins into the garbage bag. "Our family is a world of women. My father died at forty-eight, so you never had a grandfather. Your own wonderful father is gone. My brother drowned at sea. You have no sons. You have no brothers. It's a wonder we can get along, all of us women without men."

"Maybe I can fix the disposal," Abram said. He was wearing a shirt with rocket ships on it. "I fixed our video game when it broke. Mom couldn't figure it out, but I fixed it."

"Carol buys them all the modern toys when she should be saving every penny," Aunt Gert whispered to me. "What is she going to do when all the money runs out?"

Abram had gone back to the dining room to get more dishes, and I told Aunt Gert that Carol felt her boys had been through a lot, that they deserved a few toys.

"She never should have married him in the first place," she whispered. "A hippie. His brain was all scrambled by drugs."

"Who wants to play Scrabble?" my mother called from the other room.

"I'll beat the pants off you," Aunt Gert called back. To me she said, "Why isn't your mother bringing dishes in here? She's spoiled, that's why. Did I ever tell you about the Thanksgiving when we were little and an uncle of ours brought us a chocolate turkey and told us to share it, and she wanted it for herself and she threw a tantrum?"

"I know that story."

"Your mother claims I made it up. She's always telling me I make things up because she doesn't remember my stories. Why should she remember when she had a tantrum? It's not the kind of thing she likes to remember about herself. It doesn't flatter her."

"People remember different things," I said. "Everyone's reality is different."

"Tell *her* that!" Aunt Gert said. "From you, she might believe it. Everything *I* say she considers the words of a dummy."

"Come play, Gert," my mother called. "The board is all set up."

"What about dessert?" David demanded loudly of his mother. "When do we get the birthday cake?"

"Shh," Carol said to him. "Don't give away the surprise."

"We do this every year," David said. "How can Mom-Mom be surprised?"

"When you're old, your memory goes bad," my mother explained to him. "So every year I don't remember the year before. Although this year I ought to stop counting. I'm too near the end to celebrate, don't you think?"

"We always have to celebrate life. And this is an important year, Anna, seventy-five," Aunt Gert said, pulling me with her into the dining room, where the Scrabble board was now sitting on the table among the crumbs and cranberry stains on my linen tablecloth.

"Seventy-five?" my mother said, puzzled. But then she got busy picking her Scrabble tiles, and within the first ten minutes of the game she made an eight-letter, triple-score word: "quixotic."

"Tell me something about my great-grandmother," Myra asked Aunt Gert while my mother was taking her time finding her next super-score word.

Aunt Gert learned forward and held Myra's hair off her face. "Just one barrette, darling, would show off your pretty face. Why do you want to look like a sheepdog?"

Myra brushed her hand away. "Was she smart?"

Aunt Gert looked at my mother. "Was Mama smart? No, I don't think so. She was a peasant woman. Very practical, down-to-earth. When she couldn't sleep, she'd get up and wash the floor or bake a cake. She never sat around dreaming. She wasn't affectionate either."

"She was never affectionate," my mother agreed. She made the word *syzygy* on the board, using a blank for one of the *y's*.

"She never got philosophical with us," Aunt Gert said, arranging and rearranging her tiles. "She just made sure we were well dressed and neat and always clean. She never let us out in the street unless every button was closed. That's why I take great pride in my appearance to this day. Even if I get my clothes at bargain prices, no one knows. I always look good."

"Mama was very vain," my mother said.

"That's who you get it from," Aunt Gert suggested. She made the word *banjo.* "Remember in the rest home, she wouldn't let anyone come to visit her unless she had her earrings in? There was one pair she loved best of all. Your Abram had given them to her from the store, a little cluster of gold flowers with a diamond in the center."

"I remember them," my mother said.

"She used to have the nurse's aide put them in her ears every day. When I first saw that home, it smelled so of *pishachs*, I ran out screaming. I kept Mama home for eight months after that, caring for her myself until I collapsed. I couldn't even turn her over anymore, or change her sheets."

"Didn't she lose those earrings?" my mother asked.

"Lose them! Don't you remember what happened? One of her hands was paralyzed—all the fingers were curled up. And one day with her good hand, she wrapped the earrings in a tissue and dropped them into her paralyzed hand. She was going to ask the attendant to put them in her ears. But it was a new girl. She took Mama to the bathroom. She was about to put Mama on the toilet from the wheelchair when she saw the tissue in her hand. She just grabbed it from Mama's hand, tossed it in the toilet and flushed it—earrings and all."

"Oh, now I remember," my mother said.

"How could you forget! Mama couldn't be consoled for days."

"Abram got her a new pair."

"They didn't have real diamonds. You wouldn't let him get real ones. You said the help at the home would steal them."

"I don't remember that."

"It's the kind of thing you don't remember," Aunt Gert said. "Believe me, though, I never forget anything important."

"You and an elephant," my mother said.

Danny and Uncle Harry were sitting at opposite ends of the couch. Danny said, "Would you like to play a game of chess?" Uncle Harry answered, "Why not? It wouldn't be the worst idea."

In the kitchen, I looked with despair at the turkey carcass, the leftover stuffing (nearly all of it), the plates of cranberry sauce, the half-full salad bowl, the greasy roasting pan. I had hours of work ahead of me. Where was Carol? I checked the bathrooms, the bedrooms. I heard her sons shouting in the yard where they were throwing the Frisbee. I took my jacket from a hook and went outside; Carol was standing at the far end of the yard, under the sharp and leafless branches of the plum tree. I came up beside her and put my arm around her.

"I'm okay," she said, but when she turned to look at me, I saw tears in her eyes. "I'm really okay. I've been doing really well. I was just remembering how he once said he was going to paint his face like a clown's and then shoot himself through his red mouth. He was going to die laughing at the world. He said he didn't want me to identify his body, though. It would be too much of a mess. He didn't want me to be disturbed." She laughed, and tears rolled down her face. I wiped them away with my fingers. "But I haven't been thinking of him, really. I just did suddenly, that's all."

"You can think of him. It's all right."

"I dreamed last night he was on the other side of a glass wall with Skippy. He was threatening to slit the dog's throat. I couldn't go out there to save him."

I stood with Carol in the chill air and we watched her boys running through the grass. "I'm so afraid for them," she said.

"How will I ever know how much it's damaged them?"

"You just have to love them and do what you can," I said. "And I'll be here to help."

"You'd better live a long time," she said. "I'm counting on you."

"Hey, Mommy, catch." David whirled the white Frisbee at us and Carol lunged for it. She smiled when he called to her, "Great catch! You're terrific."

"Do you think we ought to go in for the big birthday party?"

"Why not?" Carol said. "Since we can't stop Mom from getting older, we might as well celebrate the fact that she's still alive."

My mother's skirt was too tight; she and Aunt Gert were conspiring about what to do about it. "Come into the bedroom," Aunt Gert said. "I'll cut the elastic."

"Don't go into *my* bedroom," Myra warned them. She added, "Don't worry, the light is out in there—I swear."

While my aunt and mother were gone, I got the cake ready. I mixed the heavy cream in a chilled silver bowl and added sugar and vanilla. The chocolate cake was three layers high; it was loaded with chocolate chips; it was beautiful. I embroidered my mother's age on the icing with whipped cream and licked my fingers. Seventy-five. What did it feel like to have lived that long? My mother had told me she read once that anyone who survived to the year 2000 could easily live to be one hundred. I didn't want to think about myself as old as I would be in the year 2000. I called out, "Come on in, Mom," and I told Myra to coax Danny and Uncle Harry from their chess game to the table.

My mother and Aunt Gert came down the hall, arms linked, laughing. My mother was wearing the black raincoat that had belonged to Carol's husband.

"Hey!" Myra said. "You *did* go into my room."

"We didn't look around," Aunt Gert said, "although if I were your mother, I wouldn't buy you another pair of socks until you hung up everything on the floor of your room. She's too good to you."

"I had to take off my tight skirt," my mother said, flipping open the raincoat and letting us look briefly at her still-shapely legs. "Gert has to cut the elastic and add a piece before we go home. So I have nothing on." She giggled.

Aunt Gert added, "My sister, the flasher!" They smiled at each other. "It's a good thing for her I can sew."

"Sit down and don't disappear," I said.

In the kitchen I lighted the candles. There were two number candles, a "7" and a "5," and one plain birthday candle, the one to grow on. Lifting the cake platter, I marched into the living room, singing "Happy Birthday." Everyone joined in as my mother leaned forward to make her wish. She took a long time thinking of it. Then she blew; she blew again and again, long and hard, her mouth a dark tunnel. The angle was wrong. The points of fire quivered but grew tall again. The boys begged their mother with a glance to be allowed to help; then they assisted, pushy in their certainty, blowing so hard that they tipped the candles over, extinguishing them like trees downed in a hurricane.

"May you live to be a hundred," Aunt Gert said.

My mother snapped, "Don't wish it on me."

"When I die," Aunt Gert said, "I want an open casket. I want everyone to see me and cry over me."

"I want mine closed," my mother said. "I don't want anyone grabbing a loudspeaker and shouting to the world, 'She's gone!'"

"I want everyone I know at my funeral."

"I want only my children there," my mother said. "I know I mean something to *them.*"

"You don't want *me* to be there?"

"I imagined I would be at yours, looking in your open casket," my mother said.

They stared at each other.

"I'm two years younger than you," Aunt Gert said finally. "So since we can't know what God has in mind, you'd better let me know now if I'm invited."

"You're invited," my mother said, "as long as you don't make any flowery speeches."

"Time for presents," David interrupted. "Then we can eat the cake." He came running to my mother and handed her a small white box.

"What could it be?" my mother said. "I wonder what on earth it could be. Don't tell me, my very favorite thing. A chocolate turkey!" She leaned forward and kissed David. Abram stepped forward and held up an identical box. "This is an extra turkey for Aunt Gert so she doesn't feel bad."

"Oh you darling!" Aunt Gert said. "Come over here to me, you precious child, and I'll give you a big kiss. Did I ever tell you about your grandmother's tantrum? It always used to kill her to share anything!"

"Is that so?" my mother said, her eyes looking very small. She opened her box roughly and pulled out her chocolate turkey. She laid it on the white tablecloth and brought her fist down upon it so hard that it crumbled into tiny pieces. "Here, I'm sharing." She handed the first and biggest piece to her sister. "Maybe this will make up to you for what you suffered at my hands." She looked at Carol. "You take the second-biggest piece. You should have some sweetness in your life for a change." The next pieces went to my mother's grandsons, the fatherless boys. She gave away the thin broken shell of her turkey till there were only a few crumbs left for her. She gathered them up by brushing them off the edge of the table into the white box. She closed the lid and set the box aside.

"I don't want any transients at my funeral," she announced to Gert. "Don't get on the phone and start calling everyone you ever met at bus stops or at card parties or in the Jewish bakery. I planned my own wedding, and I have a right to want what I want at my own funeral.

"Okay, okay," Aunt Gert said. "Calm down. Don't get into a fit. You might have a stroke, like Mama."

"I just want everyone to hear. You are all witnesses. So don't dress me up in some lace gown and put me on display like a store dummy."

"Believe me, I couldn't care less what you do when you're

dead," Aunt Gert said. She took a small bite of her fragment of chocolate. "Come back to the bedroom and I'll fix your skirt so you don't go home naked like Lady Godiva."

When they came down the hall a little while later, we were all watching slides of the children when they were little. My aunt and mother were engaged in an argument about who was wearing the outfit that cost the least. They sat together on the couch, Gert and Anna, sisters, and debated over the whir of the slide projector.

"I got this blouse for fifty cents at a rummage sale," Aunt Gert said. "It's a thirty-dollar blouse."

"My skirt was seventy-five cents at the thrift shop," my mother said. "And my shoes, one dollar."

"My slip was a dime," Aunt Gert said. "My whole *outfit* was only two-fifty."

"Well," Carol interrupted. "You think that's cheap? *My* dress was one-fifty at Goodwill. It must be in my blood. I never wear anything that isn't a tremendous bargain."

Uncle Harry and Danny were making goggle eyes at one another, but smiling just the same. Then on the screen I saw my father, in the bloom of health, riding on a broomstick across a wide green meadow, with my firstborn, Bonnie, beside him on her hobby horse. She was three. He was fifty-five, in the last year of his life. Click. There I was, at only twenty-seven, my hair in a long braid, wearing pink stretch pants and pointy-toed sneakers. I felt Danny come up beside me and put his hand on my shoulder. "You were so cutie then," he whispered in my ear. "I remember exactly how you looked then, *exactly!*"

Click. My mother and father appeared in front of me, sitting on our swingset. My mother was on my father's lap—he was pumping the way he taught me to do, with legs out wide—and my mother's delicate legs were hanging down inside his. She looked frightened. Click. There was Bard, holding Myra upside down by her sausage-legs-in-tights. He was grinning into the sun, his eyes red as a wolf's.

"I remember that day," Myra said. "I remember it perfectly clearly."

"Me, too," David piped up from a corner of the darkened room.

"You can't remember it," Carol said softly. "You weren't born yet."

"Well, it feels like I remember it," he said. "So if I want to, I will."

The slides went by faster as Uncle Harry clicked the remote-control button. Time shot by in a blur; I had one child, two children, three. Danny was young and strong, Danny was a little heavier, Danny had gray hair. The Thanksgiving-dinner scenes came on the screen, ten years in a row. Aunt Gert's and my mother's hair became whiter and whiter. The people changed; children were added, parents subtracted. Bard, the last year, was there at the head of the table with a halo of light around his head, staring at us with his red, tortured, sunken eyes. And finally there was my mother and her various birthday cakes—devil's food, chocolate chip, fudge, mocha cream, and her mouth open and blowing as if she were trying to extinguish the world.

"Mommy." Myra stood in front of me, bending to whisper into my ear. "Mom-Mom is seventy-six on this birthday, not seventy-five. We made a mistake."

I closed my eyes and counted. "You're right," I said. "But let's not say anything and get everyone upset."

"But you know what that means," Myra insisted. "It means that she didn't get her one candle to grow on."

I got up quietly, and taking my daughter's hand, I led her into the kitchen. While the light from the slide projector flickered and flashed like lightning in the room beyond, I enacted a little ceremony with Myra, lighting one candle for my mother, the one to grow on, and letting Myra blow it out.

(1984)

Hold Tight, My Love

~

THERE ARE TIMES, JANET thought, *we are sorry we have children because of what they have to face in life.* She was sorry she had ever handed her daughter the newspaper, for in it was the news of Jimmy Cole's death.

Janet remembered the day eight years before when Myra's quail had died. The bird had taken seed from seven-year-old Myra's hand, then suddenly lost its ability to stand; it fell, writhed in panic, and became still. Janet, seeing her daughter's stricken face, had launched into a speech about the cycles of nature, the life spans of various creatures, the need to accept death because it was part of life and made it more meaningful. She had ended with a little pep talk about being stoic (Myra's quail wouldn't have wanted her to grieve) and getting on with the business of living.

Now she had to do the impossible again: take responsibility for the fact that death existed. How could any mother justify the cold fact of death to her beloved child?

She wished she had ignored the article, just thrown the newspaper out. Perhaps then Myra would not have found out about Jimmy Cole's death until the fall, when school started again. Janet felt she had spoiled something for Myra, destroyed the sweetness of the summer ahead.

She also regretted having spoken almost casually, as if she

were mentioning a movie that was playing downtown. She assumed Myra didn't know the boy, or perhaps only knew *of* him.

Her daughter was at an age when she pretended to be emotionless and spoke to Janet in monotones. Most of the time she was in her room with the door closed, listening to music. Sometime after her thirteenth birthday, she had turned from a child who was vibrant, noisy, and communicative to a silent figure, most often showing her back as she walked away from her mother. If Janet so much as touched her shoulder affectionately, she would shrink away. And this had been a child who for years had blessed Janet with strangle-hold hugs, leaps into her lap, and big, sloppy kisses.

"Here's something about a boy who goes to your school," she had said over the raw potatoes she and Myra and just peeled. "It says he died having heart surgery for a condition he was born with, a three-chambered heart. Did you happen to know him?"

Wtih the same lack of affect she showed in everything, Myra had glanced dispassionately at the paper as if her mother were handing her yet another article of educational value, about a coming eclipse of the sun or the mating habits of Chinese pandas. Janet had bent down to pick up a potato that had fallen on the floor, and when she looked up, Myra was gone. Janet cut the peeled potatoes and put them in the pot to boil.

A few minutes later, she looked out the window and saw her daughter in the hammock at the far end of yard between the bottlebrush trees. She hung there, with the newspaper page clutched in her hand, staring up at the sky. Janet took a deep breath and let it out slowly, watching Myra, the hammock rocking ever so slightly.

Much later, Janet went outside. She approached the hammock uncertainly—she never knew how her daughter would respond to her these days.

"Did you know that boy?" she asked.

Myra nodded, keeping her eyes fixed on the empty blue sky.

"Was he a friend of yours?"

"My best friend."

Janet was astonished. She thought Myra's best friend was Katie, who Myra had met in nursery school. She didn't know Myra knew any boys well at all.

"But you never mentioned him. He never came over here."

"I've been meeting him in the library every week after I go to the orthodontist. You even saw me talking to him there last week just before school ended. You *saw* him, Mom, and you didn't even notice him."

"I saw him?"

"I was talking to him over by the Young Adult books. You kept wanting me to leave. You wanted to go home and *cook* something."

"That skinny, boy?"

Abruptly Myra turned her head away and waved her mother off with a disgusted flap of her hand. The curve of Myra's back, pressed against the flimsy weave of the hammock strings, pained Janet so that she could hardly catch her breath. She tiptoed back toward the house over the brittle grass, which was already turning brown in the summer heat.

She searched her memory; she remembered vaguely that she had been in the library last week looking for a specific Italian recipe, and Myra had come in from the orthodontist's office, just down the block on the main street of town. Janet, pleased to bump into her daughter, offered her a ride home.

"My term paper is due on Friday and I have lots of work to do here," Myra had said. "I'll walk home later."

"What did the orthodontist say?"

"What did he *say?*" Myra had snapped. "I've only been *going* there for three years. Do you think he ever *says* anything?"

"Don't bite my head off," Janet had said. "I thought maybe he said something about the progress your teeth were making."

Then Janet saw the skinny boy wave to Myra from a table near the record collection, and Myra had turned her back and walked away, dismissing her mother.

Janet wished now that she had given the boy more thought,

but she was intent on finding the recipe. She sat down at a table with her pile of cookbooks and glanced up only once. She saw the boy leaning against a bookshelf talking animatedly to Myra. She now tried to recall her impression of him and remembered only a very thin, pale, intense person. His back had been rounded, his posture terrible. He wore glasses. The tension in his body as he spoke seemed to reflect an earnestness and passion that was absent in Myra's lank, relaxed form. Yet on Myra's face Janet saw something quite unexpected—a sudden, sweet smile, that flash of happiness that had been her radiant trademark as a little girl.

At the time, Janet dismissed the boy as uninteresting: too young, not handsome. Yet now she remembered the brief stir of jealousy she had felt, seeing his power to draw a smile from Myra.

What was it the article had said? He had died at the Heart Institute Hospital, during surgery that had been indicated since childhood but that his parents had chosen to have done now at the recommendation of the doctors. "In a condition like the anomaly of a three-chambered heart," his doctor explained, "you choose a day to do it and you go for it. You don't agonize; you know it has to be done someday if the child is going to have a normal life. You don't look back."

That night, Myra went to bed without dinner.

"I wish I hadn't shown her that article," Janet said to Danny after she had knocked on Myra's door and gotten a muffled "Leave me alone" for an answer. "I've ruined her summer."

"It isn't your fault," Danny said.

"What isn't?"

"That her friend died. That she has to face death. You can't protect her from these things."

"Of course it's my fault! Yours, too," Janet insisted. "We gave birth to her, didn't we? Every time she suffers like this, it's our fault."

"What about every time she's *happy?*"

"When was the last time *that* happened?"

"She's at a difficult age," Danny said. "Even this bad experience is good for her. It will help her learn to cope with hard times in the future."

"How can bad things be good for *anybody?* Only a person with a heart of stone could say such a thing!"

"Only a mother," said Danny kindly, "would expect perfect happiness for her child."

∼

"Mom," Myra said grudgingly the next morning, "would you take me to the funeral tomorrow?"

"Are you sure you want to go?" Janet replied hastily. "Funerals can be very depressing, and—"

"*Yes, I want to go,*" Myra said. "If I could drive the car myself, I wouldn't ask you, but I can't. I still *need* you!" She stood there angrily, almost desperately, and then turned her back to Janet and walked, head bowed, down the hall to her room. When Janet passed outside her door a few minutes later, she could hear Myra crying softly.

∼

"Why don't you tell me a little about Jimmy?" Janet said as they drove to the church. "Only if you want to, of course." She glanced over at her daughter, who sat as far away from her on the front seat of the car as she could get. Myra had put on a white dress and the low-heeled white leather sandals she had last worn at her junior high graduation. In her hair was a thin black ribbon, tied at the top of her head in a small bow.

"What is there to tell? He lived and now he's dead."

"What was he like?"

"He was remarkable, that's all!" Myra said. She punched the armrest with her fist. "He was the most wonderful person. I wrote his mother a letter about him."

"You did? What kind of letter?"

Myra opened her purse and took out an envelope.

"It tells her how much I cared about him. How much I'm going to miss him. I'm going to give it to her today at the funeral."

"Myra," Janet said cautiously, "I don't know if that's wise. She may have too much to deal with today to be able to concentrate on how much you might miss him. After all, you need to remember that she's his mother. Think of how *she* will miss him."

"Mothers don't have a monopoly on love! Why do mothers think they're the only ones who love their children? Most mothers don't even *know* their children! I knew Jimmy better than she ever could!"

"Does that mean he knew *you* better than I ever could?"

"Of course he did! Almost anyone knows me better than *my parents!* Do you think I tell you everything?"

"No, I don't."

"Well, I can't," Myra said, sitting back, as if she had just delivered a fact of life with which they both had to deal.

They drove in silence the rest of the way to the church. As Janet was parking, Myra said, "Jimmy wanted to be a writer. He had the best sense of humor. And he played the violin so beautifully, it could make you cry. He wanted to be buried with his violin and his typewriter. I hope his mother and father arranged for it."

"How do you know that?"

"He told me, last week in the library. He didn't think he was going to make it through the operation. He was pretty sure he would die."

"He told you that?"

"He told me lots of things. He said it was okay if he had to die. He was willing to take the risk. He was really tired of being so weak and pale and always out of breath. He wanted a regular life if there was even a *little* chance. He didn't want to be some big jock athlete or anything, but he wanted to be a writer, and he wanted to be able to laugh a lot, and if the operation was successful, he knew he would have lots more air in his lungs, and then he could really laugh."

Janet looked at Myra's face. It was tight, her mouth just a thin line. She looked oddly old.

Myra tucked the letter carefully in her purse, opened the car door, and walked ahead of her mother into the church. Janet chose a seat in one of the back pews, moving in far enough to leave room for Myra, but Myra continued walking along down the center aisle to the front of the chapel. She wavered there a moment, as though her thin long legs couldn't support her, and then she reached forward to touch what Janet thought was the polished wood of the pulpit—but then saw, with a wild leap of her heart, that it was the coffin.

Tears burned Janet's eyes, spilled over onto her cheeks. *Nothing is more terrible than losing a child,* she thought. She wanted to rush down the aisle and take Myra in her arms, hold her with all her strength, protect her, keep her safe in a nest of hugs for all time.

Myra took a seat in the front pew, beside three people who must have been Jimmy Cole's mother, father, and brother. Janet could only see the backs of their heads. She restrained herself from going up to give Myra advice, to tell her daughter that it was improper for her to sit with the family. Could anyone convince her that she was a lesser sufferer? That she had no right to as big a grief as Jimmy's family?

The service began, and a minister in a black robe spoke of loss and the essential laws of being born and dying, how from dust we come and to dust we return. It reminded Janet of her speech about the quail. Then a woman whom Janet recognized as Myra's English teacher stood at the pulpit and read an essay Jimmy had written on the subject of habits he could not stand in people he loved. When the teacher read a line about his father clipping his toenails in the living room, a ripple of laughter ran through the church. The teacher wiped her eyes and said, "Yes. Good. Laugh. Jimmy loved laughter; that's what he wanted to make the world do—laugh. So don't feel guilty about laughing. Even here, even today. If he could have it his way, we'd all go out of here laughing. We won't be able to do that just now, but maybe later, much later, when we think of Jimmy, we can remember his wit, and intelligence, his courage and his humor.

Maybe then, if we can't laugh, at least we can smile."

Smiling and crying, she stepped down and made way for four students from the high school orchestra, who came forward with their violins, viola, and cello to play a somber piece of music by Schubert.

Afterward, the minister got up to make his closing comments. Janet tried to get a glimpse of Myra, but she was blocked from view. The service ended, and a man in a blue suit, apparently in charge of the funeral arrangements, came forward to give directions to the small cemetery where Jimmy was to be buried. When Janet finally caught sight of her daughter, Myra was embracing a classmate, a girl who rested her head on Myra's shoulder and sobbed so bitterly that Janet felt the hairs rise up on her arms.

"I'm bleeding," Myra said when they met outside at the car. "I don't believe this, but a band on my braces just snapped, and a wire is tearing into my gum." She held a tissue to her mouth. It colored brightly with blood.

"We'll go right to the orthodontist's."

"No! I can't miss the burial!"

"Well, I can't let you bleed like this either. The orthodontist is on the way to the cemetery. He can probably fix it right away—we'll ask him to hurry." Janet thought she might have to add other reasons to convince Myra, but Myra rested her head against the back of the car seat and closed her eyes as if she had given up.

"It's okay, I'll take care of you," Janet said helplessly. "You don't have to worry."

When they finally arrived at the entrance to the cemetery, the procession of cars was just leaving from the gate. Janet stopped the car. How could Jimmy's mother have left him to workmen? Janet wondered. How could she not be here now to witness his burial?

The funeral director was all business in his blue suit with the little flower in its lapel, waving his hands at the earthmover, directing the driver to bring the machine to a halt beside the high black mound of earth piled next to the grave.

Janet held her breath as she took a step closer to the coffin. *Someone's child was in it.* The thought was unbearable to her. She looked at Myra, and saw that she had silently taken the hand of the girl beside her. This was another friend Janet didn't know her daughter had, another person her daughter might also love. Her head spun at the thought of this whole other life Myra had.

The workmen were busy with the ropes and pulleys. One of them turned a handle, and the coffin began its descent into the grave. Suddenly Janet heard Myra speak. "Turn the coffin around please," she said, her voice strong and clear. "Jimmy told me that if he died, he wanted to be buried facing the rising sun. So the head of the coffin has to face east." The three boys beside her raised their heads and stood up straight, as if threatening to make the change themselves if necessary.

"Thank you," Myra said when she saw that neither the workmen nor the funeral director was going to argue with her. "Good," she added as they made the change. When they were done, they looked to her for further directions, as if she were in charge and knew the way.

"Now you can go ahead," she said. When the pulleys and ropes had lowered the coffin as far down as it would go, she stepped toward the earthmover and looked up beseechingly at the driver. High up on his yellow throne, the young man had the sweetest face Janet had ever seen: delicate and serene, with eyes as blue as the sea. Janet thought of a three-chambered nautilus floating in the depths of the blue ocean; she thought of Jimmy's three-chambered heart. Above the hum of his engine, she heard Myra say to driver, "This is a fifteen-year-old boy being buried here. He shouldn't have died. We all loved him."

The young man in the white T-shirt nodded. "Don't worry," he said. "I'll be very careful." With the greatest gentleness, he maneuvered the machine so that the teeth of the shovel slid silently into the black earth. He rolled the machine to the edge of the grave and gently, gently, dropped the earth with a soft raindrop sound onto the polished wood of the casket. He backed away, still controlling the earthmover with grace as he scooped up the next shovelful of earth. Before he proceeded, he looked toward Myra, raising his eyebrows. She nodded with approval.

Janet watched her daughter in awe. Myra had somehow made the transition; she was in control, she could handle this life and what came with it. The knowledge almost brought Janet to her knees.

When the grave was covered with earth and the workmen had wet down the soil with a hose, the driver of the earthmover gently scattered one more layer of dirt over the grave. He then saluted Myra and dipped his head in farewell. She smiled very slightly, and stared after the machine as it rolled away down the path.

"Okay," she said to her three friends when the air was silent again. "We've seen Jimmy off. He's safe. We did it the way he wanted."

One by one, the boys hugged Myra, even with Janet watching, and then walked toward the gate, looking awkward in their formal suits.

Myra opened her purse and took out the letter. She unfolded the sheet of paper and read what she had written. Then she acknowledged her mother for the first time since they had arrived at the cemetery. "Thanks for coming with me today, Mom," she said, raising her eyes to meet Janet's. "It would have been scary without you here." She replaced the letter in its envelope, knelt down, and matter-of-factly laid the white paper rectangle on the damp earth. She weighted it with a rock.

"I'm leaving this here for his mother," she said, her voice gentle and grave. "I have a feeling she might come back here later, before it gets dark. I know you would, if it was me. So I'll leave this letter about Jimmy for her to find. Maybe it will help." She looked up at her mother from where she knelt. "I hope you think that's okay, Mom," she said, brushing some dirt from her white dress and standing up.

(1987)

How Can She Get Along without Me?

~

JANET WAS KNEELING ON the floor of Myra's bedroom attempting to stuff her daughter's down comforter into an ancient yellow-and-brown-striped cardboard suitcase. The suitcase had belonged to Janet when she was in college; in a burst of sentimental fervor she had offered it to Myra as a gesture of passing the torch. As far as Janet could tell, Myra was not impressed.

"Hey—how about a hand here?" Janet said. As she stuffed one section of the comforter into the suitcase, another popped out. Myra sat on the edge of her bed, sniffling from a summer cold, her eyes red, a tissue clutched in her hand.

"Forget it, Mom. I can't possibly take that comforter with me to college."

"Why not?"

"It has those elephants on it."

"What's wrong with them?" Janet asked. "This is your wonderful down blanket."

"Those elephants are stupid-looking. I'm not taking it."

"Fine," Janet said, standing up, unfolding her stiff knees, straightening out her skirt. "Just pack what you want—okay?"

"I think I'll buy a new quilt," Myra announced, blowing her nose.

"*Today?*" Janet said. She lowered her pitch half an octave and tried to speak reasonably. "I mean, when exactly were you thinking of doing that?"

Myra shrugged. "Maybe tomorrow."

"*Tomorrow?* We have to leave *early* tomorrow, Myra. Your college happens to be four hundred miles away."

"I can buy a quilt when I go out to get my haircut. In fact, I'm going right now."

"*Are you serious?* I've been suggesting all summer that you get a haircut and, now, at four p.m. on the day before you leave, you're telling me you want to get one?"

"I didn't decide for sure till now."

"Oh, I see," Janet said, taking a step and tripping over her daughter's backpack. She grabbed onto the doorknob for balance. She wasn't going to lose control; she wanted Myra to remember this as a happy home. "Do you think you'll be able to get an appointment for a haircut this late?"

"At the barber college I can. They take you anytime. You can drive me, Mom. I'll get my shoes on."

"By the way, I need extra-long sheets for my bed in the dorm," Myra said as Janet drove downtown. "Did I tell you that?"

"No," Janet said.

"I thought I told you."

"You didn't. This is the first time you've mentioned a thing about it. Maybe you have a lot on your mind."

"Not really. Well—I guess I can buy them up there," Myra said. She sneezed. "Do you have a tissue, Mom?"

Janet felt around in her sweater pocket and handed her daughter a handkerchief.

"Is this clean?" Myra asked.

"For God's sake, Myra!" Janet cried. "It is *clean!* What on earth has gotten into you? First it's a haircut, then it's sheets! If you had allowed yourself even the *smallest* margin of safety . . . if you had done any of the things you were supposed to do . . ." She tore her eyes from the road and glanced at her daughter. "*Why* haven't you gotten ready, Myra? You've had all summer. Don't you *want* to go away to college?"

"What do *you* think? I can't *wait* to go!"

"Then why haven't you packed a single thing?"

"I was going to do it all today," Myra explained, dabbing at her nose with the hanky. "How was I supposed to know I would wake up with the flu?"

"It's not the flu, it's only a cold. But this haircut! To decide so late!"

"Mom! How was I supposed to know I would really hate my hair so much all of a sudden?"

A woman barber in a white nylon smock pumped Myra up in the barber chair while Janet took a seat on a wooden bench. A half-dozen apprentice barbers were snipping and trimming at their stations. The barber wrapped a striped towel around Myra's neck and laid out her golden hair in a circle, readying it for the sacrifice. All through high school Myra had worn her hair blunt-cut, at her shoulders, letting it swirl around her face like a swarm of mosquitoes. Whenever Janet had suggested delicately that this shapeless mass might find its natural, flattering curl in a layered cut, Myra had refused to consider it. Now the barber sprayed Myra's hair with water, and began meticulously measuring a strand of hair with a ruler on the back of her comb. She took a tiny snip and stopped to measure again.

"Is this going to take a long time?" Myra demanded.

"Do you want it to look good?" the woman snapped, spraying Myra's head with a hard squeeze on the nozzle of the water bottle.

Myra made a pained face. "I can't stand sitting still too long," she moaned.

As the barber cut and snipped, bits of hair stuck out around Myra's head, making her look wet and bedraggled, as if she had just hatched from an egg. Janet felt something clutch in her chest. Clearly, her daughter was too immature to go away to college—

Janet needed more time to fatten her up, fluff her out. She wanted to rush to Myra and take her in her arms, assure her—the last child, the baby of the family—that it would be best to stay home a little longer, stay and mess up her room, use her board games, even play her records long into the night. "I'll get earplugs," Janet thought frantically. "I promise you, you can play heavy metal. You can have all the slumber parties you like. I'll bake chocolate chip cookies every day. I'll buy you those ridiculous hatchet earrings if you still want them. Only don't go away. Not yet. I'm not ready!"

In the car, headed toward home, Myra threw back her head and screamed. "That woman ruined my hair! My life is destroyed!"

"It's really very becoming," Janet said, hanging onto the wheel. "Kind of feathery. It's actually quite interesting."

"*Interesting* is the *worst* thing you could say! It means you think it's hideous. I'm definitely a freak. I'll never be able to go out in public again."

Good, Janet thought. That means I get to keep you.

The next morning, after they had forced the lid of the trunk down by sitting on it en masse, Danny graciously handed the car keys to Myra and offered to let her drive. From where Janet was sitting, squashed into the backseat with the neck of Myra's guitar nudging her head, and the stereo speaker jutting into her ribs, she could see Myra—through the space between the bucket seats—clutching the steering wheel, a blue tissue in her long fingers. Every few seconds she let go of the wheel to sneeze violently, and the car swerved. Danny put his hand back between the seats and felt around for Janet's knee, which he patted reassuringly.

"Watch that big truck up ahead," he said in a kindly tone to Myra, who sneezed three times in a row and appeared to pass the truck with eyes closed.

Janet wondered if their life insurance was paid up. Myra could not be seeing clearly. She had stayed up all night, not so much packing as kicking the things she wanted to take with her into a mountain in the center of her room.

Janet tried unsuccessfully to cross her legs, then gazed out the window. Could it be that she had actually prayed for this day to come? Huddled in the cave of her daughter's mighty possessions—a sleeping bag under her feet, a tennis racket across her knees, a record collection threatening to slide off a pile of pillows and bury her—Janet admitted it: This *was* the day she had longed for during those endless years of strep throats, orthodontist appointments, broken arms and stomach flu. Their last child, going away to college—an event she had earned; a day, supposedly, of great joy, of freedom.

A sob caught in her throat. How could that unfamiliar, large, sneezing person, with that very peculiar haircut, who was driving—much too fast—be the same child who had ridden horsie on Danny's back, or, laughing her silver laugh, tickled Janet as she stood at the sink washing dishes.

"I just hope I can stand my roommate," Myra said. "She's probably a three-hundred-pound retard."

"Why not try to have a good attitude?" Danny suggested.

"That's easy for you to say. You won't have to live with her."

"No, I just get to live with your mother again, after all this time." He looked over his shoulder at Janet and smiled at her.

"Yeah, I bet you can't wait. With my stereo gone, you can finally have some peace. I bet you'll have a party to celebrate."

"Not a party exactly," Danny said. "Maybe a kind of reunion." His eyes sought Janet's, but she lowered her head and looked out the window. They were passing the cattle farm on Highway 5— thousands of steers, rump to rump, stretching as far as the eye could see, sending on the wind an indescribable odor toward the highway. It made Janet's eyes water, or so it might seem to anyone who wondered why she was blowing her nose loudly and wiping her eyes. Moving the guitar away from her ear, she settled back, limp, giving up control, letting her daughter drive them all into their future.

≈

"PIZZA PARTY at 7 in the lounge! Be there!"

Janet read the sign beside the elevator each time she staggered from the car with another load of Myra's belongings. How had her daughter collected all this stuff? Myra seemed to have brought every hanger in the house, every pillow, blankets dating back to her crib (but not her down comforter), stuffed animals Janet thought had come unstuffed long ago and blended their sawdust with the earth. Another mother, carrying a portable TV, stumbled into the elevator with Janet, and smiled. "My son's," she explained. "He doesn't want to be without any conveniences."

"What floor?" asked Janet, offering to push a button.

"Sixth."

"My daughter's on that floor, too."

"Isn't it amazing?" The woman brushed a strand of gray hair off her forehead as the elevator climbed. "They use the *same* bathrooms—the boys and girls. In my day, they would have called out the militia if a male had appeared within twenty feet of the girls' dorms."

"They used to yell out '*Man in the hall!*' when I was in college," Janet said. "If a janitor had to fix something, they'd start yelling warnings ten minutes before they let him come in."

"Can you believe it?" the woman asked Janet. "It feels as if I'm only eighteen myself. How can we be here, doing *this*?"

"I know just what you mean."

"It's unreal."

"It's real all right," Janet said. The elevator stopped and they stepped out. Janet pointed discreetly down the corridor. "That's my daughter." Myra stood talking to a boy at the end of the hall. She looked majestic—tall, poised, her hips canted out quite marvelously in a way Janet had never seen. Her sneezing had stopped; her new haircut made her look older and almost exotic. Her breasts, beneath her blue T-shirt, were round and confident-looking. A smile had come out on her face, like a blossom on a previously unflowering tree.

"That's my son," the woman whispered. "God! Good luck to us!" She reached out her palm and Janet took it. They squeezed hands, hard.

Danny carried in the last carton of books and dropped it on the striped mattress of the twin bed Myra had chosen to be her own. Breathing hard, he sat on the bed to rest; Janet followed his gaze as he looked out the window. The view was vast—it took in the clock tower, the grassy campus, a darkening sky. Myra was busy setting her lamp up on one of the desks.

"So—"Janet said, "I suppose everything is out of the car."

"Right, I checked," Danny said.

"So—I guess that's it."

Myra promptly echoed her words. "Yup, that's it."

Janet glanced around, looking for one more useful thing she could do. "We could wait here till your roommate comes. We'd like to meet her."

"Don't worry about it," Myra said. She spread her arms as if to herd them to the door. Janet felt Danny take her hand and begin to drag her over the threshold, out of the room. She pulled her hand away, hung back, delaying, watching her daughter, waiting. Then she stepped forward, arms outstretched.

Myra took a step back. "I can't kiss you, you might catch my cold."

"I'll chance it," Janet said, but just then someone knocked on the open door—the boy from down the hall.

"Going down to the pizza party in a little while?" he asked.

"Sure," Myra said. She fluffed her hair with her fingers.

"I'll stop by in about fifteen minutes, then," he said. "Okay?"

"Sure, that would be good." Myra turned to her parents. "I have to unpack now. I have a lot to do."

Danny took Janet's hand again, very firmly. "Well—have a good year, hit the books now and then," he said, his voice louder than was necessary.

"I will. Bye, Mom. Bye, Dad." She waved, an impatient flicker of her fingers, and was already bending to open a carton of records.

Danny pulled Janet along the hall. Her feet felt soldered to the floor with each step. In the elevator, going down, she felt a wild and desperate panic. "I can't do it," she said to Danny. "I can't leave her."

"It's not a choice you have," he said.

Outside the dormitory, Janet squinted up at the tall building, trying to find her daughter's face at one of the windows. They were all blank. She stumbled, her vision distorted by tears, as Danny guided her along the path to their car. Suddenly she heard a yell.

"Mom! Mommy!"

"What?" she cried, like a shot. She knew that voice as well as her own heartbeat. She spun around and saw Myra hanging out of a window. "Don't lean out so far!" she cried, a pure reflex, as she peered up the side of the building.

"But Mom. . ." Myra's voice was uncertain.

"What *is* it?"

"I didn't pack my toothbrush."

"Oh God." She glanced at Danny. To her daughter she called, "Don't worry about it. Just buy a new one."

"A new one?" Myra called back, as if she were trying to absorb a terribly difficult concept. "But Mom . . ." She was nearly hanging out the window. "I can't do it till tomorrow!"

"That's okay. Do it tomorrow. You'll be just fine."

"Okay," Myra said, drawing in her head. She stuck it out again and blew them kisses, then disappeared.

"She'll be fine?" Janet asked Danny. She laughed oddly and staggered against him. "How can she be fine without me?"

In the car, she saw that Danny was smiling as he pulled into the street. She leaned a little closer to him. "Well—who knows?" she said. "Maybe we'll all be fine."

(1986)

Ma's Moving In!

~

EVERYONE JANET KNEW HAD a horror story to tell: If something scary or dangerous hadn't happened to one of her friends, that friend knew someone else to whom something awful had happened. It was the nature of the times. But Janet never expected on those terrifying tales to come from her own mother, as it did during their regular evening call:

"How are you, Ma?"

"I had a little adventure today, don't get excited," Anna said. "I'm still alive, this time I was lucky, maybe I shouldn't even tell you about it."

"Tell," Janet said fiercely. Her heart was beginning to pound.

"I was walking to the little grocery store on the corner when I heard footsteps behind me. I turned around—"

"What were you doing out on the street alone, Ma?" Janet cut in. "I thought you agreed only to go out walking with your neighbor, Rosie."

"Rosie had a cold, so I went to get us both a quart of milk."

"But *I* shop for you. I bring you whatever you need!"

"A person, even an old person, should be able to take a walk in broad daylight, darling, even a person whose daughter sees that she lacks for nothing."

"Who was walking behind you? Did he attack you?"

"I'll get to it, just let me tell you."

"Did he hurt you? Did he *mug* you?"

"I'm trying to tell the story, darling, I have to build up to it."

"I don't want a novel, Ma, I want the facts." Anna never reached a story's climax in less than forty-five minutes, even if she was only telling Janet she had burned the bottom of the coffepot.

"It was a very nice day, early in the morning, a nice breeze was blowing, it wasn't even smoggy . . ."

"Ma . . ."

"Okay. So I heard footsteps, and I looked around, and this very well-dressed man was walking by me, so I said 'Good morning,' and for a minute or two we were walking next to each other. Then I said, 'Do you live around here? You don't look familiar.' Then he said he was looking for Cantor's Delicatessen, he had heard they were famous for their corned beef sandwiches."

"You shouldn't *ever* talk to strangers, Ma—you know that."

"Of course I know that, who taught it to you? But what was the harm? I told him where it was, but I was thinking, what a funny time of day to want a corned beef sandwich. It was early, no later than nine, who would want a corned beef sandwich for breakfast? So I told him they have very good blintzes, they'd taste better, they don't have all that garlic . . ."

"What's the difference, Ma—it's a person's business whatever he wants to eat. It's not your responsibility to teach a stranger better eating habits."

"I was right to be suspicious," Anna said smugly. "He looked fishy to me, and I was right. You know what he did?"

"What?" Janet felt her heart skip a beat.

"He went into that little grocery store and held them up with a gun. By the time I got there, he was on his way out with the money in a bag. He waved his gun at me, Janet! He said, 'You better keep your mouth shut, old lady! You never saw me, and if you say a word to the cops, I'll come back and get you!'"

"Oh God," Janet said, "Is your door locked now, Ma?"

"Of course."

"I don't want you going out alone any more."

"Janet, either I'm alive and can walk around in the world, or

I'm locked in this apartment and I'm dead," Anna said. "But muggers you don't have to worry about, Janet, because I never carry my purse with me. I just wear a sweater with deep pockets, so I can carry my heart medicine and my blood pressure pills and my ID. You know why I carry my ID?"

"So you won't get lost?"

"Of course not. I carry it for the same reason I always wear clean underwear. In case I get hit by a truck."

$\sim$

Some time ago Janet had tried to convince her mother to come and live with her and Danny. At the time, their two younger daughters were still at home and loved the idea of their grandmother moving in: Anna told wonderful stories and played the best games of Scrabble. But Anna had fiercely refused: She wanted her privacy and her independence. And Janet had felt relieved for the very same reason—she wanted and needed hers. But that was then. Anna could still see well then; Anna still thought clearly then (if not along the same lines Janet did); Anna hadn't been nearly eighty years old then.

The night after the phone call, as Janet and Danny dined late at the small kitchen table, a swan-shaped candle burning gracefully between the bowl of pasta with pesto and the bottle of burgundy, Janet said, "Danny, I have to talk to you about something." He looked up at once, giving her his full attention. It gratified her how easy it was to get his attention these days, now that the last of the children had left for college. "I think it might be time to ask my mother to come and live with us again," she said.

Danny paused to take a gulp of wine. Janet decided she could use a sip, too. She took a big one.

"A man with a gun held up the little grocery store where my mother buys milk," she continued. "She saw it, she was right there. He threatened her; he said she'd better not go to the cops or he'd come back and get her. Danny, crime in her neighborhood is out of sight. I don't want to wait till something really awful happens to her before we can get her out of there."

"I don't think she'll move out of her apartment until something major *does* happen," Danny said. "She's too stubborn."

"I know. But she just isn't safe. Plus, it's getting very inconvenient for me to have to shop for her twice a week, and to have to drive to L.A. every time she needs to see her doctors. I'd feel much less tense if I had her here. At least in certain ways." Janet reached across the table and touched Danny's fingers. "On the other hand, you know how I love being alone with you now that the kids are gone. It's been like a honeymoon."

Danny grinned. He held out his wine glass and clinked it against hers. "A toast," he said, "to your aprons."

"To my *what*? What are you talking about?"

"I'm thinking of how one night last summer you made dinner for me wearing only an apron."

"It was one hundred and four degrees that night!"

"We could easily have another heat wave soon."

"What you're saying is you don't want my mother here."

"Not really," he said. "I'm saying I like our life this way. I *also* know how you and your mother don't see eye to eye."

"Well, of course she annoys me sometimes, but I think I could handle it," Janet said. "Maybe you couldn't, is that what you're saying?"

"Have you ever considered looking into a retirement home for her?"

"Are you kidding, Danny? Do you know what my mother once said to me? 'If I ever have to go into one of *those places*, make short work of me. Get me to a bridge, so I can jump right off.'"

"They're nothing like that," Danny said. "They're not those torture chambers of yesteryear."

"You want to live in one?"

"Pretty soon," Danny said with a smile. "You know, my student Jake lives in Country Gardens—that's that place on Edinburgh Avenue, about ten minutes from here. I once gave him a ride home from school and had lunch with him there. The food is really pretty good. Maybe we should take your mother to look at it sometime."

"Never!" Janet said. "Don't ever even mention it, Danny, *please*.

She'd think we were trying to murder her. I promised, I gave her my solemn word of honor, that she'd never have to live in a place like that."

"But it isn't 'like that.' You both have some strange ideas about these places."

"Never mind," Janet said. "Let's drop the subject. I don't think my mother will *ever* move, not unless she gets hit by a truck and she has to."

The fact was that Anna was hit by a truck on Tuesday afternoon of the following week as she stepped off the curb at Melrose and Fairfax. From her hospital bed, as Janet sat holding her hand, she told Janet that for the first time in her life she had flown like a bird, but had hit the ground like a rock. Blood was in her mouth. She saw a man with a mustache jump out of his truck and take her under the arms and drag her back onto the sidewalk. She was about to thank him for his kindness when he stamped his foot and screamed at her, "Lady, are you crazy? Are you blind? Don't you know enough to wait for the light? Now I'll be late, I'll lose my job at Fatburgers!"

"You crossed on red?" Janet asked in amazement.

"I thought it was green," Anna said. "My eyes do tricks on me."

"But what were you doing out by yourself, crossing the busiest street in L.A.? Right after I told you not to go out walking alone!"

"I was going to vote," Anna said. "My civic duty. I wanted to get that bum we have as councilman out of office and vote in that nice young woman. She looks like a teenager, but she has very good policies."

"Oh God, Ma."

Anna sighed and lay back on her three pillows, her head bandaged, her face purple with bruises. The papery skin on her arms was blotchy with tiny hemorrhages from the violence of her fall.

"You know, Ma, you could have been killed," Janet said. She

bent her head suddenly and kissed her mother's fingers, terrified by the thought she had just voiced.

"Something has to get me eventually," Anna reasoned. "No one gets out of this life alive."

"But is it worth being killed for the sake of *politics?*" Janet demanded.

"Better than from cholesterol," Anna said, "Or, God forbid, a stroke."

"I don't know what to do with you, Ma. What now? When you get out of here, I can't let you go back home."

"Where else would I go?" Anna asked in all seriousness. "You want to put me away in one of those *homes?*"

"I told you, Ma, I would never do that. Ever. You could come and live with us," Janet said. But as she said it, a little green demon rose up in her head and hissed, *"Now? Now that the children are finally away at college? Now, when you and Danny could be free to be alone, to travel? NOW?"* said the demon. *"NOW? Are you crazy?"*

"Are you crazy?" Anna said. "In two days we'd be enemies. You cook with garlic, I hate garlic. You don't separate your light clothes from your dark ones. You don't use a good reading light, your posture is killing your spine. I'd get tired out taking care of you."

The nurse came in to change the dressing on Anna's forehead and shin. As she wound new gauze around Anna's leg, she said to Janet, "Your mother is going to need physical therapy when she gets home. She'll need help getting this working again. And that knock on her head left her with a bad case of vertigo. She'll need a good deal of supervision until she gets her balance back. She'd better use a walker for a while, because if she falls and breaks her hip . . ." Her voice trailed off.

"What happens then?" Janet asked.

"Well . . ." She hesitated, then told it straight out to both of them: "Some old folks never really get over a broken hip." She patted Anna's thigh. "But you have a good daughter here. That won't happen to you, Mrs. Goldman.

"Well, you heard the nurse, Ma," Janet said to her mother after she had left the room. "You can't be on your own for a while. When you get out of here—and I don't want any arguments—you'll have to come and live with us."

~

Living in Janet's house, Anna was polite. Janet had never seen her mother so polite. The first morning, as Janet served her coffee and toast at breakfast, her mother made a long speech: "Such service I'm getting from my daughter. What a good daughter I have. What a nice breakfast. And what a nice son-in-law, to have his mother-in-law barge in like this. What a patient and generous son-in-law he is."

After this, Anna began to speak of them always in the third person, as if they weren't there. "How good they are to take in a crippled old person," she would say. And Danny would stare across the table at Janet in amazement—he had never seen Anna this obsequious, this cowed, this deferential.

Each day there was an exhausting menu discussion. "What would you like me to make you for lunch, Ma? We can have macaroni and cheese, or salmon croquettes, or I could make you a hamburger and baked beans, or how about a salad?" For herself Janet usually had a cup of yogurt at lunch or some fruit and cheese. But her mother had lost weight since the accident, and the bones of her wrists seemed about to emerge through her skin. Janet racked her brain three times a day for tempting meal ideas; she had become a full-time cook against her will. She reeled off lists of foods that her mother had once relished, even ones that weren't the most healthful. "Do you want lox and cream cheese? Bacon and eggs? I could make you French toast . . ."

"Whatever the cook makes is fine," Anna would address the ceiling. "Not that this invalid has an appetite." She would stand up and fasten her hands on the rubber grips of the shiny walker they had rented for her. "But make it later, the patient isn't hungry now," she'd say, and begin to make her halting, uncertain way across the tiles to the kitchen.

After each meal (at which Anna ate almost nothing) Danny and Janet sat silently, watching her make her slow progress back to her room. Shuffle and roll, shuffle and roll. It reminded Janet of when they had brought a little wheeled walker for Bonnie when she was ten months old. Once Bonnie had got the knack of it, she had rolled like a speed racer through the house, spinning her red plastic steering wheel and beeping her little horn in wild abandon. For Bonnie it had been upward and onward. But for Anna it was the opposite. After two months of living with Janet and Danny, her morale had taken a sharp downhill turn. Her depression was palpable. The day she agreed to have her furniture put in storage and give up her apartment, her hands began to shake. She stopped wearing lipstick or even combing her hair. She wore her old flowered, quilted robe day and night. Listlessly, she stared at the television Janet had put in Bonnie's old room, where she was staying; she refused to come into the family room to watch the big color TV.

"Do you want to call Rosie, your neighbor?" Janet suggested. "See how she is? Or shall we look at my baby picture album? Would you like to hear the tape I made of Daddy singing 'Happy Birthday' to Bonnie when she was two?"

But even the mention of Janet's father did not move Anna to respond, whereas in the past she had always said one of two things: "I don't need to hear your father's voice and get all upset," or, "Let me hear his voice and cry a little. I miss him, my God, I miss him so much."

One morning Janet was in the backyard checking on the progress of the orange blossoms and the baby plums when she found herself crying. Her mother was inside, lying on Bonnie's bed, staring blankly at the ceiling; she had not even gotten up for toast and coffee. When Janet had called down the hall, "Breakfast-time. Where are you, Ma?" Anna had answered, "In limbo. That's where she is."

Janet tore a few baby plums off the tree. They were green and plump. It wasn't even that she was thinning them out for their own good; each was alone on its branch. She just got rid of them, wishing instead that she could get rid of old age and the losses that came with it. Her helplessness, her powerlessness to change anything was overwhelming. She dug her nails into the plums and threw them to the ground. Then she began to sob in earnest; violent gasps burst from her throat. She rushed into the house, into her bedroom, where she dove under the covers, burrowed down like a wounded creature, and sobbed till she felt as if she had no breath in her at all. She imagined her rib cage trying to open itself and set free her aching heart.

~

One evening they heard Anna making her way down the hall to the bathroom. Danny and Janet were about to begin dinner; Anna no longer ate with them in the kitchen, though she allowed Janet to bring food to her room. She would sip at soup, eat a few spoonfuls of Cream of Wheat, but she would push most everything away within half a minute. Yesterday at the doctor's they'd determined that, although her balance was better, she had lost fifteen pounds since leaving the hospital. "It's up to you, Anna," the doctor had said. "You want to stay alive? You have to eat."

Now, when they heard the rolling wheels of her walker, Danny called, unnaturally loudly, "Want to come in here, please, just for a minute, Mom-Mom?" He used the affectionate name the children had always called her but which had always slightly embarrassed him. Still, Janet knew he preferred it to the more formal "Anna" or the not-quite-easy-for-him-to-say "Mom." Janet looked up from the kitchen sink, where she was draining the string beans. She was puzzled that he had called out to Anna, since, where her mother was concerned, he usually let Janet do most of the talking.

At first there was no sound. Then they heard the plastic wheels rolling over the tiles in the hall.

"Come and sit down here with us," Danny commanded in a stern way that was quite out of character. "Leave that walker-thing there. You don't really need that, Mom-Mom. The doctor said you can walk on your own."

Anna came into view; her white hair was wild and feathery, giving her the look of a seed pod blowing in the wind. "Old people can go downhill if they fall," Anna intoned for their benefit. "Once an old lady breaks her hip, that's it . . ." Her face had shrunk to a little white, wizened apple.

"But you're not going to fall, and you're not that old," Danny said. "You have years ahead of you. There's no reason you shouldn't enjoy them." He waved something at her—a colored brochure.

"What's that?" Janet asked, alarmed. She'd caught a glimpse of a photo of exercise equipment. Was Danny about to suggest Anna join an athletic club as some kind of joke?

"I want you to listen to this, Mom-Mom," he said. He began to read very loudly: "We invite you to visit Country Gardens, one of the most popular retirement retreats in the inner valley. *We take the strife out of life!* We give you the charm of your own one-bedroom apartment, each completely equipped with fire door, sprinkler systems and smoke detector. We have a modern beauty and barber shop, hobby and exercise room, nurse on duty, 24-hour security guard, laundry on every floor, library, and social director."

Anna had paused in the doorway. Danny went on reading at top volume: "Our exquisite dining room overlooks a colorful garden; lunch and dinner are served daily by waiters and waitresses. We give you carefree living, relieving your relatives of worry about your security and well-being."

"She's not deaf," Janet said. "Don't shout at her."

"I'm not deaf," Anna said. She came further into the kitchen. "What's that you're reading?" she asked Danny.

"Play Ping-Pong and shuffleboard in the gardens," Danny continued, talking at top speed as if his time in a game show would be up and he would lose his chance at the jackpot. "Enjoy the main lobby for greeting family and guests, and the card and billiards room for making new friends. We have already had three weddings at Country Gardens, among residents who have met each other here!"

Danny glanced up at Janet. She frowned and shook her head at him. "He doesn't mean anything by reading you that, Ma," she said. "He isn't suggesting you move out. He's perfectly happy to have you living here, as *I* am. I'm sure you know that." To Danny she said, "If this is some kind of joke, then you've lost your mind."

"It's no joke," Danny said. "I've told you how much Jake likes it."

"Who's Jake?" Anna asked. Janet was amazed to see her mother interested enough to ask a question.

"One of my students," Danny told her. "He's the one who gave me the brochure. He's eighty-five, and he thinks the best way to stay young is to be interested in things, so he takes Dial-a-Ride down to the college. He's taken several of my courses, and I think he's also taking ballroom dancing this semester."

"He actually lives in this place?" Anna asked, waving at the brochure. "It doesn't sound like it's one of those last-stop places where everyone waits around to die. It sounds like for millionaires." Janet saw that her mother's eyes were bright again, and alert . . . her mother's aware, intelligent eyes.

"He's lived there for five years," Danny said. "The rent is actually quite reasonable, considering what you get. A few weeks ago when I gave him a ride home, he invited me to have lunch in the dining room. They had enchiladas on the menu, and chicken pot pie."

"My mother would never eat enchiladas," Janet said to Danny. "She doesn't even eat—"

"How come you're talking about me like I'm not here?" Anna demanded. She came forward without her walker. "Give that to me," she said to Danny. "I'd like to read it for myself. Not that I would consider such a thing, you understand."

He handed the brochure to Anna, along with the magnifying glass he kept on the windowsill for reading classified ads.

"I don't need that" Anna snapped. "My eyesight is just fine!"

They drove over to Country Gardens Retirement Home on Sunday afternoon, the day a complimentary lunch was offered to prospective tenants and their families. Janet sat stiffly in the back seat of the car. She felt she had disappeared into the air as far as Danny and Anna were concerned. For the last few days, in the kitchen, in the living room, in front of the TV, Danny had talked to Anna about the advantages of living in Country Gardens, and

Anna had given him reasons why she could never consider it. Yet she had *listened* to him.

During these talks Janet had stayed silent, peeling and shredding and boiling various things in the kitchen, serving and washing up, loading and emptying the dishwasher, sewing buttons on shirts. She felt unable to approach Danny about what a terrible thing he was doing, pushing Anna out of their home. It didn't matter that Anna seemed interested in Country Gardens; the truth of what Danny was proposing surely hadn't hit her yet. Hadn't Janet *promised* her mother never to put her in one of "those places?" Then, at the thought of how unhappy their lives had become since Anna had moved in, how unhappy *Anna* was, too, tears would well up hotly in her eyes.

Now Danny turned the car into the parking lot of the Country Gardens' modern, four-story building. As Janet stepped out of the car and prepared to help Anna, she felt as if a neon sign were flashing "THIS WOMAN IS ABOUT TO ABANDON HER MOTHER!"

But Anna had no sense of this. She didn't even wait for Janet to open the door. She fumbled with the handle and stepped out carefully into the sunshine. She seemed to be summoning her confidence. She'd dressed that morning in a tan, pleated skirt, a white cotton shell, and a light-pink sweater. Her hair was shining, fine as silk; and she had put on a touch of light-pink lipstick. As thin and delicate as she was now, she had the look of a schoolgirl. Danny offered her his arm, but she refused it. "Remember?" she said. "My balance is much better now." She smiled just a brief smile at Danny, then her face turned soft and vulnerable.

"Jake is meeting us in the lobby," Danny said. "You'll know him by the flower in his lapel. He dresses like an old-time vaudevillian: he's short and tough and feisty."

"But he has brains?" Anna asked.

"I gave him an 'A' in my class last semester," Danny said.

"That's good enough for me," Anna answered. "I like a man who can think."

Janet trailed behind her husband and mother. They seemed to have forgotten her anyway. Beside the reception desk in the lobby she saw a parrot in a wrought-iron cage. To her astonishment, her mother walked over to the bird and whistled softly. He cocked his head, and whistled back.

"There," Anna said. "Animals and I get along."

"There's Jake," Danny said, indicating a dapper little man who'd appeared and was waving cheerfully to them. He wore a carnation in the lapel of his striped jacket. He bowed to Janet and kissed her hand as Danny presented her. As for Anna, did she actually giggle as Danny introduced them? Jake gallantly offered Anna his arm, and this time she did not refuse guidance. Danny stepped back to walk beside Janet.

"I hope you don't think I can really consider this—putting my mother in an institution?" she whispered to him as they followed Jake and Anna down a carpeted hall toward the model apartment.

"Does this look like an 'institution?'" Danny asked her. "Can't you see the change in your mother already? To tell you the truth, I can hardly wait until we're old enough to move in ourselves. They have movies every Friday, and little trips to see desert flowers or the Queen Mary, and they serve crab quiche once a week, which you never make me. They—"

"I think I get your gist," Janet said.

Jake stopped and held open the door to the model apartment. "They don't even pay me to be your guide!" he said. Then he proudly showed them the amenities: the marble-topped vanity in the bathroom, the kitchenette with built-in refrigerator and microwave, a small balcony overlooking the hills, a good-sized bedroom with linens and maid service provided.

"Thank God I still have my furniture in storage," Anna said to Jake. "I think it would fit in here very well."

"You realize how much cheaper it would be if my mother continues to live with us," Janet whispered to Danny. She had picked up a price list at the desk and now pointed out the monthly rent to him.

"The cost depends on how you reckon it," Danny whispered back. "You haven't looked too well or seemed too happy to me lately."

"I didn't think you'd noticed," Janet admitted.

"Don't I know you?" Danny asked. "Don't you *know*?"

On the verge of tears again, Janet leaned against him, and he kissed her forehead.

"I still don't see how I can put my mother away."

"Put her away?" he asked. "Look at her, Janet, look! Does it seem as if we'll have to do it by force?"

Jake was showing Anna how the microwave worked. "See—it beeps when it's done. You can have yourself tea in two minutes. A miracle!" he exclaimed.

"If we live long enough, we'll see plenty of miracles," Anna agreed. She looked to Janet like a new person—a miracle indeed. The way her mother was walking and talking seemed miraculous. Color was back in her cheeks. Her face had come to life, as if the muscles had been commanded to take back their old shape. She was still very thin, very frail, but perhaps that would be remedied: Jake was telling her about the meals at Country Gardens in the exact words of the brochure: "Three delicious entrees offered for lunch and dinner. On Sundays, a sumptuous buffet with a dozen salads, roast beef and turkey."

"You know," Anna said to Jake, "I think I'm getting hungry."

"Ma," Janet said, as much to reassure herself as Anna, "we can go back home, and I'll make you lunch. We don't *have* to eat here."

But Anna seemed oblivious. "You like the people here?" she was asking Jake.

"Some are no-goods, some are nice; just like in the world, you have to be picky," Jake said. "It's a whole little community here. And the food, the food is good, especially the cherry-cheese blintzes."

"So what are we waiting for?" Anna asked. She turned to Janet. "You know, you yourself could use a little weight on you, darling," she said, putting her arm around Janet's waist. "Let's go try out the food. We're entitled to a free lunch, and after all, I'm practically a new tenant."

(1989)

Bye Bye Baby

~

WHEN JANET'S CHILDREN WERE little, they slept in three small bedrooms down the hall. At night, when Janet finally laid her exhausted head upon the pillow, she thought, peacefully, happily, "Three little heads in three little beds." Never mind that from time to time one of these little heads would appear at her bedroom door: *bad dreams, can't sleep, tummy hurts, ghost under the bed.* Sometimes Danny would turn over, crack one eye, then leave it to her.

In those years not all men had heard the news that raising children was their job as well as their wives', but she and Danny had worked out a satisfactory arrangement, a fair enough division of labor. And on the whole, she'd loved those days, and thought they would last forever.

How powerful the illusion had been! On any given day—say, when the girls were ages one, three, and five—it was obvious that a full year later, they would still be little—only two, four, and six. Eons would pass and they might be only four, six, and eight. Always they would be babies, and always hers. She would have them till the end of time.

Now she no longer had them. What was that piece Bonnie had once played on the violin for her high school play—a song from *Kiss Me, Kate?* "Where is the life that late I led? Where is it now? Totally dead!"

Thank heavens, not dead, but certainly gone. The babies had vanished. Even Myra, the youngest, had been in college since the fall. Her leaving had hit Janet hard, much harder than she expected. By comparison, the departure of the older girls had been a piece of cake. Bonnie and Jill, before they had left home, had been fiercely independent (and even irritating and hostile while they were at it), an attitude which, if not endearing, at least allowed Janet to believe they could take care of themselves. (Sally, Janet's psychologist friend, had told her nature programmed obnoxious behavior into teenagers—so that when they finally left home, their parents were delighted to see them go!)

But Janet had been pained to see Myra go, this special, sensitive child of hers, her "baby." Without Myra at home, nothing was the same. What did she miss? Certainly the sweet, early days, like the afternoon Myra bought a label-maker and printed out her first message: "I love you, Ma!" which she glued up over the kitchen sink. She made another label and pasted it to the oven door: "Mommy makes the world's best blueberry muffins!" Perhaps Janet missed even the emergencies, like the broken arms.

One night Myra had rolled out of her bed with a thud that woke Janet from a sound sleep. Whimpering, she appeared in Janet and Danny's bedroom doorway, her cheeks tear-soaked, her posture full of misery as she stood there in her flowered flannel pajamas with little white-soled feet attached.

"Can I come in with you, Mommy? I fell out of bed. My arm hurts."

"Well, come on, but just for a little while." Janet held back the edge of the down comforter; Myra climbed up and settled in the crook of Janet's arm. She lay her head on Janet's breast but was unable to get calm.

"Myra, sit up a minute. I want to look at your arm." Janet lit the lamp. There was nothing to see, not even a bruise.

Still the sobs continued. At 3:00 A.M., Janet got up and made a splint for Myra's arm out of the rectangular lid of a plastic cookie container. She gave her a baby aspirin. By dawn's light it was clear what they had to do: they rushed off to the hospital,

Danny at the wheel.

Six weeks in a cast, and the arm healed straight and beautiful. In fact, here was that fine arm now, waving at Janet from the window of a crowded red Toyota just pulling up at the curb. Janet waved back from the window beside the kitchen table, where she had been clipping coupons from the newspaper.

Myra used that same strong arm to open the rear door and hurl her heavy-looking duffel bag onto the grass. Then she stuck her head back into the car; her behind wiggled as she shifted from one foot to another, giving goodbye kisses. Her college friends, also going home for spring break, were unfamiliar to Janet. Yet Myra couldn't seem to leave them. Janet, standing now on the doorstep, felt a pang; her own arms were ready to hug, but she would have to wait right there until Myra was finished with her friends.

A young man in the backseat reached up to ruffle Myra's hair. (Was it possible he was wearing an *earring*?) Finally, more waves and farewells: "I'll call you tomorrow." "Yes, but don't call too early." (Laughter.) "Yeah, we'll go to the beach or whatever." "Great." "Talk to you soon." A puff of black exhaust burst out of the tailpipe as the car pulled away.

"Hello, darling," Janet said as Myra came up the walk. "How good to see you." She cringed at the formality of her words, kissed her daughter carefully, without fawning too much, without stroking her shining hair, without gazing with too much adoration on that gorgeous face she so loved. *Mine. My child. My baby.*

The hug was satisfying, but didn't last long enough. Myra disentangled herself and entered the living room like a visitor, gazing around. She was wearing white slacks with a soft lavender sweater Janet had never seen. She wanted to ask when she'd bought it, if it had been on sale, if she really needed another sweater, but she held her tongue. She noticed Myra had put on some weight; she no longer looked gangly and adolescent. She looked, in fact, changed since Christmas break, when the whole family had met in San Francisco. "Nice chairs," Myra said. "New?"

The chairs were a pair of recliners she and Danny had bought on sale, both light blue, now that there was no one to climb on them with sticky fingers. Even the cats were no longer a danger to the furniture—they had grown old and slept all day on the soft, frayed cushions of the old fold-out couch in what used to be Bonnie's room.

"Yes, Daddy and I are doing some fixing up these days. We have a little more time to attend to things we ignored for so long."

"Now that we're all out of your hair," Myra suggested. "Right?"

"Something like that."

"I wish everyone could be here," Myra said. "With Bonnie and Jill so far away, it'll just be you and Daddy against me."

"Let's hope *not*," Janet said, feeling her heart skip a beat. "Why would that happen?"

"I'm just not the same since I've been away, Mom. I hope you can live with it."

"With what?"

"With me," Myra sid. "Whatever. But can we go to my room now? I'd like to put my junk down."

Her room. Indeed it stood as it was the morning Myra had left for college at the end of summer. The artifacts of her childhood were everywhere: the Linus and Lucy candles, the green ceramic turtle collection, the plastic slot machine that Janet and Danny had brought back for her from Las Vegas, the backpack and canteen, leftover from Girl Scout days. The other girls had packed away most of their childhood things in boxes before they left for college. Janet now kept her sewing machine in Bonnie's room, and Danny had his computer on Jill's desk in the other vacant room. But Myra's room had become, if not exactly a shrine, something like a museum display.

Now Janet followed Myra into her room and noticed with a shock that moths had hatched in the big glass jar of ancient birdseed. How long could they live without air? They were flashing about, like smokey black specks of soot, near the lid; she would have to let them free. Myra was kneeling in her closet, tossing out—one shoe after the other—a pair of saddle shoes from ninth grade that she had cherished.

"Are you looking for something in particular?"

"My Star Trek communicator," Myra said. Her head disappeared under a bunch of old dresses as she searched her oak toy chest in the back of her closet.

"Your *what?*"

"I was telling a friend about it, how I had this elaborate game I used to play with Jill and Bonnie."

"Star Trek games," Janet said. "I thought college girls talked about boys or how awful their parents were. At least, that's what we did in my day."

"Who said my friend is a girl?" Myra asked.

"Well, sorry, forgive me," Janet said.

"Oh, great, here it is, I found it!" Myra backed out of her closet, bumping her head on a teddy-bear bag. She was holding a small plastic box with fake gold knobs painted on it.

"Communication time. Enterprise to Earth," Myra said. "Over and out." She looked up from her game. "I hope you don't come in here while I'm away and poke around in my *things*," she said. Then, before Janet could think of a reply, she added, "And look, Mom, could we get one thing straight before this visit gets under way?"

"Like what?"

"Could we please not have any major discussions while I'm home?"

"What would constitute a *major discussion?*" She tried to keep her voice neutral.

"My grades, my future plans, men in my life, why I forgot to thank Grandma for my birthday present, stuff like that. Who I want to room with next year."

"Who *do* you want to room with? A boy?" Janet said. She couldn't help herself.

"I'd rather not get into it right now. Okay?"

"Could we get into it later?"

"I don't know yet," Myra said. She looked at the stuffed whale on her bed and shook her head. "I can't believe the kid who used to live in here was me."

"She was you," Janet said. "And she was wonderful."

~

At 2:00 a.m., Janet heard footsteps in the hall.

"Wake up!" Janet whispered fiercely to Danny. "Someone's in the house."

"Our child," Danny said.

"My God, I forgot!"

"That's because you've gotten used to being alone with me." He reached under the covers and found a sensitive place on her belly.

"Don't," she said. "I can't do this sort of thing when there's a child of ours at home."

"Then think of how I felt for the last twenty years or so," Danny said, kissing her ear, "when there were three of them here!"

"I'm serious," Janet said. "This will just have to wait until we're alone again."

"So when is she going back to school?"

"Danny," Janet said. "She just got here. And I have to ask you something very important. What if she wants to room with a boy next year?"

"A *boy*?"

"That's what I said when she told me."

"She told you?"

"Well, she intimated she's considering it. And there was some boy in the car. She seemed to be, well, close to him."

"Do you know anything about him?"

"I think he wears an earring."

"Oh, God." Danny put the pillow over his face. "No," he said, pulling the pillow away again. "I will not support her in college if she moves in with some guy. If she's old enough to live with a man, then *he* can put her through college."

"He's only a student," Janet said. "Or so I assume."

"No," Danny said.

"Then tell me this," Janet demanded, poking his ribs. "If you had a *son*, and he wanted to live with a girl in college, would you stop paying for his education?"

"No, I guess not," Danny said.

"So? What's the difference?" She waited, but not too long. "Isn't your daughter's education as important, at *least* as important, as a son's would be?"

"You're in favor of it then."

"No, I'm not actually. I don't think I am."

"This is too complicated," Danny said. "Can't we talk about it in the morning?"

Just then, from the kitchen, they heard the electronic beep of the microwave.

"She's probably hungry," Janet suggested. "But let's be reasonable, Danny. This is a world in which a girl needs an education more than ever before. And lots of girls are living with their boyfriends these days. All my friends' daughters are doing it."

"Then you want her to live with a boy?"

"No," Janet said. "Of course not. It's crazy at her age. On the other hand . . ."

"Hmmm," Danny murmured. He grabbed his pillow and turned over to get comfortable. Janet poked him. "Don't fall asleep till I tell you this. *You* were a boy I wanted to live with. In college. Remember the sign-out cards in my dorm when I was a freshman? Remember the night watchman who locked you out of the dorm at 10:00 p.m. sharp? Didn't we wish we could live together long before graduation?"

"That was us," Danny said. "We were in love. We were sensible."

They could now hear popcorn popping in the microwave, little machine-gun rat-a-tat-tats.

"She's sensible, too. She's our *daughter.*"

They heard the stereo in the living room blast on. By the time Danny had thrown his legs out of bed and put on his robe, Myra had turned the volume down.

"Since we're up, do you want to go in and have some popcorn?" Janet suggested.

"No, thank you," Danny said. "But would you like to move to a motel for the next week or so?"

In the morning, after Danny left for work, Janet made spice muffins and honey butter for Myra's breakfast. She remembered Myra at five, when Janet had taught her to make a braided egg-bread—how delighted Myra had been, laughing as she kneaded the dough, looking adorable with dots of flour on her cheeks and nose. There were still things Janet could teach her, weren't there? But Myra's bedroom door remained closed. For lunch Janet made salmon croquettes, and ate them alone.

At two o'clock, someone with a deep voice phoned. "This is Bob. Is Myra up yet?"

"She doesn't seem to be," Janet said.

"Well, she always sleeps late," Bob said. "I wouldn't worry."

"You wouldn't?" Janet asked him.

"I'm looking forward to meeting you and your husband," he said. "Myra thinks you're both terrific."

"She does?"

"And it's awfully nice that you invited me to stay with you for a couple of days."

"Look—why don't I have Myra call you? If you'll give me your number . . ." Janet said.

"Oh, I'm just sort of bumming around with my friends," said Bob, "so I'll just call her later on."

As Janet was rolling chicken pieces in crushed Rice Krispies and bits of pickle relish (her own original recipe), Myra appeared in the kitchen, her cheeks flushed from sleeping hard, her hair standing up in lopsided curls. "Don't even *look* at this flowered nightgown," she warned. "In school I sleep in my sweats, but this was all I found in my closet."

"That closet is a virtual treasure chest, isn't it?" Janet said. She dipped a drumstick in beaten egg, and rolled it in the bowl of cereal and relish.

"What's that going to be?"

"Dinner," Janet said. "You already missed breakfast and lunch."

"I'm a night person," Myra said. "I discovered that about myself at college."

"And what else have you discovered about yourself at college?"

Myra caught her tone. She opened the refrigerator and took out some yogurt. "Mom," she cautioned.

"I know. No major discussions. Your friend Bob called about two hours ago."

"Really?" Myra smiled. Janet was reminded of the day they had surprised Myra with the desert tortoise (they were legal then) and she had done a backward somersault on the rug. That was the kind of smile she had on her face now.

"Can you tell me just a little something about him? I don't mean too *much*, nothing major, of course—maybe just where you met him."

"I met him in the dorm bathroom. He was brushing this teeth in the sink next to mine."

"I see." Janet added a little bit of cinnamon to the crumbs.

"God, Mom, what are you *doing?*"

"Writing a cookbook," Janet said. "I'm calling it *Recipes to Laugh Yourself Sick Over*." She added just a pinch of horseradish to the crumbs. Then a few ramen noodles. "I understand Bob is going to be our houseguest."

"Did he tell you that? Well, I was going to get around to asking you if that would be all right."

Janet rolled two chicken wings in the crumbs, reflecting privately on how odd chicken wings really were.

"*Is* it all right, Mom?"

"I'm worried about what your dad will say. And what sort of arrangements you're planning on."

"Oh," Myra said. "I guess you mean sleeping arrangements."

Janet did the breasts and the thighs. She decided to add some lemon slices to the baking pan. Then she added a few sprigs of mint and some boysenberry tea leaves, for a surprise flavor.

"I knew it was going to be hard to come home," Myra said suddenly. "Christmas was different, being in San Francisco. But this time, the R.A. on my floor warned me. She said, 'Your parents will think you're from Mars. Or you'll think they're from Mars.'"

"I was born in Brooklyn," Janet said. "That's far enough away as it is."

"The fact is I'm not your baby anymore, Ma," Myra said. "I just feel when you look at me that you want to brush the hair out of my eyes."

"I do," Janet said. "For eighteen years I brushed the hair out of your eyes. Why should I have to stop now?"

"Because you have to," Myra said. "It's the law of the jungle or something." She took her yogurt cup and a spoon, and walked down the hall. She called over her shoulder, "If the phone rings, I'll get it. Okay?"

"I feel rejected, I feel unnecessary, I feel useless, I feel miserable," Janet recited to Danny in bed that night. "I waited all day to see her, and then just before dinner she got dressed and some kids came by for her, and off she went, and now she's gone till God-knows-what hour."

"Aren't you glad she has friends?"

"Delighted. But who *are* they?"

"I guess she feels it's her business."

"So now you're taking *her* side."

"You know, Janet," he said, "the truth is I'm not used to thinking about her this way anymore, not on a day-to-day basis. Neither are you. Try not to let it get to you. Try to think of her as an adult."

"Some adult."

"Can't you just go to sleep?"

"No," she said. "But you go right ahead, Danny. I'll just lie here, worrying, until I hear her come in."

"When she's at school, you don't even know *if* she comes in."

"It's easier *not* knowing."

"Come here," Danny said. He arranged himself around her in their sleep posture, pulling her back into the larger curve of his chest, belly and thighs. She sighed in pleasure, despite herself. "Remember when she used to sleep with her silky blanket?" Janet asked. "I couldn't even get it away from her to wash it. I had to tiptoe in and sneak it out from under her at midnight."

"Mmmmm," Danny murmured.

Then Janet must have fallen asleep. She woke to the faint smell of wood smoke and the sound of low voices in the living room. The clock read 3:00 a.m. She put on her robe and went very slowly down the hall. She was composing a speech to deliver to Myra, about consideration and respect. She was waxing eloquent in her mind as she went along in her slippers when she saw, in silhouette against the glow from burning eucalyptus logs, her daughter and a boy—Bob?—sitting near the fireplace. They were face to face, their foreheads—but nothing else—touching. Myra's unruly bangs curled against his straight, light hair. His earring glinted in the firelight. They were studying some essence—not exactly one another, but some idea or sensation. Something was being created in this moment that Janet was not meant to witness.

She tiptoed back to bed. She crept under the down comforter and draped herself against Danny's back. He was peaceful and solid as a rock.

"I'm ready to talk about Bob," Myra announced two days later.

"It's okay," Janet said. "You don't have to. He can stay here a few days if he wants to."

"He can?"

"He's your friend," Janet said. "And I think he's nice. I've talked to him a little." She was making a new recipe, a cauliflower and cheese quiche with licorice trim. For some reason Janet could not understand, Myra's return home had sent her into a fit of creative cooking.

"He could use Bonnie's old room, or, if you don't want him that close to mine, he could have Jill's."

"I thought you would want him in *your* room," Janet said, in a perfect monotone.

"Are you kidding, Mom?"

"Why should you do anything different here than you do at school?"

"I don't live with Bob at school!"

"You don't?" Janet looked up into Myra's earnest blue eyes, and recalled how they'd looked when Myra had nursed at her breast, so many lifetimes ago.

"I'm only a freshman, Mom. Most of my friends don't move in with their boyfriends until their second or third year at school."

"But you might next year?"

"We're just talking about it, that's all. I know Daddy would have a fit."

"You're not worried about me?"

"I know you trust me," Myra said. "You know I'd be responsible and careful and all that stuff. And I *would*. But Bob and I aren't sure yet if we want to do that."

"Your father and I waited a long time and it didn't kill us," Janet said.

"But it *almost* did, right?" Myra laughed, and Janet, in spite of herself, burst out laughing, too.

"You're right! It almost did!"

"God, Mom, what's that monstrosity you're cooking?"

Janet waved a licorice whip at Myra and Myra ducked. "It's a gourmet delight, that's what it is," Janet said. "Not that you've noticed all these dishes I've been making to please you."

"Oh, but I have, Mom. I've just been so busy with Bob and everything. But one night we came home really late and found this luscious strawberry cream cheese pie in the fridge. Bob said he'd never tasted anything like it! I hope you don't mind that we finished it off."

"My God, I forgot all about that pie!" Janet said. "I never even missed it."

"That's because you were so busy on your next creation. I know you've been doing it to please me, Mom, to give me some home cooking. You're really so good to me."

"I am?"

"But Mom—this!" Myra said, motioning to the quiche. "This is really gross! I think you've got to sacrifice it and start over. Or better still, why not let me make dinner tonight? I know a great nacho dip recipe—we always make it in the dorm microwave late at night. I can probably salvage this cheese you were using."

"You want to make dinner?"

"I've always loved to cook," Myra said. She smiled. "I have your cooking genes, Ma. We always had so much fun in the kitchen together."

Janet agreed. She brushed the hair out of Myra's eyes.

"There you go again," Myra warned, laughing.

"I'm entitled," Janet said. "Aren't I? Just once in a while? I mean, how often do I see you?"

In answer, Myra gave her a powerful hug.

"This is awful for me," Janet admitted. "I hate giving you up, darling. I hate the law of the jungle."

"But the jungle is so wonderful," Myra said. "It's just so beautiful out there—isn't it?"

Janet looked out the kitchen window. Far off, she could see the tops of the low hills covered with clouds. In their own garden, weeds were choking the flower beds and termites had hollowed the trunk of the pecan tree. But there were also oranges, big as suns, on the orange tree. She was not going to lecture Myra on what she knew of animal behavior and other natural phenomena. Certainly not now, and probably never.

(1990)

This Old Heart of Mine

~

"WHERE IS IT WRITTEN?" Janet said. She was stirring some anise seeds into spaghetti sauce, a flourish she had never tried before. Her youngest daughter, Myra, who lived in a co-op dorm in Berkeley, had brought her a new cookbook a week earlier, when she had been home for winter break. The book paired two art forms—painting and cooking. Glossy reproductions of Italian masterpieces—oil paintings displaying sumptuous feasts—were accompanied by recipes for "zuppe" (soups) and "carne" (meat) and rich sauces and desserts. Interspersed throughout the book were lush photographs of Italian villages, with their rolling hills, olive trees, tiled roofs, and great cathedral domes. She could almost hear the tolling of the bells.

"What did you say?" Danny asked. Like a little boy in his mother's kitchen, Janet thought, he was sitting at the table in his usual chair, doing what he usually did while she cooked dinner: grading his students' papers and then doing the crossword puzzle on the comics page of the newspaper.

"I didn't say anything."

"You said, 'Where is it written?'"

"My shopping list," she said, thinking fast. "I don't know where I put it." She hadn't realized she had spoken aloud—and this wasn't the moment for honesty.

She dropped some basil, then some finocchio seeds, into the *salsa semplice di pomodoro* #2, and tasted it; in the past she had used only garlic and oregano, but times (as Myra had pointed out to her more than once in the past week), they were a-changing.

"Times," she said ominously to Danny, "they are a-changing."

"Huh?" he said.

Where is it written?. . . Her glance fell on the framed needlepoint that had been hanging in the kitchen for the last twenty years—who on earth had put it there? "KISSIN' DON'T LAST: COOKIN' DO" . . . *Where is it written that all meals shall be served to this man from the day of his birth onward and that he shall serve none to anyone? Where is it written that women, first his mother, then his wife, and on rare occasions his daughters, not to mention all the waitresses in all the coffee shops he's eaten in over the years—where is it written that women must prepare and serve him his food till kingdom come? That all manner of food this man consumes shall be chopped, sliced, diced, sauteed, broiled, boiled, and poached for him by women? Shall be washed, grilled, stewed, deep-fried, and microwaved for him? Shall be . . .*

"Is dinner almost ready?" Danny asked.

She ripped her two-pronged fork from the hook on the wall and brandished it.

"Another cereal bug?" Danny asked with friendly concern. For the last week she had constantly been shaking cereal bugs out of dishes and off utensils. The weevils were breeding in her cabinets as if there were no tomorrow. She kept announcing she would have to clear out all the cabinets, throw out her flour and grains and cereals and breadcrumbs, change the shelf paper, and seal everything in airtight containers. "But it would be useless," she added. "They'd just come right back. You can't fight nature."

Whenever a bug showed up, she went through her recitation of what an enormous, impossible job it would be to eliminate them. Danny, if he was around in the kitchen (eating odds and ends or doing his crossword puzzle), always offered to help, but always at some future date. "Let's not do it today," he said now. "You have enough to do as it is, Janet. Don't worry about it— there's no need for you to get tired out. Besides, I don't mind a bug or two in my soup. They're a good source of protein." As if he had not said this (or something like it) ten thousand times, he glanced at her, hopefully, waiting for her to smile.

She was out of smiles. Something had changed and it wasn't Danny. He had been this way, exactly, forever. She ought to be used to him by now—his jokes, his habits, his good nature. They'd married before the great revolution, in a time when new-lyweds worked things out based on the one simple premise, not so remarkable in their generation: he would work, she would stay home. He would take care of the lawn, she would take care of the house and children. But now, because of his bad back, Danny had a gardener who took care of the lawn and, though all three girls were gone and she didn't have to be in the kitchen so much, she still was, or it seemed she was, and for the past week, she hadn't been able to stop the refrain in her head: *Where is it written?*

It was Myra and her young man, here for a week, who had precipitated this crisis. Together, the two of them had cooked up a storm. Janet could hardly come into the kitchen even to get her daily pills (she was taking estrogen and calcium for the usual reasons) before they chased her out.

"You're not cooking a *thing* while we're here, Mom," Myra announced. "I told you when we came home that we're not making you into our slave. Especially after what we did the last time we came."

Janet remembered vaguely some innovative dishes she had tried during Myra's previous visit: quiche with licorice trim, and chicken breasts breaded in pickle relish and Rice Krispies. But that had only been a frantic attempt to get Myra's attention, which could not, by any means, be wrenched away from Bob, who was then brand-new. Bob, however, was a regular now, and Janet had no culinary acrobatics planned; if anything, she had thought about making her old standbys: roast chicken or spaghetti and meatballs.

Danny held up his wristwatch. "I did that puzzle in six minutes. I beat my own record." He waited, chin up, eyes bright, for her approval.

"Danny, did it ever occur to you that I might sometimes want to do the crossword puzzle?" The question was out of her mouth like a snake. She could feel that black thing starting up, the sudden motor of doom, and once started she knew she could not stop it—not without something awful happening: tears, or the flinging of something expensive across the room. "And while we're on the subject of the newspaper, did it ever occur to you that I might want to read the front section first in the morning and NOT the food and fashion section? Don't you think I care about what's happening in Kuwait? Or that the economy's going down the tubes?"

Danny stared at her, his eyes wide, as if she had turned into a circus act.

"And did it ever occur to you that I hate it when you eat a bag of corn chips just before dinner?" She really dove into it now: "I hate that habit of yours, it makes me furious. Whenever you're hungry, you wander into the kitchen and start throwing things into your mouth—peanuts, potato chips, chocolate chips, whatever's around and portable. When I get hungry, I recognize that it's time to feed both of us, so I cook us dinner!"

"Janet—what are you talking about? For one thing, all you have to do is ask and the crossword puzzle is yours. For another, why shouldn't I eat something if I feel hungry? And if you're tired of cooking, you know we could go out to eat more often— you don't have to cook every night, I always tell you that. But even if I eat an elephant before dinner, I'd still eat your dinner. Have I *ever* not eaten your dinner? You've cooked me the best meals for years and years . . ."

"And I'm plain sick of it!" she cried out. She stopped, shocked at the tone of her voice. The spaghetti water was now boiling over. What she saw in her mind—and what enraged her—was the image of Bob and Myra in the kitchen, slicing green onions together, chopping bits of white mushrooms together, making calzone or chicken Kiev or some co-op recipe with cheese and avocados and zucchini, and shoving little snippets of food into one another's mouths. Had Danny shoved any food into her mouth since that chunk of wedding cake so many years ago? She could not be stopped, her mind was churning up so many accusations there was no telling where this would go. She might end up on "Divorce Court."

"Dinner's ready," she growled. "But I'm not hungry," she added. "So eat it yourself."

The thing about men, Janet reflected on her way down the hall, is that when you announce a problem to them, they always feel obliged to present a solution. Whenever she told Danny, for example, that she thought her thighs were a little too heavy, he'd pop back with a solution: "Try skipping chocolate chip cookies for a while." Of course, what she really wanted from him was either (a) his assurance that her thighs were not heavy at all, and were just as beautiful and as shapely as they had been when she was twenty, or (b) at the very least, sympathy—and an acknowledgment that neither of them was as thin as they used to be.

But what she always got—and she should have known it was inevitable—was his idea of a remedy.

Now, as she knew he would, he came after her into the bedroom, where she had crawled into bed and drawn the down comforter up over her head. Lately she spent a fair amount of time curled up in just this spot—dug in, buried under, out of it. Let him just dare to make that silly joke now about getting "down in the mouth!" But what he said was almost worse, dumber:

"I just had a thought. Maybe what you need is a new kitchen," he said. "I think maybe what would cheer you up is a major remodel." He sat down on the edge of the bed, on her side, and hunted for the shape of her back under the covers.

"Don't sit on the down!" she cried from underneath. "How many times do I have to tell you? You'll flatten all the little feathers. Why can't you just leave me alone?" She knew she was going very far, maybe too far. If she kept on this way, he *might* leave her alone. How nasty was anyone allowed to be to one's mate before the injured party called it quits?

But Danny continued unperturbed, which made her even angrier. "If we enlarged the kitchen," he was saying, "built in some new modern drawers—you know, the kind on tracks, or installed cabinets with revolving shelves so you could find things in minutes . . ."

"So the bugs can play merry-go-round?" she snapped. "No thanks."

Danny was silent for a moment. "What *do* you want, Janet?" he said quietly. "You're so sad lately. I was just sitting there doing my crossword puzzle, and you were cooking dinner and everything was wonderful, we were so happy, and all of a sudden . . ."

"You always tell me—'We were so happy, and all of a sudden . . . !' Maybe we weren't always so happy, maybe I've never been happy!"

"Never?" She could hear the pain in his voice. "But why not?" he asked. "I love you. We have a nice life. We just had our daughter home and we had a wonderful visit with her. We have great kids. We're not sick. We're not poor. Why aren't you happy?"

Why? Didn't he know about the human condition? About how children grew up and abandoned you, about how daughters got sexy and beautiful just as you were getting thick and a little old? About how parents died, and cancer flourished, and the future got shorter and shorter? About . . .

His hand came under the comforter and found some part of her, her bare arm, and stroked it. "Can't we just have dinner, Janet, and then have a nice evening?"

It seemed such a reasonable request. So logical and intelligent. She almost forgot what had started all this.

"Let's just have our nice life," Danny said. "Don't spoil it."

"I don't want to spoil it," she confessed. Under the covers, she moved his fingers up to her face to wipe away her tears. "I don't want to," she begged him. "So why am I?"

She began to cry four or five times a day. She'd be peeling potatoes, or clipping coupons from the food section of the paper, or writing checks for the utility bills, and she'd think of her mother, living by herself in a retirement home, or she'd think of her father's sweet face and remember that he had died young, of leukemia, at the age she would be in just a few years. She'd be reading in the paper about a young man who'd been killed in a motorcycle accident, and she'd begin to sob wildly, reaching for a dishtowel to absorb the sea of tears.

She'd watch the talk shows and think, here I am like everyone else: midlife crisis, empty-nest syndrome, low self-esteem, symptoms of depression. Solution? Needs a job, needs a lover, needs a housekeeper, needs a pet, needs a new kitchen. She wondered what kind of addict she was after seeing the whole range of them confide their secrets: food addicts, sex addicts, shopping addicts, drug and alcohol addicts, gambling addicts. None of their vices seemed to be her cup of tea. What was she, where was she headed, why had she lost her direction, and was there help for a sad person who had no real reason to be sad?

Danny no longer seemed like the villain. Now her anger was directed instead at the religious fanatics who rang her doorbell on Sunday morning, dragging little children (boys in suits and ties, girls in frilly dresses and patent-leather shoes), hawking some formula for salvation and eternal joy. She was angry at computers that called in the middle of dinner and took marketing surveys for companies that wanted to get richer. A spoiled package of hot dogs threw her into a rage.

Nothing seemed worth the trouble. Her mother, calling one morning from the retirement home on a day when two sisters who lived there, one eighty-nine and one eighty-seven, had been killed in a car accident (she didn't say which one had been driving), summed it up neatly for her: "What's the difference what we do, Janet? That's what it comes down to in the end. It's all a big nothing."

There. She had the ultimate meaning of life from the being who gave her life: "It's all a big nothing."

She called her daughter, Myra, at college, to deliver this essential message, the wisdom that must be passed from generation to generation. "Myra," she said. "This is your mother."

"What's wrong, Mom? You sound kind of funny."

"I'm not sure I should have had children," she said. "I'm not sure this world is such a good place, after all."

"What other world is there, Mom? What's going on? Is Daddy there?"

"He's just a man," Janet said. "Men don't have the main responsibility. They don't raise the babies."

"Mom, are you alone there? I think you better call someone to come over. Aunt Gert? Your friend Linda?"

"I don't need company. That's the last thing I need. What I need is to get into bed. Look, darling, I'm really fine. I'll call you in a day or two."

She didn't need to get into bed. She realized it as soon as she was in bed and saw how limited the possibilities were. The view of the ceiling, with the bloated green paint bubble, was always the same. The view of Danny's chest of drawers, with a ceramic figurine of a bespectacled professor on top ('World's Best Teacher,' given to him by one of his students), was the same. The dusty mirror over her dresser, with a heart drawn in the dust by Myra, was the same. This wasn't getting her anywhere.

She got out of bed and walked through her house. The girls' bedrooms, still full of their junk, no longer caused her a thud of pain. They were just rooms now, not shrines to days past. Her sewing machine, on which she had run up dozens of hems for the children, hundreds of seams, seemed an artifact of a distant historic age. In the living room she stared at the Danish coffee and end tables she had loved so much when she and Danny were first married . . . but now they bored her. She hardly noticed anything around her. What she needed was some new sights.

By instinct, she ended up in the kitchen. Old or new, ancient or remodeled, she definitely didn't want to be in this kitchen for the next year. She wanted—*she needed*—a vacation from this kitchen. But where did she want to go? Maybe to some other kitchen?

Sitting on the counter was the cookbook from which she'd taken the new recipe for authentic spaghetti sauce from the Tuscan hills of Italy, the one with anise seeds and basil.

She wouldn't mind being in a kitchen in Italy. In a kitchen with a view of Tuscan hills and orange-tiled roofs and the domes of great cathedrals in the distance.

When Danny came home, she was cooking *cappelletti con salsa di funghi e pomodoro, insalata di fagiolini* and *torta di pistacchio*.

She smiled at him when he came in from the garage, calling

out his usual announcement: "I'm hoo-em. Here I am." She didn't even frown when he tossed his briefcase on the kitchen table. (She always had to carry it down the hall to his study when she was setting the table for dinner.)

"Here *I* am," she said. She waited while he took off his jacket and sat down. She poured him a glass of orange juice. Then she sprang it on him. "Danny, why don't you consider taking a sabbatical next year—a year abroad? We've talked about it for the last twenty years, but we never wanted to pull the children out of school, or we didn't want to board the cats, or we were afraid my mother would miss us too much, or we thought it would cost too much . . ."

"I thought the main reason was you never wanted to rent the house to strangers," Danny said.

"I still don't. I'd have to clean it from top to bottom and store our good things and get a headache checking references. But I *would*."

Danny was looking at her face. "Are you serious?" he said. "I've always wanted to go."

"Me, too," she said. "I'm finally ready." She set down the wooden spoon and took his hand in hers. "I spent all morning figuring this out. If you apply for your sabbatical now, next fall we can go to Europe. I can take the 'Italian for Travelers' course at the college this summer."

"You're not worried about how much it will cost?"

"Look, if we have enough money to remodel the kitchen, we must have enough to live in Europe for a while. Life is short, Danny. If we don't see the world while we can still walk, we won't ever do it."

"But how did this all happen?" Danny reached for a nearly empty bag of potato chips and started throwing the crumbs from the bottom into his mouth.

"You know how sad I've been," Janet said. "I think I figured out why—I'd run out of having any kind of future. The kids all have things to look forward to, and you do, but I've been running in place for years and years and now I need to go forward."

"To Italy?"

"Yes. For a while. Can you think of a better place? You've always loved Italian opera—now we can see the real thing. We can go to Florence and see the great paintings in the Uffizi, we can have adventures, we . . ."

"You know we'll have to come home in a year . . ."

"Of course, Danny. We'll want to."

A cereal bug spun down from out of nowhere and landed in the water she was boiling for the *cappelletti* (little pasta hats). In the twinkling of an eye, she scooped him out with her spoon and watched him shake off his wings and take flight, right up into the cereal cabinet.

"Spirited little fellow, isn't he?" she said.

(1991)